Regency Brides Collection

2 Sparkling Regency Romances

Betrayal
by Georgina Devon

Jack Chiltern's Wife
by Mary Nichols

Regency Brides

A collection from some of Mills & Boon
Historical Romance's most popular authors

Regency
Brides
Collection

Georgina Devon & Mary Nichols

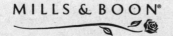
MILLS & BOON®

*First published in Great Britain 2004 by
Harlequin Mills & Boon Limited,
Eton House, 18-24 Paradise Road,
Richmond, Surrey TW9 1SR*

REGENCY BRIDES COLLECTION © Harlequin Books S.A. 2004

The publisher acknowledges the copyright holders of the
individual works as follows:

Betrayal © Alison J. Hentges 1999
Jack Chiltern's Wife © Mary Nichols 1999

ISBN 0 263 84082 4

138-1004

*Printed and bound in Spain
by Litografia Rosés S.A., Barcelona*

BETRAYAL
by
Georgina Devon

Georgina Devon has a Bachelor of Arts degree in Social Sciences with a concentration in history. Her interest in England began when the United States Air Force stationed her at RAF Woodbridge, near Ipswich in East Anglia. This is also where she met her husband who flew fighter aircraft for the United States. She began writing when she left the Air Force. Her husband's military career moved the family every two to three years and she wanted a career she could take with her anywhere in the world. Today, she and her husband live in Tucson, Arizona, with their teenage daughter, two dogs and a cockatiel.

Also by Georgina Devon
in Mills & Boon Historical Romance™:

THE RAKE ★
THE REBEL ★
THE ROGUE'S SEDUCTION ★
THE LORD AND THE MYSTERY LADY

★ novels have linking characters

Look for Georgina Devon's
AN UNCONVENTIONAL WIDOW
Coming December 2004

Prologue

Waterloo, 1815

*W*ar *is hell.*

Major Lord Deverell St Simon ran his hand over his face, smearing rain water and mud across his nose and jaw. It was hot and muggy, and he hated Napoleon Bonaparte's guts. His troops were demoralized and he was close behind.

Damn Napoleon. Damn him to *hell* for starting this war with his plans of world rule. Damn him.

If it were not for Napoleon's escape from Elba, they would not be here. But the Little Emperor never quit.

Even now, there were occasions when Dev could see Napoleon just over the next hillock as the bastard urged his troops to victory. Because of him, Britain's finest were ready to give up their lives. He was the reason they had been fighting for four days, and the massive losses on both sides were devastating.

Smoke lay like fog over the churned, bloody dirt. Death was a miasma Dev waded through while stifling the urge to vomit. Bodies, human and equine, littered the ground, grotesque in their death dance.

The rain started. Again.

Still, Dev made himself grin at his fellow officer and friend, Captain Patrick Shaunessey. 'We are almost through this, Pat. Don't give up now.' The words were for himself as much as for his comrade, and he was honest enough to realize it.

Pat grimaced, his carrot-colored hair sweat stained. 'Never say die,' he said, bitterness tingeing the words.

Dev shrugged and shook his head like a dog, sending drops spattering out from his light brown hair. 'You'd say the same, Pat, except you are more tired than I.'

For the first time that day, a smile quirked up one corner of Pat's mouth. 'And I didn't stay at the Duchess of Devonshire's ball until there was no time to change into my uniform.' His blue eyes gleamed as he looked pointedly at Deverell's gunpowder-stained evening shirt.

Dev grinned, knowing his friend needed the bantering to ease the strain of battle and death. He needed it too. 'They don't call me Devil for nothing. I had no intention of leaving the Duchess's ball early and cutting short my pleasure.' His teeth formed a white slash in his exhaustion-lined face. 'There were any number of ladies ready to console a man about to face war.'

The Captain's snort of amusement was lost in the roar of wind ripping through the poplars. Rain pelted down, turning the already muddy ground into a morass that would impede anything that tried to move. The artillery, with their heavy guns, would have a devil of a time.

Glancing behind and to the right, Dev caught sight of the Duke of Wellington. The Duke was mounted on Copenhagen, his chestnut gelding, and wearing his familiar dark blue coat, white breeches, white cravat and cocked hat.

'Wonder what the Iron Duke wants?' Pat muttered, raising up just enough to see over the ridgeline of Mont Saint Jean, the place Wellington had chosen for his final stand against Napoleon.

'We'll know soon enough,' Dev said.

The sun broke through the clouds, turning the damp ground into a mist-shrouded enigma. Dev considered taking off his black jacket, but thought better of it. White made as good a target as the typical British red uniform coat.

'Dev, Pat,' Lieutenant Colonel Sir James Macdonell yelled, 'come here. We have orders.' Both men exchanged a telling glance as they rose.

Macdonell was a large Highlander, with a reputation for accomplishing what no one else could. His mouth was grimly tight. 'Wellington has ordered us to hold the Château de Hougoumont.'

'With what?' Dev asked, realizing that the château's open position made it a hard place to defend.

'He has given me command of the Scots and Coldstream Guards, the best we have. The château occupies a strategically important place. As long as we hold it, Napoleon must split his forces in order to get to Mont Saint Jean.' Macdonell made eye contact with each man. 'It's our best chance to defeat Napoleon. We must hold it or die trying.'

A *frisson* of excitement ran up Dev's spine. He had never been one to ignore a challenge, not even one such as this. 'Then we will do it.'

'I knew I could count on you,' Macdonell said. 'See to your men and supplies. We have to be in place before Napoleon realizes what is happening.'

After Macdonell left, Dev turned and winked at Pat. 'This is it, old friend. We are about to earn our place in the history books.'

Pat's face was pale but determined, his blue eyes clear.

'You always were one for action. I hope this isn't your last.'

Dev clapped Pat on the back, ignoring the uneasiness his friend's words created. 'I'll stand you to a bottle of Brooks's finest port when we're through this.'

'And I'll hold you to that,' Pat said.

Dev sobered as he saw the fear return to his friend's face. Dev knew his eyes mirrored Pat's. 'Good luck and God go with you,' he said quietly before turning away.

Dev made haste to round up his troops and get them positioned. Coming from the east, they passed through an orchard before entering the walled portion of the property where the château, a chapel, and a barn stood. In reality, Hougoumont was barely more than a farmhouse, its grey stone walls bleak under a sky that had suddenly turned leaden.

The men broke loopholes into the buildings and walls for their Brown Besses to shoot through and then set about cleaning the rifles. Next, they built small fires in an attempt to dry their clothes, which were soaked from the earlier rains.

Dev made his rounds, uncomfortable in his wet jacket and breeches, but unwilling to stop long enough to dry them. Macdonell counted on him, and he would not let the man down. They would be prepared for Napoleon's onslaught.

Once, he passed Patrick and grinned. Pat gave him a brief salute and continued his preparations.

It was after eleven in the morning when they saw the French. The enemy stormed through a hedge and into the fifty feet of barren ground that stood between them and the château. Dev ordered his men to fire. The French dropped, good British lead in their chests.

Time was a blur to Deverell. His men loaded and fired,

loaded and fired. Dev paced amongst them, shouting encouragement, giving direction.

Without warning, a group of Frenchmen reached the gate of the château. A gigantic French lieutenant swung a sapper's axe at the gate. The gate splintered.

Dev rushed forward, knowing that if the French breached the gate the battle was lost. He swung his sword in sweeping arches, using it like a machete. Around him other British soldiers did the same.

From the corner of his eye, Dev saw Colonel Macdonell put his shoulder to the gate and begin to push it closed. Dev followed suit. Men leaped to help.

Somehow the gate was closed. Dev only knew his existence had become a red haze of death and blood and survival.

The French trapped inside Hougoumont were killed or taken prisoner, the château secured once more.

The excitement that had held Dev drained away. He moved toward the grey stone wall with the intention of resting.

'*Merci.*' A weak voice caught his attention. It belonged to a French drummer boy. He had been slashed in the arm and blood ran in a red rivulet down his sleeve. He was only a child.

Dev yanked the cravat from his neck and tied it securely around the boy's arm, then yelled for one of his men. 'See that this soldier is kept alive.'

The British ensign who took the prisoner was not much older than the Frenchman. Dev shook his head in resignation. Death and dying.

The day wore on. The French artillery pounded the château. Afternoon was well progressed. Ammunition was low.

Dev wiped sweat from his brow and prepared to exhort his men further, when smoke arose from the building behind him. The French artillery had hit a haystack. The flames spread to the barn where the wounded lay. Horses ran into the flames. Men and animals screamed.

Dev felt hot, then cold. 'Pat,' he yelled to his comrade, 'see to our men. I must help those poor devils.'

Dev ran toward the fire. Another man joined him.

Dev plunged into the barn, grabbing the first person he reached. The man's moans were pitiful, but Dev ignored them. Better to cause him pain than to lose him to the fire. He deposited him outside and went back.

Where was the French drummer? He had been near the door.

'Boy?' Dev yelled in French.

The answer was a ragged cough, but it was enough. Dev turned left. A figure staggered toward him, and Dev caught the slight youth. Smoke curled around them and burned Dev's lungs as he sped toward the door.

Overhead the timbers crackled. A large snap reverberated through the murky air. A hand grabbed Dev's leg. He slung the drummer boy over his shoulders and gripped the fingers still clinging to his leg. With a grunt, Dev pulled the other man to his feet and propelled the lumbering figure forward.

Noise reverberated through the building.

A large overhead timber gave way, crashing to the floor, bringing a curtain of fire with it. Dev threw the youth forward at the same time he shoved the older soldier toward the doorway.

Pain ripped through Dev. His right leg gave way and he tumbled to the ground. Smoke filled his mouth and burned his lungs.

His last conscious thought was: *this* is hell!

Chapter One

Pippa's gaze darted around Brussels's crowded, stinking streets. Wounded men lay everywhere. She could only be glad she was here. The times she had helped the local midwife and the county surgeon had given her skills which might save lives, or at least ease the passing.

Her twin might even be here. Wellington's letter saying Philip was dead had been sent from here. Philip might be amongst the British fighting Napoleon, and Wellington might not even know.

Her mouth twisted. It was a far-fetched idea. The note was dated weeks ago, and everything pointed to her twin being dead. But she knew her twin was alive, she felt it, and this was the only place she had to start.

A cry of pain caught her attention. It was from a man, his head wrapped in bandages turned brown by dried blood. Flies buzzed around him. His cracked lips opened, and his tongue ran over them, searching for moisture that was not there.

Pippa rushed to him. Kneeling, she felt the heat of fever emanating from him. She took a dipper of tepid water from a nearby bucket and, supporting the soldier's head with one arm, tipped the liquid into his mouth. He gulped greedily.

'Thank ye, lad,' the man said, his voice a hoarse whisper.

''Twas nothing,' Pippa murmured, for the first time regretting her decision to disguise herself as a youth. She had done so because young men were allowed in many places where women were barred, places where there might be people with information regarding her brother. Nothing mattered more than finding Philip.

Yet, if she wore skirts, she could tear off her petticoats and make a new bandage for the man's wound. As it was, she wore a pair of Philip's old pantaloons and one of his shirts, her breasts bound by linen to give her the appearance of a man. She had nothing she could take off without exposing herself.

'Blast,' she muttered, putting aside her wish for petticoats. Steeling herself, she made the decision to remove the filthy bandage. The man would be no worse without it, and probably better.

'Hey! Boy! What do you think you are doing?'

Pippa heard the voice as background noise. She was still too new at her masquerade to realize she was the 'boy'.

'You, boy,' the gruff voice said angrily as a beefy hand gripped her shoulder and swung her around so she landed on her knees.

Pippa did not like being touched. She liked even less being interrupted when she was with a patient.

'Unhand me,' she said, lowly and furiously.

'Touchy for a mite of a lad,' the man accosting her said, dropping his hand.

Scowling, Pippa stood and dusted the dirt from the knees of her buff pantaloons.

The officer looming over her—and she was not small— was a bull of a man, with a scowl the equal of hers. A shock of dark brown hair fell over equally dark eyes.

His frown deepened. 'Leave the men alone. We have

enough problems without your meddling.' He squatted by the soldier. 'And this one is sorely hurt.'

Pippa's anger seeped away as she watched the surgeon gently tend to the man's wound. 'I can help, sir. I've trained with our county surgeon and know many of the local midwife's pain remedies.'

Disregarding her, the surgeon soaked the bandage with water from the nearby bucket and then carefully unwrapped it. 'He would be better off without this.' Dismay moved across his craggy features, followed quickly by stoic acceptance.

The surgeon took off his coat and made it into a pillow, which he carefully laid the soldier's head on. Next, he washed his bloody hands in the water and dried them. Only then did he deign to give Pippa a critical once-over.

'You are naught but a boy, dressed in his older brother's clothes. I'd sooner trust yon private—' he jerked his head in the direction of a man who was going around giving the hurt soldiers water '—with an amputation before I'd let you treat these injured men.'

His callous words bit into Pippa, but she held herself straighter and met the other's hard gaze with one of her own. 'I know enough to realize you have ruined the drinking water by washing your hands in it. Now you must send someone to fetch a fresh bucket.'

'Any fool knows that.'

'You should also consider giving him a tincture of henbane to ease the pain and promote relaxation and sleep. You could do the same with opium or laudanum, but I doubt there is enough of either to go around.'

The surgeon's eyes narrowed. 'How old are you, boy?'

The barked question took her by surprise. It should not have. Only very young boys have downy cheeks and slim shoulders. She had tried to pad her shoulders, she could do nothing about her cheeks.

Going on the offensive, a trick her twin had taught her early in life, she met the surgeon's eyes boldly. 'Old enough to be here.'

For an instant the man's wide mouth quirked up. 'Plenty of spunk.'

Two moans pierced the air, each from opposite sides of the street. The surgeon glanced from one wounded man to the other, his face torn by indecision. The hook of his nose seemed to turn down.

'All right, boy. This is your chance. I cannot tend both men simultaneously.'

Anticipation made Pippa's hands shake. She looked from man to man and found her attention drawn to a bright brown thatch of hair. Her twin had hair that color, not black as her own because they weren't identical. Could it be Philip?

She took a step toward the man, saying over her shoulder, 'Yes, sir.'

The surgeon didn't stop her. 'Mind you don't do anything that will harm the bloke,' he stated, his dark eyes boring into her back. He raised his voice. 'Or I shall have you thrown out of the city on your arse.'

'Ingrate,' Pippa muttered under her breath as she hastened to the patient who might be her twin.

She knelt beside the man, disappointment clenching her hands. He wasn't Philip. But he was sorely injured.

The man's moans increased in volume, and his arms and legs thrashed about, throwing off a dirty blanket that had been draped over him. His right calf was a mass of torn muscles and protruding bone. If she did not act quickly, putrefaction would set in and he would lose the limb. The moans stopped the first time she probed the wound.

She glanced at his face to see him watching her with pain-racked hazel eyes. Rivulets of sweat poured from his high brow. He was more handsome than she had ever imagined a man could be. Pain twisted his features and furrows creased his forehead and carved brackets around his mouth, a mouth that might have been wide and sharply defined if it were not flattened by agony. His jaw was square and clenched. His cheekbones were high and flushed with fever. Perspiration slicked his hair.

'Don't cut it off,' he said, his voice a deep, dry rasp that made her fingers shake even more.

In some ways he reminded her of her brother; strong and clean of limb, with the exception of his right leg, and similar in colouring. But the feelings this man aroused in her, in spite of his helplessness, weren't sisterly. Nor were they welcome under any circumstances, much less these.

Forcing her attention back to his wound, she saw that amputating the limb was his best chance, and yet she found herself agreeing with his command not to remove it. This man had a fierce light in his eyes and a muscular wiriness that spoke of activity. He would not appreciate living without his leg.

By the time she pulled the last fragment of bone and the final piece of torn cloth from the wound, perspiration drenched her shirt. His piercing gaze bent on her face as she worked did not help. Never had a man stared at her so intently, and never had a man's attention affected her so completely.

She dared glance at him again, only to wish she had not. His face was creased in agony, and she knew it had been a supreme effort of will that had kept him conscious during the cleaning.

'That leg will have to come off,' the surgeon said in a gruff voice.

Pippa had not heard him approach. Starting, she twisted around in her squatting position and looked up at him. 'I think I can save it.'

The surgeon shook his head. 'If we were in a small town or he was the only patient, I might agree. But 'tis not so, lad. If the leg stays, it will fester and kill him. Better he lose a limb than lose his life.'

Pippa frowned. She had heard the surgeon at home say similar words, but…

Perhaps the surgeon was right.

The man's broad shoulders shook and the leg beneath Pippa's fingers twitched. His eyelids fluttered, their thick sandy eyelashes creating a sharp shadow against his pale skin. His eyes caught and held her attention, commanding her.

'Don't let him take my leg,' the man whispered, his voice coming hoarse through cracked lips. His hand gripped her wrist and squeezed to emphasize his order. 'I would rather die.'

Even as he said the words, his eyes closed and Pippa realized he was trusting her to do as he ordered. He did not have the energy to fight the surgeon. It was up to her to save his limb.

Her twin came instantly to mind. Philip would not want to lose his leg. He would call himself half a man. This man would do the same. She knew it with a certainty she did not want to question for fear that she would find herself gone insane; that she would find herself more involved with this man than she had any reason to be.

Chewing her bottom lip, Pippa stood and faced the surgeon. 'You heard him. He would rather die.'

'You would risk his life on a whim?' The surgeon's bushy brown eyebrows formed a bar across his wide face. 'I was right not to entrust anyone's care to you.'

Pippa flushed, half-embarrassed at her statement and half-angry at the surgeon for doubting her skills. 'The way a man feels about his life is as important as whether he has one.'

The surgeon's scowl deepened, his attention going to the patient. 'You did a thorough job of cleaning the flesh. Can you set the bone?'

Pippa nodded, sensing that she had won.

'You,' the surgeon bellowed to a nearby soldier, 'bring an eighteen-tail bandage and splint.' Turning his frown back on Pippa, he said, 'If this man dies, you will have to live with your conscience. Now, show me what you can do.'

Pippa bit her bottom lip and studied the surgeon. He met her gaze squarely. He was laying a heavy burden on her, but one doctors and healers faced every day of their lives. She could and would accept that burden.

Reaching into her herbal pouch, she withdrew some garlic oil and mixed it with fresh water. She poured the mixture over the wound to protect against putrefaction. Her patient flinched, and when she looked at his face she saw he had bitten his bottom lip until it bled. But his eyes were open and watching her.

Conscious of his gaze on her, she flexed the leg to straighten the bone for setting. Without a sound the man flinched and then went limp. He had finally passed out. She breathed a sigh of relief for his sake. Quickly and competently, she set the bone, put on soft lint to absorb the drainage and crossed the eighteen tails of the bandage so that the leg was completely wrapped. Lastly, she applied the splint.

By the time she was done, her hands shook and sweat ran in rivers down her spine. It was a hot, muggy day, but she knew it was the fear of failure that had worn her down.

She did not want this man to have his leg amputated. She wanted him to awaken a whole person, wanted to see the fierce determination and fire in his hazel eyes once more.

'You know he will limp—if he survives.' The surgeon's gruff voice intruded on her thoughts.

'And it will pain him most in damp, cold weather,' she added, standing and taking a deep breath to steady her nerves.

'Perhaps we can use you after all. I could not have done a better job of cleaning and setting the leg.'

It was a concession she had begun to think would never come. Pippa released the breath she had been unconsciously holding and broke into a radiant smile. 'You won't regret it.'

He looked at her from the corner of his eye and shook his head. 'You are as pretty as a maid. See that you watch yourself. Some of these men are none too particular.'

Pippa turned red. 'Yes, sir.'

Her attention flitted to the unconscious man. What would he think of her as a woman? It was a question she was fearful of having answered.

'I'd be doing you no favors if I didn't warn you, lad.'

'Thank you,' Pippa muttered, trying to deepen her voice.

The surgeon looked at the patient. 'This one is your special case. See that you let me know when gangrene sets in and the limb must be removed. You have until then to try and save the leg.'

'I will do all I can,' Pippa vowed, watching the steady, shallow rise and fall of the hurt man's chest.

'Meanwhile, there are others who need your services and your herbs.' Turning from her, the surgeon bellowed, 'Jones, stay with this lad and see that you get him what he needs.'

A tall, thin, battle-scarred sergeant ambled up. 'Knew we

was robbin' the cradle for the fightin', Major, but thought we wasn't in need of babies to tend the sick.'

'This young man has just performed as well as any army surgeon I know,' the older man said. 'Don't go giving the lad trouble or I'll have you confined to the hospital.'

Jones shuddered. 'Horrible place. Dark and hot and stinking.'

'A living morgue,' Pippa whispered, her stomach churning. 'Those poor men.'

'Ah, Lord.' Jones rolled his eyes. 'The boy has that fervent look in his eyes. Now he'll want to go nurse the bastards there.'

'You are absolutely right,' Pippa said firmly, squaring her shoulders and jutting out her chin. 'Show me the way, Jones.'

'What about this one?' the surgeon said, stopping Pippa in her tracks. 'Do you intend to leave him here, exposed to the elements?'

Pippa's gaze travelled over the patient. He was tall and well-formed, with broad shoulders and narrow hips. He was a spectacular man. She didn't want him going to the filth and squalor of the hospital.

He is your patient, she told herself. Patient and nothing more. He might not even live.

With difficulty, she forced her concentration to his medical problem. Because of the bands of muscles in his legs, it had been difficult for her to relax his calf enough to open the wounds so she could clean them. It was a good sign because of the strength it showed he had, but he had already been exposed to the wind, sun and rain too much. For the benefit of his limb, he should be sheltered.

'If you can spare the men, Major,' she addressed the surgeon the way the sergeant had done so, 'I'll give them directions to my lodgings. He…he can stay there. 'Tis a single room only, but all that could be had.'

'It'll be done,' the Major said. 'And see if anyone recognizes him. He must have rooms of his own somewhere.'

It took some time before they found men to transport the unconscious soldier to Pippa's lodgings, but when that was done, she set off for the hospital. She knew the men in the confines of the hospital would have less chance of survival than the ones littering the streets. Contagion spread easily in the crowded, dark places and probably the worst of the patients had been taken there.

She was right.

Loud moans woke Pippa from an exhausted sleep. Her head still ached from too many hours over the past weeks spent in the small, smelly quarters of the hospital, and it took her some time to become reoriented.

The room was dark except for a sliver of moonlight entering through the single window, which she had opened in an attempt to get any slight breeze. It had not helped. Heat and humidity hung over Brussels like a pall, and she was sticky and miserable.

The moan came again.

It was her patient. Pippa rose from her pallet on the floor and hurried to the single bed where he lay. A sheen of moisture lit his forehead and the sheets were damp. His linen shirt clung to him, outlining the muscles of his chest and shoulders.

Pippa bit her lip and forced her attention back to his face. Even in the silvered light of the moon he looked flushed. She poured a small amount of bark into some water and knelt beside the bed. Gently she lifted his head and put the mixture to his lips. He swallowed thirstily.

'That will ease the fever,' she murmured to him, not

expecting an answer. He had yet to regain consciousness since having the leg set, and she did not expect him to do so now.

'Nothing will ease hell's flames,' he muttered, opening his eyes.

Their intensity held her spellbound. Although she knew they were bright from fever and sickness, they seared to her soul. She reached to put the empty container back on the nightstand and missed. It crashed to the floor.

'Oh!' Exasperation coloured the word. Now she would have to clean up the mess before she stepped or sat on a piece of glass.

'Unless 'tis a goddess,' the man whispered, continuing his confused train of thought. He caught her hand and brought it to his lips.

Pippa's attention snapped back to him. His gaze was roving over her face and down to the nightshirt she wore. The muslin sheath was loose, but the material was thin enough to show the swell of her bosom. She had removed the confining linen wrap because of the heat and now regretted the comfort that one action had given her in the moist heat. His intimate perusal was making her heart pound. She told herself it was fear that he would discover her charade.

'You are mistaken, sir. I am a youth, not a maid.'

'And I am the Prince Regent,' he muttered, his mouth curving into a rakish grin. 'No man of my acquaintance has such translucent skin. Nor eyes of such lustre. Green as new grass in a summer meadow. Or are they silver?' he muttered, his voice turning querulous as he sought to focus in the dim light. Giving up, he closed his eyes. 'God, but I hurt!'

'You have been grievously injured,' Pippa said, forcing her voice down an octave. 'I...I have been tending you.'

Her subterfuge was wasted. He had passed out again.

Her worry of exposure was immediately replaced by worry for his leg. Was it worsening? Lighting a candle, she quickly examined him. The wound had finally scabbed over several days ago, but the bandage needed changing. Thank goodness there had been enough materials for her to have extra. She changed the dressing quickly and efficiently. Next, she had to lower his fever.

She soaked a cloth in water, wrung it out, and wiped it across his brow and cheeks and down his neck. Hopefully this would bring the fever down while the bark worked from inside. The water was warm, but it was better than doing nothing. She dipped and wrung the cloth again.

If he were not so well muscled and completely inert, she would move him and change the bedding, but she had learned early that he was too heavy for her. Instead, she lifted up his nightshirt as best she could and ran the cloth down his chest and across his ribs, tempted to follow the trail of brown hairs that led beneath the covers. Intellectually she knew that cooling his groin would ease some of the heat from his body, but just the idea of doing so made her stomach knot.

She did not know what was wrong with her. She never had reacted to a patient this way. Never.

She was a healer.

Eyes averted, Pippa carefully peeled back the cover. Soon she would have to look at him, but first she could moisten the cloth. She did so with meticulous care. The last thing he needed was to have sheets wetter than they already were from his sweat, or so she told herself.

Taking a deep breath, she turned to face him. Her gaze travelled slowly down his body, past broad shoulders and flat belly—lower. He was lean and narrow. She gulped and turned hot and cold and hot again.

He was magnificent. Everywhere.

She was a healer. It was her duty to sponge his flushed skin until it cooled, and she would do exactly that.

It seemed a long time before his fever began to break, and every minute was alternating pain and pleasure. Was he as wonderful a person as his body was perfect? She almost feared he would be. He was definitely charming. No man had ever kissed her hand.

He was very likely a rake.

Her hands moved automatically while her mind raced. Perhaps when her quest for her twin was over, she would go to London for a Season. She had refused to do so these many years because she had no wish to find a husband. Now, to her chagrin, she found the idea had some interest. But that was the future. First she had to heal this man and then she had to find her brother. After that would be time enough to think further.

Resolutely, she covered her patient and returned the cloth to its bowl. Next she cleaned up the broken glass she had forgotten about.

When she crawled back into bed, she felt as though she had been riding to hounds and all her energy was spent. All because of him. The way he affected her made it hard to breathe and even harder to think impartially.

Never had she been this attracted to a man, much to her grandfather's irritation since Earl LeClaire wanted her married. All she had ever cared about was her healing. Now she had found a man who stirred her blood—and she was impersonating a male.

It was a situation she could do nothing about, and morning would come soon enough. She needed rest as tomorrow would be another busy day.

But sleep eluded her. And when it came, her dreams were of a tall, smiling rake who pursued her down a tree-shaded lane. Spring filled the air with the scent of freshly scythed grass; grass the colour of her eyes.

Dev woke slowly, his head spinning, his leg throbbing. Heat was a palpable blanket of discomfort, so he tossed aside whatever was covering him, only to discover he was still twisted in something.

'Bloody hell,' he muttered, frustration and pain increasing his normal impatience. Where was he? Why did he hurt? Why couldn't he move?

Hougoumont. Flames. Pain. The woman.

Memories roared back, bringing agony instead of comfort. But he was alive, he had survived that battle fought in hell. Was it over? Had they defeated Napoleon? What of Patrick?

He tried to sit up and pain shot from his right leg to his groin and up his spine. He fell back, cold sweat breaking out on every part of his body.

Slowly and carefully, he lifted his head only and gazed down the length of his body. He wore a nightshirt that reached down to his thighs, ending—

His right leg was encased in a wooden splint from foot to knee.

He groaned and let his head drop. He vaguely remembered someone saying it would have to come off and him telling a lad not to let it happen. It seemed the youth had done what he asked. Relief washed over Dev.

It was instantly replaced by anxiety. He was alive and whole. Was Patrick? Had he saved the French lad?

And what about the woman? The one who had cared for him. Or had she? The memory was not solid. It seemed to float in and out of his mind. Maybe it was a dream. Perhaps it had been the lad, if there had been a lad. He was delirious.

Yet, the image of a beauty with ebony hair and green, green eyes haunted him. Her face was an oval with high cheeks, a wide mouth and flawless skin. Unless there was no woman, and his mind was playing tricks with him— which was quite possible under the present circumstances.

Perhaps he was even crazy. He would not be the first to go insane after a battle. His older brother, Alastair, had suffered nightmares for years that made him relive the battles against Napoleon in Spain.

Wearily, Dev rubbed a weak hand over his brow. If only someone were here to tell him what was going on.

The sound of an opening door caught his attention. Turning, he saw a youth pause in the act of entering the room.

Chapter Two

Pippa stopped flat. Her patient was awake and alert, his gaze fixed on her. Taking a steadying breath, she stepped into the room and closed the door behind her.

His cheekbones were rouged with fever or exertion, but his eyes were aware and intelligent. 'Who are you? Where am I?' he demanded in the tones of one used to being obeyed.

She smiled in spite of herself even as she bristled at his order. He reminded her much of Philip, her twin. Moving to the bed, she said, 'My name is Pippen LeClaire, and you are in my room.' At his frown, she added, 'No one knows who you are, and I am the only one with room for you. I could not leave you in the street or have you taken to the hospital with the other wounded.'

The scowl faded from his face when she laid the back of her hand lightly on his forehead to feel for fever. He had none.

'Then I have much to be grateful to you for. And my name is Deverell St Simon.' His brow furrowed again, and his eyes took on a faraway look before coming sharply back to her face. 'Are you the lad who saved my leg from amputation?'

She nodded.

'Then I owe you my life,' he said gravely. 'I would not have wished to live a cripple.'

'You owe me nothing,' Pippa said hastily, feeling uncomfortable at his solemnity. 'I am a healer and helping others is something I must do. Besides,' she said as matter-of-factly as possible while her heart pounded in discomfort, for she had known exactly how he would feel and that scared her. 'You will never move comfortably and most likely that leg will plague you until you die.'

He attempted a shrug that made him grimace. 'Much better than wearing a wooden peg.'

Pippa, seeing the stubborn set of his jaw, forbore comment and hoped fervently that he would continue to think so. 'You have been unconscious and delirious for nearly a fortnight and must be ready to eat a feast. If you will lay quietly, I will ask the landlady for some gruel.'

'I won't eat pap!'

Instead of arguing, which she knew from past experience with her twin would be fruitless and only end in a fight, Pippa turned away and left the room. He was weak enough and hungry enough that he would eventually eat whatever she brought him.

Dev watched the youth leave. The boy had an odd feminine look about him, with a face that was free of beard and hips that were a trifle too wide for his shoulders and moved a tad too much for masculine purpose. Pippen reminded him of the woman he had seen in his delirium—a ridiculous thought.

Exhaustion ate at him. Sighing, he fell back on to the cushions and told himself Pippen could not help that he was made the way he was. It was not as though the lad was the only man ever born with more female traits than was good.

Dev promptly fell into a restless half-sleep where cannon and musket shot echoed in his ears, and the stench of burning flesh swamped his nostrils.

A short time later Pippa re-entered the room with a tray. Warm tea and a steaming bowl of beef-flavoured gruel would do wonders for her invalid.

Putting the tray on a nearby table, she saw her patient—Deverell St Simon, she told herself—had slipped back into a troubled sleep. Sweat dotted his brow and his hands clenched the sheet in bunches. The urge to soothe him was as overpowering as it was bewildering. All her life she had felt the need to help others, but never had the desire to care for another made her body shake. Why, she knew nothing about this man except his name, and that meant nothing to her.

She took a controlling breath and laid a hand on his shoulder. He jolted awake.

'Who—?' He broke off, his eyes wide, his body jerking upward. 'Angel?'

His eyes searched her face, bringing a blush of awareness as his attention lingered on her mouth before sliding down to where her breasts would be if she had not bound them.

Pippa pushed him gently down on the pillows. 'Calm yourself,' she murmured. ''Tis only me, Pip—Pippen.' She had almost said her own name, she was sure because of his blatant regard. She must be more careful, constantly on guard. It would not be easy. 'I have brought you some food.'

His eyes lost their startled look and his gaze fell away from her face. Some of the tension left his body. 'For a moment I thought you were someone else. A…a woman.'

Pippa kept her countenance smooth, showing only mild interest. 'What would a woman be doing in here?'

He turned away. 'I don't know. I thought a green-eyed lady cared for me while I was unconscious.' He looked back at Pippa. 'She had your face. Only I would swear, she had the sweet curves of a female.' He sighed. 'But enough of daydreaming. Right now I could eat the landlady's entire larder.'

Pippa chuckled, letting the relief she felt at his change of topic ease the tightness that had mounted in her shoulders during his talk of a strange woman. He was remembering the time she had sponged him. 'You will eat lightly. I don't want you throwing everything up no sooner than you get it down.'

He grimaced.

Pippa put her fists on her hips, feet shoulder width apart, and looked at him. Belatedly she realized what she was doing. The pose was natural with her when dealing with her brother, and invariably it put her twin's back up. It would probably do the same to her patient.

With a sigh at her own mishandling of the situation, she quickly sat down on the only stool the room had and ladled up some of the gruel. She put the spoon to his lips. Instead of opening his mouth, his nose wrinkled in disgust and he scowled at her.

'Please,' she said. 'You need food to get well, and you need food that is easy on your digestion. Later, when you are better and your stomach can handle mutton, I will allow you a complete meal.' When his face softened, she added the clincher, 'I don't have the time or energy to care for you longer than necessary. I'm already late for my shift at the hospital.'

She watched his countenance as irritation warred with consideration. Consideration won. Pippa had been right about the way to handle him. It was the way she would have dealt with her twin.

Dev swallowed the gruel quickly, and Pippa was sure that if he had the energy and the bad manners, he would pinch his nose closed. Afterwards, she sponged off his face as professionally as she could when his nearness made her stomach knot. That finished, she tucked the covers around his chest to protect him from a draught.

Her face flamed at the familiarity of the gesture and the feel of his muscled shoulders under her fingers. It was a relief to turn away and prepare a draught.

'Take this,' she said, pivoting back and tipping the glass to his lips.

'I'm not an invalid,' he groused, wrapping the fingers of one hand around the glass Pippa still held.

Mind-startling awareness travelled from where they touched to explode in Pippa's chest. She stepped abruptly away and chattered, 'The drink is laudanum for sleep and pain and bark for the fever and inflammation. When I return, I will change your dressing, but 'twill not be until late tonight. If you need anything, ring this bell and the landlady will come.' She laid a brass bell with wooden handle by the bed.

'Thank you,' he said solemnly. 'I won't ever forget what I owe you.'

''Tis nothing,' Pippa mumbled, grabbing up her coat and heading for the safety of the hospital.

The less time she spent in her handsome patient's company now that he was awake, the better for her peace of mind. She was here in Brussels to find her twin, not get herself embroiled with a man who might be anyone. But even if he was the Prince Regent himself—which he wasn't because he was much thinner than that corpulent royal—she would not be interested. She was going to dedicate her life to healing.

Best, when she returned, to find out if he had lodgings

somewhere and arrange for him to be moved there. Surely there was someone who could look after him. That decision made, Pippa found herself alternately unsettled at the thought of him alone and relieved that he would no longer be a constant temptation to her.

Arriving at the crowded hospital, she set to work with a vengeance. There was always so much to do and not enough people or supplies to do it with.

Bent over the ripped arm of a sergeant, Pippa concentrated on removing the dressing with as little pain as possible. Gangrene had set in.

'How is it?' the man asked, agony etching furrows in his brow.

Pippa looked from the arm that would need to be amputated to the man's face. It was all she could do to keep tears from slipping down her face. 'You will need the surgeon to look at you,' she said calmly, quietly, hoping the sergeant didn't see the truth in her eyes. 'For now, I am going to clean it and let it lay unwrapped. The air will do it good.'

What she didn't tell the man was that it would not matter what she did, and the surgeon would be glad of the time saved by not having to remove a bandage. Too many soldiers needed operations. Sighing, Pippa stood and knuckled the kinks in her lower back.

'You, young man,' a French-accented female voice said imperiously. 'Come here.'

Pippa was getting used to being called a boy and turned to see if the woman was speaking to her. A small, blonde Pocket Venus with the biggest, bluest eyes Pippa had ever seen, knelt less than ten feet away with a soldier's head in her lap. The woman was dressed in the height of fashion in a sprigged muslin dress, all of which was covered by a voluminous apron. Definitely a lady, but the accent was wrong for a British hospital.

Pippa strode to her. 'Madam?'

'Lady Witherspoon.' She motioned Pippa down. 'This man needs a bath and I cannot give it. The water is right here and a piece of soap.'

Pippa nearly choked. This was one of the few duties she had managed to avoid. 'Ah, milady…'

Before she could finish her explanation, the lady had gone on to the next patient. Pippa stared after her, feeling awkward and trapped. Luckily, she saw Sergeant Jones and waved him over.

'I cannot lift the man properly,' she gave him her regular excuse, one he'd heard frequently.

Jones gave her his great lopsided grin that showed a missing canine tooth. 'Then you take that bloke over yonder. Has shrapnel all in his head. Them head wounds are the bloodiest nuisances. Turn my stomach with all their weeping they do.'

Pippa agreed willingly, but before going asked, 'Who was that lady? Her accent is all wrong.'

Jones didn't even bother to look where Pippa indicated. 'Frenchie. Married to our Marquis of Witherspoon. Several of the men have spit on her, but she never says a harsh word. Almost as though she's doin' this to make up fer somethin'.' He grunted as he rolled the patient on to his side. 'She's been helpin' regular as clockwork. Not as good as you, mind, but then she's a woman—and Quality.'

Pippa suppressed a grin at his lumping her with the 'men', while she digested the information. 'Then why have I never seen her?'

Jones slanted her a knowing look. 'Fine woman, but not fer the likes of me 'n' you, lad. Besides, she comes in the late afternoon. You're with the Major making rounds.'

Accepting Jones's assumption and explanation, Pippa went to her next patient. At least her disguise was perfectly safe. If the man she spent the most time with, and who did all the really personal care of the wounded, thought she was male, then everyone else did too.

Many hours later, Pippa walked the darkened streets of Brussels. Her back ached, her feet hurt, and she'd cried enough tears to float one of His Majesty's ships. The man had lost his arm, screaming in pain in spite of all the rum she and Jones had forced between his clenched teeth. She hated it when these things happened.

Her reaction made her question her commitment to healing. She should be strong and not cry. She should be able to focus on doing what was necessary and go on. The local surgeon had said she felt too much of her patients' pain, that she needed to distance herself emotionally—and that was before she came here and saw all this carnage.

She raked her fingers through the short length of her hair, her hand running on even after the strands ended. A month since she'd whacked off her waist-length hair, and she still tried to comb it as she had for many years. Another tear slipped.

Pippa stopped in the middle of the road and stomped her foot. She was acting like a watering pot. This would never do. She had things to do. Sick men to help and a brother to find.

Philip.

Somewhere her twin still lived. Instead of spending all her time worrying about the man lying in her bed or crying over things that had to be done, she should try again to see Wellington. Last week was the most recent time she'd sought an audience with the Iron Duke, and last week was the most recent time her request had been denied. Tomorrow she would try again.

Finding Philip was her sole reason for being here in Brussels, disguised as a boy and unchaperoned. Nothing else mattered.

Her grandfather thought she was here with Aunt Tabitha, but Aunt Tabitha was in London, blissfully unaware that Pippa was supposed to be under her chaperonage in Brussels. That was the way Pippa wanted it.

She had cut off her hair and taken the clothes Philip had worn as a youth. They were no longer in fashion, but a country man might still wear them. Disguised as a boy, she had booked passage on a packet crossing the channel and made her way here.

A young woman would never be told anything but what was proper, and she had a funny feeling that what had happened to her twin was less than respectable. Nor would a woman have been allowed the freedom to come and go as she had been while asking about her twin in the hopes that some clue to his whereabouts would emerge.

But if someone ever found out what she had done, her reputation would be gone. No one in Polite Society would ever receive her. No decent man would ever ask for her hand, no matter how wealthy she was. Not that she wanted to marry. She wanted to heal the sick and had turned down numerous offers from Aunt Tabitha to come to London for the Season. Still, she did not want to be beyond the pale.

She sighed. She had to stop this useless worrying, it did her no good. Shaking her head to clear the melancholy thoughts, she squared her shoulders. Spirits somewhat under control, Pippa strode purposefully to her lodging.

She paused just inside the door of her darkened room, allowing her eyes to adjust. The moon shone through the lone window like a silver flame in a big lantern. A splash of white light fell across the bed where Deverell St Simon lay, his face flushed and glistening from sweat.

'Patrick! Damn it man, where are you?' His anxious words cut through the night. 'I can't see you!'

A nightmare. Pippa forgot her earlier resolve to have him gone as soon as possible and rushed to his side.

She put a hand to his forehead. Fever. She should have prepared another draught of bark and left it with the landlady with instructions to give it to him. Instead, she had let her attraction to him make her careless. Guilt twisted her stomach even as she wrung a damp cloth in the nearby bowl of water which she had placed just for this type of occurrence.

Remorse brought still more tears. She dashed them away with the heel of her hand and concentrated on cooling and soothing her patient. She was overly tired and needed a good night's sleep, something she would get shortly.

'Deverell,' she murmured, 'everything is fine. You're in my bed, not on the battlefield. Patrick is not here.'

Her voice seemed to calm him. He stopped thrashing and no more words came.

Pippa crossed to her bag of herbs, lit a single candle and prepared more bark. Kneeling at the bed, she dripped it into her patient's mouth.

His eyes opened, catching her in their brilliance. 'Angel,' he whispered. 'My angel of mercy.'

Pippa started, nearly dropping the half-full glass. 'No! That is...' She took a deep calming breath. He was delirious. ''Tis me. Pippen. The boy who is taking care of you.'

'Pippen?' Bewilderment replaced the admiration in his eyes. 'Oh, yes. I remember now.'

Pippa lifted his head and tipped the rest of her concoction down his throat. 'That will help you,' she said as he sputtered.

'Choke me, more like,' he said with a faint smile that did dangerous things to her equilibrium.

She let his head fall. 'Some laudanum will ease the pain in your leg and help you sleep.'

'You should take some for yourself, Pippen.' His hazel eyes, full of compassion, held hers. 'You look exhausted. I'd wager a monkey that since I've been here you have not gotten a decent night's sleep.'

His words were too close to the truth for comment. Instead, she held out the opium.

'I need to go back to my own rooms,' he said. 'There is no reason you should have to give up your bed and your privacy for me.'

He took the small glass from her. Pippa didn't fight him, understanding that he needed to show he was not completely helpless. His hand shook, and he very nearly spilled the contents before getting it to his mouth. The small act exhausted him, and she grabbed the empty glass as his arm fell.

'You will get stronger every day.'

'Can I be transported to my rooms?'

'Most probably. But it would not be comfortable.'

His eyes darkened. 'I can stand pain, Pippen. I am not a milksop to be constantly coddled. I am a man who has taken care of himself for many years.'

'Tell me where your rooms are, and I'll find out tomorrow if they are still available.' Now it was her turn to frown. 'But I'm not sure this is a good idea. You need someone to care for you.'

He grinned. 'You can check on me. It isn't right that I have taken your bed. Where have you slept while I've been here?'

Pippa nodded to a screen. 'Behind that is a pallet. It's big enough and comfortable enough.'

Dev gave the tiny room a cursory look. A single window provided what cooling breeze there was. There was a plain oak wash-stand, a small stool and table. A single candle illuminated the area around the bed. Nothing was expensive, but it was utilitarian. The screen took up space, but he understood why Pippen would want it. No one, not even family, liked living this close together.

'This room isn't big enough to house my father's hunting dogs, let alone two men,' he said.

'Your father must be very grand, indeed.'

'The Duke of Rundell.'

Pippa sat abruptly on the stool. 'The Duke of Rundell?' Even she had heard of the most powerful duke in Britain. That meant Deverell was definitely an officer. He might know her twin. Excitement clenched her hands and made the breath catch in her throat.

'Do you...do you know Philip LeClaire?'

His brow furrowed. 'No. I've heard of the LeClaire name, but that's all.' He gave her a narrowed look. 'Why do you want to know?'

She took a deep breath and plunged into her rehearsed lie. 'He is a distant cousin and we were told he was dead, but I know better.' For once the words came easily to her tongue. 'I am searching for him because his grandfather— my great uncle—is ill and needs him home.'

'Who told you he was dead?'

'The Home Office sent a letter two months ago saying Philip was dead. But it isn't true. I know it.'

'Steady,' Dev said.

Pippa took a deep breath and just barely kept her voice from catching. 'Earl LeClaire suffers from apoplexy. He had a seizure just six months ago, and the letter nearly brought on another. The doctor has ordered complete bed rest. I fear that if I cannot find my t—cousin soon, the Earl will have another. One that might be the end.' Only sheer will power kept her from more tears. 'I have to find Philip. I have to.'

'I will help you,' Dev promised. 'When I am able to walk we will go see Wellington. If anyone knows where an officer is, and I assume an earl's grandson is an officer, the Iron Duke will.'

Gratitude overwhelmed Pippa. 'Do you know Wellington?'

A lopsided grin eased the lines of pain around his mouth. 'Not really. But he's a crony of my father's and my commanding officer. I think he will see me.'

'Thank you so much.' This man would finally get her into the illustrious hero of Waterloo. The barely checked tears flowed. 'You must think me a sissy to be crying like this.'

'I think you a young man who has carried too much responsibility and needs a good night's sleep. Something I doubt you'll get on that pallet.'

Pippa gave him a watery smile. 'That's where you are wrong. I am so tired I could sleep on a heap of rocks.'

'Then go to bed,' her patient said, 'and let me get my rest.'

Pippa went behind the screen and sprawled on the blankets. Excitement made her pulse speed. Deverell was going to do for her what she had been unable to accomplish. He would get her into Wellington. But tonight she had to put the hope aside and rest.

The room was close and humid. The discomfort from the heat was intensified by the binding she wore around her breasts and the fact that she was still in her shirt and breeches. She had slept this way since Deverell had regained consciousness, but the lack of rest was finally wearing her down.

This constant crying was not like her, and she realized that if she did not get some rest, she would not be able to keep going. It was a thought she could not bear. Too many people needed her healing skills.

She had to undo her breasts and sleep in less restrictive clothing in the hopes of being cooler. But what about Deverell? Did she dare? What if he needed her in the night? She sighed. She could give him more laudanum.

'Deverell,' she whispered, 'are you awake?'

'Yes,' he whispered back. 'You need to sleep. I need to think.'

'You are fighting the laudanum,' she scolded gently. 'I can give you more. You need rest.'

He snorted. 'You have already given me enough to fell an opium eater. No, thank you.'

She heard him shift. 'Do you need help getting comfortable?'

'No, thank you again,' he said. 'Will you take a message to Wellington's headquarters tomorrow? Tell him I'm alive and find out where Patrick is? Ask him to meet with us.'

'Of course, if that will make you sleep tonight.'

'It will certainly help.'

'Consider it done.'

Now perhaps he would sleep so she could put on her loose nightshirt and be able to rest herself. Within minutes she heard his light snoring, a sound that strangely enough did not bother her.

She gave him several minutes more before acting. Freeing her breasts from their restraint was like taking a deep breath of fresh air. Comfort eased some of the ache in her back and legs as she laid down.

She would feel better in the morning. Tomorrow she would be her old self.

*   *   *

The next day, Pippa wondered how she ever thought she would be her old self while Dev still lived with her. Even taking off his bandage was an ordeal she dreaded nearly as much as he seemed to. Most patients faced anxiety when bandages were removed, and normally she dealt with their emotions better. But this was Dev. She was beginning to realize that when he was uncomfortable so was she. And for some reason she did not understand, he was very upset about this. There was no underlying excitement or joy as she was used to seeing.

She looked down at his strained face. 'This shan't take long. And it should be relatively painless.'

He nodded, his mouth white around the edges. 'Pain isn't the issue, Pippen.'

She stopped unwrapping the linen bandage that covered his lower right leg. 'Then what is?'

'Nothing.' He turned away.

Dev gritted his teeth to keep from telling Pippen all his fears. The boy had no idea what it was like for a man to look into his future and see himself as an invalid. He was used to being active and doing what he pleased when it pleased him. Much as he might tell himself differently, he knew his wounds would make a difference. The knowledge was like a sore that ate at his peace of mind.

'Dev?'

Pippen's enquiry pulled Dev from his melancholy thoughts. There was no reason to burden the lad with his problems. Pippen was doing more than necessary for many British soldiers here in Brussels. He was just another one of the youth's patients—or would be if he hadn't ousted Pippen from his bed.

Dev released the breath he'd unknowingly held. 'Never mind, Pip, just unwrap the blasted thing so I can see just how ugly it is.'

Pippen's too green eyes darkened in something suspiciously like pity. 'It will be like any other wound that's healing, but not completely well.'

It was an effort not to snap at the boy. With carefully measured tones, Dev said, 'I don't need your pity, lad. Your skill as a sawbones has been more than sufficient.'

Pippen nodded, refraining from a response.

Under the bright afternoon light of a hot Brussels afternoon, Dev's leg was slowly revealed. In much less time than Dev had thought possible, his limb lay stretched out on the sheets. Vivid red lines slashed across his flesh, interspersed with splotched welts where the skin was healing after being burnt.

'Not a pretty sight,' Dev said softly.

'No worse than many others I've seen. You are fortunate that it has healed cleanly and you still have your leg.'

Pippen's gentle words did nothing to assuage the bitterness knifing through Dev's gut. Exhaustion smashed into him, and he fell back on the pillows, one arm flung across his eyes. The last thing he wanted to see right now was his deformity.

'The swelling is almost gone.'

Dev nodded.

'I think it looks fine,' Pippen stated.

Dev ignored Pippen's attempts to gloss over the wound. He didn't want to talk about his leg. Maybe in a couple days, after he got used to the looks—like he'd got used to the pain and then later the constant ache—he would be interested in talking to Pippen about what the scars would look like after the redness went away. Maybe. Not now.

He said nothing while Pippen bathed the leg.

'I think we can stop wrapping it,' Pippen said, his tone thoughtful. 'The fresh air will be good for it.'

Dev grimaced. Without the bandage he would be able to

see the carnage that was his leg. When it was wrapped, he could fool himself that it would return to normal. Even with the discomfort, he had been able to tell himself the leg would be fine when it healed. But seeing it, with the scars and puckered flesh, would be a constant reminder that it would never be normal again.

He stared at the dingy wall, wishing Pippen would go away.

'Dev?'

'Go away, Pippen. Go see if you can get a message to Wellington. See if anyone knows what happened to Captain Patrick Shaunessey.' He managed to keep from saying, Go away and let me wallow in my self-pity.

For long moments, the lad said nothing and Dev could feel his gaze. 'As you wish, Dev. I shall tell the landlady to bring you something to eat. Stew, if you like, and a big chunk of fresh bread.'

Dev forced himself to smile and meet Pippen's eyes. 'That would be more than welcome. Now, please go.'

He heard, rather than saw, the door close. With a grunt of pain, he pulled himself up in bed. His leg lay spread out, immobile and stiff. He looked his fill, willing himself to accept the disfigurement. He bent at the waist and carefully ran one finger along the line of the worst scar. The welt twisted and buckled, the angry red trail ending just above his knee. He barely felt his touch.

Growing braver, he ran his palm along the damaged skin, noting the roughness. Little pricks of pain darted along the length of his leg. At least he could feel something. That had to be good.

Exhaustion ate at him. This was more movement than he had done since regaining consciousness. Yet he gritted his teeth and continued to study his leg.

He had always been active. The army had been the ideal

place for him. As the youngest son, many had expected him to join the clergy, but he was too energetic. Knowing he would never be happy in so sedate a position, his father had bought him a commission. Dev had never regretted that decision. Not even now.

He could have crippled himself riding to hounds or in a coaching accident. At least he had gained his wounds by fighting for his country, by protecting something he felt strongly about, by defending England.

Determination clenched his fists and tightened his shoulder muscles. He would heal. He would do everything he always had. He would ride a horse. He would dance the night away. He would bed a woman.

So help him, he would not waste away into the life of a cripple. He would not.

Chapter Three

Deverell's previous landlord shrugged his ample shoulders, that perennially Gallic motion expressive of great regret. 'I am sorry for it, but Monsieur St Simon never returned from the battle. I am a businessman. I rented his rooms.'

Pippa felt like crumbling. This was the second piece of bad news today. Just minutes before, she had been denied access to Lord Wellington and anyone else who could have answered Deverell's questions. The setback would not please Dev.

Now she was being told that Deverell would have to stay in her small, cramped room. He would continue to disturb her in ways she was unaccustomed to. Desperation gnawed at her. 'Do you have any other rooms available?'

'*Non.* The English are coming like the droves of sheep they raise.' A grin split his thick, wide lips. 'Very profitable, to be sure.'

Pippa nodded. She had spent all morning preparing herself to move Dev. She had told herself it was for the best. Being the son of the wealthiest duke in Britain, he could easily pay someone to watch him around the clock. She didn't have to be that person. She had squared her shoulders and girded her loins, so to speak. And now this.

She felt an inexplicable mixture of emotions. Regret, apprehension…elation. As much as she had known closer proximity to Deverell would not be good for her peace of mind, she found herself glad that he would have to stay with her. At least, for a while longer. This way she would know he got expert care, and she wouldn't have to worry about someone harming his leg, which was not entirely healed. Why, he couldn't even use a cane yet, so could not walk.

They were paltry excuses for the real reason she was glad, but she refused to acknowledge any other.

'Well,' she said briskly, 'do you still have his things?'

The portly landlord drew himself to his full height, which was several inches shorter than Pippa. 'But of course. When I let his rooms, I had all his belongings packed away in case someone came to claim them. I have, also, a note. Sent from London,' he finished, a sly, curious gleam in his dark eyes.

'From his family, no doubt,' Pippa said. 'I would like his possessions, please.'

It was a short matter of time before Pippa's errand was completed, and she was back in her room. With Dev's possessions, her meagre space was more cramped than ever. Having been raised on a country estate where all of the public rooms were large enough to train horses in, and the private chambers were not much smaller, Pippa found herself feeling claustrophobic. There was too little space and too many objects in this single room. Not to mention Deverell.

Trying to stow his gear under the bed, she accidentally knocked the mattress. Dev opened his eyes, their usual bright clarity muddy from sleep. His light brown hair lay like thick satin across his broad forehead. He grinned and Pippa thought her knees would fail.

'You're back from the hospital early,' he said, grimacing as he pulled himself up in bed until he lay propped up against the pillows.

'You should not do that yourself,' Pippa scolded, rushing to help him get comfortable.

'I have done this before.' His gaze darted to her, his knuckles white where he gripped the sheet. 'Did you find out about Patrick?'

Pippa gulped. He wanted so badly to find out what had happened to Patrick. 'I know you're eager for information, but no one I could reach knew anything. I couldn't get into Wellington or even his aide.' She sighed and added softly, 'As usual.'

Dev frowned, but his grip on the sheets eased. 'Well, no news is good news, or so the saying goes. Patrick is very likely doing better than I am.'

'I would not be surprised,' Pippa said, wanting to ease his anxiety about his friend. 'I understand how it is when you are worried about someone.'

He smiled at her. 'I know you do, and we'll do something about that. Wellington will see me. I promise you that.'

She returned his smile, her stomach doing funny things. 'I know. I wish I could have helped you today.'

'You helped by trying. How about my rooms?' He gave her a devilish grin. 'If I remember right, that was another errand I asked you to do for me.'

Chagrin pulled her mouth down. 'And again I have no good news. The innkeeper gave your rooms away.'

Dev fell back into the pillows. 'That is not surprising. I shall just have to find others.'

Pippa shook her head. 'There are none to be had. Brussels is filled with every Englishman and woman who wanted to travel to the Continent in the past years but could not because of Napoleon.'

'I should have thought of that,' Dev said. 'Oh, well. We will make do.'

'That we will,' Pippa said, picking up the concoction of bark and water she had left on the table by the bed and giving him a purposeful look. 'You were supposed to drink this.'

He returned her gaze complacently. 'It tastes bitter.'

Without conscious intent, she assumed her position of hands on hips. Exasperation made her voice breathy. 'You are like a child about this medicine. If you don't drink this for the pain, you won't be able to rest. If you don't rest, you will be longer healing.'

Dev cocked one devilish brow. 'You fuss like an old woman, and you're not even old enough to grow a decent beard. And speaking of which…did you get my gear? A shave would be the very thing to make me feel human again.'

Pippa's heart, which had speeded up at his reference to an old woman, eased as her patient's thoughts turned to his grooming. 'I have all your things, and a heavy load it was. Most of it is in your trunk in *Madame*'s cellar. Only a portmanteau is here. Are you one of those dandies who must dress to perfection for everything? Although you certainly weren't dressed correctly for the battlefield.' She shook her head in private amazement at the fact that he had fought in evening dress.

Dev smiled, a rakish baring of perfect teeth. Memories of enjoyable times sparkled in his eyes. 'I dare say I wasn't the only one out of uniform. A group of us went directly from the Duchess of Devonshire's ball. And I'd do it again.'

Pippa left him to his memories while she pulled his portmanteau from under the bed and rummaged through it,
looking for his shaving equipment. She found his razor, a
small mirror, a lathering brush and finally a tin in which
she found his soap. The exotic scent of bergamot, an in-
gredient for perfumes distilled from the rind of certain or-
anges, surrounded her. It was a very distinctive smell, and
Pippa found herself entranced by it.

'Is this what you use to shave?' she asked, holding the
soap out to Deverell.

Dev's attention came back to the present. 'Yes,' he said,
the bergamot bringing back memories.

He had first worn the scent the night he met Sam. She
had seemed like a goddess on the stage, all aflame with the
passion of her role. Losing her to his oldest brother, Jonathan, Marquis of Langston, had been the hardest thing in
his life. Until now.

He sighed and forced his thoughts back to the present.
A good cleaning would make him feel better.

'Help me sit up higher, Pippen, and then bring a tray
with hot water and towels.'

Pippen gazed at him, doing nothing. 'I'll help you sit
straighter, but you cannot shave yourself.'

This boy to whom he owed his life had a very definite
way about him. Any minute now he would spread his feet
and plant his fists on his hips, a stance he took when he
was determined to have his way.

'I can shave myself very well, thank you,' Dev said in
his chilliest tone. 'You cannot do it.' He gave the youth a
once-over that made the boy blush. 'You have probably
never wielded a razor in your life. And you aren't about to
start on me.'

The lad drew himself up and assumed the pose. 'What

if you slit your own throat? You are still weak and shaving is a very precise art.'

Dev felt his lips twitch. 'Are you a valet when you're not healing? If so, tell me and I will let you clean me up.'

Dull red spread over Pippen's unfashionably tanned skin. The boy was in the sun too much. 'No, but I have done the service for…for Earl LeClaire. Upon occasion.'

Much as he was inclined to argue, Dev found that his small store of energy was fast depleting. 'Show me how you sharpen the razor.'

With methodical motions, Pippen stropped the razor over the sharpening strap. He had a grace of wrist that Dev could not remember seeing in any man other than his middle brother's valet. But then Alastair was a Corinthian and well thought of in the *ton*, so his man was the best to be had.

When the razor glistened in the bright sunshine pouring through the single window, Pippen gave him a 'what now?' look. Dev sighed.

'Proceed as you would with Earl LeClaire and if you falter, I will stop you immediately…if I am not mortally injured.'

The words were as autocratic as he could bring himself to be with the boy. Pippen looked too vulnerable for his own good, and when his chin trembled like a child caught with his hand in the toffee, it made Dev wonder how the lad had got to Brussels on his own, let alone how he had been so successful as a healer for Wellington's victorious army.

Then there were the boy's soft looks. Dev very nearly shook his head in wonder before catching himself. Pippen had taken off the hot towels, which had been wrapped around Dev's face to soften his beard, and lathered his cheeks, jaw and upper neck. Now he was applying the razor to Dev's skin with a look of complete concentration.

Yes, his saviour looked almost like a madonna. The boy's hair was pitch black and too long for fashion, with curls that sprang in all directions. Some lady of Quality would want Pippen for ulterior motives. But some man of questionable virtue would want the youth for even more nefarious schemes.

Pippen's long, slim fingers firmly guided the razor up Dev's neck in one smooth motion. A slight line drew Pippen's ebony brows together and accentuated the pure green of his eyes. They were the colour of the emeralds Dev's mother had set aside as a wedding gift for his bride. The jewels would suit Pippen.

The thought was a leveller.

Dev closed his eyes. What was he thinking? He had never been a lover of boys. His last love had been Samantha, who was decidedly female and several years his senior. Since losing her, he had flirted with every eligible girl in Brussels and shared less acceptable activities with the ineligible ones.

No, these wayward thoughts were due to exhaustion and the fact that Pippen was too feminine and delicate. A state no man should enjoy being. He would do his saviour a favour by telling him to toughen up and get to Gentleman Jackson's for some bouts with the great man. Perhaps, when he was recovered, he would take Pippen there and introduce him. He might even stand as a mentor to the youth during the Season and get the lad some town bronze. He owed Pippen much.

Bit by bit, Pippa slid the razor over Dev's bergamot-scented skin. Some patches were difficult because of the length of his beard. She had shaved him with a borrowed razor early in his illness when he had been too weak to know what she was doing and then a couple weeks later before he regained consciousness. Now she was unbearably aware of him and did as little grooming of him as possible.

The exotic smell of bergamot seemed lodged in her senses and locked in the tiny space of the room they shared. It was an unusual scent. Her brother used sandalwood or, when he tired of that, lemon. Even as she toweled away the remains of the soap, Pippa knew that every time she came into contact with bergamot she would remember these moments and Deverell St Simon.

To divert herself from this dangerous track, she said, 'There was a missive for you at the inn. I forgot until just now.'

She dug into the pocket of her jacket and withdrew the cream-coloured sheet of paper that had been folded into a screw and handed it to Dev. He took it eagerly and read it while she put away his shaving gear.

'What day is it?'

'The twenty-ninth of July. Why?'

'My mother is here in Brussels. Her note says she expected to arrive the first week of the month.' His voice was full of joy and lightness. Genuine pleasure eased the lines around his mouth that were threatening to become permanent. 'She gives her direction and orders me to come to her when I get her letter.' He smiled. 'That is just like her, assuming that, no matter what the carnage of Waterloo, I would survive.'

'She is an optimist.' Pippa wished she had the Duchess's unfailing faith. In a way she did. Everyone thought her brother dead, but she would not believe it. That was very like the Duchess's determination that her son would live through hell.

'Very much so. Do you have paper and ink? I need to send her news.'

'*Madame* will have something, although not as grand as that your mother used.'

'Mother won't mind. She is not a snob.'

Pippa fetched the writing materials and tried not to watch Dev as he jotted down the note. Such joy lit his features that seeing it made her glad. He had come to mean so much to her. It was disturbing.

When he was done, she took it herself. 'I will go straight away and deliver this.'

'Thank you. Stay for a message,' Dev ordered, grinning like a boy about to take his first pony ride. 'And don't be surprised if my mother sees you herself and then instantly orders her coach brought around. She is very impulsive.'

Pippa nodded. Her grandfather and brother often accused her of jumping before she looked. There was the time a labourer's small daughter had dropped her puppy into the trout stream. Pippa had plunged into the icy water without a thought for her own safety. The mountain snows had melted, and the stream had been nearly a river. The current had caught Pippa's skirts and dragged her hundreds of feet until she had managed to grab an overhanging tree branch. Later she had caught an inflammation of the lungs, but she had saved the puppy. That more than compensated for a week in bed with the sniffles and a fever.

If Dev's mother was equally rash, she could deal very well with her ladyship.

Dev was not far off the mark, Pippa found out thirty minutes later. The butler had barely shown her into the salon when a petite, vivacious woman burst through the door.

'Where is Deverell? Is he all right? Why did he not come with you?'

Alicia, Duchess of Rundell, was strikingly beautiful.

Shorter than Pippa, she was willowy thin. Her thick black hair was cropped fashionably short in front. The glossy waves shone blue in the late afternoon sun that poured through the large double windows. Her irises were the clear grey of polished silver and ringed by ebony lashes that were so abundant as to make her eyelids appear heavy. Her full, red lips were parted in a welcoming smile as she came to Pippa and grasped her hands.

Taking a step back and studying Pippa, the Duchess said, 'Why, you are nothing more than a child. What is Dev doing to rob the cradle for his minions?'

Pippa squelched her first impulse to curtsy and instead did the best bow she was capable of with the Duchess still grasping her fingers. 'Your Grace, I am all of four and twenty.' The Duchess gave her a quizzical look and Pippa realized her mistake. 'That is, I am a late bloomer. My entire family matures slowly. That is—'

'I understand perfectly,' the Duchess said, releasing Pippa's now clammy hands. 'You don't want anyone to know how young you really are.' She patted Pippa's arm. 'I will keep your secret, child. Now tell me where my son is and how he is doing.'

Before Pippa could speak, the door opened again. 'Excuse me, your Grace,' the butler intoned, 'but I thought you and your guest might like refreshment.'

'Goodness, yes, Michaels.' The Duchess gave Pippa a rueful smile. 'My staff endeavour to keep me from making too many *faux pas*.'

Pippa grinned. Yes, she could like this woman whose concern for her child superseded all else. In as few words as possible, Pippa brought the Duchess up to date. The last word was barely out of her mouth when the Duchess jumped up and rang the bell.

When the butler once more entered the room, Alicia,

Duchess of Rundell, said, 'Have the carriage brought round immediately, Michaels, and prepare two rooms. I am bringing Lord Deverell back, and his young friend here—' she waved a graceful, manicured hand at Pippa '—will be staying with us indefinitely.'

Pippa nearly choked on the tea the Duchess had poured and liberally laced with cream and sugar. 'Your Grace, I cannot impose on you. I have my own room and am quite happy.'

'Stuff! I dare say you will be much more comfortable with us, child. Brussels is a wonderful city, but after the battle and with all the riff-raff, you will be safer here.' She turned a stern look on Pippa's rebellious face. 'Don't argue with me, young man. You did not say so, but I believe you are responsible for Deverell being alive today. You will come to us.'

Pippa carefully set her cup down. 'Your Grace, I am perfectly happy and safe where I am.'

'Not another word.' The Duchess stamped her foot. 'I swear, you are as difficult as my own boys. Now, come along.'

Without a backward glance, the Duchess exited the room. Her muslin skirts swirled around her fashionably clad feet, and the perfectly coiffed back of her head led the way. Pippa followed.

She would go with Deverell's mother to fetch him, but she would not move here. 'Twould be too easy for her deception to be discovered in a household like this. Servants were everywhere and they saw everything. No, she would not be coming to stay with Deverell and his mother.

Several hours later, chagrin filled Pippa as she explored her new room in the Duchess of Rundell's town house. How Deverell's mother had got her here she still did not know. It must be from raising three boys that, if the Duchess were correct, had been hellions before growing into wonderful adults and husbands and fathers. According to their mother, they were everything that was admirable, with a few perfectly understandable flaws.

Pippa shook her head.

A discreet knock on the door caught Pippa's attention. She opened it to find a footman. He bowed and said, 'Pardon me, Master Pippen, but Lord Deverell requests your presence.'

Instant fear that the move had been too much for her patient sent Pippa flying to her bag of herbs. She should have never left him. She should have made him wait another day before relocating. She should have stayed by his side instead of coming to see her room. The admonishments twirled in her brain as she hurried after the servant.

Deverell's room was down the hall and to the left. In all, it was not very far. Pippa was winded by anxiety when she entered the chamber and came to a standstill.

Dev lay propped up on copious pillows, laughing at something his mother was saying. There was no sign of pain or discomfort that she could discern from this distance.

'Ah, Pippen,' he said, waving her forward. 'My mother thinks I am suffering, and I am trying to convince her it isn't so. You tell her.'

Pippa moved to the bed and looked from the Duchess's worried countenance to Dev. On closer examination, he had the tiny line between his brows that always intensified when he was hurting. And his eyes looked strained around the corners. But he wanted her to assure his mother that he was fine. She looked back at the Duchess.

Many aristocratic parents left the care and raising of their children to servants. Often that meant the ties between them and their children were not great. She had been lucky in having her grandfather. He had taken care of her and her twin after her father's death in a coaching accident. Grandfather had given them over to nannies and tutors, but he had also spent time teaching them about the estate and their place in the world. He had played children's games with them, and he had read to them. Church on Sunday had been a weekly activity he had insisted they share as a family. It seemed that Dev had had similar care from his mother.

Consequently, Pippa knew she could not lie to his mother. Not even for him.

Pippa chose her words carefully. 'Your Grace, Deverell has been grievously wounded. He's mending now, but 'twas nip and tuck about his leg.' She glanced at her patient to see him frowning fiercely at her. She decided to ignore him. 'We were able to save it, mainly because Deverell is strong and stubborn. He didn't want to lose the limb. That can be a powerful motivator for recovery. He weathered the infection that set in and the leg will heal. Still, he is not fully recovered. Even now he is in pain.'

'Blast you, Pippen. See if I ever cover for you.'

'Deverell St Simon,' the Duchess interposed, 'how dare you talk so to the young man who saved your life? Now be quiet while *Pippen* tells me the truth about your injury.'

Pippa took another deep breath and looked from her patient to his parent. 'He will always be plagued by the leg and may not regain complete movement in it. He would help himself…' she slanted him a reproving glance before turning her attention back on the Duchess '…by taking the draughts I prepare for him instead of leaving them untasted on the nearest table. They would ease the discomfort and promote restful sleep.'

'Do you have one prepared now?' the Duchess asked.

Pippa hid her smile behind a cough. She had hoped Dev's mother would ask that question. 'I can prepare one quickly, your Grace. A bit of laudanum will help him sleep tonight. He needs rest after being moved.'

Dev glared at her as she prepared the mixture, his pointed regard making her hands shake just a bit.

''Tis for your own good,' she told him firmly when the preparation was done. She handed him the glass.

'I know that well enough,' he growled. 'But I don't like the feeling of helplessness the drugs give me. Even though they dull the pain, they remind me that I have a deformity.'

Pippa stared at him. She had known he was headstrong, but until this instant she hadn't realized why he disliked the medications. He was going to find it hard going when he was healed enough to move around, but not well enough to do as he saw fit.

'I am sorry for that,' she murmured, wishing she could do something for him besides give him the painkillers. Noticing that the Duchess had moved away from them, she added, 'I am sorry that I had to spoil your plan to shield your mother. Your sentiments toward her are very admirable, but she deserves to know. This way, when you don't bounce out of bed in the next couple days, she won't be surprised and worried.'

Dev grunted. 'You're right, Pippen, but all of us have got in the habit of protecting her from the harsh things of life—if we can.'

His words brought a rush of warmth to Pippa's heart. Would she have been so protective of her mother, had her mother not died birthing her? The question brought back all the old guilt over being the death of her mother and the determination to atone for that deed. Even though no one had ever blamed her for her mother's death, Pippa had occasionally blamed herself. She knew death in childbed was common and that her mother's demise was not her fault, but still her mother's death was the reason Pippa had first wanted to learn midwifery and later medicine. She wanted to help others and hopefully prevent parents from dying and leaving behind their children.

She shook her head to clear it of the old memory. A long time had passed since she had last had these thoughts. They were probably brought on by watching Dev with his mother. That the two loved each other was obvious. That she was getting maudlin was even more obvious. She needed to go to her own room and do exactly what she was telling Dev to do—rest.

Resisting the urge to smooth the hair back from his forehead, Pippa stepped away from the bed and packed her herbal bag. 'He should be fine now.'

'Thank you, Pippen,' the Duchess of Rundell said, coming over and taking Pippa's hands. 'I will never be able to thank you enough.'

Pippa felt awkward and embarrassed. She didn't want anyone's gratitude. She just wanted… She glanced at Dev and saw his roguish grin. She just wanted things she had never wanted before, things she couldn't have. Not now.

'You don't need to thank me.' Pippa gently pulled her fingers from the Duchess's grasp. 'I am glad I could help Dev.' She stepped back. 'If you will excuse me, I am very tired.'

'Of course, child,' the Duchess said. 'Sleep as late as you need.'

'Sweet dreams,' Dev added, his hazel eyes twinkling with devilry.

And what type of dreams did he expect her to have? Pippa thought sourly as she made her way back to her room. As far as Dev was concerned, she was a young man who couldn't even grow a beard. She knew from living with her twin that not being able to grow facial hair was tantamount to being a baby.

Pippa closed her door behind herself and looked around the room she had been given. It was masculine in its simplicity. A large oak four-poster bed took up the centre while a matching armoire hogged one entire wall. A Turkey rug covered most of the wood floor, and blue drapes that echoed one of the rug's colours hung from the high ceiling to puddle fashionably.

What would Dev do if he knew she was a girl, and her room at home was done in peaches and soft greens? He would be scandalized. If she was unmasked, she would be beyond redemption. Dev's liking would turn into loathing. It was a thought she could not bear to contemplate for long.

Deverell St Simon's admiration and friendship meant too much. To lose them would be unbearable.

Chapter Four

Pippa shifted the very fashionable hat she had just bought to cover her too short hair. Then, with a determined tread, she pushed open the bank's door and entered the cool interior. The sprig muslin morning gown that would have been better for a good ironing left her arms and much of her neck bare to gooseflesh.

She had packed the gown, reticule and kid slippers in her portmanteau for just this occasion, and had had a devilish time of it keeping the women's clothes hidden. The Duchess of Rundell had assigned a maid to put her clothes up, and Pippa had had to shoo the girl out any number of times, telling her she had already unpacked.

Her letter of introduction that would allow her to draw funds on her father's account was in her reticule. Nearly all the money she had brought with her from England was spent and tomorrow Dev was taking her to meet Wellington. From there she would continue her search for her brother, and that would require more blunt.

The use of blunt, a cant word Philip had taught her, brought a smile to her lips. She would find her brother. She would.

'Pardon—' a French-accented woman's voice intruded on Pippa's vow '—but have we met before?'

Wariness tightened the muscles between Pippa's shoulders as she turned to face the speaker. The Marchioness of Witherspoon stood not less than two feet away, studying Pippa like a naturalist studies a bug pinned to a specimen tray. The Frenchwoman must have noticed the similarity between Pippa and Pippen from the hospital.

A shiver skated down Pippa's spine as she forced a smile. 'I don't believe so. I would have surely remembered if we had.' She made a slight curtsy and tried to edge around the woman. The sooner she was away, the sooner the Marchioness would forget the memory.

'Non, non,' the Marchioness said, her small white hand shooting out and coming to rest on Pippa's arm. 'Do not run, *chérie*. I mean you no harm, only…' Her head cocked to one side and her blue eyes studied Pippa. 'I could swear I have seen you before. In Brussels, perhaps?'

Pippa shook her head. 'No, milady. We have never met.' She moved her arm so that the woman's hand fell away. It was like having a chain opened. 'Excuse me, but I have an appointment.' That was not the truth, but she hoped to soon have an appointment.

Before the Marchioness could detain her further, Pippa spurted forward. The last thing she needed was for someone to penetrate her disguise.

Even as her palms turned clammy at the possible ruin, an image of Dev as she had left him formed in her mind. Her step slowed and her gaze saw nothing in the bank. For the first time since she'd met him, Dev had been dressed to go out, his tall, lean form shown to advantage by buff-coloured buckskins that fit his legs to perfection and a bottle-green coat of superfine that showed his broad shoulders to advantage. Smudge-free Hessians had hidden the scars on his right leg—not that they mattered to her. She sighed.

Would he find her attractive dressed as a woman? She berated herself immediately.

Whether Dev would be interested in her was not an issue. Deverell St Simon was not her reason for being here. Nor would he want to be, considering how she was flaunting the conventions of their society. Best to put all thought of him from her mind.

Suiting action to thought, Pippa presented her letter of introduction to a clerk. While she waited, she watched the people around her. To her surprise, the Marchioness was still on the premises. She seemed to be depositing a large sum of money which was causing a stir with the young man taking it.

Briefly, Pippa wondered why the woman would be depositing money when the normal course of action for an Englishman or woman while in a foreign country was to draw on their British bank. Before she could dwell long on the problem, she was approached by another clerk and escorted to a large desk where the bank manager smiled benignly at her.

The Marchioness's actions quickly slipped her mind as she concentrated on her transaction.

Her task done, Pippa retraced her footsteps to the small closet in the hospital where she had stashed her boy's clothing. It was a matter of minutes before Pippen emerged, carrying a wicker basket, the letter of introduction safe in the breast pocket of the jacket. Her first instinct was to dump the basket and revealing clothes in the nearest heap of trash.

It had been safe to bring the dress with her and keep it in her portmanteau until she had moved into the Duchess of Rundell's town house, where servants were constantly cleaning and straightening her belongings. The dress would have to go. The letter of introduction was much easier to hide and irreplaceable. She could always buy another dress.

On her way out of the hospital, she saw a woman kneeling by one of the patients. From the threadbare look of the woman's dress it was obvious she didn't have much money. Yet love shone from her eyes as she gazed at the man whose head lay in the pillow of her lap. Tears tracked down the woman's cheeks even as happiness made her face glow.

'Hush, darling,' she said. 'All that matters is that you are alive. I love you no matter what.'

Using the only hand he had left, the soldier gathered his love's fingers to his lips. Moisture blurred Pippa's vision. Another couple weathering the horror of war.

Without another thought, Pippa crammed a pound note into the basket and edged toward them. Unobtrusively, she set the wicker container beside the woman and slipped away.

Outside, the August heat quickly evaporated the moisture from Pippa's eyes. The sunshine was golden and warm on her skin, easing the tightness in her chest. The brisk walk to the town house lifted her spirits.

'Master Pippen,' the butler said, bowing her into the house. 'Her Grace wishes your presence in the morning room.'

Pippa grinned at Michaels. Since moving here, she and the old retainer had become fast friends. Michaels had taken her under his wing and endeavoured to remind her of the proper behavior for a young man of Quality, as he did the Duchess when she failed to do the proper thing. Pippa would be sorry to leave him.

She gave the butler her hat. 'Thank you. I suppose that means I must go there immediately.'

'It is customary.'

Pippa's too large Hessians, which she padded with socks in the toes, clumped on the polished black marble floor as she made her way. A footman opened the door and announced, 'Master Pippen, your Grace.'

'Fustian, Jones,' Her Grace said. 'There is no need to introduce Pippen.' The footman nearly smiled before catching himself and closing the door. 'Come here, child.'

Pippa nearly shook her head. The staff was completely devoted to their mistress, but her lack of formality was often a burden they did their best to correct.

'Good afternoon, your Grace,' Pippa said, making a leg before taking the outstretched hand the Duchess held to her.

'Call me Alicia. How many times must I tell you that? You saved my son's life, we won't stand on formality.'

'Yes, your Grace.' Alicia was too familiar. When Dev's mother frowned, Pippa said, 'I am sorry, milady, but as much as I know you would like it, I cannot bring myself to be so familiar with you as to call you by your Christian name.'

Michaels might often think Pippa lacked correct manners, but 'twas not so. Her grandfather had drilled her and Philip in the behavior required by their stations. They did not call duchesses by their first names. Not unless they had run tame all their lives in the lady's household, which was not the case here.

'Child, I shall surely lose my temper with you if you persist in this stubborn adherence to polite manners that is not necessary between us.' She pulled Pippa down to sit beside her on the pale blue silk-covered settee. 'Why, I begin to feel like a mother to you. And the first thing we need to do is get you some evening clothes. I am having a small dinner party tomorrow to let our close friends know that Dev is fine.'

Pippa's face blanched. The very last thing she needed was a male tailor taking her measurements.

'Thank you, your Gr—Alicia.' Using the Duchess's given name was a desperate attempt to make Dev's mother more accepting of the following refusal. 'But I cannot put you to the trouble. Besides—' she brightened '—I won't be here much longer. Right this moment, Dev is making arrangements for me to meet Wellington. When I find out where my brother was last seen, I will head there.'

'Nonsense. No matter what you learn from the Duke, you won't be leaving here in the next couple of days.'

The door slammed open before Pippa could remonstrate. Dev strode into the room, his brown hair awry and his hazel eyes wild.

'Bloody swine!'

'Dev!' Pippa jumped up without thought and ran to him. 'What is wrong? Are you hurt? Sit down and let me see.'

She wrapped one arm around his waist and urged him to the nearest chair. As soon as he sat, she fell to her knees in front of him.

'Is it your leg? Help me get this boot off so I can examine it.'

'Leave me alone,' Dev snarled. 'I deserve to feel this pain.'

Pippa rocked back on her heels and stared up at him. The wild look was still in his eyes, but the skin around them was dark and bruised looking. His full lips were thin. He looked in pain.

'What is this all about?' the Duchess demanded, coming over and taking her son's hand. 'There is no excuse for your rudeness to Pippen.'

Pippa watched the emotions battle across Dev's face: anger, hurt, contrition and back to anger. Something was terribly wrong.

'That damned Napoleon. May he rot in hell. May the ship taking him to St Helena sink and take his carcass to the bottom of the sea for fish bait.'

Pippa reached up and smoothed the tumbled lock of hair from his brow before she realized what she was doing. The motion was so revealing, she dropped her hand, stood and paced away. The more distance between them, the harder it would be for her to do another action so unlike what one man would do to another.

The Duchess cast her a quick, appraising glance before turning her attention back to her son. 'Calm down, Dev, and tell us what has happened.'

''Tis Patrick.' The words were torn from his throat and sounded like a raw wound. 'He's…damn it. He's dead.'

Patrick was the friend whose whereabouts had been the first thing Dev wanted to know when he regained consciousness. All Pippa's resolutions fled. She rushed to him and gathered him close. His head fell to her shoulder.

'I'm so sorry. So sorry,' she crooned.

For long minutes she rocked him, trying to absorb his anguish. She could give him a sleeping draught, but that would do nothing for the grief. She knew. This was the ripped-apart feeling she'd first had when the letter had arrived saying Philip was dead. Nothing but time would ease what Dev was going through now.

Finally, Dev pushed away. 'I'm all right. You can stop coddling me.'

'Of course,' she muttered.

Pippa released him immediately and stepped away. Her face flamed at what she had done. The best interpretation anyone could put on her action would be that she cared for Dev as a brother would. The worst was that she was a woman in disguise. Best that she get away and let his mother comfort him.

'Please excuse me.' Without waiting for a reply, Pippa rushed from the room.

Alicia, Duchess of Rundell, watched the slim figure of her guest fly out before turning a worried look on her son. 'I am sorry about Patrick. He was a good man and a good friend.'

Dev stood and limped to the wall of windows that overlooked an extensive garden that was in full bloom. Rosebushes mingled with iris and sweet alyssum. The beauty did nothing to ease the tightness in his chest or the urge to smash his hand through the glass.

'His death was a waste. I was glad before that we defeated Napoleon. I am ten times gladder now.'

Alicia followed him and put a comforting hand on his arm. 'You are right.'

Dev gripped her hand. 'And what am I to do with young Pippen, Mother? You saw the way he comforted me. It was more intimate than I would have expected.'

Alicia met his troubled gaze squarely. 'What are you going to do? You are the one who laid his head on the… lad's shoulder.'

Dev sighed. 'So much sorrow and so much confusion. The boy is too soft and too compassionate for his own good.'

'Perhaps,' the Duchess said with a strange smile. 'But right now, you need rest.' When his mouth opened on what she knew would be a protest, she put one finger over his lips. 'Don't argue with me. Do as I say for once. You will feel better for the sleep.'

To her surprise, Dev did as she urged. That, more than anything else, told her how devastated he was.

And what was he going to do about 'Pippen'?

Nearly three months after arriving in Brussels, Pippa finally stood outside the door to the Duke of Wellington's office. She owed this meeting to Deverell who lounged in a chair along the wall, his wounded leg straight out in front. A brass-handled cane leaned against his thigh.

His mouth was a thin line, the residue of yesterday's news about his friend. He had not come down to dinner last night, and her heart had ached for him.

Outside the day was hot and humid, a storm moving in. Every once in a while, Pippa caught Dev frowning and she knew the weather change was causing his leg to ache—although it could as easily be the grief over Patrick. This was something he didn't need right now. He was not fully healed. But then, none of the people suffering from the battle of Waterloo needed the pain.

'When we return home, I'll get you some laudanum. Just a little to ease the pain.' She was mildly surprised that she had called the Duchess's town house home, but it felt that way.

He looked at her and forced a smile. 'My leg is nothing, Pippen. I will be fine. I don't like waiting, that's all.'

She nodded even though she knew that was only a small part of his discomfort. In the last weeks, she'd learned that Deverell St Simon was impatient but he was also kind to others. He'd had his outburst yesterday, and now he was not going to subject anyone to his feelings. He was protecting her the same way he protected his mother.

A lightheartedness that was out of place in the current situation suffused her. The emotion was scary. As soon as she found out where Philip had last been seen, she would leave. She had to. It was better that way. For everyone.

Dev was so handsome. His brown hair had grown longer in the past weeks and brushed the bottom of his jacket collar. One shank of it fell attractively over his high forehead. Pippa had long since lost count of the number of times she'd wanted to smooth it back, but the gesture was too intimate for a lad to do to another man or a maiden to do to anyone. Yet, she had lost control yesterday and done exactly that. The emotions she felt for Deverell St Simon were overwhelming.

She sighed and looked away.

'A penny for your thoughts?' Dev asked, bringing her gaze back to him.

'Nothing that would interest you,' she muttered.

'Lord Deverell,' a young, eager aide to Wellington said as he stepped into the room, 'the Duke will see you now.'

Dev grabbed the cane in his right hand and used it to lever himself up from the seat. Pippa bit her bottom lip and resisted the urge to rush to him and help. That was the last thing a proud man like Deverell would want.

'Your companion, too,' the aide added.

'Thank you, Peter,' Dev said, motioning Pippa to precede him.

The office was as spare as the man it housed. The Iron Duke, the hero of Waterloo, sat behind a large desk, all his papers in neat piles. His dark hair was cut short, his dark eyes drooped at the corners and his long nose was the epitome of the aristocratic British ideal. He was neatly dressed with no creases visible.

Dev went to attention. Pippa stood several steps behind, studying the most famous man in the world.

'Lord Deverell,' the Duke said, 'take a seat. You, too, boy,' he added without glancing at Pippa.

'Thank you, sir,' Dev said, sinking into one of several plain wooden chairs. He stretched his hurt leg out and hooked his cane on the back of the chair where it would not be in the way or seen.

Pippa took another seat, sitting on the edge. She clasped her hands tightly in her lap to stop their shaking.

'What do you need?' Wellington asked in his abrupt, down-to-business manner.

'Sir, I'd like to introduce Pippen LeClaire, a relative of Earl LeClaire. He's in Brussels looking for the Earl's grandson, Viscount Staunton. Supposedly, the Earl received a letter from the Home Office saying the Viscount was dead. The news nearly killed the Earl, and he sent Pippen here to find out what was going on.' Dev cleared his throat as though what he intended to say next made him uncomfortable. 'It seems the Viscount has a twin sister who does not believe he is dead.'

Wellington looked at Pippen. His gaze was so penetrating, she felt pinned to her seat. For a brief moment she even thought he could see through her disguise.

'What precisely is your relationship to Philip LeClaire?'

She held his disconcerting gaze without flinching. 'I am a distant cousin. The closest male relative besides the Earl, his grandfather.'

Wellington asked several more questions in an effort to establish her connection. 'Do you have a letter of introduction?'

Pippa gulped. She did, but it gave her real name and said she was accompanied by her aunt Tabitha. 'No, sir. The Earl was too upset to think about such a thing. All he wanted was for me to sail immediately.'

Wellington studied her for several more long minutes. 'Major St Simon, do you vouch for this person?'

Dev sat straighter. 'I owe Pippen my life, as do many of your men. The lad has worked in the hospital for the last five weeks. Ask Major Smythe, the surgeon.'

Wellington looked from one to the other. 'The Home Office sent that letter because Viscount Staunton is believed dead. We don't know that for sure, but he dropped from sight two months ago. He was last seen in a Paris tavern.'

No one had actually seen Philip die. The tension that had built in Pippa burst. She jumped to her feet. 'Thank you, sir. Thank you. If you will tell me the name of the tavern, I'll go there immediately.'

A slight smile curved the Duke's thin lips before disappearing and leaving his face grim. Wellington was not known for his friendliness or social abilities. He was a general.

'I need to speak with Major St Simon now. I will tell him the information you need.'

The urge to fall into a curtsy, as though leaving royalty, was strong. Instead, Pippa bowed deeply. This man had given her a place to start her search and renewed her hope.

With a spring that hadn't been in her step for weeks, Pippa left. She would wait for Dev outside in the sunshine that matched the sudden lifting of her spirits. Nothing could mar her optimism now.

Dev watched Pippen leave. The lad had a lift to his walk and a smile on his face that had not been there before. Once more, the boy looked almost feminine with that glow in his eyes. He shook his head. This constant thinking that Pippen was too much like a woman was not good. He had been too long without female companionship, something he would remedy shortly.

'Major,' Wellington said, breaking into Dev's thoughts, 'you have been promoted to lieutenant colonel for your bravery at the Battle of Hougoumont.'

Dev suppressed the shout that came to his lips. Even though his father had provided for him, initially buying him a captaincy and setting up a trust fund, and his maternal grandmother had left him a small inheritance which allowed him to live like a man about town, he was still a younger son whose future was the military. This advance before he was thirty put him well on the road to success in his chosen career.

'That is great news. But I didn't do anything unusual. Every man there showed bravery.'

'True. But you lived. The others who survived have also been rewarded.'

Dev sobered. Yes, he was still alive. Unlike Patrick. The memory, so recent and so raw, felt as though someone had grabbed his wounded leg and squeezed. It was an effort of will over heart to keep his sight from blurring. His head bowed.

'Damn Napoleon,' he swore softly. 'Damn that Corsican to hell.'

'We have,' Wellington said. 'For a man of Napoleon's ilk, St Helena will be like hell on earth. He won't escape again.'

'Thank God, and all our men who died.'

'Quite right,' Wellington said. 'And because of this, I have a mission for you.'

Dev's head snapped up. He grasped at something to do that would keep his mind from Patrick.

'I want you to go with Pippen LeClaire and find Viscount Staunton. I believe Staunton is a traitor.'

Dev stared, his mind a riot of conflicting thoughts. 'Why?'

'We thought Staunton was spying for us, but he was last seen by one of our men talking to a known French agent. Later that evening, another one of our men was found dead. Someone had to reveal his identity. I think that person was Philip LeClaire.'

Anger boiled in Dev. 'A British peer betraying his country. That is the worst type of treason. The man should be shot.'

'Precisely. We want Staunton found and brought to London, but…' a thin smile stretched Wellington's mouth '…to be tried and hung as a traitor to the crown. Had we caught him during the battle I would have had him shot.'

'I will find the scoundrel, sir,' Dev said, his earlier anger still roiling and making his gut twist.

'I know you will. Because Staunton is the grandson of a respected and liked Earl, not to forget a very powerful man, you will report directly to me. While I am nearly a hundred per cent sure that Staunton is the traitor, his family is too influential for this type of action to be bandied about. No one—and I repeat, no one—is to know what you are doing.'

Wellington picked up a sheet of paper and began reading what was written on it. Dev knew he was dismissed. He eased himself up and resisted the urge to rub the ache in his leg. His disgust and fury over a British peer betraying the country that had made him everything he was gave him the strength to walk out of the room without limping.

As soon as the door closed behind him, Dev used the cane. One look at Pippen's radiant face told Dev the upcoming journey was not going to be easy. In fact, it was going to be the hardest thing Dev had ever done. He was going to betray Pippen's trust in him, and he owed Pippen his life.

Sudden exhaustion made Dev's shoulders slump and his leg hurt even more. Using the cane, he made his way to the chair he had used earlier and nearly fell into it.

Pippen did a jig on his way to stand in front of Dev. 'Is this not exciting? 'Tis the best news I've had in over a month. I am leaving tomorrow for Paris. I won't be coming back to Brussels.' The words babbled out of the boy's smiling mouth. 'Oh, yes. I must send a message to Grand—Philip's grandfather to tell him the latest information.'

Dev groaned.

Pippen fell to his knees in front of Dev, concern wrinkling his brow as he began to gently massage Dev's lower leg through the thick leather of the Hessian boot. 'Oh, you are in pain. Let us go home and I will give you something.'

Dev stared at the boy, his gaze going from the black hair to clear green eyes and on to lips that were too full and too pink and finally to Pippen's slim fingers that were surprisingly strong. They eased the discomfort of his wound. Lying was not going to be easy.

'I am going with you,' he said. 'Wellington promoted me to lieutenant colonel and told me to take some time to heal my leg. I am going to use that time to help you, as I promised I would.'

Joy filled Pippen's face to be instantly followed by another emotion Dev could not name. 'Don't feel that you have to do that, Dev. I know you're trying to help me as payment for the care I have given you. You don't need to. I am a healer, and I would have done the same for anyone.'

'But you didn't,' Dev said quietly. No, Pippen had saved his life, and now he would use Pippen to do what must be done. Patrick and others were dead because of men like Viscount Staunton. A jolt of remorse shot through Dev, quickly followed by sorrow over Patrick and renewed determination to find the traitor.

If there was one thing Dev had learned in the past six months, it was that life is never easy.

Chapter Five

'Don't work too hard,' Dev said, forcing himself to tease Pippen as the lad took off for the hospital. The boy grinned over his shoulder. 'Damn!' Dev swore softly. He was going to destroy that happiness.

But he had no choice. Not really.

An image of Patrick as he'd last seen him rose in his mind. Patrick had been hot and tired and scared. As they all had been. He was exhorting his troops to hold Hougoumont.

Dev's breath caught.

Damn. Damn. Damn.

He could do nothing for Patrick now except bring to justice one of the men responsible for the carnage. But he could find out about the French drummer boy he'd tried to save from the fire. The lad had been younger than Pippen.

Hours later, Dev found himself on his mother's doorstep with the French boy, named Raoul, in tow. The lad had been in one of the makeshift prisons for Napoleon's army.

The door opened and the butler's imposing body met them. 'Lord Deverell.' Michaels's gaze roved over the French boy. 'And friend.'

Dev rolled his eyes. Leave it to Michaels to be droll. 'Take Raoul here to the kitchen and see he gets a good meal. Then find something for him to do.' He cast a wicked look at the appalled servant. 'He knows how to do a drum roll.'

'Just so, milord. But does he know anything else?'

'How should I know?' Dev entered the house and handed his cane to a waiting footman. 'I don't know the boy. And he doesn't speak English.'

Michaels drew himself up to his full height. 'And I do not speak French.' Under his breath he muttered, 'Bloody frogs.'

'I heard that.' Pippen's voice came from the salon doorway. 'Shame on you, Michaels,' he said, striding into the foyer. 'Who is this?'

'A boy who lost out in the war,' Dev said, his good humour replaced by a tinge of bitterness.

'Poor child,' Pippen said, moving to the boy's side. 'For he's no more than that.'

'Obviously,' Dev said. He turned his stare on the butler. 'Well?'

'Yes, milord,' Michaels intoned, reluctant to do as ordered.

'Now.' Dev's voice brooked no further delay.

The butler bowed and shooed the French lad away. Over his retreating shoulder, the boy said, *'Merci, monsieur.'*

Pippen turned to Dev. 'You have saved that boy's life. Did you stumble on to him or what?'

Dev ran his fingers through his once immaculate hair and headed for the salon and the decanter of port he knew reposed there on a sideboard. He poured himself a glass and drank the entire thing down.

'That boy was in the burning barn.' Images of the inferno crept along the edges of his memory, images that had eaten along the edges of his dreams but not yet busted through. He broke into a cold sweat.

Pippen stepped up to him and put a hand on his arm. 'The barn where you were injured?'

Dev stared into nothing. Flames dazzled his eyes. 'Yes.'

He broke free and turned to pour himself another glass of the strong wine. He gulped it.

'Did you rescue him? Was he one of the people you were cited for bravery for saving?'

Pippen's fingers bit into Dev's arm, drawing him from the past back into the present. 'I don't know. I tried.'

'Then you did,' Pippen said decisively. 'And you've saved him once again.'

Dev shook his head to clear the thoughts away. 'Perhaps. Only time will tell.'

'Time will tell that you went to the trouble to find that boy. Most would not have.' Pippen's voice brooked no argument.

Dev shrugged and turned away. 'I had to. I had to help someone. Patrick is…' he choked on the finality of the word he had intended to use and substituted others '…Patrick is beyond my help.'

Before Pippen could offer the comfort Dev saw in the youth's green eyes, Dev twisted away and left the room. He didn't want comfort from a lad who was barely out of the school room. Most particularly when the admiration in Pippen's gaze would soon turn to hate and disgust.

'Child.' The Duchess of Rundell's voice stopped Pippa from entering the salon where tonight's few guests mingled. The Duchess, as usual, was late.

Pippa turned and made a leg. 'Your Grace…ah, Alicia.' The Duchess smiled her wonderful, warm smile that never failed to elicit an emotional response in Pippa. Dev had his mother's smile.

'I see you did not go to the tailor I recommended,' the Duchess said, taking Pippa's arm. She slanted an amused grey gaze at her guest. 'I am not really surprised.'

'You aren't?' Pippa had thought Dev's mother would be irritated at her for attending the dinner in the same clothes she wore everywhere. But going to a tailor had been out of the question.

The Duchess chuckled softly. 'No, child, I am not. Dev may be blind, but I am not.'

Pippa stiffened. Surely she could not mean what Pippa thought she meant. After all these weeks, no one had hinted that they had the least suspicion Pippa was not what she claimed to be. Not even the maid who cleaned her room seemed to know, and that was nothing short of a miracle.

Before Pippa could probe her hostess's enigmatic comment, the Duchess signalled the butler to announce them. In the grand manner that only a woman secure in her position as the wife to the most powerful duke in Britain can achieve, Alicia swept Pippa into the room. No easy feat considering that Pippa's feet dragged.

Pippa had not wanted to attend this dinner, but when the Duchess had cornered her at breakfast and reminded her of the occasion and how having a friend nearby would help ease Dev through his first social engagement after his wound, Pippa had wavered. Dev had walked into the room just then. He had limped to the table and rested his cane against the back of a chair.

'I heard you two talking,' he'd said, turning to eye Pippa. 'You will come. If I have to attend my mother's little gathering, then so do you.'

'But—'

'Your clothing won't be correct, but that's nothing.

Don't want the frippery these continental tailors produce anyway. We will get you the best from Stultz when we're in London.' He'd gone to the sideboard and loaded a plate with eggs, kippers and toast. Before sitting, he'd poured himself a tankard of ale.

'But I don't want new clothing,' Pippa had declared.

He'd taken a mouthful of eggs. 'Going to get you some. Stultz does all the military men's coats. You aren't exactly army, but with all your healing and doctoring, you might as well dress like the men you're helping.' He took a bite of kippers and washed them down with the ale.

Pippa'd glared at him.

'Now, children,' the Duchess had intervened, 'stop this arguing. Pippen is old enough to do as he wishes. As for you, Deverell, you need to try on your evening attire to see how it fits after the weight you've lost.'

A persecuted look crossed his face. 'Did. The jacket is loose, but fits the shoulders. Horton is having the breeches taken in at the waist.'

'Good,' Alicia had said. 'You will be the most handsome man here tonight.'

Something like anger had lit his eyes, but was quickly extinguished. 'Wish you hadn't done this, Mother.' As soon as the words were out, Dev had flushed as though he regretted them. 'That is, with Pippen and me leaving early tomorrow…'

Pippa had known he didn't want to attend this dinner in his honour any more than she did. Probably less. Everyone would be watching him, looking for differences, expecting to find them. His heroism and subsequent wounds were well known.

She could not leave him to face the curious stares on his own. Even knowing the Duchess would be with her son had not been sufficient. Pippa had needed to be with Dev.

The strength of that emotion was something Pippa had refused to study. Tonight, as she pulled herself back into the present and walked into the room where the Duchess's dinner guests mingled, she once more refused to analyse why she had to be with Dev in his first foray back into society.

Even realizing that some of the people here tonight might know her grandfather had not kept her from Dev's side. The guests might even know more about her family tree than Dev and his mother did, and, if so, they could expose her. The danger was not exhilarating. But she had to be here, to stand by Dev.

Meeting face to face with the Marchioness of Wither-spoon and her husband upon entering the room did nothing for Pippa's peace of mind. The Marchioness was as beautiful and dainty as ever. Her blonde hair curled fashionably about her rosebud face. Her evening dress of pale blue muslin, overlaid with a silvery gauze material that echoed the cool brilliance of her crystal-speckled turban, showed her figure to perfection.

Her husband was a complete contrast. At least forty years her senior, his coat was peacock blue superfine, but the waist was tighter and the skirts fuller than men wore today. He echoed, in a mild way, the style of his youth. His heavy-lidded brown eyes and long nose conspired to make Pippa feel he looked down on her, even though she was his height.

'Jane. George,' Alicia said, pulling Pippa forward, 'I want you to meet the young man who saved Deverell's life. Pippen, the Marquis and Marchioness of Witherspoon.'

Pippa made a hasty bow to each.

'Alicia, *chérie*, I have met your paragon. Only...' the Marchioness's blue eyes took in Pippa's unfashionable clothing and hair before smiling kindly '...I did not know the pride and joy of the hospital surgeons was your protégé.'

'Jane, I owe him everything. Without him, Deverell would have died on the streets of Brussels.'

Flushing uncomfortably, Pippa demurred. 'No, no, your Grace. I only cared for him. Nothing more.'

'Such modesty in a young man,' the Marquis said, his dry, soft voice feathering over Pippa's already raw nerves. 'The youth of today is too often loud and full of themselves.'

He was of an age with her grandfather, but while the Earl had a joviality about him and an interest in others, this man was cold. His words were more a derision against persons of her age than a compliment to her. Beside him, his wife's pretty mouth tightened, but she said nothing. Her eyes beseeched Pippa to understand. Pippa gave her a slight nod.

'Mother—' Dev's voice intruded on the awkward conversation '—what are you doing to poor Pippen to make the lad redder than the lobsters you ordered for dinner?'

Before the Duchess could reply, Dev draped his arm around Pippa's shoulders and steered her away. They didn't stop moving until the distance of the room and the thirty guests in it stood between them and the Marquis of Witherspoon and his wife.

'Thank you,' Pippa said with heartfelt gratitude.

'Least I could do. Owe you my life.' A footman passed by and Dev snared two flutes of champagne. Handing one to Pippen, he said, 'Here's to getting through this evening.'

Grinning, Pippa added, 'And to finding my cousin.'

'That, too,' Dev said in a hollow voice.

Pippa looked at him, but he smiled at her, that lazy, parting of lips that made her body do funny things. She forgot everything else.

Dev raised his glass and so did she. He downed the liquid in two gulps and reached for another.

'Should you have so much?' she asked, sipping hers and relishing the tickle of bubbles in her mouth and down her throat.

He shrugged. ''Tis as good at numbing the senses as the horrible stuff you pour down me every night and tastes a sight better.'

She supposed he was right. In a whisper she asked, 'Are the Marchioness and Marquis of Witherspoon in love?'

'A love match? Doubt it.' He drank his second glass only slightly slower than the first. 'Don't know them well, but he treats her with a cold politeness that makes it unlikely.'

'She works at the hospital.'

'Does she? Interesting. I wouldn't have thought it of her. She's quite the thing in the *ton*. They don't run in my circles. More like the ones my older brother frequents—or she does anyway.'

Pippa shot a glance in the direction of the couple they discussed, only to see the Marchioness on her own with two younger men paying homage to her beauty. 'But she is French. I would have thought that would make her unacceptable.'

Dev replaced his empty glass on the tray of a passing footman and took a third. 'You think? Don't. Her being French only makes her exotic. Old 'Spoon married her when she was barely a child, back in 1804 or thereabouts. Her family was killed on the guillotine, and she was living with distant cousins when he visited Paris.'

'For not knowing them, you know a lot about them.' Pippa wasn't sure what made her sound so waspish. Dev's interest in other women was nothing to her. To prove it, she gulped the last of her champagne and boldly waved the footman over and took another.

He grinned, a rakish parting of lips. 'Everyone knows a little about her. As I said, she's one of the leaders of the *ton*. An intimate with Sally Jersey and that group.'

Even Pippa had heard about the Almack patronesses, of which Sally was one of the more vocal ones. 'She does run in high circles.'

'Exactly.' Just then the butler signalled that dinner was ready. Dev put his empty glass on a nearby table. 'Best find a lady to escort into the meal. Not that my mother is a stickler for such things, but some of the other women here are.'

On that word of warning, he moved to the Duchess and offered his arm, his limp less pronounced than it had been that morning. Pippa looked nervously around the room. Luck was with her. One of the gentlemen offered to escort two ladies in, one on each arm. It was not normally done, but no one commented, least of all Pippa. She slunk in last and found her seat on the Duchess's right.

Dinner was subdued and excellent. She thoroughly enjoyed the Duchess's conversation and banter.

Dev sat at the head of the table in lieu of his father. He drank the last of his red wine, which went with the meat course, and the butler poured a fresh glass of white wine to go with the fish course. His eyes sparkled golden in the candlelight. He flirted with the young woman on his right who responded with a giggle and a heightened colour in her cheeks.

Pippa looked away.

Alicia, Duchess of Rundell, raised one sooty brow in enquiry as she caught Pippa's attention. Pippa inclined her head and smiled. The last thing she wanted was the Duchess's acute interest on her. She feared that Dev's mother already saw more than was comfortable.

'Pippen,' Alicia said in an aside, 'the ladies will be leaving shortly. You may go with us—' she smiled '—in deference to your youth.'

Relief eased the discomfort that had been churning in Pippa's stomach. She had dreaded having to stay behind with the men drinking port and brandy and smoking cheroots. The sense of reprieve was short lived. If she went with the ladies there would be talk.

'Thank you, your…Alicia, but I will either stay with the rest of the gentlemen or go up to my room. I have an early day tomorrow.' She glanced at Dev. 'So does your son.'

'Of course. So silly of me to forget that the two of you are hieing off to Paris before the rest of us have even gone to bed.'

Pippa smiled as she was supposed to.

Taking a fork, the Duchess rapped on her empty crystal goblet. 'Everyone, let us forgo the pleasure of separate entertainment after dinner.' She sent a roguish grin around the table. 'I suggest that we go into the salon, roll back the carpet and dance. So much more fun, you know.'

Surprise, followed by interest and then delight, flitted across the face of each guest.

'Perfect,' Jane, Marchioness of Witherspoon, said softly in her French-accented voice. 'Only you, Alicia, would think of, and then do, so original a plan.'

Others concurred.

With a laugh, Dev stood and circled the table to offer his arm to his mother. 'May I have the first dance?'

She rose and accepted his escort. 'No other. Unless it were Pippen.'

Pippa stood so quickly her chair toppled over. 'Thank you, your Grace, but I concede your first duty is to Dev.'

She stood still and watched them exit, Dev expertly wielding his cane, and wondered why the Duchess had so suddenly changed her plans. It was almost as though she had reacted to Pippa's statement about going to her room.

A giggle from her left snapped her attention back to the other guests. The young woman, girl, actually, who had been seated by Dev was looking at her with expectant brown eyes. Pippa sighed mentally.

'Miss Perryweather, may I escort you into the salon?' She offered her arm, thankful she was tall for a female. Having to act the part of a man was hard enough, it would be mortifying if she had to look up at the ladies while doing so.

'Yes, you may, Mr LeClair,' the girl giggled.

Inside the parlor, Pippa seated her charge and excused herself. The last thing she wanted was to be constrained to ask the chit to dance. Her dancing master, after pulling out his hair at her reluctance, had barely managed to teach her to follow a gentleman's lead, let alone how to lead.

Spying the Duchess, Pippa made her way quickly to that lady. 'Your…Alicia. Ma'am. I would be glad to play the pianoforte. Surely you need someone to do so, and it would be a shame if someone who truly enjoys dancing had to miss out when I am but an indifferent practitioner of the art.'

Dev, who stood beside his mother, laughed out loud. 'You? Don't tell me part of your training was playing musical instruments.'

Pippa coloured but stood her ground, her chin raised. 'Me. I am not superb, but I am adequate. For a small gathering of this type, my skills should be up to the requirement.'

'Deverell.' The Duchess rapped his arm with her closed fan hard enough to make him draw in his breath. 'Stop teasing Pippen. The boy cannot be worse than you.' She turned a gentle smile on Pippa. 'Thank you for offering, and I will take you up on it. I was going to do it myself, but much prefer to dance.'

Pippa gave Dev a triumphant look before going to the pianoforte. Michaels put the second candle in its holder, then lit the wicks. He cast Pippa a look of pity.

'I hope you don't embarrass yourself, Master Pippen.'

'As I told her Grace, I am adequate. I don't play with passion, but neither do I hit a lot of wrong notes.'

Ignoring the butler's raised white brows, she flexed her fingers and began warming up. All of the music was for the waltz, a new dance that was only recently allowed in polite circles. She had occasionally played some of the pieces because they were so flowing and beautiful. As soon as she started the first piece in earnest, couples stood up.

Between dances, Pippa managed to glance around. Each time, Dev was soliciting a partner, and each time she could not prevent the twinge of envy that made her hit the keyboard a little harder than necessary.

When dancing, he held his partners the *de rigueur* twelve inches away, but Pippa knew that was close enough to feel one another's body heat and for the woman in his arms to smell his bergamot soap. Her imagination provided the scent, turning her insides to warm cream.

What would it be like to be held in Dev's arms? She hit a wrong key and chastised herself. She would never know.

He moved with grace to the music. Only once or twice did his right leg buckle when he turned his partner. As the night progressed he faltered more and more until finally she could stand it no longer.

Why he was being so stupid as to continue dancing when it pained him, she did not know. But she would certainly put a stop to it.

Pippa finished the last piece with a flourish. Before anyone could request another, she stood and bowed.

It was as though the Duchess understood perfectly. She clapped and said, 'Bravo, Pippen. A fine demonstration, but I declare I am monstrously tired.'

The guests, with mild looks of surprise on their faces, took the hint. Over the next thirty minutes they drifted to the door. Pippa suppressed her grin of appreciation. Deverell's mother knew exactly how to handle every situation.

When the last of the guests were gone, Pippa turned to Dev and let her irritation out. 'How could you be so stupid as to dance every one? 'Tis a wonder you did not fall flat on your face, taking your partner with you.'

Irritation creased his brows, but he only turned his back to her and walked away. Pippa planted her feet and put her fists on her hips and watched him. He limped. Badly.

The temptation to let him go beckoned her like hot chocolate on a cold morning. Discomfort might teach him not to exert himself beyond his capabilities, but it would not ease the reason that drove him to perform beyond his means.

She sighed.

A light hand took her shoulder and turned her to face the Duchess. 'Go with him, child. He has need of your skills. I will be up shortly.'

The Duchess's eyes were filled with such compassion that Pippa knew there was nothing she could do but help Dev. She would have done so anyway. This just dissipated her ire with him sooner than it might otherwise have done.

She caught Dev as he was halfway up the main staircase. He leaned heavily on the bannister with one hand and eased himself up the steps one at a time. She ran to him, finding herself slightly out of breath by the time she reached him.

'Here,' she said, taking his free arm and laying it across her shoulders, 'use me.'

He looked at her with chilly affront. 'I don't need some

still-wet-behind-the-ears pup to help me. Especially one who has just tried to scold me when he has no authority.'

Contrition blunted Pippa's initial retort. It never did any good to fight. 'I was worried about you. You are my patient, and you weren't taking care of yourself tonight.'

'I was doing very nicely and taking care of myself exactly as I wished.' He moved up one stair.

Pippa could feel the tenseness in his muscles and hear the slight, sharp intake of breath as he brought his bad leg up to join his left. Still he left his arm on her shoulder. She took that as a good sign.

'You were dancing more than you ought. Why, you are barely out of bed and should always use a cane.'

'I'm not a blasted invalid,' he snarled, taking two steps in rapid succession.

Pippa's heart twisted. This was so hard on him. More than ever, she was glad she had been able to save his leg.

'No, you are not,' she said calmly. 'But you are still healing. In time you will be able to dance.'

He slanted her a bitter look. 'But not as well as once I did.'

She met his heated stare. 'No, not as well. I am sorry for it. For your sake.'

Her compassion seemed to ease the emotions that rode him. His face lost some of the tightness around the mouth, and he even managed a weak smile.

'I know you are, Pippen. You did more than anyone could have expected. Without you, I would've lost the blasted thing.'

His hazel eyes held hers. Pippa felt as though she was falling into their ever-changing depths. One minute they were light brown, flecked with green. The next they shone like golden candles. She wanted to stay like this for eternity.

The heat of his body penetrated the layers of clothing between them, and the scent of bergamot filled her senses. Underlying everything was an awareness of him as a man that she had never felt for another. He might be leaning on her, but the strength of his shoulders could crush her, and the muscles of his chest were taut beneath the fine lawn of his shirt.

A dark growth of beard shadowed the strong line of his jaw. His breath was sweet like the champagne he had been drinking all evening. The urge to lean into him was great.

He shook his head and frowned down at her. 'Pippen, you are a strange lad. Strange. There are times when I wonder—'

'Children, this is not the time for a serious discussion. Dev is nearly off his feet.'

The Duchess's voice shocked them so that Pippa jumped away, and Dev had to clutch the bannister to keep from toppling. Pippa grabbed at him, and he once more wrapped his arm around her. With his mother clucking behind them, they mounted the rest of the stairs and made their slow progress to his bedchamber.

The door was opened by Horton, a footman who had taken the place of Dev's previous valet who was still recovering from his own war wounds. Pippa guided Dev to the bed where he collapsed. She and Horton got his boots off.

'Horton,' she said, turning away while Dev wrestled with his cravat, 'bring me hot water and fresh cloths.'

'Yes, Master Pippen.'

The servant left and Pippa turned to face her charge. He looked like a fallen angel. Brown shocks of hair tumbled across his wide brow and red delineated his high cheekbones. No wonder he was known as 'Devil'.

'Help me with these breeches,' Dev ordered, getting off the bed.

Pippa gulped. The last thing she wanted to do was help him undress. In the past weeks, she had seen all of Dev and been sorely pressed to resist temptation. Now that he was well and aware of everything around him, she knew it would be even harder to resist the sensations his body elicited in her.

From the doorway, the Duchess said, 'Why don't you wait for Horton, Deverell?'

Pippa shot her a questioning look. Dev's mother smiled benignly back.

Dev glanced from one to the other. ''Tis not as though Pippen hasn't seen everything I have to offer. You, however, could leave the room, Mother, and spare my blushes.'

The Duchess laughed. 'I saw you in diapers, my boy. Wait for Horton. Pippen is too tired to support your weight any more tonight.'

Dev gave Pippa one more searing study, then agreed. 'As you wish.' He sat back down on the bed and sank into the mounds of pillows. 'I shall be asleep before he returns with everything Pippen requires.'

His eyes were shut, and Pippa could hear the soft sound of his breathing when Horton returned. She told the servant to help Dev get undressed and under the sheet. Then she and the Duchess went into the hall to wait.

'Shall I come back in with you?' Alicia asked. 'Or will Horton be enough?'

It was all Pippa could do to keep her jaw from dropping. Somehow the Duchess suspected her secret. 'There is no need, Alicia. I have put hot compresses on Dev's leg before.'

His mother gave her a mischievous look. 'When he was awake and watching?'

Pippa sighed. 'Once. Mostly I did them when the leg was still healing and I needed to draw the pus out. Now the heat will ease some of the ache from over-exertion.'

'My son is very stubborn,' Alicia said softly. 'It is one of his strongest virtues, even though it sometimes drives him into the wrong situations.'

Pippa's lips twisted wryly. 'Such as tonight?'

'Exactly. He was proving to himself that he could still do everything. He loves to dance and was very good at it.'

'He is still more than passable, ma'am.'

'To you, perhaps. But he knows better.' She put one delicate hand on Pippa's arm. 'Give him time, child. He will come around.'

As Pippa opened her mouth to make some innocuous reply, the door opened and Horton bowed to them. 'Your Grace. Master Pippen. Lord Deverell is ready.'

Alicia's hand dropped from Pippa's arm, and she smiled at her. 'I am going to my bed. I want to be up in time to see the two of you off.' She leaned over and, before Pippa knew what she intended, kissed her on the cheek. 'Take care of him for me, child. He is my youngest and I nearly lost him.'

'Always, milady.' The words were out before Pippa realized she was going to say them.

Alicia touched a finger to Pippa's cheek. 'I know.'

With that, Dev's mother left. Pippa stared after her, listening to her own words repeat themselves in her head. Always. What was happening to her?

'Master Pippen?'

Horton's voice snapped her back. Stepping briskly into the room, she asked, 'Is the hot water by the bed?'

'Yes, sir.'

'Thank you.'

Pippa went to the side of the bed closest to Dev's leg

and lifted the sheet aside. The scars were nearly healed, the angry red easing into pale pink. She knew that with more time they would turn white and be barely noticeable. She wrung out one of the clothes and laid it across Dev's limb.

'Ah, that feels good.' Dev's eyes caught hers. 'You always know what to do.'

She smiled at him. 'I have had many years of practice with the people on my gran—on Earl LeClaire's land. The county surgeon thought I was too young—' and a female, she silently thought '—and would not have the determination to work hard, but I proved him wrong. The midwife often let me assist.'

Dev raised one eyebrow. 'She let a boy help in birthing?'

Pippa realized her mistake too late. 'She let me help some,' she fibbed. 'Not a lot. Let me see the compress. 'Tis probably cool by now.'

Dev smiled at her in a knowing way, but did not try to bring the conversation back to her training. She changed the cloth and paced to the fireplace in an attempt to put distance between them.

'Horton,' Dev said, 'you may go to bed now. Master Pippen will finish up here.'

Pippa swung around. She was going to be unchaperoned in his bedchamber. Her heart raced before she managed to tell herself it was not the first time. Only…only before he had been unconscious most of the time. Nor had the Duchess been around with her enigmatic comments that made Pippa think Dev's mother knew her secret. What would the Duchess say if she knew about this?

Pippa shook her head to clear the maggots out of it. The Duchess knew nothing. She was just distraught over Dev being hurt. That was all.

The door closed quietly behind the servant and they were alone in the room, their gazes locked. Pippa stood poker straight, hot and cold chasing each other down her back. She told herself she was overreacting. The naked man in the bed, with only a sheet covering his lower body, was Dev. She had seen all of Dev there was to see. She had even touched all of him. But that seemed like an eternity ago.

She licked dry lips.

'You have some of the most feminine mannerisms,' he said, his voice grating with irritation. 'Has no one ever told you to stop them?'

She stopped and glared at him. 'Such as?'

He looked at her through slitted eyes. 'Such as licking your lips. Women lick their lips, not men.'

She stalked over to him. 'I have seen men doing it.'

'Not much,' he stated baldly. 'You will have to stop that if I am to take you to London for some town bronze,' he said.

'Town bronze?' she echoed him.

'Exactly. When we are done finding your cousin, I want to take you to London and give you the entrée to the *ton*. 'Tis the least I can do.' He slanted her a roguish grin. 'How else do you think I am going to get you jackets made by Stultz, as I promised this morning?'

'I did not think anything of it. You were irritated over this dinner party and merely talking.' Nor could she go even if he were serious. When she found her twin, she was returning home. The last thing she needed was to continue this masquerade.

He frowned up at her. 'I said I was taking you to London. I don't go back on my word. You would do well to remember that, Pippen.'

Taking affront at his overbearing attitude, she stated, 'Neither do I.'

'No man of honour does,' Dev said. 'And you may too

often do things that remind me of a woman, but you are a man—or a boy,' he finished with a cheeky grin.

The breath Pippa had been unintentionally holding whooshed out. Imitating a man was not as easy as donning the clothes. She should be glad she hadn't given herself away, instead of this sense of disappointment. She was here to find her brother, not make Deverell St Simon notice her as a desirable woman. No matter how attractive she found the man.

'And stop standing over me like a parent over a recalcitrant child,' the subject of her thoughts said. 'Any minute now you are going to assume the position.'

'What?' One minute she was telling herself to stop wanting him and the next he was spouting still more gibberish.

His eyes glinted. Almost as though he were teasing her. 'Hands on hips. Feet planted apart.'

'Oh.'

He let out a long breath and it was as though all the energy he had used tonight came out with the air. 'Never mind, Pippen. Finish what you've started and then we need to rest.'

By this time Pippa's emotions were a riot of contradictions, with the only constant being her feelings for Deverell. It was more than past time for her to get some sleep and put some distance between herself and this man she found so appealing. For once, she did as he ordered without feeling any irritation at his imperiousness.

Dev continued to stare into the darkness long after Pippen was gone. His leg was a dull ache that no amount of Pippen's hot compresses, rubs or herbs could ease. Nor did the large amount of wine he had consumed help. Just as no amount of coddling would change the fact that he was a cripple—from now until the day he died.

He flung an arm over his face, wishing he could blot out the fact of his infirmity as easily as he could block out the flickering light of the single candle by his bed. But he could not.

Instead he thought about Pippen. If anything could make him put aside his bitterness over his wound, it was his sense of shame over his intended betrayal of the boy. Pippen had saved his life and trusted him with finding his missing cousin, while he, Deverell St Simon, a man who had always held honour above everything else, intended to betray that trust. In a just cause.

If only the person he would be hurting was not Pippen. He owed the youth more than he could ever repay. He had told the lad he would take him to London for town bronze.

A bitter bark of laughter shook him and made his leg flair. He ignored the pain. Pippen would no more go to London with him when this was done than the boy would torture a patient. Pippen would hate him, and rightly so.

But he had to find Viscount Staunton and bring him in for retribution. The man was a scoundrel of the worst sort. A peer who had betrayed his own country and the men who had made him what he was. Because of Staunton and men like him, Patrick was dead.

A sneer curled Dev's lip. Betraying Pippen's trust would be soul wrenching, but bringing a traitor to justice would recompense the deceit he must play. Avenging Patrick would be enough. He had a job to do, and he would do it.

Chapter Six

Dev was in one of the foulest moods of his life when he sat down for a quick breakfast. He shovelled eggs, toast and ale into his mouth with a concentration he hoped would blot out the other members at the table. He found himself unable to meet Pippen's clear open green gaze.

Blast the boy! Wellington would snort in disgust if he were privy to Dev's doubts and regrets. The Iron Duke had a one-track mind: the preservation of Britain. Any traitor that stood to hurt the country was expendable in the great man's opinion. In Dev's, too. If only the traitor weren't Pippen's lost and loved cousin.

He took a gulp of ale and turned as polite a face as possible to his mother. 'Pardon me, Mother, but I didn't hear what you said.'

She laughed. 'You were always my child who daydreamed. I remember when you were ten and wanted to run away and join the East India Company. You would go into the home woods and pretend you were in the jungles of India. You pretended to hunt tigers, played by the poor grooms.'

Dev grimaced. 'That was a long time ago, and I know the difference between reality and daydreams now.'

For a moment the Duchess's face clouded. Then she forced a smile and changed the subject. 'Dev, don't you think Pippen's eyes are the exact shade of the emeralds I have put aside for your future bride?'

Dev nearly choked on a mouthful of eggs. 'Mother. Where did you get that idea? Pippen's a boy. His eyes don't look like any jewels.'

The Duchess shook her head slightly, amusement curving one corner of her mouth. 'Observation. Only observation.'

Dev glanced at Pippen. The boy sat like a mute, his body still, mouth pinched and both cheeks splashed with colour.

'You've embarrassed him,' Dev said, beginning to see humour in the situation. At least the banter took him out of the darkness of his thoughts.

'Have I?' the Duchess asked, her brow wrinkling in concern. 'I did not mean to.'

Pippen gave a shaky laugh. 'No, not embarrass…exactly. 'Tis not every day that my eyes are compared to emeralds.'

'Shouldn't think so,' Dev said, taking a bite of toast. 'Most men don't like having any part of themselves compared to jewels.'

'But it is true, none the less,' the Duchess said. 'Your eyes are the exact shade of the emeralds.' She smiled at Dev. 'My father gave them to me when I married the Duke, and I am saving them for Dev. I gave the black pearls to Alastair when he married Liza.'

Dev slanted his mother a quizzical look. 'Why all this talk of marriage and necklaces? It isn't exactly the topic I would have thought we would be discussing this morning.'

'No, it is not,' Alicia said. 'But I thought of it. Let us change our discussion. Where will the two of you be staying your first night?'

'Don't know,' Dev said. 'Depends on how far we get

and if the weather holds. The last thing we need is rain if we are to make good time.'

'And we had best be getting started,' Pippen said in a small voice, almost as though the lad were afraid to speak for fear of what would be said next.

'Right,' Dev said, rising and throwing his napkin on to the table. 'I hope you made a good meal of it, Pip, because we are not stopping for a long while.'

For a second the boy's eyes flashed, but he spoke mildly enough. 'I made as good a showing as possible. And we should be stopping every few hours so you can get out and stretch your legs.'

'Get out?' Dev queried, one brow raised.

'Yes. You must walk around some. Sitting all day in a jolting coach will do your leg no good.'

'Coach?' Dev felt his temper starting up.

'You should ride in a carriage,' Pippa said matter of factly, as though there was no question of what would be done.

'I think not.' Without waiting for further comment, Dev pivoted on his good leg, used the cane to steady himself and strode off. His ramrod-straight back brooked no discussion.

Once outside, the sunlight and breeze eased some of the tension inside him and Dev came to a stop. He rotated his shoulders and told himself not to react so strongly. The boy was only trying to help. It was not Pippen's fault that the last thing Dev wanted to do was make this trip.

He sighed and ran his right hand through his hair. It seemed that lately he'd been doing a lot of things he didn't want to do.

'Milord,' the groom said, having come up without Dev being aware. 'The horses are saddled and the spare clothes you and Master Pippen need are packed in the saddle bags. Exceptin' yer coat.' He held out the garment.

'Thank you, Tom.'

Dev took the many-caped greatcoat of buff cloth and wondered if he should wear it, or lay it across the saddle. He decided to lay it before him when Pippen came out of the front door. The boy wore only the brown coat he always wore.

'Where is your heavier coat?' Dev demanded. 'We are bound to run into nasty weather, and then you'll be glad of the extra weight.'

The boy flushed. Again. Dev shook his head. There were times he wondered what kind of upbringing the lad had received.

'I don't have a coat.'

Turning aside, Pippen strode to the gelding that would be his mount. He paused for a long moment before putting his foot in the stirrup and mounting. The movement lacked grace and were it not for the impeccable training of the horse, Dev was sure Pippen would have missed his seat and landed on his bottom in the road.

'Tom,' Dev said, 'have Horton fetch my black greatcoat. Master Pippen will be glad of its warmth before this journey is over.'

The groom hurried to do his bidding.

Pippen glared at Dev, then his face softened. 'Thank you for your thoughtfulness. I've no doubt it will come in handy.'

''Tis the least I could do,' Dev said, turning to mount his own horse.

He had not been on a horse since the battle, but old habits die hard—if at all. The only awkwardness was getting his injured leg to move as it should. For an instant, as he balanced on his left leg he thought his right leg would not swing over the animal's back. Then, as though his mind gave the injured limb strength, his leg arched over and his booted foot came to rest against the stirrup.

As he settled in his seat, he did his best to suppress the jolt of pain that wanted to twist his mouth. He must get used to the discomfort of mounting and riding a horse. He'd be damned if he intended to spend the rest of his days travelling in a coach.

To turn his thoughts from his throbbing leg, he watched Pippen on the second gelding. His seat was not solid and he twitched. The boy looked awkward as a youth caught looking at a pretty girl's ankle. If Dev didn't know better, he'd say Pippen had spent little time riding. But that was impossible. The lad lived in the country and was of good birth. He should be proficient on horseback.

Just as they prepared to urge their horses forward, the Duchess erupted from the front door. She rushed to Dev so that he had to lean down.

She grabbed his face and kissed him. 'Take care. I nearly lost you once, I could not bear to do so again.'

With a gloved finger, he gently flicked away a tear from his mother's face. 'I shall do my best. Take care of yourself and give my love to Father.'

'I shall,' she said, smiling wistfully up at him before turning to Pippen. 'Be careful, child. And watch over my headstrong son.'

Pippen nodded. Even with the several feet separating him from the youth, Dev could see moisture glistening in the boy's eyes. Damned if he wasn't as much of a watering pot as a girl.

Disgust twisted Dev's mouth as he urged his mount on. The sooner they started, the sooner they'd finish. He heard the clop of horseshoes on the cobbles behind him as Pippen followed.

* * *

Pippa frowned as she watched Dev enter the tavern. It was evening on their second day of travelling. They were on the outskirts of Paris, and Dev was in a foul mood as the result of too long spent in the saddle. But Dev had refused to listen to her when she'd told him to stop and rest at a smaller inn three hours ago.

Men! They were stubborn as mules and belligerent as bulls when their minds were set on something and it was denied them.

Last night had been just as bad. Dev had nearly fallen getting off the horse. If she hadn't had just as much trouble and very likely bigger saddle sores, she would have berated him for going so long before stopping. But never having ridden any way but side saddle, she had been too miserable to do more than see their horses were stabled, prepare each of them a draught to ease their pain and then stumble into the small bed in the tiny private room Dev had been able to procure for her.

Bringing her attention back to the present, Pippa sighed and told the ostler in her barely adequate French, 'See that you rub them down and feed them plenty of oats.'

The French youth nodded as he led the horses away. Pippa wished Dev were as easy to manage. She winced as she walked toward the door.

The tavern's public room was hot and crowded. Even though it was well into September, the weather was warm and the room didn't need the extra heat from the large hearth fire. The sting of smoke made her squint as she searched for Dev.

He stood near the bar, talking to a buxom serving wench. He had a smile on his lips and a look about his eyes that she had never seen before. A twinge of anxiety made Pippa stride toward him.

'Dev,' she said, coming up to his side and tugging at his sleeve.

'Not now, Pip,' he muttered, never taking his eyes off the wench. 'Do you work late tonight, Giselle?' he asked in French.

'Only till everyone has had their fill,' she answered in her native tongue.

The woman grinned at Dev, showing two crooked but white front teeth. Her black hair was caught up in a knot and her eyes were large and blue. There were poppies in her cheeks and plenty of curves under the clean white blouse and brown skirt she wore. She had not the look of a loose woman, which Pippa imagined added to her appeal. Philip would have done exactly as Dev was. The knowledge was no comfort.

'Dev,' Pippa said in an attempt to catch his attention, 'we need rooms. An inn this close to Paris will fill quickly.'

He frowned at her. 'Then procure them. You don't need me for that.' Before he finished speaking, his focus was back on the woman.

Fast losing a temper she had not realized was slipping, Pippa stated, 'I may be able to get the rooms, but I won't carry up your baggage.'

'Then get one of the servants,' Dev said in the autocratic manner he sometimes used. It was a sign of just how occupied he was with this seduction.

Pippa snorted, but realized that for the moment there was nothing more she could do. And why should she bother? Deverell was a grown man and entitled to amuse himself where he wanted. The serving woman certainly seemed interested. Giving herself a mental shake that extended to her shoulders and made the cape of her riding coat swing, Pippa went to find the owner.

*   *   *

Less than an hour after paying for adjacent rooms, she heard the door to Dev's room open and shut. While waiting for him to come up, she had prepared a distillation of bark to ease the pain she knew he suffered. She picked up the drink and crossed the hall.

Her knock brought a muffled, 'Come in.'

Entering, she said, 'I've brought you something for the pa—'

Dev stood by the open window, his back to the door. He was clad only in breeches and stockings. The ridges of muscle in his back flowed with each stroke as he washed himself with a damp cloth. Knit breeches showed the narrow leanness of his hips and tight lines of his legs. The sight brought back memories of him lying in her bed with only a sheet to cover his nakedness. Suddenly it was difficult to breathe and the room was like an oven. Pippa licked dry lips.

Dev turned to her, the yellow light of the two candles that stood on each side of him bronzing the hair that dusted his chest. Pippa forced her gaze away, looking anywhere but at his exposed flesh.

'Oh, it is you.' Disappointment dulled the gleam in his eyes.

'Only me,' Pippa said, her sight snapping back to him as she stepped further into the room. Her hackles rose for no reason she would admit to. 'Did you expect your serving wench so soon? I heard her tell you it would be some time.'

'What is the matter with you?' he said, putting down the cloth and going to sprawl in the single chair.

'Nothing.' Pippa gave herself a mental scolding. 'I've brought you something to ease your discomfort—you would ride longer than you should have.'

'You nag like an old woman, Pippen.'

Pippa felt the blood drain from her face. Had she given

herself away by…by…? She refused to name the emotion that had sent her tongue lashing.

Dev leaned over to pull on his Hessians and winced. 'What you need is a woman,' he added in the voice of a man goaded beyond endurance.

'Your wench when you've finished with her?' Pippa snapped. She slapped the glass on the small table beside Dev and stepped away. The scent of bergamot wafted from him. It would always remind her of him.

Dev's eyes narrowed. 'You've a mighty sharp tongue tonight. Take my advice and do as I intend to do. You will find it eases many troubles.'

'Hire a whore for the night?' Pippa sneered, hands on hips. 'What does that prove?'

Dev's scowl deepened. 'That you are a man. Something I'm beginning to wonder about where you are concerned.'

Throwing caution to the wind, Pippa stood her ground. 'And what if I don't have those urges? So? Does that make me less of a person?'

'Be careful what you say and to whom. Those proclivities might be indulged by some, but the law's against them.' Dev pulled on his remaining Hessian, the line between his brows deepening. 'Blast!' he muttered. 'Can't even pull on a boot.'

He hurt. Contrition smote Pippa. She'd been haranguing him when she should be taking care of him. 'Here,' she said brusquely, 'drink this. 'Twill ease the pain. Then, instead of whoring, you should rest.'

'Back to that, are we?' Dev said, pulling on his linen shirt. 'Well, I've had enough of your orders. Tonight I am going to do what I please, and the devil take you if you try to interfere.'

Pippa's sympathy for his discomfort washed away like a river plunging down a mountain. 'No wonder they call you

Devil Deverell. You are more interested in your pleasure than your health.'

He grabbed her right arm in a bruising grip. 'Listen well, Pippen. I won't stand your nagging tonight. I am a man and I intend to live like one, not like some papping baby who must be coddled from dawn to dusk and then tucked into bed.'

With an expletive that Pippa had only heard in the stables, he flung her from him. Never had she seen him so angry or so careless of another. Before she could try to stop him, he strode out of the door, slamming the heavy oak panel behind him.

The fury drained from her in a rush, leaving her so weak she sank like a rock on to the chair Dev had vacated, and cradled her head in her two hands. Dev felt maimed, less than a man because he walked with a limp and couldn't ride a horse at the speed and for the duration he once could. She had mistakenly thought that by saving his lower leg, she had kept him from this. She had known he resented the limitations the weakened limb imposed on him, but she hadn't realized how truly deep his bitterness went. Until now.

By bedding the serving woman he would prove to himself—and to others—that he was still a man and could still do what men do. Understanding brought no comfort.

She didn't want him making love to another woman. She wanted to give him that comfort and to share that intimacy with him. Her hands dropped to her lap and began to shake as she stared into space, picturing what it would be like to sleep with Dev. Heaven. And hell because he did not care that way about her.

Pippa rose and went back to her room. She flung herself down on the bed, pillowed her head on her crossed arms and stared at the ceiling. Even knowing that he would not enjoy making love to the serving wench as much as he anticipated because his leg would pain him brought no ease. She wanted to be the woman he kissed and held.

Pippa's stomach twisted into coils, and her head started pounding. She squeezed her eyes closed, shutting out the sight of the dingy white ceiling. But she could not stop seeing Dev kissing the Frenchwoman. Pain made her breathing shallow and sleep impossible. She rolled to her side and stared into the dusk-shadowed room.

With a sigh, she sat up and rubbed her throbbing temples. She would drink the bark she'd prepared for Dev. Without it, she would never sleep. She might even take a little laudanum to help her calm down. There was nothing she could do to stop Deverell. She had to live with what he intended.

She told herself his actions didn't matter. He was a grown man and could do anything he chose. All she cared about was that he help her find Philip. Philip's disappearance had brought them together and finding her twin was all that mattered. And as soon as they found her brother, she and Dev would part, never to see each other again.

For when she found her brother, Pippen must disappear and Lady Pippa LeClaire would return home from her visit on the Continent and continue to help the local midwife. That was the life she wanted, the only life she'd wanted since childhood. Deverell St Simon made no difference to her future. None whatsoever.

She needed to sleep. She needed to forget this obsession with Dev's love life and with her own desire to be the woman he turned to. She needed to get the bark from Dev's room.

Walking on feet that insisted on dragging like leaden faggots, she went to his room where she had left the bark. She expected him to still be downstairs waiting for his lady, so she entered without knocking.

Locked together like twining snakes in a pool of golden candlelight, Dev and the wench kissed. His shirt was off and her blouse was around her waist, his hands kneading the fullness of her breasts. Their breathing was loud in the silence.

Pippa gasped and her chest contracted in sharp agony. She felt betrayed. It did not matter that she had known Deverell intended this. It did not matter that she was supposed to be a boy. Nothing mattered except the agony of seeing him doing things to another woman that—she took a great shuddering breath—she wanted him to do to her.

Dev's head snapped up and he roared, *'Out!'*

From the shelter of his shoulder, Giselle gaped, her hands inadequately covering her voluptuousness. *'Merci.'* She pushed away from him and clumsily pulled up her blouse.

'Damn you, Pippen,' Dev said, advancing on her when she did not immediately flee the room. He grabbed her shoulders and shook her like a storm shakes a tree. 'I told you to leave me alone.'

His fingers bit into her flesh. His eyes flashed dangerously, and his jaw formed a harsh angle. He was furious. And he had been drinking. His breath had the sweet scent of red wine.

She had never seen Dev drink to the point that a wild light lit his face. The drink would dull some of the physical discomfort he felt. Now, more than ever, she understood how much he needed to feel like a virile man.

'Take me,' she whispered, knowing as she spoke the fateful words that they were the only thing she could do. Making love to him herself was the only way to keep him from spending the night with the French servant. Making love to him was the only way she could show him that his leg meant nothing to her. His leg did not make him less of a man. 'Make love to me.'

His face darkened.

The bedroom door slammed. Pippa and Dev jumped, but neither looked away from the other.

Dev released her and moved away. He turned his back on her and ran his fingers through his dark hair, disarraying it and making it sweep across the nape of his bare neck in such a way that Pippa was hard pressed not to reach out and smooth it.

'Dev—'

'Get out!' He swung back to face her. 'Get out now. I don't know what I have done to make you think I'm a catamite. But I am not.'

She took a step toward him. The beginning of a smile lifted one corner of her mouth. He misunderstood her, which meant her disguise was safe. But she no longer cared. All she wanted now was to feel him kiss her as he had kissed the other woman. She was too far on this road to change her mind. Nor could she. If she failed to seduce him and prove to him that she desired him, then she would fail to heal him. He needed to make love to her. She wanted him to make love to her.

Dev backed up. 'You have accomplished what you set out to do. I won't be sleeping with Giselle tonight.' His lips twisted. 'But neither will I sleep with you.' He took a deep breath and his voice became calm. 'Go away, Pippen. And don't worry. I will keep your secret.'

Her smile widened. 'Dev,' she said softly, 'I have something to show you.'

He scowled and put out one hand as though to ward her off. 'I am not interested.'

'You will be,' she murmured, taking hold of her courage even as she began to undo her shirt. One by one, she slipped the wooden buttons through the holes until the muslin hung open to her waist where it tucked into her breeches. She shrugged out of it.

Dev's eyes widened.

Slowly she unwound the linen strip that held her breasts captive. Her attention never left the face of the man before her. She saw when comprehension lit his grey eyes into twin flames. The length of cloth fell to the floor.

'Out!' Dev growled. 'Get out before I thrash you. Or—' his voice lowered '—I take what you are flaunting.'

Pippa swallowed hard. He had never intimidated her before. This was not the time to allow him that advantage. For his own good, she had to convince him to love her. Because she…loved him.

The realization took her breath away. Seeing him locked with the serving wench had made her admit that what she felt for him was more than a healer for a patient.

Because she loved him, she had to heal him. Body and soul. Until he felt attractive to a woman, Devil Deverell would not feel whole. Like riding his horse for longer than was good, he needed to make love to a woman to be whole.

Feeling her face flame and the heat lower to her chest like a rash, Pippa sat in the chair and pulled off her brother's too large Hessians. She yanked off the extra pair of socks she wore. Next she unrolled her stockings. Standing again, she unbuttoned her breeches and shimmied out of them. She was down to her small clothes.

Dev stood immobile before her, his face unreadable. 'Why are you doing this?'

His voice was tautly controlled, but she sensed anger and frustration and something else. Something dark and sweet and powerful.

She licked dry lips and chose her words carefully. 'Because I want to. Because I have lived with you for more than three months.' Her hands began to shake when he remained frowning. 'For a month of that time, I cared for you. I learned your…' Another flush marched across her fair skin. 'I know your body intimately. I know how you are formed, and I…I think I know what brings you pleasure.'

He lifted one brown eyebrow in sardonic disbelief.

Pippa struck her unconscious pose, hands on hips, feet shoulder width apart. 'Well, I do. I know you like to be touched. You like having your hair smoothed from your forehead. You like sweets—'

'You know nothing of me,' he said across her words. 'You don't know what I think, and you certainly don't know what I enjoy in bed.' He took a deep shuddering breath. 'Now, get out.'

Pippa took a step toward him. Determination firmed her tread and kept her gaze on his face. Storms tossed in the hazel depths of his eyes and warned her that while he wanted to bed the Frenchwoman, he was not going to willingly do the same to her.

If she left him now, he would not heal. And the next night or the next inn they stayed at he would find another willing woman, another woman who wasn't her. Dev making love to someone else was an unbearable thought.

She moved until her breasts brushed lightly against his chest. 'No.'

Before he could say another word, she wrapped her arms around his neck, pulled his head down to hers and kissed him. It was an inexperienced meeting of lips, and instead of responding as he had to Giselle, he remained motionless, his arms at his side, his mouth sealed.

Pippa broke an inch away. 'Help me, Dev. Let me be your woman tonight. Let me ease your pain.'

He shoved her violently away and flung himself into the

only chair. 'I don't need or want your pity, Pippen. Or whoever you are,' he added sarcastically.

'Pippa,' she said softly.

Dev stared at the woman before him. Minutes ago she had been the youth Pippen. Granted, he had frequently thought the boy too feminine for his own good. He remembered the green-eyed angel he'd imagined while lying on the edge between death and life. That apparition had been Pippen…or Pippa.

He perused her body and felt his loins responding. Too much wine made his thinking less than sharp and made it much easier for his body to do things his mind said no to. His mouth twisted.

Damn, he'd had too much to drink. He had intended to dull the aching throb of his leg so that he could better enjoy and pleasure Giselle. Now the slight disorientation made him even more susceptible to the woman standing so openly before him.

She was tall for a woman, although average for a boy. The face he had thought too smooth and beardless for a man was bathed in the golden glow of the candles, luminous in its purity. His gaze lowered. Dev swallowed hard and knew he should look away from temptation.

Her breasts were smooth and full without being voluptuous. Her waist was slender as a willow, and her hips flared so that all he could think about was nestling his against them. A groan rose in his throat.

He wanted a woman tonight. Had wanted one for months. Tonight was the night he had determined to make love to prove he was still a man, that he could still enjoy being with a woman and giving her pleasure as he took his own.

As though sensing his weakness, Pippen…Pippa knelt at

his feet. The warm, musky scent of her permeated his being.

'Let me help with your boots. I know how it hurts you to take them off.' Suiting action to words, she pulled them off one by one.

Dev studied her. In all their weeks together she had never flirted or sent him looks that smouldered with awareness. Now in one night she was everything enticing. The deep green of her eyes held promises no woman had ever made, of more than a romp in bed, of knowledge and awareness of him as a person. The dark cleft between her breasts was a mystery he longed to explore. Even her short hair seemed exotic. The urge to tousle it made his hand move out and up until his fingers buried themselves in the thick, ebony strands.

Her eyes met his boldly, and she leaned into his caress until she nestled between his sprawled legs. She slid her torso up his chest as he unconsciously pulled her head to his. His need was so great it was like a vise around his chest. Great shuddering chills raced from their hot contact to all parts of his body.

'Do you know what you are doing?' he asked. 'Or are you seducing me by instinct?'

A short, nervous laugh was his answer. He knew her too well to really think she was experienced.

She trailed tentative kisses along the line of his clenched jaw. The urge to take what she so boldly offered swamped Dev. The two bottles of fine French wine he had consumed bade him to succumb.

With a groan as much of pain as passion, he cupped her face in his hands and met her mouth with his in a kiss of fierce desire. When she opened to him, it was as though he plunged over a precipice, his stomach cartwheeling and his head spinning.

Pippa didn't know if she was standing or kneeling. Dev's touch made her head spin and her toes curl.

His tongue slid into her mouth, sending sensations shooting through her that she had never experienced before. She wanted to consume him and be consumed in return. She wanted to have everything he could give her. She wanted to give everything back to him.

Her hands roamed restlessly along his shoulders. Her fingers slid down his chest to twine in the golden brown curls that studded his muscles.

His mouth moved against hers, sliding from side to side while his hands held her head steady for his penetration. She moaned.

He drew instantly back, his eyes glazed, his voice rough. 'Did I hurt you? I'm sorry. I've never been with a woman who's—'

'Shh,' she interrupted him, pulling his head back to hers, his mouth down to hers.

When she could barely breathe and her skin felt prickly with tension, he stood, drawing her up with him. Their bodies moulded to each other. She felt his hips cradle against her stomach as he fitted her even tighter to him. Inexperienced as she was, she recognized his hardness pressing against her.

A tiny thrill of exultation made her smile. He wanted her. Tonight he would be with her instead of another woman. It was all she wanted.

'Help me,' he murmured, releasing her mouth and her body to fumble with the buttons on his breeches.

With eager fingers, she helped ease the tight fitting clothing from him. He stood before her, proud and virile. She had seen him many times before as she nursed him, and she had known then that he would be devastating when he was healthy. But she had not realized just how much he would affect her.

Pippa's breath caught.

He opened his arms to her and she stepped into them. It was like coming home. A sigh slipped between her lips just before he sealed them with his.

They slid to the floor, their bodies never losing contact. Side by side, they lay exploring each other's secret pleasures. His teeth scraped across the rim of her ear, and it was more intense than any touch of a hand. When his palm cupped her breast, she thought she would expire.

'Talk to me,' he crooned. 'Tell me what you like.'

She had no words to express what he made her feel, only tiny gasps and soft moans. Her head tossed from side to side as he ravaged her with his mouth, teeth and tongue. He slid down her until he knelt in the V of her legs. His hands roved over every curve and indentation of her. She thought that surely she would explode.

'Please,' she begged, not knowing what she asked, but that she needed something only he could supply.

'Soon,' he whispered, his voice hoarse with passion. 'Soon. I can't wait much longer.'

Her back arched as he stroked down her ribs to her hips and along her flanks. When he took one of her breasts into his mouth, she bucked. So intense was her pleasure that she felt herself melt inside. A throbbing began in her loins.

'Do something. Please,' she moaned.

'Soon,' he promised.

She thrashed beneath his ministrations. Tiny sounds escaped her throat. Her fingers gripped his waist and pulled him closer. She wanted to feel him against her.

'Spread your legs,' he said, inching closer.

When she complied, he pressed against her, sending heat coursing through her limbs. She reached for him to guide him in. As her fingers closed over the hard length of him, he groaned.

'Pip...' he dragged out his nickname for her. He licked lips gone suddenly dry. 'Don't...' He gulped. 'Don't hold me that way. It's too...much.'

His words aroused her even more. 'What do I do instead,' she gasped as he nipped her shoulder.

'Wrap your legs around my waist,' he said, his voice barely audible.

She did as he said and felt him slide into her. It was the most exciting thing she had ever experienced. He filled her to bursting. Instinctively she surged up to take him completely.

A sharp pain stopped her in mid-thrust.

'Oh!' she gasped, drawing back.

His hands gripped her hips like vises and prevented her from easing away. 'No,' he murmured. 'This will only hurt for a second. I...' he took a deep breath '...promise.'

Before she knew what he was doing, he plunged into her. One quick thrust and he was completely sheathed in her. They lay that way for long moments. He rained tiny kisses along her eyes and down her jawline. His hands played along her torso, cupping and kneading her swollen breasts.

Her pain turned to pleasure, and she began to move against him. She began returning his kisses. Her hands gripped his hips and held him to her.

'What now?'

He chuckled, ending with a groan. 'Just what you're doing.'

They moved in rhythm as though they had spent all their lives making love. The gentle slap of skin on skin filled the room, mixing with the sounds of two people reaching the ultimate physical joy.

Tension mounted in Pippa until her moans crescendoed just as Dev thrust deeply and made her explode into a thousand tiny fragments. Her gasps mingled with his shout.

They lay entwined as the candle gutted and went out. The only light came from the moon shining through the window. The cooler evening air brushed across their sweat-slicked bodies.

Pippa stirred. Only now that the heat of passion was slacked did she begin to feel embarrassed by her boldness and the results. Dev's naked body pressed to hers in the most intimate of embraces.

'I…I need to go back to my room,' she murmured, feeling the heat of mortification warm her face and chest.

He nuzzled into her, his sweet wine-scented breath wafting across her neck. 'Not yet.'

He rose and pulled her up with him. They stood, torso to torso, hip to hip, thigh to thigh. 'Come to bed, Pip. Let me show you how wonderful lovemaking can be when there is no pain.'

She hesitated.

He bent and kissed her. It was a gentle, slow touching that evolved into something deep and primitive. His need reached out and caught her heart. She was lost.

Pippa lay awake long after Dev's soft snoring told her he slept. She still could not totally believe what she had done. All her life she had reached out to people in pain and tried to ease their suffering. But never had she put their needs so much before what was best for her.

It was because she loved Deverell St Simon.

She sighed and closed her eyes on the moon-drenched room. The scent of impending rain wafted through the open window. A horse whinnied in the stables. Her senses were acute. Too acute.

She could still feel Dev's lips on hers, his body in hers. The memory was shattering.

Love. Physical and emotional. She had given him everything she had to offer, and he had taken it. She would do it again.

Chapter Seven

Dev surfaced slowly. A beam of early sunlight slashed across his face. For the first time in months he was relaxed. His leg was only a minor ache, not the usual incessant throb. He felt good. Damn good.

And warm.

Someone snuggled against his side, one leg thrown over his. He turned his head.

A woman's face nestled in the hollow of his shoulder. Her short, curly black hair clung to him. Her full red lips were slightly parted, and her warm breath caressed his chest.

Memory flooded back. Pippen. Or Pippa. Or whoever she really was. It hurt to think.

He had a raging headache. Two bottles of port had submerged his good sense, but not his ardour. Dev nearly groaned. The desire to kiss her awake was making his loins tighten in sharp response to her nearness.

Her breasts pressed against his ribs, and the hot apex of her legs caressed his thigh. Oh, yes. This was more temptation than he was used to resisting.

But who was this woman really, and why was she looking for Staunton? Was he really her cousin? All he knew for certain was that she was a healer and had saved his life. And she was of gentle birth. She might have done a risky and hoydenish thing by pretending to be a boy, but her manners and the way she carried herself spoke of Quality.

She moved. Her thigh slid down his, sending sparks coursing through him. Surely this was hell. He dared not touch her intimately again. He shouldn't have done so last night, but his judgement had been impaired. The sight of her white limbs glowing in the moonlight had shattered his resistance, just as her body had shattered his mind.

Without warning, her eyes opened. They widened. She gulped.

There was a softness about her that Dev had glimpsed before, but never focused on. Her mouth was full and red, swollen from his kisses. Her eyes were brilliant.

'Mother was right,' Dev said, all his questions disappearing in the wake of his response to her. 'The emeralds will be perfect on you.'

She blinked. The thick black lashes Dev had too often thought effeminate acted like elaborate fans, brushing her blushing cheeks.

'Emeralds?' Her voice was husky. What had been a light tenor for a young man was really a woman's beautiful alto.

Dev felt his body tightening. What a blind fool he had been.

'Yes. The emeralds I intend to give you when we are wed.'

'Wed?'

He resisted the urge to stroke the hair back from her face. 'Yes. Wed. After last night it is the only thing we can do.'

Her eyes narrowed and she pushed at his chest. 'After last night? You mean you feel obliged to marry me because of what we did.'

'Of course. A gentleman does not sleep with a respectable, single woman and then not marry her.' Dev scowled at her, wondering why she was being difficult about this. There was no other option.

She pushed harder. 'I don't wish to marry you.'

'But you will,' he said, remembering why they were in Paris. She would hate him after they found Staunton. The thought pushed all ideas of dalliance from him. 'Get up and get dressed,' he said curtly. 'We have a few things to discuss.'

'Besides marriage?' she countered. But she sat up, her back to him.

He couldn't help himself. The delicate curve of her back, the sweep of her hips caught him. He traced a finger down her spine to the cleft just above the swell of her *derrière*.

She drew in a sharp breath. She seemed to lean toward him, and Dev sensed with a man's instinct for knowing when a woman wanted him that he could slip his arm around her waist and they would once more enjoy the pleasure they could give one another. The urge to have her was a sharp agony that quickened his pulse.

He let her go. 'We have things to straighten out,' he said, his voice a raw husk. 'Like who you really are.'

She didn't look at him as she pulled the sheet up and wrapped it around her slim body. With a grace he had occasionally noticed when she dressed as a boy, she moved to her discarded clothes.

'Please don't look,' she said, keeping her back to him.

Dev turned away. He might want nothing more than to drink in the beauty of her, but he was a gentleman. Gentlemen didn't watch a woman dress when asked not to, just as a gentleman didn't sleep with a virgin and then not marry her.

'All right,' she said.

He rolled back around and sat up in the bed.

She gasped and her gaze dropped. He was fully aroused and did nothing to hide that fact. Dev watched the blush start at her cheeks and descend to her neck.

'I lost my modesty a long time ago,' he said, standing. He glanced at her shocked face. 'You have seen me naked, and you have seen me in this state.' A wicked grin laced his features. 'I seem to recall that you enjoyed it very much.'

She twisted around on a bare foot. 'That was last night.'

'True.' He found his breeches and pulled them up, careful not to hurt himself in the process. 'Now you owe me an explanation. Several.' As an afterthought, he added, 'I'm dressed.'

She turned around and her attention instantly went to his hips. He shrugged. 'It will take some time for that particular ailment to correct itself.'

She licked dry lips and her gaze met his. 'I suppose you want to know who I really am.'

'For starters.'

He sat in one of the room's two chairs and motioned for her to take the other. Instead, she paced.

'I am Philippa LeClaire. Philip LeClaire's twin. Earl LeClaire is my grandfather.'

Dev frowned. This was worse than he'd imagined. Once he betrayed her and turned Staunton in, she wouldn't have anything to do with him. No matter what they'd done last night.

'Now I understand your determination to find Staunton. But why did your grandfather let you come to Brussels alone and disguised as a boy? If you were found out, you'd be ruined.' He didn't add that she was already ruined by sleeping with him.

She paused and looked away. 'Grandfather doesn't know,' she said quietly.

'What?'

She shrugged and had the grace to look as though she knew what she'd done was wrong. 'He thinks I came here with my aunt, Tabitha Montcleve, for a chaperon.'

Dev shook his head. 'And what is to keep him from finding out?'

For the first time since awakening, a tiny smile tugged at her lips. 'He and Aunt Tabitha hate each other. They never speak, so he'll never know she's still in London.'

'What a family,' Dev murmured. 'Where are your parents? Surely they would never knowingly allow you to do such a hoydenish thing as this.'

She paused and said softly, 'Dead. My mother died in childbirth. That's why I became a healer. To help other women. My father died later in a carriage accident.'

'I'm sorry.' Dev rose and went to her. She stepped away from him, but he followed. 'Come here, Pip.'

She watched him steadily and must have seen the sincerity he felt because she moved into his arms. He stroked her hair and held her gently.

She took a deep breath. 'I must find Philip. I'm so afraid that if I don't…Grandfather will die too. He has a bad heart and getting the letter about Philip nearly brought on another attack of apoplexy.'

Oh, God, Dev thought. This is getting worse and worse. He felt like a cad. 'We'll find your brother, if he's alive.'

'He is. I know it,' she said fervently. 'I would know if he were not.'

'That twin thing,' Dev said, half believing because of her belief.

'Yes. When we were younger, oh, maybe ten or twelve, he took one of the dogs for a romp. He missed dinner. Grandfather and Burns, our nanny, were worried that something awful had happened to him, but I knew he was all right. I sensed it. He came home thirty minutes later, his pants and shirt torn because he'd tripped over a log and ripped them, but otherwise fit as a fiddle.' She lifted her head from Dev's shoulder and met his eyes. 'I knew he would be. Just as I know he will be this time.'

Her eyes gleamed from unshed tears. Determination etched a sharp line between her brows and edged her jaw.

Admiration and a desire to protect and comfort her welled up in Dev. Without thought, he gently took her lips with his. It was a tender touch, meant to ease some of her pain. But his need for her soon turned it deeper.

Pippa reeled under the sensual devastation of his kiss. All her resolve to act as though their lovemaking had been a pothole in the road that could be ignored fled. She collapsed against him.

An eternity later, he released her. Pippa stumbled back. Her calf hit the edge of a chair, and she collapsed into it. Stunned, she stared at Dev who still stood.

'You are marrying me,' he stated. 'I told you I keep my promises.' A grin broke through his determination. 'And no woman who swoons when I kiss her is going to get away.'

She smiled back, all her earlier objections forgotten. She loved him. Surely he felt the same, or he couldn't make her feel so completely overwhelmed by emotion.

'Come here,' he ordered. 'I haven't finished with you.'

The sun was well overhead and the room hot when Dev woke again. He eased himself from the bed and dressed. He had to start looking for clues as to where Staunton had been and to whom he had talked. The first place to start was the stables. Ostlers and grooms knew everyone who came and went in an establishment like this.

But before leaving, Dev paused to kiss Pippa lightly on

the cheek. She slept through his caress, her face flushed and her body relaxed. She trusted him implicitly. More than ever he wished he didn't have to ruin that trust, but bringing to justice a man who had helped kill many British men was more important than one person's happiness. Even if that person was Pippa.

To put the image of Pippa's disillusionment from his mind, Dev walked briskly from the room.

A coin here and another there, soon had several of the ostlers talking to him. One, a slight youth with a gaping hole where his two front teeth should be, told Dev he'd seen a man who met Staunton's description.

In his lisping French, the boy said, 'But he was French as I am, not English.'

Dev kept quiet. It was possible that Staunton spoke French like a native. The skill would be indispensable to a spy.

'He often met with Jorge.' The youth nodded his head in the direction of the water trough. 'Over there when Jorge would stop by. The first time it seemed an accident. But on the fourth time, I thought they were trading something. Jorge is often curious—just as you, *monsieur*—and willing to pay a franc or two for information.'

'Where is Jorge from?' Dev handed out another coin for the direction.

'Dev,' Pippa said from directly behind him just as the ostler finished speaking.

Dev managed to keep from jerking around and wondered how many more lies he was going to have to tell her. She stood in the shadows, but he could tell she was in her boy's clothing and that she wasn't happy with him for leaving her behind. He thanked the ostler before turning.

'So, you're finally awake, sleepyhead.'

She frowned at him, her glance going from him to the ostler who was backing away. 'I worked harder than usual.'

'Ouch,' he murmured, taking her arm and steering her outside.

'Why did you sneak out?' she hissed at him, trying to draw her arm away.

He held her steady. 'Because you needed the rest.'

'That was kind of you,' she said with an ironic twist of lips. 'But why do I feel there was more to it than that?'

He couldn't meet her open gaze. 'Because there was. I don't want you involved in this search any more than you already are.'

She dug her heels in until they stopped. 'Why?'

His brows snapped together, and he pulled her forward in spite of her resistance. 'It could be dangerous. Just as talking where anyone can overhear us could be dangerous.'

Dev continued dragging her as he tried to decide how much to tell her. They were on the street in front of the inn, the traffic creating enough noise to drown out their voices when he allowed them to halt.

'Pippa, why do you think your brother was here in Paris when all of Wellington's troops were gathering at Brussels?'

Her face took on a pinched, worried look. 'I...I had tried not to think about it.' She took a deep breath. 'But it was unusual.'

'Very.'

'Was he doing something dishonest?' She gripped his arm and her fingers dug through the heavy cloth of his jacket. 'Did Wellington tell you something?'

Dev gazed down at her. The best thing would be to tell her the truth, up to a point. If she knew Staunton was considered a traitor then she would wonder why he was helping her find him. He couldn't tell her that. Guilt and remorse slammed into him. He owed her so much. He owed Patrick and others like him more. He looked away.

'He was…is a spy. He disappeared from here.'

Her jaw tightened. 'A spy. Why didn't Wellington tell me that?'

He forced himself to meet her angry gaze. 'Because he thought you naught but a boy.'

'But he told you. Is that why you came with me? Because Wellington told you to?'

So much truth in her words. Dev clamped down on the urge to tell her everything. 'No. I came because I had already promised to help you. You know that. The only reason Wellington told me was because he knew we were determined to come here, and he didn't want me—or you—in jeopardy because we didn't know the truth about your brother.'

'Why didn't you tell me sooner?'

He sighed and ran the fingers of the arm she wasn't holding like a vise through his hair. 'I was hoping to search for him without having you along. Stupid, I know, but I didn't want to worry you more. Spies live dangerous lives.'

The lines around her mouth softened. Seeing that she believed his tale of half-truths made Dev feel worse.

'Oh, Dev,' she said softly, 'I'm sorry I doubted you. Even for a second.'

Damn, but it was hard to keep meeting her gaze. 'Then will you trust me enough to let me search for him without you? Having you along would only distract me and make it more dangerous for both of us.'

She considered for a long time. Around them, pedestrians swirled like a river around a large boulder. Horses with their riders or drawing carriages clopped along the cobbled street. Hawkers yelled their wares.

At last she said, 'I know you'll do your best. I appreciate

your help and how difficult these last days have been on you. I...I don't want to make everything worse.' Her hand fell away from his arm. 'Do you have information?'

The last was so unexpected, that Dev started. 'Yes. The ostler gave me a man's name and direction.'

'Ah...' her eyebrows rose '...that is what you were doing. If it were anyone else, I would insist on going.' She stepped away, stepped back. Uncertainty was writ plain to see on her face and in her actions. 'But since 'tis you, I'll wait at the inn.'

'Thank you,' he said, humbled by her trust. A trust he didn't deserve.

'But...' she shook a finger at him '...if you aren't back in two hours, I shall go and bribe that same young man and then follow you.'

He caught her hand and brought that admonishing finger to his lips, completely forgetting where they were or how she was dressed. 'Understood.'

He watched her go back to the inn, making sure she was inside before heading off. He was piling up more and more acrimony. The more he lied to her, the more she would hate him when all was said and done.

A pain that had nothing to do with his leg filled him. He pushed it aside. This went beyond any one individual. He had to remember that.

Some time later, he returned to the inn. Jorge had given him a description of another man, a man who fit the particulars, as Wellington had told him, of the British spy who'd been murdered. Everything was pointing to Staunton. Jorge had also given him the name and direction of a third man. Tomorrow he would go there. But right now his two hours were up.

He found Pippa in the tap room, seated in a dark corner, nursing a mug of ale. He went to her.

She jumped up as soon as she saw him. 'What did you learn?'

'Shh.' He sat down across from her and ordered a beer. When it came he took a long drink and wiped the foam from his upper lip. 'I found out that anyone can be bribed, if the money is high enough.' He shook his head in disgust. 'The man denied knowing your brother, but when I gave him enough gold to weight down a strong man's hand, he told me he had seen a man of your brother's likeness. He also gave me another name. I plan to visit him as soon as I leave here.'

'Leave here?'

He set the mug down. 'Leave here, Pip. Your brother's trail is months old. The less time we waste here, the better. I doubt he's even here now, but maybe this next man will have a clue as to where he went.'

She agreed, but when she left the tap room her step wasn't as light as normal. He knew this was hard on her.

His next errand led him to one of Paris's biggest slums. Trash filled the gutters and an eye-watering stench filled the air. People dressed in rags walked through the muck or slept in it. Dev had seen poverty in London and had done what he could to help those he met. Here he hesitated to give anyone money, for fear that he would then become a target. It was bad enough that his good clothes set him apart.

Knocking on the door of the address given to him, Dev kept an eye over his shoulder and was thankful for the pistol in the pocket of his coat. When there was no answer, he used his cane to hammer on the door. Just as he decided to leave, the door cracked open.

A woman's raspy voice asked in French, 'What do you want? Ain't nothing here for a swell.'

Dev stuck his foot in the opening and with a glance over his shoulder, held out his hand. On the palm was a franc. 'I have some questions,' he said in French, 'and I will pay well for the answers.'

The door opened wider and he slipped inside, keeping his back to the solid wood. There was no telling who was with the woman.

The room was dark and dingy. The smell of sweat and onions was like a slap in the face. His nose wrinkled automatically.

'Told you this ain't no place for Quality,' the woman said defensively.

She was as thin and rusty looking as a worn nail. Her dress was patched and in need of cleaning. Her hair hung in lank shanks around her tired, lined face. He added another coin to the one in his palm and gave both to her.

'What's this for? I haven't told you anything yet.' But she took the money and it disappeared faster than Dev could follow.

'I'm looking for Pierre Mont. Do you know him?'

Fury replaced the greed that had just lit her muddy brown eyes. 'He's dead.'

Dev nearly groaned out loud. So close. 'When?'

'A month ago. Why?'

Dev drew out another coin. 'I think he knew someone I'm hunting for.'

She snatched the money. 'What do you want to know?'

'Can you tell me someone who knew Mont? Someone he might have told a secrct to?'

Her thin mouth twisted bitterly. 'Me. He was my man.'

Hope unfurled again and Dev dug out another franc. 'How did he die?'

'Stabbed. Lived for days while the wound festered. I couldn't do nothing. No money.'

He had to look away from the grief she made no effort to hide. 'Do you know who killed him?'

She shook her head. He handed her another coin. She took it.

She licked her dry lips, and her claw-like hands curled. 'He was out of his mind at the end. Fever eatin' him up. He kept talking about some foreigner and Holland.'

'English?'

She shrugged, the cloth of her dress hanging loosely off her shoulders. 'Maybe. And Holland. Didn't seem like he meant the country, but maybe.' She shrugged again and held out her hand.

Dev gave her everything he had left. Without another word, she turned and left through a small door in the back of the room. Having no wish to stay any longer, Dev walked briskly away, using his cane for support.

It was darker outside than when he'd gone into the house. More ragamuffins were around, and there was a distinct air of danger. Dev picked up his pace and kept his right hand on the pistol in his pocket. It had two shots.

Maybe it was his speed or the look of cold awareness he had, but no one accosted him. Once or twice a man or woman edged his way, but when he stared them down they quickly retreated.

A little less than three hours after leaving Pippa for the second time that day, Dev re-entered the inn. He was exhausted. He needed food and rest, and then he would think on what the woman had told him. Holland, but not the country, and a foreigner, maybe British.

That night Pippa and Dev ate in the tavern. She hunkered down on the hard bench with her arms propped up on the scarred pine table top. Now, more than ever before, she found it hard to impersonate a boy. After Dev's loving and with his hazel eyes devouring her across the span of wood, she felt as though her body was shouting 'female' to any who looked. Even her mannerisms were reverting back to her feminine gestures. Twice today she'd caught herself tossing her head to get her non-existent hair off her face.

'Eat up,' Dev said, taking a swallow of his ale.

She noted that tonight he wasn't drinking to excess. 'I'm not very hungry,' she answered, pushing the overcooked mutton around her plate.

'Would *monsieur* care for more ale?' Giselle's husky French voice asked. She sidled closer and stopped inches from Dev, her right hand propped on one canted hip as she thrust out her ample bosom.

Pippa clamped her jaw on a brusque no. This was Dev's decision to make. Instead of looking at him and hoping to see uninterest in his eyes when he gazed at the French-woman, Pippa watched a table of men toast one another. All her determination barely kept her from turning back to Dev and beseeching him with her eyes to get rid of Giselle.

'She's gone now,' Dev said quietly.

Pippa's gaze snapped back to him. 'Oh? I barely even realized she was here.'

'Liar,' he said softly. 'Let's go upstairs.'

He stood and pushed back his stool with his good leg. Still, he winced. Pippa forgot her jealousy in her concern for him.

She jumped up and circled the table to offer him her shoulder. 'You've had a long day and wouldn't use a carriage. Nor did you get much slee—' Her scolding stopped abruptly as she realized the implications of what she had said.

'No, I didn't,' he murmured. 'But I enjoyed every second of my labours and would again.'

Pleasure mixed with embarrassment as Pippa stumbled and caught herself up before dragging them both to the floor in this public room. He made her forget propriety.

'You shouldn't say such things where people can hear,' she muttered.

His arm tightened on her shoulder. 'You're the only one who can hear me, and you already know what I'm talking about. And…' he grinned down at her '…you started the conversation.'

She had. Instead of continuing down this path, she shut up. It was a rare experience for her to know someone else had beaten her to the last word.

Silently, they climbed the stairs to their rooms. At Dev's door, she released his waist.

'I'll return as soon as I fix you something for the pain. Then you'll be able to get a good night's sleep.'

His eyes flashed and he grinned. 'There are better ways of forgetting the discomfort.'

'Perhaps.' She looked up at him through the shade of her lashes. There was a hard-angled hunger about his face that made her breathless. 'But this will also help.'

Before he could refuse, she nipped into her room. Minutes later, she knocked on his door and entered without waiting for his reply.

He stood looking out the window. The sun was setting and blood-red rays splashed across his bare chest. She went to him and gave him the draught. He downed it in one gulp before setting the empty glass on the table.

'Thank you for your care,' he said, drawing her into the safe haven of his arms.

She went willingly and leaned her head against the hollow of his shoulder. Warmth and the musky scent that was his own enveloped Pippa. She felt comfortable and cared for. Perhaps with time he would love her. He already liked her. Unconsciously, she sighed.

'What is wrong?' he asked, tightening his hold on her.

'Nothing.' The last thing she was going to do was tell him her insecurities and longings where he was concerned.

He misunderstood. 'We'll find your brother, Pippa. I promise. I got a good clue today. You know that.'

She turned into him, sliding her hands up his chest and into his hair. 'Love me, Dev. Make me forget everything else.'

Hunger narrowed his eyes and sharpened his jaw. 'I want nothing more, Pip, but I can't.'

'What?' Hurt made her voice falter. 'You don't want to?'

He groaned. 'That's not it. I shouldn't have made love to you last night or earlier today. It isn't right. We aren't married yet.'

She dropped her hands and clasped her fingers together to keep from reaching for him again. 'I understand.' She moved away.

'Pippa,' he said, reaching for her, exasperation writ clearly on his face. 'That isn't it. I want to love you more than anything else, but...'

'But what?' The anguish in his face and the bright blaze in his eyes were beginning to penetrate her sense of rejection. He did want her. He might say differently, but his body was refusing to heed his command.

He shook his head. 'You're from a good family. I shouldn't have even touched you.'

'Do you regret it?' she asked softly, deciding to use any means to overcome his late scruples.

'No.' He turned from her.

She glared at his back. 'Then what difference does another time make? I'm no longer a virgin. Stopping now won't change that.'

'No, but maybe it will make me feel less a cad.'

'Then why were you flirting with me downstairs?' she demanded, wondering if the tightness in her chest caused by his rejection would ever go away.

Deep down she knew she should leave instead of continuing to throw herself at him, but she couldn't. Her desire for him was beyond his need for her as a woman. She wanted him to love her as she loved him. She wanted him to marry her for herself and not for his honour.

She moved to him and wrapped her arms around him. 'Please don't make me beg, Dev.'

He twisted around and caught her hands. 'I could never do that, Pippa.'

With a moan mixed of pleasure and surrender, he bent his head until his lips met hers. Their arms twined around each other and their mouths melded to one another.

Pippa wanted to be as close to him as possible. Dev wanted to forget everything but the feel of her pressed to him and around him.

Chapter Eight

At Calais, they boarded a British ship bound for Dover. After long thought, Dev had concluded that the 'Holland' mentioned by the Frenchwoman had to be Lord Holland, possibly that lord's country estate since Parliament was briefly out of session. It was a shot in the dark, but they'd agreed to take it.

Now, with the ship rolling beneath their feet, they stood as close together as two men can. Pippa leaned against the rail and watched France disappear.

'I shall almost miss it,' Pippa said softly.

Dev turned a questioning look on her.

She smiled. ''Tis where you and I found each other. As horrible as it sounds, without the war I would have never met you.'

'I can't find it in me to be glad for a country that cost so many British lives.' Dev stared out at the open sea. Storm clouds hovered on the horizon. He turned back to Pippa. 'We would have met anyway. You would have come to London for a Season.'

'No, I would not have. I'm not a social butterfly, Dev. I love the country, and I enjoy my work.'

Dev surreptitiously took her hand under the cover of their

greatcoats. 'Then I must be glad for what happened, much as it pains me to say so.'

'Oh, Dev,' she said tremulously.

A strong wind caught the sails and the ship veered to one side. Pippa's feet slipped on the saltwater-coated deck. Dev grabbed her arm and kept her from falling.

'I think we would be safer in our cabin.'

Pippa, her short hair speckled with spray, agreed. She had no more than put one foot on the step leading down to their cabin when the ship bucked. Both hands wrapped around the stair rail, she groaned.

Dev, some steps below, looked up, a worried frown obvious even in the dim light from a wildly swinging lantern. 'Are you all right?'

'Barely,' Pippa muttered. Her stomach was beginning to lurch with every roll of the ship. Just as it had done on her crossing to Brussels. She had forgotten the agony until now.

Dev found their cubbyhole and held the door open for her. Pippa stumbled over the threshold, one hand plastered to her mouth.

'What the devil?' He reached for her, but she eluded him and went straight for the slop bucket. He followed.

Pippa lost her dinner.

'Pip,' Dev said, 'why didn't you tell me you get seasick?'

'Didn't matter,' she muttered, her face tinged green around the edges. Her legs felt like they were about to collapse under her.

'Lie down. Now,' he ordered when she hesitated.

She fell to the bunk, too weak to lift her feet. Dev did the service for her after pulling off her boots. Sweat popped out on her brow and he went to the water pitcher, unstoppered it and wet his handkerchief. Returning, he laid it across her forehead.

'I...' she turned a ghastly shade of grey '...think I...'

He dropped the wet cloth and grabbed the bucket. She leaned over and promptly cast up what was left. For long minutes all she could do was heave drily. Dev rubbed her back and wiped her mouth.

'I'm so sorry,' she finally managed. 'I never meant to do this. I'm not normally so poor spirited.'

'Hush,' Dev said. 'Can you sit up enough for me to get this jacket off? It cannot help you to be hot.'

'I think so,' she murmured, straining to raise her shoulders up.

That done, she fell backward, too spent to do more than murmur thank you. Dev undid the top buttons of her shirt and tucked the rough cotton sheet around her waist. He poured a small amount of water and brought it to her.

'Can you manage this?' He tipped the glass to her lips.

Pippa managed a sip. 'Bring my bag of herbs. Please.'

He gave her a quizzical look, but fetched the item. She rummaged until pulling out a small vial that contained a light brown substance.

Seeing Dev watching her, Pippa said, 'Ginger. A little of this in the water will help settle my stomach.' The ship rocked and she grimaced. 'I should have thought of this sooner.'

She instructed him on the amount and then drank down the concoction. 'More water, please,' she croaked after the last of the medicine. 'The ginger burns.'

'Burns?' Dev handed her a little water.

'Yes,' she managed to say around sips. ''Tis like pepper, only it does not make you sneeze.'

Minutes later she fell into a light doze. Dev perched on the wooden side of the bunk and smoothed the damp tendrils of hair from her face. A smile tugged at his lips. Their positions were reversed, and he found that he liked caring for her.

His leg ached from the long ride they had made yesterday, coming from Paris. The only place to lie down was the bunk Pippa now slept in. With a wider smile, Dev gently moved her inward and lay down beside her. She snuggled close until her head rested in the crook of his shoulder. She always managed to find that spot, and Dev was coming to expect her near him.

Contentment relaxed his muscles as he fell asleep. Even his throbbing leg seemed less intense.

Later, they woke, flushed with the nearness of each other.

'How do you feel?' Dev asked, rubbing his hand up and down her arm.

'Much better.' Her gaze met his. 'Much better.'

'I am glad,' he murmured, leaning over and taking her mouth with his. 'Very glad.'

Luckily, he had locked the cabin's door when they first entered.

Hours later, they disembarked at Dover and headed for an inn where Dev was well known. At the door, he turned to her. 'Stay out here, Pip.'

She scowled at him. 'Why?'

'Because I don't want anyone seeing you who doesn't have to.'

'Why not? Are you ashamed of me? Do I look disreputable after my shipboard activities?'

He sighed. 'No, but the fewer people who see you as you currently are, the better.'

Understanding dawned. 'You are protecting me,' she said.

'Hush. The less said in public the better.'

Before she could tell him he was being overly cautious, he left and the door closed in her face. Pippa watched the hustle and bustle as time passed. She had just decided to go inside and search Dev out, when he hailed her from inside a coach that had just driven into the front yard.

She hurried to the vehicle and pulled open the door.

'Come on,' he said, 'we haven't all day. Our things are already loaded. Your herbs are in here.' He waved to the corner opposite him where her bag rested.

She clambered in. 'Why are we travelling this way? I thought you were too determined to prove yourself to sink this low.' She softened the words with a smile.

'I think I have proven myself enough for one day. I don't need to continue showing you I'm a man by riding a horse when there are better ways to use my energy,' he murmured wickedly, referring to their activity after wakening on the ship.

'Perhaps,' she agreed, sitting beside him, glad that her love for him had eased his feeling of inadequacy. 'But then again, that was a while ago.' She turned innocent green eyes on him, placing one hand lightly on his chest. 'I have never had the experience in a carriage, and I think it might be very interesting.'

He looked at her in amazement, but she could see his pupils dilating and feel his heart picking up speed beneath her palm. She knew her wish would come true.

It was a long, cold journey to Lord Holland's country house. Autumn was on its way and with it came shorter days and wetter travel. The sound of wheels on gravel was most welcome.

Exhaustion atc at Pippa. She knew that if she felt this badly, then Dev must be worse. His leg had to be hurting.

'Dev,' she murmured, sitting away from him and looking out the window, 'we're here. How are you feeling?'

He stretched before joining her at the window. 'As good as can be expected. Thank goodness you showed me the error of my ways.'

She turned a puzzled face to him. 'Me?'

'Yes,' he said tenderly, smoothing a curl from her forehead. 'You showed me there are other ways than killing myself on horseback to prove my wound is insignificant.'

Warmth suffused her. She caught his hand and brought the palm to her lips. 'If we weren't nearly at our destination, I would show you again.'

He kissed her lightly on the mouth. 'Or I would show you.' The carriage slowed to a halt. 'But not now. The last thing we need is for someone to see us.'

She nodded regretfully and released his hand. Turning the subject, she said, 'I hope my brother is here. I've been gone from home many months, and I know my grandfather. My letters might be written to soothe him, but I doubt they do. I need to find Philip.' Her voice fell to a barely audible whisper. 'For Grandfather and for myself.'

Dev heard the softly spoken words and his gut twisted. He turned abruptly away.

Soon he would have to ruin her regard for him. He could not help it. Staunton had done irreparable damage and, if left free, he would continue to do so. Napoleon might be on St Helena, but he had plenty of sympathizers who would be more than willing to see him free again.

The carriage stopped and Pippa flung open the door and leaped before the ostler could get the step down. Dev, unable to match her feat, exited sedately. To his amazement, his pride was not hurt.

They had barely taken ten steps before the front door

was opened and the butler ushered them inside. Their hosts met them shortly.

'Lord Holland,' Dev said, extending his hand and moving forward. 'Thank you and your lady for having us.' He made a bow to Lady Holland.

'Any time, Deverell. When your brother's letter arrived asking me to let you rusticate while your leg healed, I was glad to do what I can. How is Jonathan? I have not see him since Parliament adjourned.'

Dev smiled ruefully. 'I don't know, sir. I haven't seen him since his marriage.'

'Ah…yes.' Lord Holland gave Dev a knowing look before turning his attention to Pippa. 'And who is your companion? Another one of Wellington's heroes?'

'Most definitely,' Dev said, moving aside for Pippa. 'May I present Pippen LeClaire?'

Pippa made a bow to Lord Holland and then to his wife. That woman studied Pippa from head to toe.

'You look in need of a bath and food,' Lady Holland said in her abrupt way. 'We keep country hours here and dress for dinner.'

Pippa gulped. 'I am used to eating at five, milady. But—'

'But Pippen does not have formal dress, Lady Holland,' Dev said decisively. 'His clothing was lost in the turmoil of travelling from Brussels to here. Besides which, Pippen cared for many of Wellington's injured troops.'

Lady Holland gave him a shrewd look. 'So, you are telling me that, as a war hero, it is my duty to receive him at my table regardless of his dress?'

Dev said nothing, but met her eyes squarely.

'There is no need for this,' Pippa said hastily. 'I can eat off a tray in my room. Please—'

Once more she was interrupted. 'Young man,' Lady Holland said, 'I will do as I see fit in my own home. And I have decided that you will be an oddity. We meet for drinks fifteen minutes before. Do not be late.'

Dazed at the swiftness of the lady's change, Pippa stared at Lady Holland's disappearing back. Behind her the butler coughed.

'If you will follow me, milords, I will show you to the rooms prepared for you.'

Dev and Pippa thanked Lord Holland and followed the servant.

Pippa surreptitiously watched Dev as they climbed the stairs. He was already exhausted. She knew traversing two flights of stairs was not going to help his leg.

When she saw him wince and his left leg buckle just a little, she said softly, 'Here, lean on me.'

He did so without protest.

The butler deposited them at their doors, which were side by side. Pippa went into her room and immediately spied a door that she was sure would connect with Dev's. She rushed to it and rapped smartly. Seconds later, he opened it.

He grinned rakishly at her, his dimple begging to be touched. 'How convenient.'

She laughed up at him. 'Why would they give us connecting rooms?'

He shrugged. 'Probably because I told Jonathan to tell them you are taking care of me, and I need you close by.'

'Ah,' she said. 'How clever.'

'I thought so,' he murmured, entering her room and looking around. 'Quite cosy.'

She glanced around. A large four-poster hugged one wall. Thick carpet softened the waxed gloss of wood floors. Heavy blue damask curtains closed out the cold night.

'I shall be very comfortable. And how is your room?' she asked, edging by him.

His room was larger and more richly furnished, as befitted the younger son of a prominent duke. In addition to a bed, wardrobe, dresser and washing table, he had several large overstuffed wing chairs grouped around the fireplace.

A knock on his door made them both jump. 'Who is it?' Dev asked.

'Milord,' a deep male voice, muffled by the heavy oak of the door, said. 'I have brought you a light supper.'

Dev raised a brow at Pippa. She could stay or return to her room. She decided to return to her own room. She was more tired than hungry, and when her food was delivered she would politely decline. She should have done so downstairs, but had been too taken aback by Lady Holland to think straight.

Dev waited for the connecting door to close before bidding the servant enter. 'Set the tray on the table,' he said, thinking how nice it would be to stretch his leg out before the roaring fire. The heat would ease some of the ache.

The servant did as instructed, but not without casting a curious glance around the room. His eyes met Deverell's. For an instant, Dev felt as though he were being studied. Then the man's gaze fell away. Even after the servant left, Dev was left with the impression of a tall man with hair a shade darker than his own and vivid green eyes that reminded him of Pippa's. Strange.

Pushing the image away, Dev sank into one of the soft chairs and devoured his food. The warmth from the fire eased the discomfort in his leg, and he knew that if he didn't reach the bed soon, he would fall asleep where he sprawled.

Nor was this the time to go to Pippa. They must be careful if they were to keep her identity secret.

Dinner that evening was a lively affair. The prominent Whigs of the day were well represented, along with wits, scientists and artists. Pippa was entranced by the conversations. The only thing marring her pleasure was a sense of urgency about finding her brother. She found herself watching everyone, listening for any word that might indicate his nearness.

'Mr LeClaire,' Lord Holland said, 'tell us about your healing. Dev says you were indispensable after Waterloo.'

Pippa flushed, realizing she was the synosure of all eyes. 'Why, milord, I believe Deverell does exaggerate.'

'Very pretty,' Lady Holland said. 'And yes, Devil Deverell often exaggerates, but somehow I don't think this story has been.'

Pippa felt herself heat up even more. 'I only did what anyone else would have done. I have some small knowledge of herbs and healing. I helped where the doctors and surgeons needed me.'

Even as she spoke, Pippa felt a sense of unease. As though someone studied her. She finished quickly and turned her attention to the fish. Her good manners tried to surface in a compliment to the chef, but she suppressed them. The last thing she wanted to do was draw more attention to herself.

Still, the hairs on her nape rose. She cast surreptitious glances around the room to no avail. The focus of the group had now shifted, and Dev held centre stage.

After dinner, the group retired to the salon, for which she was grateful. There were very few ladies. A fact that hadn't surprised her. As a divorced woman who'd married her lover, Lord Holland, Lady Holland was not considered good *ton* and Society's sticklers did not frequent her home. There were some women, and Pippa found that she would have been more comfortable with them. They were intelligent and discussed more than the current fashions and who was married to whom.

The night passed slowly, and Pippa made her excuses, knowing the rest of the guests would chat and play cards into the small hours. Making her way up the stairs, she hoped Dev would soon retire. She wanted to be in his arms.

Her wish was not long in coming true. She had barely taken off her coat and shirt and begun to unwind the cloth that bound her bosom when the connecting door opened. Dev stood in the doorway, his hair mussed and his evening dress replaced by a blue satin robe.

She smiled and he entered.

Without thought, she went to him. The kiss was long and deep, all her anxiety and need distilled into one intense meeting.

'Well,' he said softly, when they finally pulled apart enough for him to look at her, 'what brought that about?'

Desire and contentment curled in her deepest heart as she looked at his beloved countenance. 'I missed you.'

He smoothed the tangled curls from her face and kept his fingers enmeshed in their silken strands. 'Then miss me some more,' he murmured, gathering her even closer.

Much later, they lay on her bed, tangled in the sheets and each other. Passion slaked for a short while, Pippa stroked the wiry hairs of Dev's chest. Occasionally, she pulled one just to keep him from slipping into sleep.

'Minx,' he murmured, catching her fingers after the last tweak. 'Do you intend to keep me awake all night? For I warn you—' he moved quickly and pinned her to the bed with his body '—if you keep this distraction up, we shall have a repeat of what started all this.'

She giggled. 'I am more than happy to indulge your excesses.'

As his head bent to hers, and happiness welled up inside

her, Pippa began to think that maybe she should marry him. She loved him, and perhaps what he felt for her would become love. Then she forgot everything but the feel of him.

Several days passed much as the first. The company was lively and Pippa enjoyed herself immensely. Although she thought she would find pleasure anywhere Dev was. Still, she occasionally had the disquieting feeling that someone watched her, in spite of her never finding anyone looking at her who was not also ready to talk to her.

The third night of their stay, Pippa sat in the single chair her room boasted. She edged it closer to the fire and fought the melancholy that threatened to drown her. She'd had such high hopes when they disembarked from the ship at Dover. She had been convinced she would find Philip here.

A sigh escaped her. If only Dev would finish downstairs and come to bed. Tonight, more than ever, she needed his warmth and care.

She got up to prepare herself a tonic of chamomile, hoping it would relax her, and froze. The handle to her chamber door was moving. Someone was trying to enter. Someone who hadn't bothered to knock.

'Who is it?' she asked, irritated when her voice came out squeaky.

Instead of answering, the person pushed open the door and stepped into the room. A tall man, with light brown hair and dressed as a servant, confronted her. His green eyes burned into hers.

'*Philip!*' The recognition was sudden and sharp. Tears of joy blurred her vision. She catapulted herself on to his chest. 'Philip.'

'Easy, Pip. Easy,' he murmured, holding her close.

The solid muscle of him assured her he was real and well. She drew back enough to look at him.

He smiled down at her. 'I see you're still the reckless, determined to be anything but a girl, hoyden I know and love.' He hugged her. 'I am glad to see you are doing well, sister.'

'And I you,' she said, squeezing him again. 'We thought you were dead. They sent us a letter saying you'd been killed in battle.'

His full mouth, so much like hers, thinned. 'Who is "they"?'

'The Home Office.'

He released her without warning and turned back to lock the door. He then moved to the connecting one leading to Dev's chamber and did the same.

'We have much to discuss,' he said, angling back to her. 'First, why are you here, dressed as a man, and what are you doing sleeping with a man of Devil Deverell's reputation?'

Her mouth fell open, followed by confusion, quickly followed by irritation. 'What do you think I am doing here? Looking for you! As for Dev, what do you know about him that you feel free to judge him?'

He scowled, drawing his dark brown brows together. 'The last thing I need is for you to be arousing suspicion by looking for me. Secondly, I've been to London. I know the youngest son of the Duke of Rundell is considered wild, to say the least. Only a few months ago he chased some actress until his older brother had to intervene to keep him from marrying her.'

Stunned at the revelation about her lover, Pippa slumped on to the nearest thing. Thankfully the bed was high so that when her knees gave out she didn't have far to fall.

'He tried to marry someone a few months ago?'

'An actress.' Philip pulled the single chair near the bed. 'Now do you understand why I had to risk giving away my cover in order to stop this affair the two of you are having? He's no good for you.'

'How do you know all this?' she asked, wondering if the numbness she felt in her heart would eventually go away.

'I told you,' Philip said, impatience putting an edge to his voice. 'It was the *on dit* of London until Deverell went to Brussels. Then his brother married the woman and made the situation into a scandal.'

'Does he still love her?' she asked, her voice soft and vulnerable.

'How should I know?' Exasperation dug lines between Philip's brows. 'I doubt it since he is carrying on with you.' His voice turned cold. 'Something that has got to stop or I'll call the cad out myself and ensure that he is in no condition to continue.' Anger thinned his mouth. 'I shall call him out, anyway, after this is over. Someone must protect your honour.'

She stared at him, hearing his words but not comprehending them. If Dev had wanted to marry an actress, he must have been very much in love with her. Could that type of emotion disappear so soon? Or was he still pining after her, but wise enough to know she was now beyond his reach?

Even more importantly, what did he feel for herself? She had begun to hope he cared for her, that his offer of marriage was more than a way to make up for having bedded her. That hope crashed against the ache in her heart. Deverell was only trying to do the honourable thing.

'Snap out of it,' Philip said, rising from the chair and shaking her. 'He isn't worth it. I want you out of here immediately. I will take you to the stagecoach and put you on one home to Grandfather.'

It was an effort to make herself concentrate on what her twin said, but she knew she must. What was between her and Dev had nothing to do with the situation Philip was in.

She pushed his hand off her shoulder to stop the jostling he continued to give her. 'I cannot think with you shaking me up.'

He sat back down. 'I don't believe you have thought once since leaving home. What maggot got into your head?'

A tiny flare of anger sparked her temper. 'I might say the same about you. What do you mean by skulking about and letting us think you were killed? Do you know what that nearly did to Grandfather?'

He had the grace to look uncomfortable. 'I am sorry for it, but could not help it. I am…was…a—'

'Spy?' she provided with a twist of her mouth. 'That is what Dev thinks.'

'Does he? I wonder why?' A thoughtful look held Philip's handsome features.

'Because we tracked you here from Paris, where Wellington sent us to find you.'

His eyes narrowed. 'Why is Deverell St Simon with you? This isn't his style.'

The pain Pippa had been trying to ignore by concentrating on her twin's plight resurfaced with a vengeance. She held it tightly in rein. 'Because he thinks he owes me his life and wants to do whatever he can to help me.'

'So he sleeps with you? That is rich!'

'Stop it!' Pippa jumped off the bed and paced the short distance to the fireplace. She rounded on her twin. 'Stop denigrating Dev.'

'He will be lucky if I don't kill him. With that leg of his, it wouldn't be hard to beat him at swords or even pistols.'

Fury exploded in Pippa. 'How can you be so cruel?'

'How can he be so callous? He is using you, Pippa.'

Weariness descended on Pippa like a winter storm. Her shoulders slumped. 'I must talk to Dev about these things.'

Philip jumped up. 'You must get away from here and him. Go home and tell Grandfather I'm well and will return when I'm able.'

She glared at him. 'You go tell him yourself. Seeing you will do more for his health than any message I could take.'

His eyes narrowed. 'Then you come with me. And don't tell Deverell St Simon where you are going.'

'Leave without a word?' She blanched.

He crossed his arms over his chest. 'Yes.'

Pippa turned away from her twin's furious face. 'I couldn't do that, Philip. I trust him. What you have told me about the actress has done nothing to make me not trust him.'

'Has he told you he loves you? Is that why you slept with him? Because if that is so, then you are a fool.'

She sighed and still couldn't turn to face her brother. 'No, he has said nothing about love. But he wants to marry me because of what we have done.' She swung back around. 'That shows honour.'

Philip shook his head. 'Honour would have kept him from touching you in the first place.'

Heat mounted her cheeks. She could not tell even her brother, the person who had been closer to her than anyone else before Dev, that she had seduced Deverell.

'Have you ever been in love, Philip?'

Now it was his turn to look away from her. 'Once.'

'And did it make you do foolish things?' she asked softly, knowing that she would do anything for Dev.

He clenched his fists. 'Yes. Damn it.'

The handle on the door connecting her room to Dev's shook. Then heavy banging came loud and clear.

'Pip, are you in there? What is going on?'

Dev's voice penetrated the wood panel. Pippa shot a harried glance at her twin who put one finger to his lips.

'Let me tell him,' Pippa asked. 'He will help you.'

'I don't need his help. Or yours for that matter.'

'Is what you are doing that secret or…that dangerous?'

More than anything she wanted him to tell her no. She had just found him alive and despite their argument, she worried about him.

'What I do is my own business. I don't trust him.'

'I do,' she said softly.

'So you say.' Philip moved toward the door leading into the hallway.

'Please.' She tried one last time, wondering if she would tell Deverell without Philip's permission.

'I will think on it.'

Her patience snapped. For all she knew, Philip would leave the house and disappear as soon as he left her room. Then she might never find him again until he chose to be discovered. Or until he turned up dead, and even then she might never find out about it. They had been more than lucky to stumble onto someone who knew he was headed here.

She made her decision. 'You can stay here and meet Dev now, or I will tell him who you are, and we will go to Lord Holland and have the house and grounds turned inside out until you are found.'

Amazement quickly turned to fury in Philip. 'Whose flesh and blood are you?'

'Yours, Philip, but I cannot take the chance that you will disappear on me. Grandfather needs you. He nearly died when we got that letter. If I return without you, I don't know what will happen.'

'Pippa!' Dev's voice penetrated the door. 'What is going on? Let me in.'

Pippa kept her focus on Philip. 'What will it be?'

With ill grace, her twin nodded. Not taking her eyes off Philip, Pippa opened the connecting door. Dev, looking suspicious and worried, stepped through. He stopped cold when he saw the other man.

'You,' Dev said.

'What?' Pippa said. 'Have you seen each other before?'

Philip made a mocking bow. 'We meet again, Lord Deverell. Only this time I bear no tray of food for your comfort.'

'Who is this man?' Dev asked, moving to put a protective arm around Pippa. 'And why is he in your bedchamber?'

'The place you make your own?' Philip said sarcastically, taking a step closer.

Dev looked from one to the other. The hair was a different color, but the eyes were the same brilliant green, the lips full Cupid's bows. Even their stance bore a resemblance, the same hands on hips, feet shoulder width apart.

'Philip LeClaire, Viscount Staunton,' he said, positive he was correct.

'At your service,' Philip said with a sneer. 'Now let my sister go.'

Instead of releasing Pippa, who stood stiffly in his embrace, Dev studied the situation. Staunton wasn't a small man, which didn't surprise him, since Pippa was not a small woman. With his wound, he would be hard pressed to tackle him.

He grimaced to himself. Still one more time when his being less than whole made things difficult. Thankfully, he had slipped a pistol into his left pocket when Pippa's door had been locked. He withdrew it now.

'What are you doing?' Pippa asked, one hand raised in shock.

Dev, anticipating that she might intervene for her twin, reluctantly stepped from her. 'Move away from the door, Staunton,' he ordered.

Philip, his sneer turning to surprise, did as told. He cast a fulminating glance at his sister. 'And you trusted him,' he said bitterly. 'Remind me to tell you about the Frenchman I trusted.'

'What are you doing?' Pippa demanded again, her voice rising. Her hair seemed to stand on end, so agitated was she.

Not taking his eyes off Staunton, Dev moved closer to the spy. 'Sit in the chair.'

Rather than do as he was told, Staunton stopped with the chair between them. His gaze held Pippa's. Dev knew there was going to be trouble and cursed his infirmity.

'Don't make me hurt you,' he said through lips gone stiff.

'I don't understand,' Pippa said, her voice only marginally calmer. 'I thought you were trying to help me find my brother, Dev. Not capture him.'

The urge to run his fingers through his hair was strong. Denying it added to Dev's tension. 'Your brother is a spy who has betrayed his countrymen to death.'

'You are crazy,' Staunton said.

'You are wanted for treason,' Dev replied.

Shock froze Staunton's features. Pippa gasped. Dev took advantage of the situation and moved to the bell pull over the fireplace.

Seeing him, Pippa moaned in despair. 'You can't do this.

He isn't a traitor.' She turned desperate eyes on her brother. 'Tell him the truth.'

Instead, Staunton bolted for the door.

Hating what he was doing, but knowing he had no other choice, Dev fired. The ball went into the thick oak wood door not more than five feet ahead of Staunton, just as he had intended.

'The next one will hit you,' Dev said through clenched teeth.

Staunton turned, feet planted apart, face tense. He took the measure of his opponent and said, 'You would, too.'

Dev nodded. 'I lost too many friends at Waterloo to allow a man like you to escape.'

Outside the room commotion reigned. Footsteps pounded down the hall. Voices rose in surprise and panic. Minutes later the door burst open and two armed footmen stood framed in the threshold. Their shocked gazes took in the chaos of the room and the deadly confrontation.

'Take this man into custody,' Dev ordered before anyone could find their wits to speak.

As one they moved on Staunton who did nothing to resist them. 'You have won. For now.'

Immediately after, Lord and Lady Holland arrived. 'Frightful mess,' Lord Holland said. 'Was he trying to rob you?'

'No, sir,' Dev said, setting his pistol on the nearby mantel. 'I would like to explain the situation to you in private.'

'How diverting,' Lady Holland murmured. She moved to Pippa. 'Are you hurt, Pippen?'

Numbly, Pippa shook her head.

Staunton was bound and taken to the butler's pantry where the silver was kept, it being decided that that was the easiest room to guard. Dev promised his host an explanation first thing in the morning.

The room cleared quickly until only Dev and Pippa remained.

She turned stricken green eyes on him. 'I trusted you.'

Chapter Nine

Dev reached for her, but she sidestepped him. 'Pippa, I'm more sorry than I can ever explain.'

'You are a devil,' she spat at him. 'You betrayed me and, more importantly, you betrayed my brother.'

'I did what I had to.'

'You did what you wanted to.' She took a step toward him. Her fist swung up and caught him squarely on the jaw.

'I deserved that,' he said quietly, wishing she would hit him again. The agony in her eyes made him feel even worse than he had anticipated.

She turned away and great racking sobs shook her body. 'I hate you,' she said, the words muffled by her hands. 'I hate you so much I could kill you.'

'I would do anything for you, Pippa. I owe you my life. But I cannot let your brother remain free.'

She rounded on him like a tornado. 'And to think I told Philip to trust you—as I trusted you. He didn't want to. He was cleverer than I.' Her mouth twisted. 'I loved you. I thought you could do nothing I would not admire. How stupid I was.'

Dev's stomach twisted. Love. It was a word, an emotion, he had avoided when he thought of her. He had been protective of his feelings after what had happened with Samantha. He had taken pleasure where he wanted without allowing himself to feel deeply. Oh, he had vowed to marry Pippa, but he hadn't let her into the part of him he had walled off when Samantha married Jon. He would be glad of that, if her pain didn't hurt him so much.

'Pippa, he revealed the identities of two British spies in Paris. Both men were killed.'

'I don't believe that. Philip would never do that.'

Dev shrugged, knowing there was no way he could convince her, but determined to do so. So he tried again.

'Then who would? We found a man who remembered Philip. Wellington told me another spy escaped, telling him that Philip was supposed to warn the remaining two and then make his way north to Brussels. The other two are dead and Philip never returned.'

Pippa scrubbed at her eyes. 'I don't know why those things happened. Why did you not ask Philip before having him bound and imprisoned?'

Dev groaned and ran his fingers through his hair. 'Because the two of you didn't give me a chance. If you remember, Philip didn't trust me. He was going to escape when I came into the room. I had no choice. I'll ask him tomorrow, but no matter what his answer, I must take him to London. I gave my word to Wellington.'

'Your word,' she spat at him. 'For what it is worth.'

Dev drew himself up straight, anger replacing the pain he felt for her. 'I have never broken my word, Pippa.'

She cast a contemptuous look over him. 'No, I don't suppose you have. You didn't promise to keep my brother safe, only to help me find him.'

'Enough.' Dev slammed his hand against a table. 'I have had enough of your recriminations.'

'Well, I have had more than enough of you!' She crossed her hands over her chest. 'Get out of my room.'

Instead of leaving, he studied her. Tear tracks ran down her cheeks, but her chin angled defiantly up.

'I'll leave if you promise not to do anything foolish, like trying to rescue your brother.'

She glared at him. 'I'll promise you nothing.'

Dev's eyes narrowed. 'I know you, Pippa. You are a hoyden who will stop at nothing to achieve what you want, and right now, you want your brother free.' He took a step toward her. 'Promise me.'

She sniffed disdainfully. 'I won't make a promise I might not keep.'

'Then I'll stay here.' He sat in the single chair and stretched his bad leg out. It was starting to throb.

Eyes wide, panic beginning to replace the previous anger, she said, 'You cannot stay here. I won't allow it. Get out.'

'Promise me.'

In one lightning move, she dashed to the mantel and grabbed the pistol. 'Get out. Now. Or I'll do to you what you threatened to do to my twin. I'll put a bullet in you.'

The hard line of her jaw. The tightness in her shoulders. The desolation in her eyes told Dev she would do so with relish, or thought she would.

'Then do so,' he said, leaning forward to massage his painful leg.

She took a great, hiccuping breath. Her eyes stared fixedly into his. She raised the pistol and aimed it at his heart.

Dev watched emotions flit across her features, but the only ones he could name were frustration and resignation. Slowly, her arm dropped.

'Once more, you have won,' she said in a tired voice. 'I

can no more shoot you than I could have let you lay in a Brussels gutter.'

She dropped the pistol to the floor. 'If you'll leave my room, I promise not to do anything tonight.' Her voice strengthened with a flash of her old determination. 'But don't think I won't do everything in my power to rescue my brother. Because I will.'

Slowly, awkwardly, his leg aching and making him clumsy, Dev rose, then bent to retrieve the pistol from the floor. He winced when his right knee threatened to buckle. He saw her gaze flit to his wound, but she made no move to help. For the first time since he'd awakened in her Brussels room, Pippa was failing to succour him. She was gone from him. A small coldness entered Dev's heart.

'I'll be in my room, Pippa. And I trust you to keep your word.'

Without waiting for her to comment, he left.

Pippa watched Dev limp from her room. The urge to go after him and rub his leg and give him a posset to ease the discomfort was strong, but overlying everything was her anger and sense of betrayal. Nothing in their time together could erase the emotional devastation his arrest of Philip had brought.

More weary than she could ever remember being, more exhausted emotionally than she had ever been—even caring for all the dying and wounded at Brussels—she stumbled to the bed and fell across it. It was just as well she had promised Deverell to do nothing tonight. She didn't think she could rise, even if her own life depended on it.

Tears of loss wet her cheeks. In the last days, she had let herself begin to think that Dev might be coming to care for her. She had begun to dream about marriage to him, to think it might be possible. All those dreams were now bitter ashes in her mouth. He cared nothing for her or he would not have imprisoned her brother. His vow of marriage had been empty and cruel. He had known all along that when they found Philip he would betray them.

Pippa curled into a tight ball, unable to continue facing the reality of what had just happened. Her head ached and her stomach churned.

As soon as dawn pinked the sky, her promise to Dev would be over. Tomorrow, before anyone but the servants rose, she would rescue her twin. And to hell with Deverell St Simon.

Pippa dozed fitfully. Her limbs were leaden and her eyes swollen when she woke up. It was still too early for the maid to start the fire so the room was cold. She rose awkwardly and lit a single candle. By its flickering glow she gathered together the few belongings she would need, careful to take her bag of herbs.

Her promise to Dev was over.

Cautiously, she opened her chamber door only to be met by the unsmiling visage of a footman. 'What are you doing here?' she demanded.

He had the grace to look embarrassed. 'Lord Holland told me to stay here and make sure you don't leave your room unescorted, Master Pippen.'

Pippa's mouth thinned. They must have posted their guard right after her fight with Dev. Even the knowledge that the servant still thought her a youth did nothing to ease the disquiet that filled her. Instead of fighting her gaoler and creating a situation that would accomplish nothing except make the poor man feel more awkward than he already did, she closed the door. She knew where this order of incarceration really came from.

She stalked to the door between her and Dev's room and yanked it open without knocking. She strode into the room and stopped. She scanned the area. Everything was gone. The normal disorder she associated with Dev was missing.

She knew without even checking the wardrobe that his clothes were not there either. He was gone.

And with him, her brother.

She cursed her stupidity. He had probably left as soon as he exited her room last night. He had played with her like a well-worn deck of cards, and she had let him. But no more.

She rushed to the door leading from Dev's room to the hallway. With luck, she would be out the door and down the hall before the footman realized.

Luck was with her. The servant's back was turned to her and she managed to scurry down the hall and out of the house without anyone being the wiser. Reaching the stable without incident, she ordered the groom to saddle a horse so she could go for a ride. The poor man must not have been told about her imprisonment, for he did as she wished. She mounted quickly, and with one last glance at Lord Holland's house, galloped off.

Dev and her brother were probably travelling by carriage, and she could easily catch up with them. As soon as that thought came, she discarded it. She had underestimated Dev last night, she would not do so again. He probably had armed outriders to ensure that Philip didn't escape.

She would go to the nearest town and board the mail coach. She had plenty of money left from that she had withdrawn from the bank in Brussels, and she would be safer travelling with a group of people than riding alone. She would go to Aunt Tabitha in London. That was where Dev was taking Philip to be incarcerated in the Tower, for treason she knew her twin hadn't committed.

The carriage bounced with every rut in the road, and with every jolt, Dev's leg twinged. His head hurt and exhaustion ate at him like mice at ripe cheese. But he couldn't rest as long as Philip Staunton sat across from him, eyes open and body poised for any opportunity to escape.

Dev found that Staunton's steady gaze impressed him. It was a shame a man of the Viscount's quality had been corrupted. But how? The man certainly did not need money or land, and by betraying his country he risked losing everything he owned: title, land and wealth.

Staunton was an enigma he was not qualified to answer. His job had been to catch the man and turn him over for trial. If the Viscount didn't seem to fit his idea of a traitor, then it was because Staunton was good at what he did.

Dev also knew his feelings for Pippa were clouding his judgement of her brother. He pushed thoughts of Pippa away. The last thing he needed was to let his closeness to her make him unreliable. Staunton was too clever not to take advantage of every angle.

'Pippa says you are innocent.' Dev held his captive's gaze. 'I would like to believe her, but you must give me proof.'

Staunton's green eyes met Dev's without blinking. 'I have no proof. Only my word.'

Dev sighed in frustration. 'Your word is no longer good for anything. Two of our men were killed in Paris shortly after you disappeared. Wellington thinks you were responsible.'

Something like pain flickered across Staunton's face before his countenance once more became inscrutable. For long minutes he stared out the window at the passing trees and hedgerows. Finally he turned back to Dev with a strange mixture of determination and desperation on his features.

'I'll tell you what I know, but it proves nothing.'

Dev nodded. 'Perhaps between the two of us, we can find something that neither one alone would recognize.'

'Perhaps,' Staunton said, doubt heavy in his voice. 'I sent George ahead to Wellington with the latest information we had on Napoleon's march north. I stayed behind to contact the others…' He paused and the muscles in his face tensed. 'I told Peter and Alan to leave Paris immediately because I thought someone was aware of their real identities. I think they didn't get out in time. Then I went to join Napoleon's army as a French foot soldier, but before I could enlist I was attacked.'

Dev kept quiet in spite of the questions he longed to ask. Such as, where was Staunton wounded?

As though reading Dev's mind, the Viscount opened his shirt-front and pulled the material away from his right shoulder, showing a clean white scar. 'The knife went through from the back to the front. I was lucky.' His mouth twisted. 'My assailant missed the lung. Otherwise, the letter from the Home Office to my grandfather would have been correct.'

Another pothole sent Dev sliding to one side, and he cursed under his breath at the sharp pain. 'Does your shoulder still hurt?' he asked.

Staunton shrugged, then grimaced. 'Only when I do that. I use it to remind me of how precious life is and how someone betrayed me.'

'Why did you not go directly to Brussels when you were able?' Dev asked, thinking he saw the flaw in Staunton's attempted defence.

Staunton's eyes narrowed to emerald slits. 'Because someone obviously knew who I was and wanted me dead. The last thing I needed to do was come into the open, even to report to Wellington. Nor was there any information I could give the Duke that would have aided him. By the time I recovered from the attack, Waterloo was history.'

Bitterness had crept into the Viscount's voice. 'I have several suspects, but, again, no proof.'

'Who are they?' Dev demanded. 'Wellington can have them watched.'

Staunton stared at Dev. 'I'm not sure I can trust you. After all—' his voice dipped into an ominous growl '—Pippa thought she could trust you and where did it get her?'

Dev felt the blood drain from his face. 'I had a prior commitment. Wellington had already elicited my word that I would find you and bring you in for justice.'

'Justice!' A harsh croak of a laugh came from Staunton. 'The longer I am held in the Tower, the greater the likelihood that whoever is the real double agent or spy will escape.'

'Then tell me who you suspect, and I will follow them.' Dev's mouth twisted. ''Tis the least I can do.'

'I think not.'

The calm, softly spoken words lay between them like an insurmountable wall. Hazel eyes met green in a clash of wills.

Irritation welled up in Dev. 'Then who will you get to trail your suspects? You certainly cannot do it from behind prison walls.' When Staunton did not answer, understanding dawned on Dev. 'You cannot get Pippa to do it. She's a hoyden and would gladly do it for you, but that type of search is dangerous. You cannot justify using her that way.'

'And you can justify using her to slake your passion?' Staunton leaned forward until only inches separated them. 'How many times did you make love to her? What did you tell her to convince her to allow you to do so?'

There was no honourable answer to any of those questions so Dev said nothing.

'When I'm free,' Staunton continued, 'I will kill you for using her so.'

Fury boiled in Dev. 'I admit that what I did was wrong, but I intend to marry your sister.' He paused before pointedly adding, 'And what she and I did together does not threaten her life. What you intend to ask of her could get her killed. Look at what happened to you and the other two agents.'

For a second, Staunton looked doubtful, but that weakness was quickly replaced by implacability. 'We shall see. But whatever I decide, it won't be to trust you. Just as I shall tell Pippa she would be a fool to marry a man like you, one who used her to get to me. And she is no fool.'

The urge to throttle the Viscount rose strong and urgent in Dev. Somehow he resisted. The last thing he needed to do was add to the wall Staunton had built between them. Nor was it any of the Viscount's business what Dev intended to do with Pippa. He was her brother, but his grandfather Earl LeClaire was her guardian. When Staunton was safely behind bars, he would return to Lord Holland's house and get Pippa. From there, he would take her to her home and ask the Earl's permission to wed her. Pippa would fight him, but he was sure her grandfather would see the wisdom of such action.

In the meantime, he had to get Staunton to London. Fortunately, they should soon be met by one of Wellington's agents. Dev had sent a message to the Duke last night after he'd explained the situation to Lord Holland and asked for his host's cooperation. Lord Holland had also promised to keep Pippa safe. Dev hadn't told his host Pippa's real identity, only that the young man needed to be retained until he could return for him.

Somehow, bouncing down the road, Pippa's brother scowling at him and his leg hurting, Dev didn't feel completely confident that when he returned to Lord Holland's country estate things would be as he wished. But he had no other choices.

Five days later, Dev nervously flicked his riding crop against his booted leg, the uninjured one, as he paced Earl LeClaire's salon. The butler had said his master was touring the estate, but that was more than an hour ago. Patience had never been one of his virtues, and it was even harder for him knowing that Pippa might be here. When he'd returned to Lord Holland's estate, he'd been told that Master Pippen had managed to ride out the very morning after he had left with her brother.

Worry and anger had mixed in equal parts as Dev had pondered what to do. His first inclination had been to rush to London and watch the Tower. Pippa knew that was where her brother was headed, and Dev believed she would go there and try to free her twin. He also knew that in London she would be safe with her aunt Tabitha.

In the end he had decided to visit her grandfather. The Earl needed to know his grandson was alive, and Dev needed to ask him for Pippa's hand in marriage. But he hadn't expected to be left cooling his heels for so long once he arrived.

Dev's irritability was compounded by the fact that his right leg ached from riding the last two days straight with only enough rest to ensure he didn't fall out of the saddle from exhaustion. He was tempted to cross to the sideboard and pour himself a glass of whatever the Earl kept in the decanter. But good manners kept him from that transgression.

Just then, the door opened and without ceremony, a tall,

ruddy-complexioned man entered. His hair was thick and silver white, just brushing his well-worn brown corduroy jacket. Unlike Pippa, his eyes were a vivid blue. His strong jaw was outlined by muttonchop whiskers, and his full mouth would have been jovial if it weren't pinched in worry.

Dev found himself instantly comfortable with this man. 'Lord LeClaire,' he said, stepping forward, 'I'm Deverell St Simon. A friend of your granddaughter's.'

'Pippa?' The Earl came closer until Dev could see the deep lines that scored the edges of the older man's eyes and mouth. 'Is she alive? Where is she?'

The smile that had hovered on Dev's lips fled. 'She isn't here?'

'No!' the Earl roared, his face turning dangerously red. 'Nor have I heard from her since she landed at Dover.' His eyes narrowed. 'Were you with her, then? Did Tabitha introduce you?'

Dev knew he was headed for a rocky road, but how much did he reveal? From the Earl's colouring, he needed to be careful. 'Milord, perhaps you should sit down?'

'Not until you tell me where my granddaughter is.' The Earl's imposing height and ample, though not obese, girth stood firmly upright.

Dev had to follow the Earl's example, but his aching leg seemed like a waterlogged roll of paper, ready to bend at any moment. Still, he summoned the same determination that had seen him through battle and held firm.

'If she isn't here, I believe she is in London.' Dev paused, his mind racing. 'With her aunt Tabitha.'

The Earl visibly relaxed, the high colour of his face lessening but not entirely subsiding. He moved to the sideboard Dev had been eyeing earlier.

'Tabitha ain't my first choice, but she's better than noth-

ing. And the two did go to Brussels together.' He poured
a generous glass of liquor and asked, 'Care for a drink?'

'Please,' Dev said, hoping that whatever was in the decanter was strong.

The Earl handed him a glass as full as his own. Dev
gulped down half, nearly choking as the liquid burned a
trail down his throat. Whisky, the same stuff his brother
Alastair liked so well. He had never been enamoured of the
drink, but he needed its potency now. Within minutes, the
ache in his leg seemed far away.

'Here now,' LeClaire bellowed. 'Sit down before you fall
down. You're swaying like a birch in a heavy wind.'

'Just my leg. Been on it rather too long.' Still, he was
grateful to take the chair indicated and even more glad of
the warmth from the fire which was just feet away.

The Earl took a seat.

'Why did you think Pippa was here? And where did you
meet her?' He peppered Dev with questions, his gruff voice
still sounding strained. 'Do you know anything about my
grandson?'

It seemed to Dev that telling the Earl about Staunton
would be easier than threading his way through Pippa's
adventures. He told LeClaire as briefly as possible about
his grandson. Before he could launch into an abbreviated
version of Pippa's story, the Earl surged up with a roar.

'Philip is no traitor. I will have Wellington's head for
this impertinence, this insult to our family name. We fought
for William the Conqueror. That upstart Wellington.'

The Earl paced the room, his heavy footfalls ringing
whenever he stepped off the heavy carpet. Dev watched,
realizing why Pippa was so worried about her grandfather's
health. The Earl was like a volcano waiting to explode. His
face was mottled, and his white hair stood on end.

Dev levered himself out of the chair and blocked the

Earl's path, forcing the older gentleman to stop or run him down. 'Milord, you should sit down and calm yourself. I understand you suffer from apoplexy and this excitement cannot be good for you.'

The Earl glared at Dev. 'I'll do what I damn well please, and no scoundrel who has helped imprison my grandson is going to tell me anything.'

Dev, knowing he wasn't going to win this confrontation, stepped aside. He should have known it would be a mistake to come here, but his honour had demanded it. Just as his honour demanded that he ask for Pippa's hand in marriage even though he knew the Earl would refuse.

The older man continued to stalk the room. Gradually his colour eased.

'Lord LeClaire,' Dev said, 'I have one more thing to tell you.'

Pippa's grandfather came to a halt, hands on hips, feet shoulder width apart. The stance was so much like Pippa that, for a second, Dev grinned, but no longer. The reminder was more unsettling than happy. That was Pippa's reaction when she had wanted him to do something. Right now, Dev knew it would be a long time before Pippa cared enough about him to want him to do anything but stay out of her life.

'Speak up and then get out,' the Earl said, obviously at the end of his tolerance.

Dev met the older man's gaze. 'I would like to marry Pippa.'

Incredulity arched the Earl's white, bushy brows. 'You have a lot of gumption for a scoundrel. First you tell me you have captured my only grandson and that you've sent him to the Tower to await trial for treason. Now you say you want to marry my granddaughter. Well, even if she'd have you—which I doubt after what you've done to her twin—I'd sooner see you in hell than have you in the family.'

Dev clamped down on a sharp retort about the honour of the Earl's family. Antagonizing the man more would do nothing for his suit. He intended to marry Pippa, even if he had to drag her screaming to the altar.

Without another word, Dev bowed and left.

Chapter Ten

Two weeks later, Pippa stared at her image in the large mirror situated in the middle of her bedchamber in her aunt Tabitha's London house. She had arrived here a bedraggled ragamuffin, stiff and tired from travelling in stagecoaches. Between now and then, Tabitha had taken her in hand and made her into something Pippa had never imagined for herself. She was a beauty.

Where had her square jaw and high cheekbones gone? What had happened to the hard glitter of her eyes that her brother had so often told her was more like that of a bird of prey than a girl? Even the sharp angles of her figure which had allowed her to masquerade as a boy were gone. All disguised by style and illusion.

'I cannot believe that is me,' she said, her voice soft with awe. 'I've never looked this way.'

A light, tinkling laugh was followed by a movement behind Pippa. 'My dear, this was nothing. A little eye blacking, a smidgen of rouge, and the proper clothing.' Aunt Tabitha waved a small, well-shaped hand. 'Nothing. Everything was in place, just waiting for the right touch.'

Pippa turned, a smile of gratitude on her lips. 'Aunt Tabitha, you are a miracle worker. Without you I would have never known to do any of this. Just as I would have never been able to find my way into Society as quickly as you have guided me.'

Tabitha Montcleve, sister of Pippa's grandmother, laughed again and took her grandniece into a lavender scented embrace. 'Child, you underestimate yourself. I had nothing to do with this. You are the one who is wearing daring colours and being just a little *risqué*. Society loves gossip, and you are providing that in plenty. Now hurry or we'll be late for Maria Sefton's rout. And we must not miss it. She is one of the *ton*'s foremost hostesses.'

Aunt Tabitha stepped back while the maid draped a shawl over Pippa's bare shoulders. As always, Pippa was glad she had made the choice to come to Tabitha. She had told her aunt everything about her travels except that she had fallen in love with Deverell St Simon and become his lover. That was something she had to forget or she would go crazy. Nor would a lady, which Tabitha was, condone such behavior, and Pippa had found in the past weeks that her aunt's opinion mattered.

Arm in arm, they swept from the room and down the stairs. Tabitha's coach was already waiting for them, and it was a matter of minutes before they joined the line of people waiting to disembark from their carriages at Lady Sefton's ball.

Inside was a crush. People milled everywhere. The rich colours of dowagers in their purples and young ladies in demure white muslin swirled against the darker drama of the gentlemen in evening dress. Jewels of every description glittered in the blazing light of numerous chandeliers. In short, Lady Sefton's gathering was a huge success. The fact that this was the little Season, while Parliament was in session before the holidays, had not made a difference.

Pippa paused at one side while Tabitha went on to talk

with several friends. She scanned the room for anyone she might know and particularly for anyone who might possibly be one of the traitors she was determined to find for Philip.

'Lady Philippa, may I have this dance?'

Pippa started, not having noticed Mr Hopwell's approach. He was a tall, slim man dressed in the height of fashion. His brown hair was done in an immaculate Brutus, and his shirt points were high without being ridiculously so. He was also involved in the government.

'Of course,' she said, taking his proffered hand and going with him to form one of the couples. Out of the corner of her eye, she caught her great-aunt's satisfied smile. Pippa smiled back.

So far, she had managed to become one of the most sought-after young ladies in the little Season. This was ideal. The politicians and men active in government were in town, and these were exactly the people Pippa was most interested in meeting. When she had met with Philip on first arriving, her twin had told her the real spy must have connections that allowed him to mingle with the makers of England's foreign policy.

'How are you enjoying your visit?' Mr Hopwell's question forced Pippa's attention back to him and the present.

'Very well,' Pippa answered, following his lead. Thank goodness they were not waltzing. She had never been good at the dance.

Off to one side, the Marchioness of Witherspoon stood talking to a Cabinet member. She glanced at Pippa with a curious look on her perfectly moulded face. Pippa turned away.

Since coming to London, Pippa had seen the woman at several functions but had not met her. Nor did she want to. The last thing she needed was to have the Marchioness wonder where she had seen her before. That was how masquerades were undone.

The music stopped and Mr Hopwell escorted Pippa back to her aunt Tabitha, who stood up at their approach. Tabitha had come to London shortly after her younger sister married Earl LeClaire, and had soon married a well-connected gentleman. She had been a widow for the last twenty years. Barely coming to Pippa's chin, her aunt was still fashionable and lively. She was considered one of the premier hostesses in the *ton* and had frequently tried to get Pippa to come for a Season.

Aunt Tabitha smiled at Mr Hopwell and said, 'If you will excuse us.' After he bowed and left, she took Pippa's arm and drew her away. 'Child, I would like you to meet someone. I'm not on close terms with her Grace, but I have always found her to be most charming when we have met.'

Pippa raised one jet black brow. 'Her Grace? Which one, or are there that many?' she jested lightly.

Tabitha gave her a small smile of appreciation. 'There are more "your Graces" than "your Grace". It comes of having widows and dowagers. But come, her Grace requested that I bring you to one of the rooms set aside for informal meetings.'

Bitten by curiosity, Pippa followed. The demi-train on her cobalt blue evening dress swished with each step, its rich colour in direct contrast to the white muslins worn by most of the other young women present. For a moment, Pippa felt like an exotic animal out of its element, but that quickly passed. She had never been a shy young maiden, and was even less so now.

She and Tabitha slipped through a side door. By aristocratic standards, the room was small, but it was filled to the brim with trinkets and artwork. A thick burgundy rug cushioned the floor while matching curtains blocked out the winter cold. Flames licked up the chimney, providing warmth and light.

Standing a safe distance from the fire was a woman, her thick black hair caught up in a fashionable knot. A diamond-studded clip allowed several gleaming curls to tumble on to her long neck.

'Come, child…' the Duchess of Rundell held out her hand '…and let me get a closer look at you as you really are.'

Pippa faltered and would have turned tail and run if Aunt Tabitha hadn't gripped her arm. Forced to stand her ground, she sputtered, 'Your Grace.'

'Tut, tut, Pippen—or should I say, Lady Philippa. What happened to calling me Alicia?' The Duchess's lips curved into a mischievous grin.

Pippa took another step forward and felt her aunt release her arm. The quiet sound of the door closing told her Tabitha had gone.

'How did you know?' Pippa took another step forward.

With a tiny shake of her head, Alicia moved to Pippa and took her hands. 'How could I not? Even dressed as a boy, you had the slender curves and soft, smooth complexion of a young woman.' She gave Pippa a conspiratorial look. 'Not to mention the mannerisms of a woman. The time you rushed to comfort Dev after he found out about Patrick was more revealing than anything else.'

Pippa could do nothing but stare. And all this time she had thought her imitation of a man had been well done. 'Thank goodness not everyone is as perceptive as you, ma'am.'

'Particularly my son,' the Duchess said drily.

Pippa nodded, her gaze sliding away. She didn't want to bring Deverell into this conversation. In the past weeks, she had managed to put him from her mind. Or so she constantly told herself.

'Sit down, child. We have much to discuss.'

The Duchess released Pippa's hands and sat down in one of the two chairs pulled close to the fire. With a wary look, Pippa sat in the other.

'What do you call yourself?' Alicia asked. 'I cannot imagine your family calls you Lady Philippa or even Pippen.'

'Pippa, your Grace.'

'Alicia,' Dev's mother said firmly. 'Let us not start at the very beginning again.'

Pippa managed to smile in spite of her discomfort. 'Alicia. But I cannot call you that in public.'

The Duchess cocked her head to one side. 'No, I don't suppose you can since we aren't supposed to know each other. My, how you have changed.'

Pippa flushed. 'Aunt Tabitha took me in hand.'

'And a very nice job she has done. You are stunning. I understand that you are being called the Dark Aphrodite. Very appropriate.'

Pippa's blush deepened. ''Tis merely the trappings.'

Alicia's smile softened. 'The lip gloss, rouge and blacking only bring out your natural beauty. As does the bold colour of your gown. But if you were not already handsome, the extras would be overpowering. I knew, even in Brussels when you were dressed as a boy, that you would make a pretty girl. Dev will be very impressed.'

Pippa's discomfort at the compliments she wasn't used to receiving turned to cold anger. 'Lord Deverell is the last person I care to impress.'

'Ah, yes, the situation with your brother. I'm sorry, child. Dev was always my devil-may-care child, but when honour was and is concerned, there is no one else more strict than he.'

Pippa took a deep breath to try and calm herself. The last person she should denigrate Dev to was his mother. In an attempt to change the conversation, she asked, 'Why did you want to see me, and how did you know it was me?'

The Duchess looked away for a long moment, as though marshalling her forces, before turning her gaze back to Pippa. 'You are all the rage in Society, with your brother's situation and your own beauty. At first I didn't know for sure if you were the Pippen I remembered, but Deverell arrived in town recently and he told me everything, or what he considered important.'

Under the Duchess's kind, yet knowing look, Pippa found herself even more uncomfortable than she had initially been. Had Dev told his mother they'd been lovers? She doubted it, but his mother was very perceptive. She might easily have seen beyond the surface of Dev's tale. After all, she'd seen that Pippen had not been a boy.

'Dev wants to marry you, child. He thinks he must marry you and won't rest until he has accomplished it.'

Pippa stood abruptly, nearly knocking her chair over. 'Never.'

The Duchess smiled gently. 'Never is a long time, my dear.' In the same reasonable tone she continued, 'I remember you knocking over your chair in Brussels. I believe it was in my dining room when you'd been taken by surprise, just as now. But somehow, I cannot imagine that Dev's wishing to marry you is something you didn't already know.'

Pippa stood resolute against the older woman's patience and wondered if her mother, had she lived, would have been as diligent in caring for her children as the Duchess was. Knowing she would have liked greatly to have had a mother like this woman made it impossible for Pippa to stay angry at the Duchess's interference.

'You are right, ma'am. I knew Dev wanted to marry me, but that was before he betrayed me and sent my brother to the Tower.'

'It is Dev's honour. Can you find it in your heart to forgive him for what he has done and to accept him for what he is?'

The urge to do all of that was strong. No matter what she told herself in her sane moments, Pippa missed Dev. Missed him horribly. His little kindnesses. His loving. She even missed tending to his aches and pains. It was the way she imagined a wife would feel about her husband. No matter how much she reviled him now or how hurt she felt by his treachery, she could not totally cut him from her heart.

But she had to. She could never trust him again, and without trust there could be no commitment.

The Duchess's soft voice added, 'I would like you to think about what Dev is offering. I would like very much to have you in the family.'

Pippa gaped. She could not help herself. The Duchess was so forthright and honest, but she had never imagined Dev's mother would want her in the family. Nor would the Duchess if she knew everything. No mother would want her son marrying a woman so sunk in depravity that she slept with him when no vows of marriage or love had been exchanged. Yet, the thought of having the Duchess as a mother-in-law was enticing.

A light knock on the door was followed by it opening before the Duchess could say anything else.

'Mother,' Dev said, stepping into the room and closing the door behind him. 'Maria told me you were in here.'

His gaze passed over Pippa to his mother. A look of

shock crossed his features. He stopped in his tracks and his attention came back to Pippa.

'Pippa? Is that you?'

Pippa drew herself up. How dare he look so surprised. It wasn't as though he hadn't known she was a woman. The way he was reacting, one would think she had been a perfect dowd before.

'You have eyes,' she snapped. 'Who do you think I am?'

'I…you're…beautiful. That is, not that you weren't before, but…'

The Duchess's melodious chuckle filled the chilly silence. 'Close your mouth, Deverell, before you say something you can never recover from. Besides, you look like a carp caught out of water.'

'He looks like a Judas,' Pippa said softly, coldly, as she moved to the door.

Dev watched Pippa rush past him, resisting the urge to reach out and grab her. In seconds, the light scent of lilac was the only thing left to remind him that she had been here. She hadn't worn fragrance before, and he found he liked what she had chosen.

'Your timing is atrocious,' his mother said.

'My timing?' he asked, turning around to face her. 'What were you doing with Pippa in the first place?'

'Deverell,' the Duchess said, warning in her voice, 'I am your mother. Don't be demanding explanations of me.'

He ran the fingers of his right hand through his hair, messing the once-perfect Corinthian cut. 'I'm sorry, Mother. But why were you talking to her?'

'Because someone had to try and make her see reason, and it was patently obvious from what you have told me that you aren't going to be that person.' Exasperation tightened her mouth.

'What did you do?' Dev took a step toward her, beginning to fear what he knew she'd done.

'I told her she should marry you and let the past go.'

Dev groaned. 'That is the worst thing you could have done. Now her back is up and I shall be hard pressed to even get near enough to say hello, let alone talk to her.'

'Perhaps.' Alicia rose and drew her paisley shawl around her shoulders. 'We shall see. I'll call on her later this week.'

'Mother,' Dev said, at the end of his tolerance, 'you are a meddler. Please stay out of my affairs before they're beyond saving.'

The Duchess turned a hard stare on him. 'Have you told her you love her?'

Taken aback, Dev stepped away. 'No.'

'Then try. Love works miracles if you let it.'

Dev opened his mouth to answer, but nothing came out and his mother was gone before he could think of what to say. Tell Pippa he loved her? He liked her. He desired her. He owed her his life. But did he love her?

That was a question he couldn't answer.

Pippa didn't stop running from Dev until she was at the entrance to the large room where the dancing still went on. If anything, there were more people than when she had left to visit with the Duchess. What a disaster that had been.

What was Deverell doing here? And why had his appearance made her heart race like thunder clouds across a stormy sky? But she knew why.

No matter what he had done, no matter how awful his betrayal of her trust, no matter how hard she tried, she could not make herself stop loving him. Not yet.

'Lady Philippa LeClaire?'

Pippa jumped. She hadn't realized someone was beside

her. The Marchioness of Witherspoon stood not two feet away, a faint smile curving her full lips.

'Lady Witherspoon,' Pippa said, with only a small catch in her breath. What was the woman doing?

Lady Witherspoon shrugged her milk-white shoulders. 'I am being too forward, but that is not unusual. Although—' she cocked her head to one side '—you know my name, so perhaps I am not overly bold.'

Pippa kept the smile on her face. 'You are known as the "Pocket Venus" and your name is on the lips of all the gentlemen.'

'Ah.' She smiled. 'Something to be admired, no?'

Was there a hint of derision in her voice? Pippa could not be sure. 'Decidedly something that brings you to the attention of other women.'

'Yes, that is often so.' She waved a tiny, white hand in dismissal. 'But that is not why I have intruded. I wished to make myself known to you, and we have no friends in common so I had to do it myself.'

Pippa sighed in silent relief. The Marchioness didn't recognize her or she would know they had the Duchess of Rundell in common. 'I'm flattered, milady.'

'I wanted to tell you that I admire your courage. Your brother is in the Tower, yet you speak openly of his innocence. You must love him very much.'

What a strange thing to say to a complete stranger. Pippa looked at the Frenchwoman whose accent had become almost so thick as to obscure her words. Lady Witherspoon's large blue eyes were wide and worried, almost as though she worried as much about Philip as Pippa did. The idea brought an upward curve to Pippa's lips. Now she was being fanciful, another result of seeing Deverell St Simon. But still, the woman's actions were very uncommon. Yet, she found herself liking the Frenchwoman for her concern about a person whom she didn't know.

'You have a kind heart, Lady Witherspoon. Philip is my twin, and we have a twin's affinity.'

Mr Hopwell chose that moment to approach them. 'Ladies,' he said, bowing deeply, 'would you honor me by going into supper?'

Pippa considered declining, but he was familiar with many Cabinet members. Mr Hopwell was also very personable. Plus his grey eyes were filled with admiration, an emotion she decided would go a long way toward dispelling the irritation caused by Deverell's unexpected appearance.

Smiling brightly, Pippa said, 'I would be delighted, Mr Hopwell.'

Lady Witherspoon accepted the offer as well, and the three of them made their way to the supper room. Mr. Hopwell seated them and then hurried to the buffet table to fill plates with the offered delicacies.

'He is so charming,' Lady Witherspoon said.

'He can be,' Pippa answered without thinking, her mind having wandered back to Deverell. Why was he at this party?

'Can be?' Lady Witherspoon asked. 'I have never known him to be anything else.'

The puzzlement in the other woman's voice brought Pippa back to the supper room with a jolt. 'Oh, Mr Hopwell. Yes, he is very nice to be around. Always agreeable.'

'And a very good dancer.'

'That, too,' Pippa said, making herself smile.

The object of their discussion returned, giving each lady a plate piled high with lobster patties, oysters, and other delights. He waved to a footman and got champagne flutes.

'To the Exquisite Opposites,' he said, raising his glass.

'The Dark Aphrodite and the blonde Pocket Venus. May we always be blessed with your company.'

Still not used to the profuse compliments some of the men paid women in the *ton*, Pippa flushed. This was almost as bad as facing the Duchess of Rundell.

Lady Witherspoon laughed her tinkling laugh and changed the subject. 'Mr Hopwell, how is Parliament going? My husband does not attend regularly but, this being my adopted country and after what happened in my own not so very long ago—' she shuddered delicately '—I am always interested in the ways of government.'

Mr Hopwell smiled. 'I wouldn't dream of boring you ladies with such talk.'

'No, no,' Lady Witherspoon interjected, 'it would not be boring at all. Please.'

Pippa listening, wondered briefly why the Marchioness would care, but decided the woman meant exactly what she had said. She was interested. She was known as one of the most gracious women in the *ton*. Getting a man to talk about his interests was one of the surest ways of being thought charming.

As Mr Hopwell warmed to his topic, Pippa found her mind wandering back to her meeting with Dev and his mother. The memory made the skin between her shoulder blades tense. It was exactly how she had felt when Dev looked at her or touched her. Her gaze roamed the crowded room to come to rest on a man lounging in the doorway. Deverell.

Dev watched Pippa flirt with the Honourable Mark Hopwell over lobster patties and thought about calling the man out. But that would create a scandal and make people wonder what Pippa meant to him when he wasn't even supposed to know her. No, he might want to do bodily harm to Hopwell, but he wouldn't.

Still, it was damned hard to watch Pippa make eyes at the man and do nothing. What had happened to her?

'Lord Deverell St Simon?' a soft, feminine voice asked.

Dev turned sharply. A small, older woman looked up at him. Her silver hair was partially hidden by a plum-coloured silk turban, and her slender, almost frail figure was fashionably swathed in matching material. Her complexion was pale, perfect and lightly wrinkled. Laugh lines framed her full lips and accentuated her eyes. Her emerald green eyes, the same colour as Pippa's, sparkled up at him.

Dev returned her smile. 'Mrs Montcleve, my pleasure to meet you.'

She twinkled. 'I see that you are as astute as you are brave. But, please, call me Tabitha.'

'My pleasure, ma'am.' Dev made her a perfect leg, his grace only slightly marred by the stiffness of his right thigh. 'Would you care for something to drink?'

'A glass of champagne would not go amiss,' she replied, laying her hand lightly on his preferred arm.

Together they entered the supper room. Dev felt Pippa's gaze on them and smiled innocently at her. She, her grandfather and brother might think him lower than a grub, but if Aunt Tabitha was willing to talk to him then all was not lost.

He seated Mrs Montcleve and fetched her a plate before sitting across from her. 'Please excuse me for being so abrupt, ma'am, but since we have never been introduced I wonder why you have sought me out.'

She studied him for long moments. 'You are a very forth-right young man. I like that. Today's young people are too namby-pamby. In my day, we called a rake a rake and a trollop a trollop. I believe we shall do well together.'

Dev laughed outright, something he hadn't done in a long time. 'Tolerably. Are you a meddler like my mother?'

Without an ounce of contrition, she replied, 'Absolutely. Seeing young people make a muddle of their lives is the biggest waste I can imagine.' For a second she looked wistful, and her eyes took on a faraway look. 'I know what it is like to have that which you want most in life within your grasp and then to lose it. I don't want that to happen to my great-niece.'

'And why is your great-niece wasting her life?'

'Do not pretend ignorance. It doesn't become you.'

He bowed his head in acknowledgement of her hit. 'I have asked her to marry me, but she won't do so after what I had to do to her brother.'

'My great-nephew is innocent, Lord Deverell. I have no doubt that with time he will be proved honourable. Meanwhile, I expect you to woo Philippa until she sees the error of her ways. It would help immensely if you would tell her you believe Philip is not a traitor and help her prove that point.'

Dev met her gaze for long minutes, neither of them speaking. Pippa's aunt was more than he had anticipated and asked more of him than he was ready to give.

'Wellington thinks him guilty, and I cannot go against my commanding officer without more proof than Staunton was willing or able to give me.'

The older woman's foot tapped impatiently on the floor, matched by her rapidly tapping fingers. 'You are as stubborn as she. I'm not asking you to flout Wellington, only to help Pippa in her search for the real traitor.'

Before Dev could decide what to answer, a husky alto voice said, 'Aunt Tabitha, you are consorting with the enemy.'

Pippa stood not three feet away, her green eyes flashing like the finest emeralds when held up to sunlight. She looked ready to spit fire at him.

'Sit down, Philippa, before you cause a scene,' her aunt ordered.

'No, thank you. I would rather consort with a criminal. A traitor, to be exact.'

With that parting shot, she spun around and stalked off. Several heads turned to watch. Dev knew that by morning the latest *on dit* would be Lady Philippa LeClaire's snubbing of Lord Deverell St Simon. At least everyone would attribute it to his being responsible for her twin being imprisoned in the Tower. No one would know that everything was made worse because he had once been her lover.

'Foolish chit,' Aunt Tabitha said. 'But it is just as well that she is not here. I have much to say to you.'

Dev raised one brow. She rapped him with her closed fan. 'Ouch. My mother has that same nasty habit, ma'am.'

'And very likely for the same reason, young man. Now, listen well. From here on, you and I are allies. Pippa, foolish chit that she is, has been trying to discover who is the actual traitor. And Philip, selfish young man that he can be, has been encouraging her to do this dangerous act.'

Dev's hands clenched white. 'I knew this would happen. Staunton has much to answer for.'

Aunt Tabitha made a moue of disgust. 'Sometimes my great-nephew is beyond my comprehension. But he wants to get out of the Tower. What I need from you—' she impaled him with her green gaze '—is to protect Pippa. She won't listen to me when I advise caution—'

'And you think she will heed me, ma'am? I fear you are far out of it there.' Bitterness curled Dev's lip.

'Yes, I know, but you, at least, can follow her. I am too old to be out of my bed once I reach it.'

Dev leaned forward, anger beginning to form a hard knot in his gut. 'Is she sneaking out to run Staunton's errands?'

Tabitha glanced around to see that no one was close

enough to hear her whispered words. 'She is doing worse
than that, I fear. I have reason to believe she intends to
break into the homes of some of England's foremost peers.'

'What?' Dev hissed, barely keeping himself from shouting his outrage. 'That is beyond even what I would expect
of her.'

Tabitha's tapping fingers escalated their pace. 'Exactly
what I thought. I believe it is at Philip's urging.'

'That bas—scoundrel. Pardon me, ma'am. I know he is
family, but what he is making Pippa do is inexcusable.'

She frowned at him. 'Do you think I don't realize that?
That is why I have come to you. Regardless of what Pippa
says, you care for her and you owe her a great deal. I am
asking you to protect her from herself and her brother.'

'On my honour.'

A mischievous grin broke through Tabitha's irritation. 'I
count on it, for we know where your honour has left you.'

Dev bowed his head in mock answer. 'I would do nothing differently where Staunton is concerned. Now, how are
we going to work on this, ma'am?'

'I shall keep you informed through these tête-à-têtes. Tonight I came up to you because I want Pippa to see that I
accept you and intend to speak with you. In the future, she
will be upset with me, but not surprised to see me talking
to you. If I have information you need and I haven't seen
you, I will have it delivered. Most likely it will be by a
street urchin so that no one in my employ can let slip to
Pippa what I am doing.'

Dev's admiration for the spirited lady grew. He grinned.
'I see that Pippa and Staunton come by their adventurous-
ness and, can I say it, deviousness honourably.'

She chuckled. 'The right side of the blanket is the way
we would have put it in my day.'

He smiled at her, some of his earlier tension easing. With

this formidable lady's help, he would be able to keep track of Pippa. No matter what the hoyden did, he would be there. He would also get the chance to further his suit.

He raised his flute of champagne in a toast. 'To our partnership, ma'am. May we accomplish what we set out to do.'

Tabitha raised her glass. 'To your future wedding and the release of my great-nephew.'

Both drank down the liquid in one long gulp.

Chapter Eleven

Deverell lounged in the chair set well to the back of the Duke of Rundell's box at Drury Lane. From here he could see while not being seen. Just a few months before, he had come here to watch Samantha perform on the stage. It seemed a lifetime ago. He hadn't wanted to come tonight, but Tabitha's note had said she and Pippa would be here.

Below and to his right was Mrs Montcleve's box. Tabitha and Pippa sat there, the older woman waving to acquaintances. Edmund Kean was on the stage and, as usual, his acting was superb, but most of the members of the *ton* were here to socialize. He was intrigued to notice that Pippa tried to watch the play.

Dressed in a cold white muslin gown with vivid green ribbons, she stood out like a sparkling diamond. A simple, single strand choker of emeralds circled her long neck and solitary emerald drops fell from her ears. The colour of her dress might be that of a chit in her first season, but the rest of her ensemble was not.

Dev's gaze ran hungrily over her. The *décolletage* was a little too low for a young girl. The smooth whiteness of her breasts crested above green ribbon. She looked more like a dashing widow or young matron. His blood ran hot, and he remembered warm nights in Paris and long, passionate nights at Lord Holland's country estate.

She was his.

'Engrossed in contemplation of the Dark Aphrodite, the *ton*'s latest darling?' Jonathan St Simon, Marquess of Langston asked, entering the box and taking a seat.

Pulled with a jolt from the avenue down which his thoughts were headed, Dev gave his older brother a wry grin. 'It is becoming a boring habit of mine, I must admit.'

'Almost as boring as your mooncalf pursuit of Samantha was nearly a year ago.' To keep any sting from the words, Jon clapped Dev on the shoulder and drew him into a brief hug. 'We have missed you. Sam was wondering just yesterday why you haven't called.'

It was on the tip of Dev's tongue to say a gracious social lie, but he caught himself. This was his brother, married to the woman he had once thought himself irrevocably in love with. 'I didn't think you would want me to after what happened.'

Jon shook his head. 'Dev, how can you be so stupid? You made your peace with me long ago. I distinctly remember you visiting me before the wedding to give me your congratulations and impress upon me your acceptance of the fact that Sam and I were marrying. Anything else is forgotten.'

Relief spread through Dev like a warm draught of ale. The barrier he had felt between him and Jon seemed to melt away, and some of the old sense of teasing camaraderie came back.

'Since you stole away the first woman I fancied myself in love with, maybe you can help me with this hoyden.'

Entering into the spirit, Jon said, 'You mean Lady Philippa LeClaire, twin of the traitor you put in the Tower? I don't think there is much anyone can do to help you on that front.'

'I'm very much afraid you are right, Jon.'

'Don't be so glum. Break her brother out of jail and you will be a hero in her eyes. Short of that, you can storm her walls. Go visit them in their box. Confront her in a place so public that she will have to endure your company or leave. Make her do something besides avoid you.'

Dev gave his brother a thoughtful look. 'You think so?'

Jon grinned. 'It has been my experience in Parliament that very few will stand up to a blatant confrontation. They might talk behind your back, but not to your face.'

'It might be worth a shot,' Dev murmured, squaring his shoulders as though preparing to go into battle. 'The worst she can do is give me the cut direct.'

'Spoken like a true war hero,' Jon said, giving him a slight shove. 'And come to dinner tomorrow.'

'Absolutely,' Dev said, his mind already on the problem of Pippa.

He exited the box and made his way down several levels. Aunt Tabitha saw him before Pippa.

'Ah, Lord Deverell,' Tabitha said, a dimple peeking out from her right cheek. 'Come in and take a seat.' With her fan, she indicated a chair near Pippa. 'I hear you are possibly to receive a title for your bravery at Hougoumont.'

Dev's stomach twisted. Every time someone brought up that farmstead where Patrick died, he found himself fighting anger and grief.

'There is talk,' he said, knowing the edge in his voice made him sound harsh. 'But no one has offered me a title, and I don't think I would take one. Too many people— people I cared greatly for—died defending Hougoumont. I have no desire to gain from their sacrifices.'

Pippa, who had been studiously ignoring him, glanced at

him toward the end, and he thought that for a moment compassion showed in her eyes. But she turned away before he could be sure.

Aunt Tabitha made a moue of sadness. 'Yes, I can understand your feelings. Is that why you wear the black arm band?'

Dev nodded curtly. This conversation was not going as he'd planned. Bowing abruptly, he cut across anything else Pippa's aunt might want to say and said, 'Lady Philippa, would you go riding in Rotten Row with me tomorrow?'

'I think not,' Pippa said clearly.

Several matrons in the nearby box stopped talking. A gentleman who had been approaching halted. Aunt Tabitha gasped.

'Pippa,' she said, 'that is unpardonable. Please apologize to Lord Deverell.'

Pippa raised her chin higher. 'I will not.'

'Do you wish to set all the tongues wagging?' he asked softly, doing nothing to keep the hard edge out of his voice.

'They are wagging already. Everyone knows you are the man who had my twin put in the Tower.' She stared defiantly at him, her eyes flashing like emeralds.

'And they will wag even more if you refuse me so loudly and so blatantly.'

'Then let them.'

She tossed her head and turned to speak to a gentleman who had sidled up during the confrontation. The anger that had started with the mention of Hougoumont mounted. Dev saw red.

'Lady Philippa,' he said loudly and clearly, 'I will call for you at four tomorrow.'

Without giving her another chance to cut him, Dev pivoted on his heel and left. Irritation boiled in him, but he held it in check. The last thing he wanted to do was give the old biddies more to gossip about. As it was, this latest incident would be the *on dit* in every drawing room tomorrow.

Hours later under cover of dark, Pippa made her way toward the Tower. She had crept out of Tabitha's house after they returned from Drury Lane. Seeing Dev again, she had found herself weakening toward him in spite of the way she had treated him. The decision to visit Philip had been impulsive. She hoped that seeing her brother in the Tower would strengthen her resolve to resist Deverell St Simon.

The sound of scratching, as though boots scraped along cobblestones, made Pippa freeze. She glanced nervously behind her, but the fog off the Thames was so thick she could not see more than three feet. Still, no darker shadow moved within the opalescence of the swirling mist.

Leaning with her back to the brick wall, she took a deep breath and wished for the first time that she had brought a footman with her. Chill crept through the thick wool of her cape like prying fingers. A shiver skimmed down her back. But no further sound came to increase her unease.

She shook her head to clear it of the phantoms that seemed to plague her with each step she took. It wasn't as though she had not come this way many times before. She'd lost count of the visits she had made to her brother. The only difference was the time. Usually she came during the day. But that was the only thing that wasn't usual.

It was her earlier confrontation with Deverell. That was what made her skin prick and her heart race. If the truth be acknowledged, his proximity had brought back memories. Memories she wanted to bury forever.

Even now, with the creeping fog shrouding her sight, she could smell the citrus tang of bergamot and remember the first night she had encountered it. She had shaved him, the feel of his skin rough with beard under her fingertips, the urge to lean down and kiss him nearly overwhelming.

Pippa breathed deeply, inhaling the scent of moisture and…bergamot.

A hand snaked out of the night and grabbed her shoulder. She twisted, knowing who her waylayer had to be, yet not wanting to be caught. His grip held.

'Will you be forever mauling me?' she hissed.

'Will you be forever provoking me?' he countered, stepping close enough that she could see him and smell the bergamot even better. His teeth flashed in a rakish grin that did nothing to belie the hardness in his hazel eyes.

'How did you know I was here?'

One last time, she squirmed, trying to escape his fingers. His grip held firm. With a sigh of exasperation, she stilled.

'I have my sources. Ones I don't intend to reveal to you.'

She sniffed. 'Well, now that you have found me, release me.'

'I believe I have heard that order before. And as before, I'll do so when I see fit.' He edged closer, until the heat from his body seemed to engulf her. 'Where is your footman, Pippa?'

She lifted her chin. 'I can take care of myself. I did so for many long days in Brussels. And, I might add, I cared for others at the same time.'

He shook her, only enough to make her know he meant business. 'In Brussels you were dressed like a boy. And if you are going to prowl the seamier side of London, then you had best don your breeches again. A woman alone is fair game for any scoundrel.'

'Such as yourself?'

'Were I such, you would be beneath me now, not bandying words with me.'

Heat suffused her face, erasing the cold nip of the damp night breeze. 'A gentleman would not speak so to me.'

His laugh was a harsh sound that seemed to echo on the still air. 'And were you a lady, I wouldn't have to chase you the length and breadth of England. You would already be married to me.'

'How dare you!'

He glared at her, the grin of moments earlier gone as though it had never been. 'If I dared, I would do more than follow you to protect you. I would cart you off to Greta Green and be done with this intolerable situation.'

'I would leave you at the first chance.' She leaned into him, forgetting his hold on her shoulder, forgetting everything except her anger and her hurt. 'How many times must I tell you that I will never marry the man who betrayed my brother? I swear, talking to you is like talking to a simpleton. Only worse.'

Before she knew what he was about, his second hand came up and grabbed her other shoulder, pulling her to him. His face moved down swiftly, like a striking hawk, and his lips crushed hers. Emotions erupted in her. Anger warred with desire, swelling the torrent of response that surged in her.

She rose on tiptoe to meet his kiss, her mouth pressed to his. When his tongue demanded entrance, she gave it willingly. Her hands tangled in his hair and held him tightly.

As quickly as he had yanked her to him, he pushed her away. His breath came in quick gulps. 'And you deny any feeling for me? I could have you now. This instant. And you would revel in our joining.' His hands fell away and he turned his back to her. 'Damn it, Pippa.'

She stared at him, her senses still reeling, her lips still tingling. Always, he had always been able to make everything else disappear. She took a step away, afraid of what she might do if she didn't put some distance between them. No matter what he had done, she still wanted him. She still loved him.

She knuckled her mouth to keep from emitting the sob of pain that threatened to escape. Drawing herself up straight, she forced her voice to coldness. 'Now that you have proven your power over my body, will you let me go? Will you go away?'

He turned back to her, his mouth twisted, his eyes dark. 'No.'

A shock of pleasure and pain skittered through her, making her fingers shake in the folds of her heavy wool cape. 'Philip won't be pleased to see you.'

He shrugged, the dark outline of his greatcoat standing out against the white of the fog. 'He would do well to talk to me. His sending you to find this *traitor* he claims not to be is enough to make me want to throttle him myself. From now on, I'm going everywhere with you.'

'You are not,' she stated, indignation replacing the uncertainty of seconds before. 'You don't believe Philip is innocent, I would never trust you to find the real culprit.'

'Don't be more foolish than you have already been,' he said bluntly. 'Whether your brother is guilty or not, someone has tried to kill him. That same person may very well try to do the same to you.'

His words sank in like leaden weights. She had been so concerned about Philip that she hadn't thought of this. She gulped, but straightened her spine. 'Whether that is possible or not doesn't matter. Someone must do the searching for Philip, since you have put him behind bars and he cannot do it for himself. I'm that person.'

'We will see about that,' Dev stated, taking her arm and

propelling her toward the Tower. 'Let us get on with this visit. The night is far from young.'

Reaching the Tower gate, Pippa stated clearly, 'I am Lady Philippa LeClaire, come to visit Viscount Staunton.' The guard, as though used to peremptory visits by noblewomen in the small hours of the morning, moved aside. 'I know my way,' she said, dismissing his escort before it was offered.

Dev nodded at the man as he followed Pippa.

She paused at a heavy door and knocked softly. When, after several long minutes, there was no answer, she rapped harder. The noise echoed in the stone hallway.

'Your brother is a heavy sleeper,' Dev murmured. 'Nor do I blame him for ignoring so untimely a summons.'

'He will come,' Pippa said shortly. 'He has to be inside.'

Dev said nothing, but leaned against the cold stone of the wall, his right leg eased out so his weight rested on his good leg. She knew his wound ached from the cold fog. This prolonged standing would not help. Pippa felt a twinge of concern, but stamped down on it. He no longer merited her help or interest.

When more time passed, she began to worry. Surely nothing had happened. Philip's trial was not for several weeks. What was wrong?

As she wondered, a guard passed by. She stopped him and demanded, 'Has something happened to Viscount Staunton? He has kept us waiting, which is unlike him.'

The guard glanced from her to Deverell and all but snickered. 'His lordship has another visitor, milady.' His eyes were knowing. 'A woman.'

Pippa's eyebrows shot up. She gave the guard a repressing glare. 'I see. Thank you.'

She turned away, dismissing him. She didn't understand. Philip had said nothing about a woman.

Nonplussed, Pippa stood motionless while her brain whirled. There was only one reason she could think of that Philip would have a female visitor at this time of night. A blush rose up her neck and into her cheeks.

'Exactly,' Dev said drily. 'Now will you go home? I'm sure the last thing your brother wants is to see you.'

Even with so blatant a situation, it was well nigh impossible for Pippa to walk away. She needed to see Philip, to see him imprisoned and all because of the man who stood too close beside her.

She bit at her lower lip, a habit she had thought herself grown out of. She had stopped the abuse years ago. Until now. She stopped.

'Come on,' Dev said kindly, one hand under her elbow in an attempt to steer her away.

She dug in her heels. 'I will knock one last time. 'Tis not as though I don't know what is happening.'

She cast him a fulminating glance before shaking off his hand and banging again on the door. She lifted her fist to repeat the beating when the door cracked open.

'For heaven's sake,' Philip growled, standing in the small space that was only large enough for his body.

Pippa tried to peer around him, but could not. 'Philip, let me in.'

Philip's gaze went beyond her, and his brows snapped together. 'Why is *he* with you? I thought you had finished with this bounder.'

Fury hardened Dev's jaw. 'Let us in, Staunton. It is late and we already know you are entertaining a guest, so it is no matter whether we see the mystery lady or not.'

Philip's eyes bored into Pippa's. She looked away first, unable to stand the awareness in his gaze that told her he knew she understood exactly what he had been doing with the lady because she had done the exact thing with Deverell. She realized what she felt was close to shame, an emotion she had once thought she would never experience in relation to Deverell. Now it was more because she had loved him and been fooled into thinking he was someone he wasn't.

'Please, Philip,' she said softly, forcing herself to meet his look. ''Tis late and I...I want to see you. I will even turn my back so your companion can leave without being seen.'

He turned and said something to his guest which Pippa couldn't hear. The words sounded like French, but while she had the English upper-class girl's smattering of that language she was far from proficient. A female voice answered.

Behind her, Dev whispered, 'She told him it is all right for us to enter. She knows us.'

Pippa's eyes rounded in surprise.

Philip scowled. 'I see you are fluent in French, Lord Deverell. Somehow, I would not have thought it.'

The direct insult darkened Dev's hazel eyes to brown. 'Now that we have settled that you don't know everything, Staunton, are you going to let us in or waste the time your sister has spent coming here?'

Pippa heard more than dislike in the exchanged insults, she heard challenge and realized that if Philip weren't incarcerated the two men would be at each other's throats.

With obvious reluctance, Philip stepped away and allowed Pippa and Dev to enter. The room was spacious and comfortably appointed with furniture and wall hangings that Pippa had directed to be delivered from her grandfather's closed town house. Several scattered rugs cut the chill rising from the stone flooring. A large four-poster oak bed stood in one corner. Beside it reposed a matching wardrobe and wash stand. In the opposite corner a large fireplace, filled with flames, provided enough warmth to make her cape unnecessary. There was no window.

Sitting, back ramrod straight, in one of the two well-upholstered chairs drawn close to the fire, was the Marchioness of Witherspoon. Pippa's mouth dropped.

'*Chérie*, please do not look so…so startled.' The Marchioness's lightly accented voice was filled with chagrin. 'I did not want you to know, but neither did I want Philip to turn you away after all the trouble you went to coming here tonight. He wanted me to go earlier, but I convinced him to let me stay.' She shrugged her delicate white shoulders expressively. 'You see, Witherspoon is at Brighton for several days.'

'How convenient,' Dev drawled. He gave them his best, guaranteed-to-charm smile. 'For both of you.'

Philip took a step toward him. 'I will call you out for that slur.'

Dev eyed him coldly, one eyebrow arched. 'And you dare to condemn me?'

Philip drew back as though slapped, but said nothing. He whirled around and confronted Pippa. 'What do you want?'

The baldness of his question hurt, but Pippa put it aside. He was her brother, her twin. 'Only to see you. To visit, to talk over some of the things I have heard. I haven't been here in nearly a week.' She trailed off lamely. When Philip made no reply or asked her to sit, she said, 'Perhaps I should come back.'

'No,' Philip said curtly, his hand chopping through the air. 'Jane knows everything. She too has been gleaning gossip to help.'

'Everything?' Pippa asked, incredulous.

Philip paced the room, his hands stuffed in the pockets of his buff pantaloons. 'Everything. That I am a spy. That you were this man's lover. Everything.'

Disillusionment stopped the angry words in Pippa's throat. How could he have told this woman about her and Deverell? It was bad enough that he had trusted the Marchioness with his secrets, but to tell her about something that had nothing to do with him, to trust her with knowledge that could ruin Pippa in the eyes of the world was more than she could bear.

As though reading Pippa's mind, the Marchioness rose and crossed to her. Taking Pippa's cold hands, she said gently, 'Do not judge Philip harshly, please. He had no choice. I recognized you and asked him what was going on. You see…' she cast a look at the Viscount '…I am very good at remembering faces and yours is so beautiful that when I saw you here I realized you were the woman in the Brussels bank.'

Not even the compliment could ease the hurt still gripping Pippa. No matter what the provocation, she hadn't expected her twin to reveal such damaging information about her. Never Philip. Did everyone betray others without a thought for how the one whose trust had been shattered would feel?

'*Chérie*, I am sorry you had to find out like this.' She cast a reproving glance at the Viscount who had stopped his pacing to watch them. 'But I, of all people, understand what it is like to love a man. For I would do anything—anything—for your brother.'

And now to have someone say this. It was bad enough that she knew how much she had loved—no, still loved—Deverell, but that the Marchioness should say so in front of him… Pippa looked from the Marchioness to her brother, who showed no sign of understanding what he had done. She would not look at Dev.

'I think 'tis time I left,' Pippa said through stiff lips, pulling her fingers from the other woman's clasp.

'*Non,*' Lady Witherspoon said, stepping closer and laying a delicate white hand on Pippa's arm.

'Don't be a goose,' Staunton said, moving to his lover and putting a protective arm around her. 'Jane is distraught and your leaving will only make it worse.'

Pippa looked at her twin. All his concern was for the woman in his arms.

'Enough of this,' Dev said. He took Pippa by the arm and drew her away from the couple. 'You obviously don't need us here. Whatever Pippa has to tell you can wait.' He raised one brow sardonically. ''Tis not as though you will be leaving in the next day or so.'

If looks could kill, Staunton's would have felled Dev. 'Thanks to you.'

Dev made a curt nod. 'We have been down this path before, Staunton, and in front of the women is no time to do so again.'

Realizing that the men's animosity was mounting to dangerous levels, Pippa edged between them. She forced herself to smile at the Marchioness and go on tiptoe to kiss her brother's cheek, a habit from many years and one she did again without much trouble. He might have revealed her deepest secret to another person, but he was still her brother.

'Dev is right. My news will wait.' She cast Dev a look meant to keep him in place as she moved past him to the door. 'I'll come back.'

'And I will be with her,' Dev stated, following her. He opened the door and, with a palm to her back, gently pushed her through.

Irritation spurted in Pippa. 'I am perfectly capable of leaving.'

'I know,' he said, 'but you were taking your sweet time about it. 'Tis late and we have some way to go.'

'We don't have anywhere to go,' she faced him defiantly.

He shook his head. 'I know you are angry with me, Pippa, and I know your brother has hurt you. You want to be alone. Believe me, I understand that. But I won't let you go home on your own at this time of night.'

He gripped her shoulder and steered her through the halls and out of the Tower door. The night had become colder and the fog heavier. Right on the Thames as they were, the splash of water on the shore seemed loud in Pippa's ears. Suddenly she was glad of Dev's company.

They made their way through the streets without a word. It was a long walk.

'Why did you not take a horse?' he asked when they finally reached Tabitha's house. 'It would have been easier on both of us.'

Pippa winced, realizing his leg must be causing him horrendous pain. 'I was coming alone, and I didn't want anyone in Aunt Tabitha's employ to know I was gone. Taking a horse would have alerted a groom who then would have insisted on accompanying me.'

'So your aunt doesn't know what you are about.'

'No, and I want to keep it that way. It would only worry her more.' Pippa sighed. 'Thank you for bringing me home. Now I need to get inside.'

Dev nodded and escorted her to the back door where she inserted a key in the lock. 'I see you are prepared.'

She gave him a wan smile. 'As much as I can be. Goodnight.'

She left him standing there with the fitful light of a half moon playing along the planes of his face. There were lines of worry around his mouth.

He might have turned her brother in, but he was determined to care for her. In spite of knowing she should not let it matter, his concern warmed her. Tonight's revelations

about her brother and the Marchioness made her wonder if
Dev cared more than her brother.

She swiped at moisture forming in her eyes. She was
being maudlin. Philip loved her. He was her twin.

She reached her room, went inside and closed the door.
With a sigh, she sank into a chair and let her head loll
back. She was so tired and so confused.

Chapter Twelve

Dev handed the reins of his horse to his groom. 'Jimmy, keep him moving.' He grinned, knowing the boy would not do anything else.

'Yes, milord,' Jimmy said, indignation writ hugely across his narrow face.

With a determined step, Dev went to Tabitha Montcleve's front door. He didn't expect Pippa to go riding in the park as he had arranged, but he was determined to make her tell him no to his face—again. He rapped smartly on the knocker.

An aged butler answered immediately.

'Good day,' Dev said, taking off his hat and handing it and his riding gloves to the servant. 'I'm here to take Lady Philippa riding.'

The butler took the items, scepticism raising his white brows slightly. 'I shall see if her ladyship is available. Please have a seat in the drawing room.'

He showed Dev the way to a light, airy room furnished in the current rage of Greek Revival. The settee had lion-paw feet and a lyre-shaped back, as did the grouping of chairs around the fireplace. A rosewood table reposed beneath the long window that looked out on to the street.

Dev sat gingerly in one of the chairs. His mother was always decorating, but she usually stayed with more substantial furniture. His father had made it plain he would not risk his neck by sitting in a flimsy chair.

'Oh, here you are,' a trilling female voice said.

Dev rose and turned to bow to Tabitha. 'Are you Pippa's representative, come to tell me she's indisposed, or more bluntly that she won't be seen with me?'

Tabitha laughed. 'I have come to tell you she is going riding in the park. I assumed that meant with you.'

'Whatever could have brought this about?'

Instead of answering, Tabitha moved to a sideboard and poured out a generous portion of wine. 'Will you have some?'

'Certainly.' Dev crossed to her and took the proffered glass.

'I never drink sherry or ratafia,' she said. 'Too namby-pamby.'

Dev grinned as he sampled the strong port. 'I should think not. You are too strong-willed to drink something so weak.'

She laughed again. 'I can see why you are called "Devil Deverell". The name suits you. Too bad my stubborn niece can't be brought around.' She took a sip. 'Ah, that is just right. However, I believe Pippa is wavering.'

She moved to take a seat. Dev followed.

'How so, ma'am?'

'Why, she is going riding with you, is she not? That is a definite improvement.' She raised a hand for silence, got up and went to put her ear to the door. Coming back, she lowered her voice. 'We are alone for now, so tell me what happened last night. Something has softened her toward you.'

'She has told you nothing?'

'How could she? She thinks she is sneaking out without my being any the wiser. If I didn't know you would be with her, I should have to stop her. That would create a pickle. She would resent me instead of, I hope, growing to care for me.' Tabitha set her glass down and stared out the window. 'When her mother died, I tried to get Julian—LeClaire—to let me come and help raise her. He refused. Ever since, I have asked her to spend time with me in London. This is the first time she has done so. I have enjoyed it.'

'I think she has too, ma'am.'

Tabitha returned her attention to him and smiled. 'But you didn't come here to listen to the meandering thoughts of an old woman. I don't know what is keeping that girl, but while we have the privacy, you must tell me what happened last night.'

Dev set his glass down on a nearby table. He had known at the time that her brother's imparting of her past to Lady Witherspoon had upset Pippa. He hadn't realized how much. If she was going riding with him, then she must have been deeply hurt and now be turning to him.

He looked gravely at Tabitha. 'I believe I know, but I don't feel it is my place to tell you. Please try to understand. I'm sorry.'

Tabitha seemed about to say something, then stopped. She took another sip of wine. 'You have honour and a sense of privacy. I hope my stubborn niece brings you into our family soon.'

The door opened and the butler entered. 'My lord,' he paused, his gaze going to Mrs Montcleve. 'Madam, I did not know you were here or I would have had refreshments sent in.'

Tabitha snorted. 'Don't bother, Watkins. Lord Deverell and I have been drinking this lovely port.'

'Yes, madam.'

'Now get back to the reason you entered,' she prompted him, rising to pour herself and Dev another glass.

'Yes, madam. Your lordship, Lady Philippa sends her regrets, but she has a prior commitment.'

'What?' Dev and Tabitha said in unison.

The butler drew himself up straighter and met each one's gaze. 'That is what she said, madam. My lord.'

'I'll be…'

Dev happened to look out the window as Pippa ran across the pavement and climbed into a pretty pale blue phaeton. The Marchioness of Witherspoon held the reins and with a smart flick of the leathers set the carriage in motion. No tiger accompanied them.

Tabitha came up alongside him and saw the rear of the carriage disappear briskly. 'Now when did this happen?'

'I believe,' the butler intoned, 'a message came this morning for her ladyship. It bore the arms of the Marchioness.'

'Thank you, Watkins. That will be all for now.'

The butler bowed himself out.

Tabitha tapped a finger against her mouth. 'I didn't realize they knew each other.'

Dev, watching the phaeton turn the corner in the direction of Hyde Park, said, 'They had supper together with Mr Hopwell at Maria Sefton's ball.'

'I remember now. Well, young man, you had best be after them. There is no sense in letting Pippa think she can snub you like this with impunity.'

'The least I can do is put a spoke in the wheel of whatever they are plotting by being close at hand.'

'Plotting?'

Dev grinned at her. 'Did I say that? I'm sure it was a slip of the tongue.' The last thing he wanted to do was reveal to Tabitha what had happened the night before. That was for Pippa to do.

'Hum, so you say. But never mind. Be on your way.'

Dev made an awkward leg, thought briefly of how he had used to be renown for his grace, and left. Now was not the time to bemoan his wound. Pippa was up to something, and he wasn't going to be far behind.

Pippa settled herself in the elegantly upholstered carriage. The squabs were blue velvet to match the paint. 'Very nice,' she murmured by way of opening the conversation.

'Thank you,' Lady Witherspoon said. 'I am glad you came. I was afraid that you would not, after last night. Because of what your brother said, and my relationship to him.' She turned large blue eyes on Pippa before looking back at the crowded street. 'I wanted to speak privately with you and felt this was as close as we could get.'

Pippa sensed the other woman's nervousness and immediately felt the need to ease it. 'I was pleased you asked. It seemed…how do I put this delicately?' An embarrassed smile lifted one corner of her mouth.

'Ah, you are trying to be polite about what Philip and I mean to one another. There is no need. I feel you and I are like sisters. We can speak plainly.' She flicked her whip over the lead horse's head before casting a worried glance at Pippa. 'I hope that is all right.'

Pippa's hands tightened in the folds of her skirts. She truly didn't know how she felt about the situation. 'Of course that is fine. It was obvious that Philip loves you very much.'

'And I him.' She turned the phaeton between the gates that led to Hyde Park. 'For a long time. But there is Witherspoon. He would never divorce me. Nor would that be good for Philip. His reputation.'

Pippa nearly laughed aloud from sheer anxiety. 'Philip's reputation. He has none. Even if he is found innocent, it will always be remembered that once he was thought a traitor.'

'True.'

They slowed their pace and fell behind a line of other carriages, all of which were touring the park. Men and women stopped their vehicles and spoke across empty space to one another or carried on conversations with people walking. Everyone who was anyone was out.

Pippa forced herself to smile at the occupant of a nearby cabriolet whom she had met at a rout. Lady Witherspoon stopped to speak briefly with Mr Hopwell.

Pippa uncurled her fingers and tried to relax her shoulders. Rather than dwell on Philip's circumstances, she should be enjoying this outing and getting to know her companion better.

'When did you meet Lord Witherspoon?'

'I was barely sixteen, in 1804. Napoleon was at peace with England for a brief time and many Englishmen came to Paris. My *maman* introduced us and arranged the marriage. It was a very good union for me.' She sighed. 'Of course, I did not know I would meet Philip.'

'Do we ever know things like that?' Pippa asked, thinking about Deverell.

They were still now, waiting for the carriages in front of them to move. Lady Witherspoon laid a gloved hand on Pippa's. 'No. That is the hardest part about living.'

Pippa clutched the other woman's fingers in sympathy. 'Have you and Philip thought of running away? Now that Napoleon is defeated you could go to the Continent.'

The Marchioness gave a trill of laughter. 'You are very

risqué. Philip said you were no prim-and-proper miss, something I did not think after hearing about your adventures.'

Pippa blushed. What she had suggested should have been the furthest thing from her mind. But she wanted her brother to be happy.

A high-perch phaeton paused beside them and the woman in it waved. 'Lady Witherspoon, so nice to see you.'

The Marchioness looked over and a genuine smile lit her elfin features. 'Lady Stone. It has been so long. But you look magnificent. Motherhood agrees with you.'

The other woman was a statuesque redhead and a beauty. In her arms was a small bundle. Beside her sat a strikingly handsome man with black hair frosted by silver at the temples. His grey eyes were studying Pippa.

'My lord,' Pippa said coolly, nodding her head.

Lady Witherspoon coughed nervously. 'Pippa, may I present Lord Alastair St Simon and his wife Lady Stone?'

Pippa felt the colour drain from her face. The tension in her shoulders which she had managed to ease returned with a vengeance. 'Pleased to meet you, my lord and lady.' She was glad her voice didn't show her discomfort.

'So you are the young woman who is giving Deverell the time of his life,' Lord Alastair said, his voice deep and slow.

''Tis about time someone caused Deverell some heartache. Now he will definitely forget about Samantha,' Lady Stone said matter-of-factly. She shifted the sleeping baby to her other arm. 'You must come to dinner, my dear. I promise not to invite Deverell.'

Pippa didn't know what to think. She expected them to revile her, not ask her to their home.

'Leave off,' Dev's voice said from close by, moving between the two carriages. 'Pippa has enough to contend with snubbing me. She doesn't need the two of you complicating the matter by being nice to her.'

'Deverell, you scoundrel,' Lord Alastair said, reaching out a hand to shake the one Dev extended. 'Jon said he saw you at the theatre.'

'Just last night. But he neglected to tell me you are a papa.' Dev grinned wickedly. 'But then he was probably too embarrassed. You go from the fashion setter of the *ton* to being so unfashionable as to take the air with your wife and baby.'

Alastair cuffed Dev on the shoulder. 'I am setting the latest rage. Are we not, my dear?' he asked his wife.

She kissed him on the cheek. 'And that will certainly have all the toadies wondering how they are going to emulate you when most of them do not even care to be in the company of their spouses.'

Dev grinned so hugely at their antics that Pippa could see there was genuine love between him and his brother. 'Only you could set such a standard,' he said with a droll rolling of his eyes.

The baby chose that moment to waken. Blue eyes looked at the world in wonderment before screwing up into tears. A loud wail left no doubt that the pride of his parents' life was unhappy where he was.

Lady Stone tsked and gave the child her finger to suck. 'We had best get to a more private place, Alastair. Your heir has certain expectations; if they are not met, he will be even more vocal in his displeasure.'

Her husband laughed and directed the coachman to move on. 'See that you come to visit,' he called over his shoulder. 'Both of you. Singly or together.'

'Marriage has been good for my brother,' Dev said, giving Pippa a meaningful stare. 'He is more relaxed.'

She met his gaze haughtily. 'He obviously has a wife who loves him.' She turned to Lady Witherspoon and asked, 'Can we move on, please? The company has lost its sparkle.'

The Marchioness looked ruefully at Dev before urging her horses on. 'That was very rude,' she said in a low voice.

Her nose in the air, Pippa said, 'I don't care. What he did to Philip is unforgivable. It makes it unnecessary for me to treat him with civility.'

'*Chérie*, he is a good and honourable man who only did what his conscience bade him. Although…what he did to you was very much wrong.'

Pippa went to Dev's defence without thinking. 'What we did was my fault.'

'I see,' Lady Witherspoon said. 'You are in love with him.'

'Not any more,' Pippa stated.

'Philip says he wants to marry you.'

'Philip talks too much.' Pippa turned her back ever so slightly to the other woman. Feeling instant remorse for her intended snub, she shifted back around. 'I'm sorry. 'Tis just that where Deverell St Simon is concerned I am not rational.'

'I understand. I feel that way about your brother.'

The impulsiveness Pippa so dreaded in herself surfaced. 'Then will you help me find the real traitor? Together we can do more searching and clear Philip's name.'

Lady Witherspoon took a sharp breath. 'I do not know. It would be very dangerous.' Her small chin firmed. 'But, yes, I will help.' She added a cautionary, 'But we might not succeed.'

'Yes, we will. I won't let us fail.'

For once, Pippa knew in her heart that her tendency to rush into things had not steered her wrong. The Marchioness loved Philip. No matter that she had hesitated. Pippa knew the other woman would do everything in her power to help. Just as she had always known that Philip was alive, regardless of what the Home Office had believed.

Dev lounged against a solid Grecian pillar, one of several scattered around Mrs Fitzpatrick's ballroom. Three chandeliers dripped with candles, providing enough light to make every lady in the room glow. Potted palms and orange trees clustered in groupings behind which small groups of people chatted and gossiped. It was a crush.

Dev's mouth twisted sardonically. The hostess was probably beaming over her success.

'We seem to be meeting everywhere but at a family gathering,' a deep, drawling voice said.

Dev turned with a grin. 'Alastair. Didn't know you were an acquaintance of Mrs Fitzpatrick's.'

'Barely. Enough to always get an invitation.'

Dev snorted. 'Everyone in the *ton* invites you in the hope that you will grace them with your presence and they will ever after find themselves in the golden circle.'

Alastair hit him on the shoulder. 'Enough of your toad-eating. I'm here because I know your nemesis's aunt is one of our hostess's cronies. I thought you would show up tonight in hopes of pressing your suit still again.'

Glumness soured Dev's smile. 'My suit, as you so optimistically call it, is merely a need on my part to protect Pippa from herself and her scoundrel of a brother.'

'Don't be so down in the mouth. Chase her. Ask her to dance. Do it here, in a place so public that to refuse you will be tantamount to slapping you in the face. Very few women, or men for that matter, have the stomach to create so public a display.'

Dev gave his brother a thoughtful look. 'You think so?'

Alastair clapped him on the back. 'I kidnapped Liza and made her marry me. What I'm telling you to do is nothing.'

Dev gaped at him. 'You did? You never told anyone.'

'It wasn't something I was proud of. Just something I had to do.'

Dev looked at his brother with new respect. 'I might have to do as you suggest. You certainly don't regret your actions.'

'Never,' Alastair murmured.

Dev squared his shoulders as though preparing to go into battle. 'The worst she could do is give me the cut direct.'

'Spoken like a true war hero,' Alastair said. 'Now I must find Liza. And don't forget Mother's little gathering tomorrow.'

'I shan't,' Dev said, his mind already on the problem of Pippa.

He pushed away from the Grecian pillar he had been leaning against and began to thread his way through the press of Mrs. Fitzpatrick's guests. It was another crush, even in this off season. Some people played cards in another room, many chatted in small groups and quite a number of the younger ones danced.

If he recognized the strains, the orchestra was about to start a waltz, for it was one of the tunes Pippa had played so long ago in Brussels. She had been so protective of him that night, getting up from the pianoforte and ending the evening without a by-your-leave. She had courage.

She would marry him, if he had to follow in Alastair's footsteps and kidnap her. He strode purposefully toward her. Tabitha saw him first and smiled.

He returned the older woman's greeting before turning to Pippa. 'May I have the honour of this dance?'

Pippa turned a haughty face to him. 'I don't believe you have any honour to begin with. My answer is no.'

He gritted his teeth. 'Dance with me or I will drag you on to the floor. Then all of Society will wonder what is really between us.' He held out his hand.

'Pippa—' Tabitha entered into the battle '—do as he says, for he is right. At this moment they all think your refusal is because of Philip. If Lord Deverell does as he threatens, they will begin to wonder if there is more between you than your brother.'

Reluctantly, slowly, she put the bare tips of her fingers in his palm. 'If I must.'

Titters and whispers accompanied them. Let the *ton* have a field day with this, Dev thought, he no longer cared. Pippa's insults had gone beyond what he was willing to endure from her.

The music began in earnest. Couples around them started moving. Pippa stood stiffly when Dev put his left arm around her waist.

'You are making another scene by refusing to dance while everyone around us does so.' A muscle in his jaw twitched.

Reluctantly she began to move but it was like holding a wooden doll in his arms. The glare she sent him would have felled a less determined man. Dev gave back as good as he got.

'I don't waltz well,' she said through lips as stiff as her body.

'Nor do I.' His bad leg buckled so that the twirl was less than perfect.

Instantly, every feeling Pippa had ever felt for Deverell St Simon surged back. The urge to take away his pain and to hold him softened the harsh line of her mouth. Even though he held her lightly, the heat from his body seemed to engulf her senses. She wanted nothing more than to melt into him, as she always had.

They moved smoothly, successfully completing another twirl. She smiled up at him, forgetting everything but the feel of his arms around her.

'Very good,' she murmured.

'As good as can be expected,' he replied, his mouth twisted up but showing no real bitterness. 'As you so often assured me, my wound has healed well. I will never do everything I once did or do it as well, but I shan't let that stop me from doing what I want. Including waltzing with you.'

'I never thought you would.' And she hadn't. Even from the start, before she'd even known him, she had sensed he was stubborn and would do exactly as he pleased. 'I'm glad I didn't amputate your leg.'

'Not nearly so glad as I am.'

The music soared and he pulled her tight against him, both of them unconcerned with propriety. They dipped and swirled, their steps perfectly matched. Only when the music stopped did they come back to reality.

Pippa stumbled but his arm around her waist steadied her. Her eyes met his. Passion and awareness filled his gaze. If only they were meeting for the first time, she thought. If only Philip weren't between them.

Her breath caught. 'I need to return to Aunt Tabitha.'

'Pippa…'

'No.' She cut him off before he could say the words she saw in his eyes. 'There is too much between us.'

'Philip,' he said, his voice scathing.

She realized he regretted losing her more than the loss of his physical grace. The knowledge was a bittersweet pain in her chest. Before he could say another word, she slipped from his grasp and hurried to her aunt.

Dev didn't follow.

Chapter Thirteen

Dev felt like a thief, lurking in the deepest shadows with Aunt Tabitha's note crumpled in the pocket of his greatcoat. It was just past midnight, but the streets were still busy, and many buildings glowed with lamplight. Soot hung heavy in the air and the muffled sounds of horses' hooves and wheels echoed in the narrow alleys.

He had followed Pippa here from Tabitha's town house, where he had watched her sneak out of the back door. On the way she had stopped to pick up the Marchioness of Witherspoon.

At this moment, Pippa was barely a hundred feet in front of him, on her way to break into the house of an English peer. If she was caught, she'd go to Newgate. Unless she got shot first.

Sweat broke out on Dev's upper lip. He had to stop her.

Lady Witherspoon's slighter figure stuck close to Pippa's side. The two had been inseparable since the night in the Tower, so this combination didn't surprise him. He was sure neither one had made provisions in case they were discovered—or even thought they would be found out.

He muffled a snort of disgust.

The sound of their footsteps stopped. He pressed into the

indentation of a doorway. In the dark-encrusted night, he saw them huddle together, their voices rising but still indistinguishable. After long minutes, Pippa moved away.

'Blast,' Dev muttered. Pippa was going to break into the house on her own. Not that doing so with Lady Witherspoon along made it any more safe or acceptable, but at least the other woman could stand guard.

First he had to deal with the Marchioness. Moving swiftly, he was on her before she realized anything.

'Hush,' he ordered, clamping one gloved hand over her mouth and the other around her waist. ''Tis Deverell St Simon. I'm not going to hurt you.' To himself, he added, *yet*.

She said something into his palm.

'I'll release you if you promise not to scream or run away. Otherwise, I shall gag and bind you.'

She nodded.

Slowly Dev took his hand from her mouth. When she stayed quiet, he released her waist and stepped away.

'Merci,' she whispered. 'But you gave me a fright.'

'Imagine how you would feel if I were a footpad,' he said sardonically.

'I should be in dire peril.'

Her tone was solemn, but Dev thought he detected a glint of amusement in her blue eyes. It angered him. 'You and Pippa are dealing in things you cannot handle. Where is she?'

Her chin lifted stubbornly. 'We are perfectly capable, *monsieur*. We both have pistols.' She drew a small silver-embossed gun from her reticule and pointed it at his chest.

Dev's anger rose. In one lightning motion, he gripped her wrist and twisted. The weapon fell to the ground with a clatter that seemed to echo loudly in the still air. He stooped and grabbed it, ignoring the protest of his leg.

Standing, he goaded her, 'You were saying?'

She sighed. 'You are the second person to catch me off guard. Perhaps it would be better to have you on our side. Although Philip will not like it.'

'To hell with Staunton. Now, which house did Pippa go to?'

She mentioned the name of a very prominent Cabinet minister. 'She went through the garden. There are French doors that can be opened into the library.'

'You seem very familiar with the place,' Dev said, impressed in spite of himself. He hadn't expected them to be quite so knowledgeable about this particular gentleman's abode. 'I'm going after her.' He took a step forward, then turned back to Lady Witherspoon. 'I'll return your pistol if you give me your word that you'll return home now.'

She studied his face in the pale light from the stars. 'What about Pippa?'

'Better that I catch her and give her a thrashing than the owner of the house she's burgling. I'll turn her over my knee, but I won't imprison her or shoot her.'

The Marchioness nodded her head and held out her hand for the pistol. 'You have my word. This time.'

Dev gave her the weapon and strode off. There was no time to lose. As Lady Witherspoon had said, the garden led to open French doors. Peering in, he saw a single candle flame with Pippa, dressed as a boy, in the small puddle of light. She was bent over a desk, her fingers riffling through a sheaf of papers.

Dev swallowed an oath and moved over the threshold. She looked up. Startlement widened her eyes and formed an O with her lips. He was on her before she could move.

One arm went around her waist, one hand on her mouth. The light scent of lilacs engulfed him, infuriating him more.

She squirmed in his hold. Her voice was muted by his gloved palm. When he didn't release her, she bit him.

'Damn,' he hissed, keeping his hand on her mouth. He put his lips to her ear and said, 'Don't do that again or I shall be forced to hit you. The last thing we need is for someone to hear us.'

She glared at him, her eyes sparkling in the scant light coming through the open doors. Her body where it pressed close to his was rigid.

'If I release you,' he whispered, his breath wafting over her cheek, 'you cannot say a word.'

She stared defiantly at him, neither nodding or shaking her head. He was tempted to haul her out the doors and be done with this, but he knew how important this was to her. It didn't matter that her mission was foolish and dangerous.

He took a chance. Dropping his hands he took a small step away.

'I'm not stupid,' she hissed. 'His lordship is away, and this is the servant's night off.'

Dev rolled his eyes and moved back in on her, resisting the temptation to touch her again. 'There is always someone in a house like this. Always.'

She didn't budge. 'I'm willing to take that risk.'

The urge to forcibly take her away was strong. Instead he said, 'You finish looking while I stand guard.'

She looked at him for a long moment, then nodded curtly. Dev moved to the door. He kept an eye on her while listening. Long minutes passed. Every second he expected to hear a voice or footfall. Pippa continued to scrounge through the papers, even going so far as to pry open the desk drawers.

Dev hoped to hell they didn't get caught. She was more bold than he had anticipated.

From what seemed a long distance, he heard the front-door knocker. In a flash, he was by Pippa.

'Quiet,' he ordered, dousing the flame with a finger and thumb.

He gripped her wrist and yanked her out the doors. They sped through the garden and on to the street. He refused to stop until they were several streets away and he deemed them safe. In their haste, they hadn't bothered to disguise the fact that someone had been prying. The drawer Pippa had been rummaging through was open, as were the French doors.

'Keep moving,' Dev said, continuing to walk even though he had allowed them to stop running. His leg hurt like Hades and his temper was barely in check. 'I shall throttle your brother with my bare hands. After I have given you a thrashing.' I should have never let you continue, he added to himself.

She dug her heels in and confronted him. 'You have no control over me. I did what I had to…and I will do it again.'

'The devil you will,' he growled, grabbing her shoulders and shaking her. 'You could have been killed. Thrown in Newgate at the very least.'

'Stop treating me like a child,' she demanded, trying futilely to loosen his grip on her.

'Then stop acting like one.'

She reached up to slap him, but his arm blocked her aim. Frustration and fury ate at him. He cursed and, with a sharp yank, pulled her to him. His lips slashed down on hers, claiming her with a thoroughness that spoke of familiarity and uncontrollable hunger.

'I could have lost you,' he muttered, anchoring the fingers of one hand in her short curls. He pulled her head back to better plunder her mouth with his.

Pippa sank into his embrace, her fury at him submerged by rising passion. His scent surrounded her as he drew her even closer, until she could feel the hard need of his arousal. The kiss deepened, his tongue teasing hers in imitation of more contact.

Her toes curled in her boots. Tingles shot from her lips to centre in her stomach.

'I have missed you so,' he said, breaking away enough to run his lips against her cheek.

His mouth came back to hers. The kiss gentled. Instead of demanding entrance, his tongue moved softly against her bottom lip, asking admittance. The sensations intensified until Pippa wanted to burrow her fingers inside his shirt and twine them around the thick brown hair she knew covered his chest. When one of his hands dropped to cup her breast, she arched into his caress.

How she had missed him. The feel of him pressed to her. The scent of him. Even her worry for him had become a part of who she was. Heaven help her, but she loved him beyond reason.

She moved into his caress. 'Dev, I...' The confession died in her throat as he kissed her breathless.

'You will marry me,' he murmured. 'I have a special licence.'

His words were like an electric shock to Pippa. She jerked in his arms and brought her clenched fists up to push against his chest. What was she doing?

Pippa could not believe she had let herself react so wantonly to Dev's embrace. She had acted like a harlot, eager for her lover's fondling.

'Let me go,' she ordered, pushing harder. 'I'll never marry you.'

He held her tighter, pulling her inexorably toward him. Determination etched lines around his mouth. 'What if you bear my child? It is not inconceivable. What do you intend to do then?'

She gasped. ''Tis none of your business. If it happens. Nor would I tell you.'

'How dare you,' he raged, his face inches from her.

'Hey, guv,' a raucous cockney voice said. 'This ain't the place for carryings on like that. 'Gainst the King's law.'

With an oath, Dev released her. Both of them had forgotten she was dressed as a boy.

Pippa knew her face was bleached of colour and her lips were swollen from his possession. This is what came of loving a man beyond reason, she thought bitterly. But she did not have to continue to let him dominate her.

A carriage rattled by, its lantern casting light over them. A sedan chair went by, the two men hauling it casting curious glances their way. In the heat of their emotions, they had forgotten they were on a well-travelled street. The effect they had on one another was sobering.

''Tis late, Dev,' Pippa said, turning away from him. She felt drained of all emotion. Exhaustion ate at her. 'I want to go home.'

He took a step toward her, then stopped. 'I'll escort you.'

Irritation briefly flared in her. This wasn't worth another confrontation. 'As you wish,' she said, her voice without inflection.

It was a long walk back to Aunt Tabitha's house, and Pippa felt every inch of it. What made everything worse was that she hadn't found out anything by breaking into the Cabinet member's house. All she had done was endanger herself and end up in a fight with Deverell.

Now that the urgency of the situation and their emotions was past, she realized that he had managed to appear just in time. 'How did you know what we were doing?'

'I have my sources,' he said.

When he didn't add anything, she gritted her teeth. She wasn't going to get into another confrontation with him. She always seemed to lose. She picked up her pace.

Up ahead was the corner to Aunt Tabitha's. Pippa turned it and halted. The house was ablaze with light. A travelling chaise with four prancing matched bays blocked the front door. Servants in livery milled around.

'Grandfather,' she breathed, recognizing the purple coats the coachmen and outriders wore.

'We have got to get you away before someone recognizes you,' Dev said, taking her arm and pulling her back into the shadows. 'The last thing the Earl needs is to see you dressed like this and to find out what you have been doing.'

'He would have another attack,' Pippa said softly, worry puckering her brow. 'I must creep in the back way and get up to my room and change.'

'I'll create a diversion.' Dev moved off before she could thank him.

Unwanted admiration rose in her as he strode purposefully up to one of the grooms. Even at the distance, she heard him say, 'Someone has been attacked. Just around the corner.' He pointed in the opposite direction from where Pippa stood. 'I chased off the scoundrel, but cannot lift the wounded man on my own. I need help.'

With an autocratic wave of his hand for the servants to follow, Dev headed off. She saw him limp as though his leg had reached its limit. Compassion swamped her. He was in pain, yet he helped her. If only…

This wasn't the time to ponder what ifs. Moving quickly and surreptitiously, Pippa skirted down the street, keeping to the shadows of nearby houses. At Tabitha's, she edged along the side and into the garden in the back. Hopefully, everyone would be engaged in her grandfather's arrival.

She made it to her rooms without incidence and changed. Smoothing her hair back into some semblance of order, she took a deep breath and went to meet her grandfather.

Even from the top of the stairs, she could hear her grandfather's deep voice booming and the light response of her aunt. They were fighting. Over her.

'Are you telling me Pippa isn't here?' the Earl roared. 'I should have known better than to trust a scatterbrain to watch over her.'

'Now, Julian,' Tabitha said, her right foot tapping, 'do not think you can barge into my home and throw insults at me. I will have you escorted to the door if you don't mind your manners better.'

The butler, an older gentleman who had been in Tabitha's employ for forty years, kept a bland face, although Pippa saw his hands clench spasmodically. Sympathy for him made her descend the stairs quickly.

'Grandfather,' she said, pausing to catch her breath before flinging her arms around him, 'what brings you to London? I'm very glad to see you, but the trip cannot have been good for your health.'

He held her at arm's length and examined her. 'You look well enough, but where were you that Tabitha couldn't find you?'

Pippa smiled at him while her brain whirled. 'I was…in the garden. Taking a walk. I had much to think about and the dark and quiet help.'

He released her, but there was a slight wrinkle between his brows, and she knew he wasn't entirely convinced of her story. But he didn't enquire further.

'Well, go pack your bags, girl. I'm opening my town house and you are moving in with me.'

'Tonight?'

'Tonight,' he said in a tone that brooked no discussion.

Tabitha shook her head. 'You always were highhanded, Julian. I see you have not changed.'

'Nor have you, madam. You always spoke your mind, regardless of the consequences.'

Tabitha gave him an almost wistful look. 'Not always, Julian.'

Pippa watched the byplay between them and wondered why she felt as though they had once known each other well. Ever since she could remember, her grandfather had disparaged Tabitha, just as her great-aunt had done to the Earl. She had always thought they tolerated each other because of her grandmother. Now she was not so sure.

'Well,' the Earl said, 'don't just stand there, Pippa. Go and get a portmanteau for the night. A footman will come round tomorrow to pick up the rest of your things.'

'Yes, sir.' Pippa went to her aunt and hugged her. 'I shall still run tame here. If you allow it.'

Tabitha held her tight. 'I would be hurt if you didn't, child.' She smoothed back a curl. 'I'll miss not having you about. But...' she shot the Earl a look '...you must stay with your grandfather now that he is in town.'

'I'll miss you, too.'

Pippa turned and ran up the stairs. Tabitha had been like the grandmother she had never known. Her care and wisdom about men and life had made Pippa feel loved and secure in a way that living only with men had never done. Tabitha had understood her needs and her worries.

She would be back.

Pippa woke late the next morning. A maid had brought her hot chocolate earlier, but the still-full cup sat on the night table, cold. She rolled to her side and gazed out the window. Grey sky and scudding clouds filled the glass panes. Soon rain would fall.

The weather was as sullen as her mood.

She crawled out of bed and went to stand in front of a large mirror. Her fine lawn nightdress billowed around her feet. Frowning, she gathered the material into one hand at the small of her back so that her figure was revealed. She turned from side to side.

No change.

With a sigh, she released the fabric and went to slump in one of the feminine chairs. She gazed around the room, studying it in an attempt to keep herself from thinking. Pink and gold were the dominant colours. Satin and velvet the major materials. Everything was delicate and flowing, even the rosewood furniture.

A log popped, the sound loud in the still quiet of the room. Pippa covered her face with her hands.

What was she going to do? Until now, she had avoided the issue, but Dev's urgency last night and his mention that she might carry his child had made it impossible for her to delude herself any longer. Deverell's baby might well greet the world in eight months. She had always been regular— until this month. She was three weeks late.

She shot up and paced the room, energy surging through her. Part of her had known. The nearly imperceptible swelling of her breasts, the sense of euphoria, both had told her. Her training as a healer and midwife hadn't failed her. She had refused to admit it, even to herself.

Where there should be joy, she had only worry. All her life she had wanted children to love and raise. But not like this. Not when the father was a man she wouldn't marry because she could not trust him. And yet…

She loved Deverell. She always had, and in her heart, she knew she always would.

She sank to the floor, a thick pink-and-gold carpet easing her landing. The tears came.

A long time later, a noise outside her door pulled Pippa from her misery. She rose and went to the wash stand. She washed her face, knowing the cold water might feel good but it would do little for the swelling around her eyes.

But her decision was made. Deverell need never know. When she had cleared her brother's name, she would return to the country and her grandfather's estate. She would continue to work with the local midwife and do what she could on her own to help the sick. When her child came, she would have him and raise him with all the love she had to give. It didn't matter that she would never marry. Until Deverell, she had never wanted to put her life and future into a man's hands.

Grandfather would be upset, but he would come to love the child. Just as he would never throw her out.

The only sadness that remained was knowing her child would be a bastard. It would never know its father or have the honour of its father's name. Pippa's chest tightened painfully, and she fought off the tears that once more threatened to fall. She would make it up to her baby. No child would be more loved, more coddled, more cared for than her child. She and her grandfather would be enough.

No one would dare slight the great-grandchild of Earl LeClaire and, if anyone tried, she would see they regretted the action. She would protect her child.

She stood tall, pushing the sorrow away. She would make everything come out right. No matter what the cost.

A knock on the door jolted her.

'Pippa?' Her grandfather's voice came through the heavy wood. 'Are you all right?'

She smiled wistfully. All her life he had come to her door if she was late for breakfast. To him, anyone who missed the first meal of the day had to be sick.

'I'm fine, Grandfather,' she said, pulling on her robe. She

crossed to the door and opened it so he could see for himself.

'Well, you look kind of peaked, but there is plenty of colour in your cheeks.' He reached out and tweaked her nose, a habit from her toddler years. 'Get dressed and come eat something. You will feel much better with some eggs and kippers in your stomach.'

She grinned. 'Yes, sir.'

She closed the door behind him and leaned back against the solid surface. Food was the last thing on her mind. Fortunately she was not plagued with morning sickness, she just wasn't hungry. But she was eating for two now.

Later, dressed in a muslin morning gown, she sat across from her grandfather. 'Sir, I'm not ready to eat the house down,' she protested as the Earl directed a footman to fill her plate with a little of everything from the sideboard.

'You won't be eating me into the poor house, girl. Why, you are all skin and bones. What was Tabitha thinking to let you run yourself down like this?' He snorted and took a long swallow of ale. 'Probably dragged you to all the goings-on without regard for proper food and sleep. That is just like her.'

Pippa nibbled at a piece of toast. 'Grandfather, why do you dislike Aunt Tabitha so much? She is one of the sweetest and kindest people I have ever met, yet you never miss an opportunity to say something unkind about her.'

The Earl's complexion grew ruddier. He made a mission out of cutting a piece of ham. 'I have nothing against Tabitha. I just don't approve of many of the things she does.' He put the meat into his mouth and chewed.

Pippa thanked the footman for refilling her cup with hot chocolate. 'Is that why you never wanted me to have a London Season with her?'

He glared at her. 'Now don't start blaming me for your never coming to town. You never wanted to.'

'True.' She ate the last of her eggs. 'But neither did you want me to.'

He grunted and pushed his chair from the table. 'This is a pointless discussion. Finish your food, then get some rest.'

Startled by his sudden action, she jumped up. 'Where are you going? I thought we would spend the day together.'

His face gentled. 'Maybe the afternoon, puss. Right now I'm going to visit your scapegrace of a brother. I want to know everything he can tell me that might help his cause. I have hired the best lawyers.'

She should have known, Pippa thought as she watched his large form leave the room. She only hoped that seeing his grandson and heir locked up in the Tower wouldn't bring on an attack of apoplexy. It would be best if she went with him.

She threw her napkin on the table and hurried to her room to don a pelisse and gloves. She would be waiting in the foyer when Grandfather came down.

From his post at the corner of the street, Dev watched Pippa and the Earl get into a carriage bearing the LeClaire coat of arms. Relief flooded Dev. If she was with her grandfather, she wouldn't get into any mischief. He could go home and dry out.

Twisting around on his good leg, he headed in the direction of his town home, given to him by his mother when he came of age. The Duchess had been enormously wealthy in her own right when she married the Duke of Rundell, and she had kept that wealth in trust for those of her children who would not inherit the dukedom.

The rain had become a steady mist that obscured vision

and the streets were slick. Dev stayed far away from the well-travelled cobblestones.

In three days Viscount Staunton's trial was to begin. Dev had been notified by Wellington that his testimony would be required. The summons had arrived this morning before he left to come keep an eye on Pippa. It hadn't improved his mood.

What more would Pippa do in an effort to clear her brother's name now that the time was so short? He shuddered to even consider it.

Chapter Fourteen

Dev glanced at his cards, then scanned the room. It was cards and dinner in the home of a prominent Cabinet member, and everyone who was anyone was present, including Pippa and Lady Witherspoon. Tabitha's note had indicated the Earl would be present as well, but so far Dev hadn't seen him. Tabitha waved at him from another table. He smiled back and made her a modified bow from the waist.

'Courting the Dark Aphrodite by being sweet to her aunt?' his whist partner asked. 'Put a wager in White's betting book yesterday that you'd lose.' The young man, his shirt points too high and his hair too pomaded, snickered. 'Everyone knows she'll have nothing to do with you since you put her brother in the Tower. Can't say I blame her.'

Dev's eyes narrowed dangerously. 'No one asked you, Cathcart. Now play or get out of my sight before I lose my temper and call you out.'

All colour drained from the youth's already pale face. 'Don't get testy, Devil. Everyone knows you did what was right. You being a war hero and everything. You still wear that black arm band, though it's been five months.'

Dev saw red. He edged his chair back and began to rise, intent on slapping the fool across the cheek.

'Ignore the puppy,' the man on Deverell's right advised, cutting short Dev's action. 'No one ever said Cathcart had brains. Pity you had to draw him for a partner. Pity our hostess made us draw in the first place.'

Dev's tension defused. Leave it to Ravensford, a crony of his brother Jon's, to put everything into the right perspective. There was no sense in letting an idiot like Cathcart make him do something stupid.

Dev led the two of spades. 'Be glad I don't call you out, Cathcart. Everyone knows you can't fence, and you're more likely to shoot yourself than your opponent in a duel.'

The youth turned brick red, but kept his mouth shut. Dev considered it a minor miracle. Now, if only Pippa were as easy to deal with.

Two rubbers later, and two monkeys lighter of money, Dev pushed away from the table. 'I've had enough for the moment, gentlemen. If you'll excuse me.'

He wandered the room. In one corner Earl LeClaire and Tabitha Montcleve talked, or argued, if the white bar of brows across the Earl's face was any indication. Tabitha's right foot tapped away, a sure sign of her agitation.

Pippa was nowhere in sight. In the opposite corner, behind a potted orange tree, was the hint of a white skirt. She'd worn a simple white muslin evening gown. At first, he'd been surprised, then he'd decided that she wore it to make herself less conspicuous. He didn't like to consider the only reason he could think of that might make her do so. This wasn't the place to go looking for incriminating evidence, there were too many people around.

He made his way in that direction, only to stop at the sound of a male voice. Angling around, Dev saw that the man was Mark Hopwell. Pippa's right hand lay lightly on

Hopwell's forearm. Her face was alight with laughter at something he'd said.

Dev's gut twisted.

They made a distinguished couple. Her black hair and ivory skin were an arresting contrast to his light brown hair and swarthy complexion. With a start, Dev realized Hopwell had the same colouring he did. That could be him with Pippa, if he hadn't done his duty. The picture was too painful.

He turned away.

He walked aimlessly until he found a deserted bench off by itself, a trio of palms shielding it from the rest of the room. Sinking down, he stretched out his bad leg. The scars were white now instead of angry red. He'd even begun to think the wound didn't look too bad, not that it mattered. No one saw his leg except he and his valet. Pippa had said it would heal like this, but he had never believed her. Never trusted her word. His lack of faith didn't matter now, for she was with another man and wouldn't have him.

When had caring for her begun to hurt so much? When had he started wanting her so much it was an ache in his chest that never went away? He shook his head.

He'd always liked her, even when she'd masqueraded as a boy. He had respected her healing skills and been grateful for them more times than he could remember. Then, when she'd revealed herself to him, he had desired her. Desired her as he had never desired another woman. And there was the sense of camaraderie, of being able to do and say anything to her and knowing she still liked him. Not even Sam had generated the same feelings. Nothing near.

He had worshipped Sam, he now realized. She'd been an idealized, unreachable goal, not a flesh-and-blood woman to heat his blood and share his burdens. He'd wanted to help and protect Sam, but he hadn't wanted to ravish her and then hold her close and tell her he would keep the world from hurting her. Sam had not been Pippa.

Dev groaned and tunneled his fingers through his hair.

Had this feeling started when he saw Pippa in her new guise, her fine-boned beauty accentuated and brought into prominence by things he could never possibly understand? His mother said the bold colours Pippa wore became her. It was more than that. Dev didn't know what, he just knew there was something there that had grown over the past weeks of watching her and longing for her.

He wanted her, and he was damned if he would let Hopwell steal her away without a fight. He pushed up from the settee, determination stiffening his neck. If the two of them were still together, he would interrupt them. He was a soldier, and he would fight for Pippa.

Dev strode in the direction they had been, only to see no one there. A quick look around showed Hopwell talking to someone else and Pippa nowhere to be seen.

Dev's blood ran cold.

He should have known better than to let her out of his sight. He had come here tonight, knowing there was every possibility Pippa would try to sneak into the host's library and rummage through his papers. That was why he'd come here in the first place—to stop her.

Well, he could find his host's library as easily as Pippa could. With a quick look around to see that no one was paying attention to his actions, he slipped into the hallway.

A passing footman bowed to him before continuing into the card room. Dev knew he would have to be careful. The last thing he needed was for someone to catch him opening the doors of his host's house. It wasn't done.

The picture he conjured up tickled his sense of humour but not for long. There was no plausible excuse if he were caught, just as there was none if Pippa were found out.

He went down one hall and turned the corner. It was darker here and no one walked around. Still, a sliver of light shone from under one of the doors. He would take a chance.

He glanced both ways to make sure no one was around and opened the door. He slid inside and closed the door.

Sure enough, Pippa was bent over the desk, the glow of one candle spreading across the papers she read. The pale white of her gown looked ghostly. Lady Witherspoon, in a darker gown, stood nearby, riffling through a sheaf of papers.

'You should shield that light, it shows under the door,' he said.

Pippa jerked and her arm knocked over the candlestick. Gasping, she dived for it. Dev was beside her in an instant. She grabbed the candle and he stamped on the rug, putting out the tiny flickers of flame that had started. The Marchioness stepped back, taking a piece of paper and secreting it in the folds of her dress.

Dev caught Lady Witherspoon's action from the corner of his eye. She met his gaze before nodding her head in acknowledgement and slipping out the door he had just entered.

Pippa put the candle on the desk and rounded on him, drawing his attention to her. 'How dare you scare me like that!'

How typical, he thought. 'Better me than someone else. Just what harebrained thing do you think you're doing? Someone could come in here at any minute. And with your accomplice gone, there would be only you. What then?'

'Jane's gone?' She looked around.

'Like a rabbit down its hole,' he said sardonically. 'She, at least, has sense enough to get out.'

She huffed. 'I don't need Jane. I would think of something.'

'Like you did with me? A fire would certainly keep anyone from questioning you right away.'

She glared at him. 'You've had your laugh, now get out. I don't want you here.'

Exasperation roughed his voice. 'I came to save you from your foolish actions. If you won't think of yourself, think how your grandfather would feel if someone found you here.'

Her chin lifted. 'He would understand. He wants to clear Philip as badly as I do.'

'It isn't bloody likely that he wants to do it at the expense of his granddaughter's reputation.' He picked up one of the papers she'd been reading and glanced down it. 'Besides, there is nothing here. These are personal correspondence and not a word applies to anything the government is doing.'

Exasperation tinged her voice. 'That is only one sheet.'

'And you plan on going through all the letters? You don't have time. And what if you're caught? What explanation do you have? This is nearly as bad as breaking and entering. Nearly.'

Her hands clenched. 'I've got to do this. Time is short.'

Compassion softened his eyes. 'I know. Your brother goes to trial in two days. But getting caught rummaging through a Cabinet member's desk won't help. In fact, it will hurt. They will think you're spying for Staunton.'

'They won't. I will tell them the truth…if I must.'

He shook his head, wondering how much more stubborn she would be. 'We are wasting time. If you're determined to do this, I'll stay by the door and listen for anyone.'

She stilled, her fingers splayed on the desk. 'You would help me?'

A crooked grin showed his white teeth in the yellow glow of the candle. 'Not willingly.'

She gave him a curt nod.

Pippa watched Dev move to the door, her forehead wrinkled in perplexity. His honour was so strict, she wondered how he could bend it enough to allow himself to aid and abet her action. Yet, two nights ago he had helped her creep unseen into Aunt Tabitha's house. If he had revealed her presence, her aunt and her grandfather would have had her watched, which would have made her excursions difficult if not impossible.

She made herself look away from him. There was no sense in pondering what made Deverell St Simon act the way he did. She had very little time and a lot of papers to rummage through. Impatiently, she pushed a curl behind her ear and continued searching.

Voices muttered out in the hall, the sound reaching Pippa's ears just as Deverell grabbed her. His eyes bored into hers.

'Don't give us away,' he muttered.

'What are you—?'

His mouth cut her off. The kiss was hard and practical, no melding of lips and tongues. It had a purpose, and Pippa realized that purpose was to convince anyone who came in the door that they were having a lovers' tryst. The idea boded ill for the future.

The door opened. 'What in bloody blazes is going on?' her grandfather's voice boomed.

Pippa and Deverell jumped apart. Pippa looked at her grandfather's beet-red face and prayed he wouldn't have an attack. She rushed to him, noting that Aunt Tabitha was with him.

'Now, Julian,' Tabitha said in a voice that brooked no

argument, 'lower your voice and give the children a chance to explain.'

The Earl advanced into the room, heading straight for Deverell. 'I won't have my granddaughter consorting with this scoundrel. I told him before that she won't marry him and, by God, I'll thrash the meaning into him if I must.'

Pippa grabbed his arm and tried to make him stop going forward. 'Grandfather, there is nothing between us.'

He scowled down at her. 'What kind of simpleton do you take me for?'

She fell back, head dropped. 'Pardon, sir. You are right.'

'Stop this nonsense,' Tabitha said, her brisk voice cutting through the tension. Her gaze went from the scatter of papers on the desk to Dev. 'Clean this mess up the way you found it, Pippa. Dev, light some candles. Julian, go and close the door. 'Tis past time we had a little discussion.'

Pippa stilled. Wide-eyed, she looked at Tabitha, who looked right back without flinching. 'You know.'

'Yes, child, I do. I'm the one who has told Deverell when and where you will be.'

The breath caught in Pippa's throat. Another act of betrayal. She gazed at Dev, but couldn't stand the pity in his hazel eyes. Dropping her head, she returned everything on the desk to its original position as best she could remember.

The Earl closed the door, and Dev lit the branch of candelabra on the mantel. When all was done, Tabitha ordered everyone to sit down in the small grouping of chairs by the unlit fireplace.

Now that she was no longer in danger of being caught snooping, Pippa noticed how cold the room was. Her light muslin gown did nothing to keep her skin from turning to gooseflesh. Nor did the anger in her grandfather's face or the sympathy in her aunt's.

In a few brief words, Tabitha told the Earl what she

knew. Pippa realized her aunt knew everything except what had passed intimately between her and Dev. Her sense of betrayal strengthened.

The Earl's face was purple in the yellow light of the candles. His fists lay on the arms of his chair. 'I should have known better than to put her in your care.'

Tabitha's face turned to ash. 'How dare you! If you had raised her to be a lady instead of another boy, she would have never thought to do the things she has done.' Her chest rose and fell. 'But it is over and done. The child is a caring person who is worried about her brother. If there is anyone to blame for this imbroglio, it is Staunton. He encouraged and relied on Pippa to spy for him.'

'You should have stopped her,' LeClaire said.

'And how should I have done that? Chained her in bed at night?'

'You should have sent her home.'

'And had her worry herself sick over Staunton? I think not.' Tabitha took a deep breath. 'I did the best I could. I got Deverell to watch her and he has done well. As I knew he would.'

'Kissing her and compromising her reputation are doing well?' One of the Earl's brows rose. 'In my day, the chit would have been ruined. She would be today if anyone but us had come through that door.'

Pippa could stand no more of her grandfather's disparaging of Dev. 'Better that I be ruined than that I be caught as a thief.'

Dev broke in. 'I intend to marry Pippa. Anyone who dared impugn her name would answer to me.'

'All well and good,' the Earl said, 'but it would not change the facts, only make people speak behind her back.'

'They would have done that anyway,' Tabitha inserted.

'As it is, very few will speak badly of the future daughter-in-law of the Duke of Rundell.'

Pippa jumped up, sending her chair backwards. 'This is me you are discussing, and I am not going to marry Deverell. No matter what. He put Philip in the Tower. He betra...'

Pippa trailed off. Deverell wasn't the only one to break her trust. Her beloved brother had done so by telling the Marchioness of Witherspoon about her activities. And now her aunt Tabitha had done so by enlisting Deverell's aid and telling him and her grandfather everything. Her temples throbbed, and her jaw ached from clenching it shut.

Dev stood. 'Madam, my lord, I think it would be better to discuss this later. Pippa is tired and needs some rest.'

Before anyone could comment, he crossed to Pippa and took her arm. Not waiting to see what the other two did, he guided her out of the room and into a secluded corner in the hallway.

'Stay here, love. I'll get your cape and call for my carriage.'

Pippa pushed away from the wall she had momentarily slumped against. 'No. I'm fine, and I must return to the party or Jane will be beyond herself with concern.'

'I—'

'No.' She put a finger to his lips. 'I owe Jane peace of mind.'

Dev shook his head, but took her arm and escorted her into the card room. Pippa entered with a slight smile playing around her lips and her head high. She hoped anyone who looked her way would attribute her lack of colour to the heat in the room.

The Marchioness waved a languid hand at them before turning back to Mr Hopwell. Mr Hopwell looked inclined to leave her company for Pippa's, but Dev put a proprietorial hand on Pippa's arm. She glared up at him.

In an undertone, she said, 'I may have defended you to Grandfather, but that doesn't give you the right to touch me so openly.'

He grinned wickedly. 'And what may I do in private?'

Pippa's nerves, which she had been holding in check with severe strain, snapped. 'That is not humorous.' She shook him off and moved away.

Fortunately, the Earl and Tabitha appeared. The Earl's colour was still heightened, but it was no longer a splotched purple. Pippa hurried to them. She would not make eye contact with Tabitha or her grandfather, but asked to be allowed to leave.

'I will go with you,' the Earl said in a voice that said any argument would be futile.

'Pippa,' Aunt Tabitha said, 'I'm sorry. Please come for tea tomorrow and let me try to explain.'

The lump in Pippa's throat threatened to explode. 'Perhaps.' At the pain in Tabitha's eyes, she said, 'Yes.' Impulsively, she hugged her aunt briefly, uncaring of curious looks. 'I love you.'

'Oh, child,' Tabitha said, moisture blurring her vision, 'you are the grandchild I never had. Take care.' She turned to the Earl and admonished, 'And you leave her alone tonight, Julian. The last thing she needs are your recriminations. She has been through too much.'

For a fleeting moment the Earl looked chastened before his jaw clenched belligerently. 'I shall do as I like, madam. Just as I have for these last twenty years.'

'Old goat,' Tabitha said softly, but there was a softness about her expression.

Momentarily brought out of her own self-absorption,

Pippa studied them. What had happened between them? But she knew neither would ever tell her.

She sat silently in the swaying carriage as they made their way home. The Earl said nothing, but Pippa could feel her grandfather's censure across the chill dark space of the coach. It increased her own sense of malaise.

The outside lanterns of the coach cast a glimmering light through the windows, making the inside murky one moment and sharply defined the next. It was like Pippa's thoughts. One instant she could understand why Philip and Aunt Tabitha had told others about her secrets. The next second, she was angry and hurt that they had done so. Her world was no longer black and white, but filled with many shades of grey.

And what about Dev? He had turned Philip in, yet he had stood by her. He hadn't liked what she was doing, but he'd been determined to protect her.

She sighed heavily. Her head hurt and her mind was a jumble of conflicting thoughts.

The carriage halted, and she and her grandfather got out. In the foyer, the Earl handed his hat, cane and gloves to the butler before turning to Pippa.

'I have minded my tongue the entire journey, but I have something to say to you. Come to the library.'

Pippa dreaded the scolding she knew was coming, but followed him with her head held high. She had only done what she had felt necessary.

'Have a seat.' He directed Pippa to one of the sturdy leather wing chairs.

She did as told. The fire was banked and the Earl had only lit two candles. The room was shrouded and cold.

'Pippa, I know you feel responsible for Philip.' He paced the room once. 'But what you did was foolhardy. I can hardly believe that even someone of Tabitha's questionable sense would allow you to do so. However, it is done. But from this second on, I forbid you to continue.'

She struggled with her rebellious streak. 'There are now only two days left, sir.'

'Exactly. And if you have not found anything yet, I doubt that you will.'

She bit her bottom lip to keep from arguing. Some small part of her knew he was right, but a larger part would not give up hope. 'The traitor has to be found, Grandfather.'

He sank into the largest chair, exhaustion turning down the corners of his mouth. 'I know how you feel, Pippa, but there is nothing more that can be done. I will go to speak with Wellington tomorrow. I have an appointment with the Prince Regent for Monday morning before the trial starts. I will try to get immunity for Philip or, at worst, ask that he be let free to go to the Continent.'

Pippa's head sank. 'This isn't what I had hoped for.'

'Neither had I.'

The weariness in his voice pulled Pippa from her own sorrow. Standing, she said, 'Come, Grandfather. 'Tis past both our bedtimes.'

He rose heavily. 'Go on up. I will stay here a while.'

She saw his gaze wander to the decanter of port on the desk. 'You know that isn't good for you. I'll fix you some chamomile tea.'

He made a face. 'That stuff is bitter. The wine will be much smoother going down and accomplish the same end.'

'It will also give you a raging headache in the morning and irritate your gout. Better that I put plenty of honey in the tea.'

After several more arguments, he gave in with an ill grace. Pippa smiled as she watched him climb the stairs.

She knew there was no port in his bedchamber because she had directed the maid to remove it.

Feeling marginally better, she headed for the kitchen to brew the tea. While she was at it, she would mix a small pot of cream for the tweenie's burned forearm. The child had brushed against a burning ember while lighting the fire in Pippa's room. Working with her herbs always eased the strain and made Pippa feel better.

Chapter Fifteen

After church the next day, Pippa changed into a pomona green dress. A fetching straw bonnet with matching green ribbons framed her face. Several ebony curls peeked coquettishly out. Gloves and a spencer finished the outfit. Nothing could hide the dark circles under her eyes. Properly attired, she set out to call on Aunt Tabitha.

She wasn't comfortable with the impending visit. Even after tossing restlessly for most of the night, she hadn't come to terms with the knowledge that two of the people she had trusted the most had given away her secrets. Yet, somehow, she knew she would forgive her aunt, just as she had managed to forgive her brother. If nothing else, she would spend the rest of her life trying to forget their lapses.

Watkins, Aunt Tabitha's butler, opened the door. Pippa gave him her hat. 'How is your shoulder?' she asked, knowing he had injured it the week before while carrying one of the heavier silver serving dishes to be cleaned.

He unbent enough to smile at her. 'Thank you for enquiring, my lady. The salve you gave me has helped. I barely feel the ache.'

'Wonderful. I was hoping it would work.' She gave him

a conspiratorial grin. ''Tis what we use when a horse sprains a fetlock.'

Watkins looked momentarily taken aback before chuckling. 'Quite the thing.' A footman passed by, glancing their way to see what the laughter was about. Watkins stiffened up. 'Madam is waiting for you in the drawing room. She had Cook prepare your favourite sandwiches.'

'Please thank Cook. I can taste the cucumber already and the sweet butter.' Anxious to get her talk with her aunt over, Pippa moved rapidly. Belatedly, she realized she had outpaced Watkins who would be flustered if she didn't allow him to introduce her. She waited at the door for him.

With a flourish, he opened the door and announced her. Pippa smiled and moved past him.

Pale autumn sunlight flooded the room. Aunt Tabitha sat on a settee with crocodile legs. The table in front of her was heavily laden with a silver tea service and at least a dozen delicacies. Pippa's mouth watered in a very unladylike fashion.

'Child, come and sit down. I am famished and have barely been able to make myself wait for you.'

Pippa's apprehension eased at her aunt's informality. She took the seat offered and patiently waited for her tea, laced with plenty of sugar, and a plate stacked with cucumber sandwiches.

Not until they had both eaten enough to fuel an army did Tabitha clear her throat. 'Pippa, about last night—'

'No,' Pippa interrupted. 'Let us forget everything.'

Tabitha smiled sadly. 'That is only postponing the inevitable. In a week, a year, you will remember that I gave away your secrets and conspired with a man you claim to hate.' She set her empty plate down and clasped her hands in her lap. 'I would rather we discussed this now. I do not want you hating me some time in the future.'

Discomfort made the tucked and ruched neckline of Pippa's gown seem tight. 'As you wish.'

'Sometimes we have to do things that other people think betrays them because that is the only choice we can make and live with ourselves. Sometimes it is the best decision. But every time we do so, we risk losing a friend or lover.' Tabitha paused to gaze out the window as though looking at something that wasn't there. 'It is always hard.'

Tabitha's attention came back to Pippa. 'When I was younger, I was in love with a man I knew I would love all my life.' A wistful smile curved her Cupid's bow mouth. 'I was very young. But another woman, someone very dear to me, loved him too. I thought he would be happy with her and grow to love her so, in the end, I let him go. I chose to be sad so that she could be happy.'

'Aunt Tabitha, I'm so sorry,' Pippa said, leaning forward and taking one of the older woman's hands.

Tabitha patted Pippa. 'Do not be. I have lived a full life and found happiness. That was just an example to you. The man felt I betrayed him when I refused to marry him. But, you see, I did not feel I had any other choice. That is how I felt about your spying for Philip. I knew you would do it, with or without my help and knowledge. And I knew it was dangerous, no matter what you might have thought. The only person that I could be sure would look after you was Deverell St Simon, so I went to him.'

'That is how he always knew where I was going,' Pippa said with a martial light in her eye.

'Well, he always knew when you were leaving the house so he could follow you.'

'I would have been fine without him.'

'Perhaps. I could not take that chance. Nor did I feel I could tell you not to hunt for the real traitor. I know how you feel about Philip and, like you, I know he is innocent.'

'But why tell Grandfather?'

'That is harder to explain.' Tabitha released Pippa's hand and stood. She paced to the mantel and took down a dress sword. 'This belonged to my husband. Like your Deverell, he was an army man. He died in battle.' She paused and cleared her throat. 'This sword represented the military to him and what he knew he had to do. His duty. His honour. I felt honour-bound to let Julian know what had really happened.'

Pippa bit her lip to keep from saying how stupid she thought that was.

As though sensing her niece's reaction, Tabitha said, 'I know it would have been just as easy to keep him in the dark. I did not feel comfortable with that. He entrusted you to my care. And you must admit, the scene we walked into last night needed explaining.'

Pippa rose and took the sword. Holding it in both hands, she gazed at the shiny silver hilt and gold-and-red braid. 'A handsome weapon.'

'Very.' Tabitha took it and replaced it. 'Please try to understand, Pippa. I did not do anything last night or in the past weeks with the intention of hurting you. I did what I thought at the time was best for you. Sometimes that is not easy. Nor is it always the best way. It just is.'

Pippa looked away from her aunt's silent request for forgiveness. 'Just as Dev did what he felt honour-bound to do when we found Philip. But how can I forget that and marry him?'

Tears began to form in Pippa's eyes until they overflowed. The room was a blur.

'Oh, child,' Tabitha said kindly, drawing her into an embrace. 'Life is never easy. Sometimes we have to let the past go in order to continue living. Will you let Dev's strong sense of honour and duty keep the two of you apart?'

'I don't know. I just don't know.'

Pippa found comfort in her arms. It was like confiding in the mother she had never had. The two sat down and Tabitha continued to hold Pippa until her tears were past. When she raised her head from Tabitha's shoulder, the older woman smoothed back a stray lock of hair.

'Only you can mend the rift between you two. There is nothing Dev can do that he has not already done.'

Pippa hiccuped. 'I know, but I must think about whether I can let go of my anger and resentment.'

At the Duke of Rundell's town house, Dev waited patiently for his father to finish reviewing the account books. The room was large and dark. Bookshelves covered every wall, and where they ended walnut panelling continued to the ceiling. Brown crushed velvet curtains were pulled against the oncoming storm. Flames caroused in the massive fireplace. Unfortunately the room was so large the warmth didn't penetrate to the chair where Dev sat.

The Duke was a tall, slim, elegant man, his height hidden by the desk he sat behind. His hair was blonde with frosting at the temples, and his eyes were deep set and chocolate brown. The hands holding the papers were long, refined and very white.

'Now,' said the Duke, looking up at Dev. 'What brings you here in the middle of the afternoon? Usually you are at your club or some less reputable haunt.'

Dev resisted the urge to cringe. His father was a strict disciplinarian and known for his acerbic wit. 'Sir, I have a favour to ask.'

The Duke's thin lips curled. 'I should have known it was a service you wished rendered. Or your allowance has run dry.'

Dev's hackles rose. 'My allowance is intact, sir. I have

Grandmother's legacy, if you'll remember. I invest what you give me.'

'*Touché,*' the Duke murmured. 'What can I do for you?'

Dev never liked asking a favour of his father and this one was immense. But he had no other choice. His father was the only person he knew with enough influence to possibly change Viscount Staunton's fate. For Pippa, he had to ask.

'I know this will be difficult. You may refuse me, and I would be the last to blame you, sir. But…' Dev took a deep breath. 'Can you intervene in the case of Viscount Staunton? I would appreciate it more than I can ever repay.'

The Duke steepled his fingers. 'In what way do you want me to meddle? Have the traitor released or have him hung sooner?'

Dev couldn't trust himself to respond without anger so he said nothing. Moments dragged by.

'I assume you want him hung since you still wear your black arm band, and you sport a wound earned in a battle that might not have been fought if Napoleon hadn't escaped Elba.'

Acid dripped from the Duke's words, and Dev knew he had set himself an impossible task. But he tried anyway.

'Staunton deserves to die, sir. There is no doubt of that—if he is truly a traitor. His sister doesn't think he is.'

'If you believe her, why did you capture her brother in the first place?'

Nothing was ever easy when dealing with his father. 'Because I believed him to be guilty. All the evidence, what little we could gather, pointed to him. But now I'm not so sure.'

'Why?'

No longer able to sit still, Dev rose and paced. The drag of his bad leg was nearly impossible to see, but he could feel it. It reminded him of Hougoumont, and for the umpteenth time he wondered why he was doing this. And came back to the same answer—Pippa.

'He has had his sister break into the home of a Cabinet member and then gain entrance to the library of another during a card party.' He came to a halt in front of his father and leaned forward with his fists on the desk. 'They grew up together. Pippa says they have the emotional bond so many twins share. He wouldn't put her in jeopardy as he has done unless he truly is innocent.'

'A good argument.' The Duke reached across the wood and leather expanse of his desk to a large cut-glass decanter. He poured two glasses and handed one to Dev. 'Drink this down. It will ease some of your anxiety. Then perhaps you will sit again, and we can continue to discuss this without the tension you are currently generating.'

Dev felt heat move up from his perfectly tied cravat to suffuse his jaw and cheeks. His father had a knack for making him feel like a bumbling child. He took the drink and downed it in one swallow.

Whisky. It burned a hole down his throat to explode in his gut. He sat abruptly.

'I should have warned you,' the Duke said. 'But I thought it would do the trick. More?' He lifted the decanter.

Dev nodded. This one he would drink slower. 'Did Alastair get his preference for the drink from you, or vice versa?'

'We discovered it together. One of the things fathers and sons do.' He raised one blond eyebrow in a sardonic gesture.

The door opened and her Grace, the Duchess of Rundell, rushed across the room. Her husband raised both eyebrows at this behaviour.

'My dear, I am not going anywhere.'

She didn't stop until she reached him. He swivelled around and she sat in his lap. 'If I didn't know you were teasing me, I would be hurt at your tone of voice,' she said, her own tone both loving and reproving.

Dev watched them, marvelling at the love they had finally found for one another. He wasn't always comfortable with his father, but he loved him and was glad for the both of them.

'Perhaps I should leave,' Dev said, seeing that the two were momentarily absorbed in one another.

'No,' his mother said, getting off her husband's lap and pulling a small chair close.

Dev bowed his head in acknowledgement and stayed put.

'What brings you in here so precipitately, Alicia?' the Duke asked.

She dimpled at him. 'I'm come to beg for Dev's cause.'

The Duke rolled his eyes. 'I should have known.' His lapse of dignity was brief before his gaze pinned Dev to his chair. 'You fight unfairly. You should have told me from the outset that you have your mother's support.'

Dev's hands clenched the arms of his chair. 'Your reprimand is unfair, Father. I didn't tell Mother anything of my plan.'

'Rundell!' the Duchess expostulated. 'How very narrow of you. Dev told me nothing.' She straightened her shoulders and lifted her chin. 'I have been listening at the door. Although I could have listened from across the hall, Dev was so loud.'

'You never cease to amaze me,' the Duke murmured, the words softened by the look of love in his eyes.

'Well, I know the two of you don't get along. I didn't know why Dev was here, and I wished to be able to intervene if needed.'

Dev groaned. 'Mother.'

'Very commendable,' the Duke said. 'But 'tis true. We are not as close as perhaps we might be.'

Dev had thought the conversation uncomfortable earlier, but that was nothing compared to now. He and his father never discussed their differences. He didn't want to start now.

The Duchess grabbed one of the Duke's hands. 'Please, Rundell, say you will help.'

Her husband looked at her. 'Does it matter that much to you?'

'Yes,' she said quietly. 'I think the boy is innocent. Stubborn, but innocent.'

The Duke looked from one to the other. 'Then I shall see what I can do. But no promises. A man who is thought a traitor has very little sympathy from everyone else. Including myself.'

Relief washed over Dev. 'Thank you, sir. If anyone can get a postponement of the trial or get it set entirely aside, you are the person.'

'Don't set high hopes. Either of you,' the Duke said brusquely, looking from one to the other. 'This is very late to be interfering. I should be surprised if anything is changed.' As they both rose to protest, he held out one hand. 'Quiet. I said I will try, and I will.'

The Duchess grabbed his hand and took it to her bosom. 'I shall see that you are amply rewarded, my love.'

Seeing the amorous turn the situation was taking, Dev bowed himself out of the room. No one noticed him leave.

The next afternoon, Pippa returned from a ride in the park with the Marchioness of Witherspoon to find her grandfather sitting morosely in the library. The drapes were pulled and the only light came from the fire. A tumbler of liquor, held loosely in one hand, threatened to spill its contents on to the rug. The Earl was oblivious.

Pippa knew immediately. He hadn't been able to get anything changed. Her heart sank.

She went to stand behind him and draped her arms around his neck. 'It was no good.'

'Wellington would not hear of dropping the charges. Nor would the Prince Regent settle for allowing Philip to renounce his rights to the title and go to the Continent. I fear the results of his trial. I do not believe anyone thinks him innocent.'

Pippa hugged him tight, inhaling the scent of his soap and the citrus bite of the snuff he used. He looked ten years older than he had this morning.

'The trial before his peers starts tomorrow morning,' he said.

'We will contrive something,' Pippa said, kissing him on the cheek. 'But right now you need to get some rest.'

Mindful not to spill the liquor, she took the glass from his unresisting hand and put it on a table. Next, she helped him stand and led him from the room. If she weren't very careful, this trial would be the death of her grandfather. She couldn't bear two such heavy losses.

With her arm around his waist, they mounted the stairs. She tucked him into bed for a nap and turned to leave. He grabbed her wrist.

'Pippa, you should know. The Duke of Rundell was before me. He asked for the same leniency as I.' His eyes held her for a long minute.

'Thank you,' she murmured.

He released her hand, and she hurried away. If the Duke of Rundell had asked, it could only be because Deverell had requested him to. What did this mean?

Agitation sat on her shoulders like a bird of prey. Had

Dev decided Philip was innocent? Did he regret bringing Philip to trial? She didn't know what to think, but found herself softening toward him. He was trying so very hard to change the wrong he had done.

Perhaps there was a chance for them. How wonderful it would be to marry the man she loved. Their child would be better for it, too.

If only she could truly believe Dev regretted his actions. Everything would be perfect, or as nearly perfect as possible under the circumstances.

She spent the rest of the day in a haze of hopeful anticipation.

The next morning was cold, damp and eery. Pippa entered the courtroom with dragging feet and a heavy heart. She was to testify in Philip's defence. Character witnesses were considered almost as important as those who gave evidence about the supposed crime. Aunt Tabitha was to testify as well.

Grandfather walked beside her, his head held high and his shoulders back. His ruddy complexion was paler than usual. He stared straight ahead, ignoring the few curious glances.

Pippa looked over the group of peers who were to decide her brother's fate and recognized all of them. At one time or another, she had danced, talked or ridden with each one. The Marquis of Witherspoon was one, his face with its usual sour expression. She knew how he would vote before the trial even got under way.

Aunt Tabitha beckoned to them. She had two seats set aside. They took them, with the Earl between the women. Pippa had noticed that Tabitha seemed able to calm the Earl when nothing else could.

Shortly after, Philip was brought in with chains on his

wrists. The sight was nearly more than she could stand. To see her proud brother treated like an animal was unforgivable. She heard a soft moan of pain from her grandfather. She reached for his hand and held on tightly.

The expanse of the room separated her from Deverell, who sat with his mother. The Duchess smiled at her. Pippa did her best to return the gesture, but knew her effort was weak. Dev stared at her. She turned away from him, all of yesterday's softness erased by her brother's plight.

If not for him, Philip wouldn't be facing a death sentence. Bile rose like acid to eat away at the love she still had for him.

The rest of the day did nothing to change her opinion.

Wellington stated what he thought Philip had done.

Pippa squeezed her grandfather's hand. Together they sat as still as though they expected to be pounced upon if they made the slightest movement or sound. On the Earl's other side, Tabitha's face was as white as a sheet. Pippa knew she looked the same.

Then Deverell was called to present his information.

As much as Pippa didn't want to watch him, she could not take her gaze off him. He sat stiffly, his eyes looking straight ahead. He spoke dispassionately, neither adding nor deleting anything they had found out in Paris. The only things he didn't tell were her part and what she had done here in London. Even to her, the evidence he presented was damning.

The tightness in her chest increased until it seemed she would expire from lack of breath. But it wasn't over yet.

When Dev was thanked and told he could return to his seat, he asked, 'I would like to add something more.' When no one objected, he continued. 'While I brought Viscount Staunton in to stand trial for treason, I would like to caution that we have no absolute evidence. To condemn him to death and the abeyance of the LeClaire title is severe punishment if there is any doubt as to his guilt.'

A chorus of suppressed gasps sounded around the room.

'I am not saying he isn't guilty,' Dev said. 'Merely that we have no unarguable proof.'

Pippa's mouth twisted into a bitter smile. Too little, too late.

Tabitha leaned around the Earl and whispered, 'He has tried, Pippa.'

Eyes brittle, Pippa hissed, 'He would have done better to have second thoughts before being responsible for Philip's incarceration.'

As Dev returned to his seat, his eyes sought out Pippa's. She stared stonily at him, refusing to acknowledge the regret in his. Head held high, she looked away, going so far as to turn her shoulder to him.

Aunt Tabitha was called next. 'Philip is one of the most honourable men I know. He would never betray his country. What would he have to gain?' She continued in this passionate vein until asked to step down.

Pippa glanced around the room. The closed faces on the people present told her louder than words that her aunt's testimony had done nothing. Her hands clenched so her nails bit into her palms. She was next and had nothing to say that Tabitha had not already said. Still, she was closer to Philip than anyone—except, possibly, the Marchioness of Witherspoon.

Pippa glanced at her twin as she made her way to the stand. He nodded at her, his eyes full of encouragement. She fought the tears his confidence in her brought.

'Philip is my twin,' she started. 'I, more than anyone else, know him, and he would never commit the acts he is being charged of. From the moment we were old enough to understand our place in the world and what it meant to be English, Philip has been determined to help make his country strong. He is the eldest son of the eldest son, heir to the title and lands. He joined the army to protect that heritage, not destroy it. He would never spy for Napoleon.'

She said more, but could tell by the bored looks on several of the faces and the pity others did nothing to hide, that she was failing. Her voice trailed off, the catch in her throat threatening to become a sob. She would not cry. She would not show such weakness to a room of people determined to destroy her brother.

She stood and glared defiantly at anyone who met her gaze. 'He is innocent. If you condemn him, you will be condemning a man who would have died for his country before betraying it. You will be making a mistake.'

She walked back to her grandfather and sank into her chair. The Earl's hand sought hers and squeezed. Tabitha gave her a smile of understanding. The gestures were nearly more than she could take. Her vision blurred, and she blinked rapidly to keep the tears from falling. The trial was not over yet, and she had to be strong—for Grandfather, for Philip, who was called on last.

He rose, his chains clinking clearly in the silence. Loudly and clearly, he stated, 'I am innocent of treason. However, I have no way to prove that. I believe the real spy is in this room…' Shouts and anger met his words and it was some time before it was quiet enough for him to continue. 'You don't like what I say, but the information the French spies had could only come from someone privy to government policy. Who else? Since no one will stand and claim responsibility, I am the scapegoat.'

With a contemptuous curl of his lip, he sat. His gaze roved boldly over the assembled peers. Most met his stare.

Silence followed as Philip's peers deliberated.

Soon afterwards the sentence was pronounced. Philip

was found guilty of treason and to be hung and then drawn and quartered. The LeClaire land and title were to revert to the Crown upon the death of the present Earl.

Pippa felt as though someone had given her a mortal wound. It took all her resolve and strength not to crumble to the ground. She blinked furiously to keep the moisture filling her eyes from falling. The knuckles of the hand holding her grandfather's were white. The other hand shook under cover of her skirt.

Every eye in the place turned to them, some with pity, some with righteous gloating. She ignored them. Somehow she would stand up and walk out of this room. She would make her legs support her and her heart continue to beat. She would draw one ragged breath after another. She would show them the pride of a LeClaire. Then tonight she would take justice into her own hands.

She had forgotten her grandfather.

A sharp intake of breath, followed by a low moan were the only warnings. He collapsed to the floor.

Forgetting all her resolve of a haughty exit, Pippa fell to her knees. Fingers clumsy and frantic, she unloosened his cravat and shirt and slid her palm over his heart. She could feel it beating, swiftly and erratically. His face went from flaming red to the white translucence of a turnip. His breathing was laboured.

Across his chest, her eyes met Tabitha's. Tears streaked the perfectly applied powder on the older woman's high cheekbones.

'Is he…will he…' Tabitha took a deep breath '…live?'

Pippa fought off her own tears. She needed to remain calm. Just for a little longer. 'I don't know.'

A commotion drew her attention. Philip was struggling with his gaolers in an attempt to get to them. The Duchess of Rundell went to the scuffling group and, with an imperiousness that was magnificent to watch, demanded that he be allowed to attend his grandfather. The guards, too taken aback and unused to dealing with aristocracy of such rank, fell back.

Pippa would have risen and thrown herself into Philip's arms if a hand hadn't dropped to her shoulder. 'Pippa,' Dev said calmly and authoritatively, 'you have got to help your grandfather.'

His words penetrated the fog of pain engulfing her. She reached for her reticule and the small vial of foxglove tincture she always carried in case her grandfather had an attack. The midwife she had helped used it for many things, from dropsy to falling sickness to apoplexy. Pippa had seen with her own eyes that it helped. Her hands shook uncontrollably as she tried to open the strings of her reticule.

'Let me,' Dev said calmly, taking the bag from her. He opened it and withdrew the vial. 'Is this what you want?'

By way of answer, she grabbed it from him and wrested the cork out. Tipping her grandfather's head back, she poured the liquid in his mouth and prayed.

In a loud voice, she demanded, 'Everyone stand back. He needs room to breathe. Someone find a litter. He must go home.'

It seemed to Pippa that they waited an eternity. Philip knelt beside her and they joined hands with Tabitha. Without thinking, Pippa even took Dev's hand and held it tight, thankful for the sturdy comfort of his presence. She didn't even think of what a contradiction to her earlier feelings it was. All that mattered was his nearness in this most awful time.

Tabitha's tears fell freely. Pippa sniffled, but refused to give in to the grief welling inside.

In guilt-riddled pain, Philip said, 'I've done this to him. I am so sorry.'

Pippa's agony increased, for there was no honest answer to Philip that didn't agree with his self-condemnation. 'Don't make it worse, Philip. He would never blame you.'

Suddenly, miraculously, she felt the Earl's right arm move. 'Grandfather,' she said softly.

His eyes opened, the right more than the left. His lips moved but she couldn't hear what he said. The words were slurred.

'Tabitha?' he whispered, the effort closing his eyes again.

'I am here, Julian,' she sobbed, laying her cheek against his. 'Always.'

Grandfather and Aunt Tabitha loved each other. Awe and happiness held Pippa motionless. If only it weren't too late for them. She smiled through her tears.

Just then, several men arrived with a litter and carefully lifted the Earl on to it. He slipped into unconsciousness during the procedure, but Pippa noticed that his breathing seemed to ease. Tabitha stayed by his side, never once releasing his hand. A carriage waited outside. They settled him inside and Pippa turned to Philip.

She wrapped her arms around him. 'As soon as Grandfather is comfortable I shall come to you,' she said. 'Be prepared.'

Understanding momentarily lit his features as he kissed her forehead. 'Take care of him.'

'I will,' she promised, entering the carriage.

Through the window she saw Deverell and his mother. They stood near Philip, who was once again being held by his guards. She smiled sadly at the Duchess and waved. Deverell she ignored, although she couldn't forget the sense of security his nearness had given her during the first moments of her grandfather's collapse.

The coach moved forward, the wheels clattering on the

Betrayal

cobbles. Increasing the distance between her and Deverell did nothing to dampen the depth of her reaction to him. It seemed that no matter what he did to her family, she could not stop loving him and depending on him.

It was a curse she would spend the rest of her life trying to overcome.

Chapter Sixteen

Pippa and Tabitha took up opposite sides of the Earl's bed. Pippa monitored his pulse and breathing while Tabitha bathed his forehead and spoke softly to him. The Earl went in and out of consciousness.

Finally, in the small hours of the morning, his eyes slowly opened and he focused on the room. 'Tabitha?'

She leaned over him until she was in the field of his vision. 'Yes, Julian?'

He smiled, the left side of his mouth not quite as high as the right. 'I love you.'

'Oh, love,' she murmured, burying her face in the crook of his neck.

He tried to raise his right arm to her shoulder. Seeing that he couldn't, Pippa did it for him. His eyes thanked her.

'Why did you leave me?' he asked, his voice hoarse and barely audible.

Tabitha lifted her head and wiped at her tears. She glanced at Pippa then looked at the Earl. With a sigh, she said, 'Because it was the right thing to do. Mary had slept in your bed, and you had made love to her.' When he opened his mouth to speak, she put a finger over his lips. 'Hush, love. I know you were drunk at the time and that she disguised herself as me, but that did not change the act, only the intent. She loved you so much. To do so desperate a thing was unheard of. And you are a gentleman. You had to marry her after that. I knew it. So did you.'

'Yes,' he muttered. 'And I did my best not to hate her for it. Although I often felt I failed.'

'Hush,' Tabitha said. 'Do not fret yourself. She was happier with you than she would have been without you. I knew that, and that is what made it bearable for me to let you go.'

'So many years,' the Earl rasped, exhaustion drooping his eyelids. 'So many wasted years.'

'But no more,' Tabitha said. 'I will never leave your side again. I promise.'

He smiled before drifting into a sleep.

Over his gently rising chest, Pippa said, 'Grandfather was the lover you let go because of honour.'

'Yes, and while I missed him horribly and had bouts of anger over the pain of losing him, I never truly regretted my decision.' Her eyes met Pippa's squarely. 'I had no other choice.'

'You could have run away with him.'

'No. Neither one of us could have lived with ourselves if we had done so irresponsible a thing and hurt Mary like that. Nine months later she birthed his child. Your father. No, it was better to go through life without him than not to be able to live with myself.' She looked down at the Earl, longing and love softening her features. 'He would not have been happy either.'

'Honour,' Pippa breathed.

'Sometimes it is all we have,' Tabitha said.

'A cold life.'

Tabitha caught one of Pippa's hands. 'Think well on what you just said.'

Unable to meet Tabitha's gaze any longer, Pippa pulled her hands free and turned away. 'I have things to do,' she said over her shoulder. 'He should sleep for a while and, unless something else happens to upset him, I hope for a nearly full recovery.'

'If he has some paralysis, it will not matter,' Tabitha said. 'I will care for him always and be thankful for every day we have together.'

Such love and devotion. It made Pippa's heart ache for what she did not—would not let herself have.

'I will check on him as soon as possible,' she said, moving to the door. 'But I will be gone for a while. Maybe several days. If he relapses, give him the contents of the bottle on the table.'

'Be careful, Pippa,' Tabitha said, the solemnity of her voice making Pippa pause. 'If you are caught, you may well suffer Philip's fate, and then where would your grandfather be with both of you gone?'

Pippa swallowed hard on the fear that rose up in her throat. 'I have no other choice. I cannot leave him to be executed.'

'I know,' Tabitha said quietly.

Dev stood in the shadows, watching Earl LeClaire's town house. It was a position he was becoming too accustomed to. Behind him, his horse whickered. Absentmindedly, he reached behind and petted the gelding on the nose to quiet him. The last thing he needed was for a restive horse to reveal his position.

A cold wind blew off the Thames. There was no moon so the stars shone more brightly than normal, their glitter the hard sparkle of diamonds. He shivered and pulled the collar of his caped greatcoat up around his ears.

Soon Pippa would be creeping out on her way to the

Tower. She had no other choice. But how would she break Staunton out? That remained to be seen, for he had no doubt she would manage. The only real question was whether or not he would stop her.

It was just hours before dawn when he saw a figure slip from around the back of the house. She paused as though listening, then motioned behind her. Another figure, draped in an all-encompassing cape, hurried up to her and stopped. The second person was taller than Pippa, so he knew it wasn't the Marchioness. Probably a servant. Two horses followed.

Dev began to suspect what the plan was. He wondered when it would occur to Pippa that arriving at the Tower at such a strange time would be suspicious.

Quickly the two shrouded figures mounted their horses and headed in the direction of the Tower. Dev waited until they were well on their way and the sound of hooves on cobbles had died away. Then he followed more slowly, always careful to keep a silencing distance between them. He knew their final destination.

Dev reached the Tower in time to see Pippa hand the guard something. A bribe most likely. The two figures disappeared inside, and Dev settled in to wait. He didn't have long.

Three figures stood silhouetted in the light from the door. Pippa, the tall person whom Dev thought was now Staunton, and a much shorter individual. He wasn't surprised to see the Marchioness of Witherspoon with them.

Dev shook his head and agonized over his decision. Did he stop them, or let them escape? It seemed the guard didn't realize that his prisoner had taken the place of one of the late-night visitors. Or, if he did, the gold he'd received was adequate to make him deny any such knowledge.

The three shadows moved swiftly to the horses and

mounted. He had allowed them to make their getaway. Nor was he completely sorry. In his heart, he believed Staunton was innocent. He was even beginning to wonder if the Viscount was protecting someone. But if so, he was paying a steep penalty.

He spurred his mount onward. From now on, he would have to keep close behind them. His guess was that they were headed for a seaport. If he were doing this, they wouldn't go to Dover or another large port. They would go to a small fishing village and arrange to be smuggled across the Channel to the coast of France. From there, they could quickly lose themselves on the Continent. He quickened his pace.

Pippa thought she heard hoofbeats behind them, but couldn't be sure. They were travelling too fast for her to safely look behind. Philip was in the lead, planning on taking them to a small village where he knew a fisherman who did smuggling on the side. But it was a long ride, and they had to be well away before daylight and someone came to check on Philip.

Their capes spun out behind them as they raced toward the rising sun. Blood-red light crested on the horizon when they stopped at the first inn. They changed horses and kept on going without a rest.

It was mid-morning when they cantered through the quiet main street of the tiny village. Philip deposited them at the single tavern and left.

Pippa hunkered down over a pine table in the darkest corner of the public room. Jane sat across from her. Fatigue lined their faces and dulled their eyes. Neither spoke for a long time.

Finally the Marchioness spoke, her accent more pro-

nounced than usual. 'Were you surprised to find me with
your brother?'

Pippa looked dispassionately at her, noting a smear of
dirt that dragged across the other woman's cheek. She probably looked worse.

'No. I was only taken aback when you pleaded to come
with us. You're giving up everything for my brother and
without benefit of marriage.'

She shrugged and a sad smile tugged her lips. 'I love
him. It is something I never expected when first we started,
but it happened. It changed everything.'

'How?'

Pippa's sixth sense told her there was something the
Frenchwoman wasn't saying, something that was important. She remembered Dev saying Jane had taken a paper
the night they rifled through the Cabinet member's desk.
Why?

Jane's gaze slid away, wandered the room without ever
coming back to Pippa. 'Perhaps some day I will be able to
tell you, but not now. It is better this way.'

Suspicion, only a hint before, flared in Pippa. But there
was nothing she could do. All she was certain of was that
the Marchioness loved Philip. Anything else didn't really
matter. Not now.

The same sixth sense that had warned her about the Marchioness made her turn her head in time to see the edge of
a beaver hat and the black greatcoat of a man walking by
the single window the tavern boasted. She didn't see
enough to be sure of who the man was, but she knew. Dev
had followed them.

But why didn't he do something to stop them?

She rose and headed for the door with the intention of
confronting him. Before she could turn the handle, it
opened and Philip stepped inside. His eyes looked hunted

as his gaze darted around the murky room. Danger emanated from him.

If he knew Dev was here, he would kill him without giving Dev a chance. They were too close to success for him to do otherwise. Pippa couldn't bear the thought.

'Where are you going?' Philip asked harshly. 'I thought I told you to stay put until I returned.'

Pippa bristled. 'I'm not your servant to do as you order. I wanted a breath of fresh air. The smoke in here is making me cough.'

His eyes narrowed, but he said nothing. She brushed past him. Outside the sun was bright enough to make her squint. A quick look in all directions showed no one who met Dev's description. For a moment, she wondered if she'd been in error, her heightened nerves making her see things that weren't there.

The skin between her shoulder blades itched, and she knew she was right. Dev was here somewhere, watching them. She hoped he would be cautious as much as she hoped he would not interfere with their plans. Philip had to escape.

She took several deep breaths, seeing no reason to waste her time in the clean air, then re-entered the dark, smoky room. Philip sat at the table with Jane, his arm around her. She leaned into him. Pippa sat opposite them.

Philip's face was expressionless as he watched her. She imagined this was how he looked when he was on a mission, cold and unemotional. His only weakness, that she could see, was Jane.

'I have a room for us. We need to get some rest.'

Pippa nodded. Jane sank deeper into his embrace.

'I have arranged for us to leave tonight with a shipment of wool. If all goes smoothly, Jane and I will in France before the sun rises tomorrow.'

Pippa breathed a sigh of relief.

Philip rose and drew Jane with him. Pippa followed them up a set of rickety stairs to a small room tucked into the eaves. The single window looked out on the only street that went through the town. Philip would be able to watch anyone coming into or going out of the village.

She and Jane stretched out on the two pallets. Philip pulled the single chair to the window and straddled it with his back to the room. She noted the pistol he took out of his pocket and sat on the sill. A shiver chased down her spine.

Her brother was serious and would stop at nothing to escape. She was doubly glad she hadn't said anything about Dev. Still, sleep eluded her through the chill hours of the afternoon and early evening. Beside her, Jane tossed and turned. Philip sat motionless.

Well after dark, Philip rose. 'It is time,' he said quietly.

They left the tavern as unobtrusively as they had entered it. A light, salt-laden breeze fanned their faces. Clouds skipped across the sky, obscuring the sliver of moon. Within minutes they walked on the rock shingle of the beach. A single lantern glowed in the distance, outlining a small boat. Figures scurried around it. Philip led them toward it without hesitation.

Pippa shivered. Everything was going too smoothly. Why was Deverell letting them escape? He had followed them this far, surely he meant to stop Philip. Unless…

Hope sprang in her heart. Perhaps he was here only to see that she remained safe, like he had in London. He'd tried to keep Philip from being condemned as a traitor, it wasn't unreasonable to think he might let her brother go. If that were so, then maybe…just maybe they could finally be together. Her heart longed for him, had done so even when he was convinced Philip was a traitor and should be punished. She might be able to forgive him.

She stumbled on one of the larger pebbles and her foot slipped out from under her. With a muffled shout, she twisted her ankle and went down. She flung her arms out to break her fall and ended up scraping her palms on the rocks and shells. Sharp, burning pain shot up her arms and up her leg. Very likely, she had a sprain.

Philip turned back with an impatient grunt. He extended a hand to help her up. Pippa took it and stood. She gasped as her ankle buckled and she nearly went back down.

'Are you hurt?' Philip asked.

'I have sprained my ankle,' she managed to say through teeth clenched against the discomfort. 'But I shall be all right. Just give me a minute.'

'I don't have a minute,' he said. 'Stay here and I'll send one of the men to help you back to the tavern. You will be safe there until you can send word to Grandfather.'

She stood shakily with her weight on her good leg. Reason told her his suggestion was the only sensible one. And if Dev were here, he would find her.

'Ah, a damsel in distress,' a French male voice said, the words seeming to originate from a nearby spit of rock.

Pippa twisted around, suppressing a gasp of pain. She felt Philip tense beside her. Jane rushed to their side, not stopping until she was in the circle of Philip's free arm.

The clouds chose that moment to clear. The hard light of the waning moon combined with the harsh glitter of stars to show the small, slight figure of a man stepping away from the rock. He moved toward them with an economy of motion that spoke of control. He held a pistol aimed at them.

'Grimod,' Jane whispered, the softness of her voice doing nothing to disguise her fear.

He made a mocking, disdainful bow. 'Jacques Grimod, spymaster extraordinaire, at your service. Or should I say, your demise?' His lips split in a cold, hard smile.

'How did you find us?' Jane asked, her voice trembling as she moved even closer to Philip. 'I thought you were in Paris.'

His smile disappeared. 'That is what you were supposed to think. You are stupid to think yourself my only spy in England. I knew about your affair with Staunton. When I heard through my other contacts that the Viscount was accused of treason, I knew you would run with him.' He levelled the pistol on Staunton. 'You are a flawed tool, Jane. One I can no longer afford to use or let continue to exist.'

Staunton released Pippa's hand and pushed Jane behind him. 'Let her go. She can't harm you. If you must kill someone, kill me.'

Grimod laughed. 'How noble. I intend to. And then I will kill both women. I won't leave any loose ends. That is why I am Napoleon's spymaster. I never take anything for granted. The lovely Jane can recognize me, something not many can do.'

He pulled back on the pistol's hammer, moving slowly as a gloating smile of anticipation transformed his face to that of a mocking demon. Pippa stared in horror. Her brother's death was writ all over the Frenchman's countenance.

'Stop!'

The order momentarily distracted Grimod, who looked for the man behind the word. In the seconds following, a figure darted forward and in front of Staunton. Realizing his mistake, Grimod shot.

The sound reverberated in Pippa's ears. Her heart stopped.

Oh, God, not again. First Philip, then Grandfather and now Dev. She flung herself at him, ignoring the protest of her ankle and mindless of the second pistol Grimod still aimed at her lover. She had to cover Dev's body with her own.

She fell down on Dev, only to have him push her away and roll to one side. Another shot pierced the air, rising above the pounding of the surf. The soft thud of impact was barely audible.

Grimod folded, a rag doll that has had the stuffing pulled out. Red spread across the chest of his shirt, creeping ever further until almost no white showed. His eyes glazed over.

Frantic with worry, Pippa crawled over the sharp stones to Dev. His breathing was loud and rapid.

'Where are you hurt?' she demanded, running her hands over him. 'Tell me. We must staunch the flow. Oh, Dev, how could you be so reckless?'

Tears soaked her cheeks and desperation lent her the strength to push his fingers away when he tried to interfere with her search. She couldn't lose him now. Please, God, not now.

'Shh,' he said, finally capturing her hands in his. 'I'm fine. Just a graze to my shoulder. More painful than dangerous.'

Relief rolled over her and she collapsed against his chest, her tears soaking through his shirt. 'Oh, Dev, I thought you were going to die. I couldn't bear it.' She clung to him, burrowing her face into the hollow of his shoulder.

He held her tight, his free hand rubbing the tight muscles at the base of her neck. 'It is all right, love. I'm fine.' He kissed her temple and released her hands to smooth the hair back from her face. 'Everything is fine. Calm yourself.'

Slowly his words penetrated her terror. Clutching his shirt, she lifted her face to look up at him. There were no lines of pain around his mouth and eyes such as she remembered from when his leg wound was fresh. He even smiled. The tightness in her chest began to ease.

'I owe you a thank you,' her brother said, drawing her attention momentarily from Deverell.

Dev rose, drawing her with him. She gasped and clung to him for support. 'Are you hurt?' he demanded.

'Only a little sprain. Nothing.'

He frowned at her, but turned to Staunton. 'I owe you a debt. It seems I had the wrong traitor put in the Tower.' His gaze shifted to the Marchioness, who was still sheltered against the Viscount's chest.

'Merci,' she said, her voice a husky whisper. 'I am so sorry. So sorry.' She looked up at Staunton, her lashes wet with unshed tears. 'I never meant to endanger you. I swear it.'

'I believe you,' he said.

'Then why?' Pippa demanded, all her anger aimed at the Marchioness. 'Philip nearly died and all along you were the real spy. You even pretended to help me hunt for the "traitor".'

Dev cut through the accusations. 'Was there something on the sheet of paper you took from the library the night I caught you and Pippa?'

She nodded. 'It had information on Napoleon's imprisonment that I thought Grimod would be interested in.' Her gaze slid away from Dev's hard stare. 'I had to spy for him. He had my mother.'

'Ah, love,' Staunton said tenderly, wiping a tear from her cheek.

She caught his hand and kissed his palm. 'If I did not spy for him, he was going to kill her. I could not let him do that. So I did as he ordered. To the bitter end. Please forgive me.'

Staunton brought her fingers to his lips and returned her caress. 'There is nothing to forgive. You had no choice. I knew that.'

'What?' Her shocked eyes met his.

'One of my informants knew about you. He warned me.'

'You knew?' Pippa demanded, furious at her brother and hurt by what he had done to her. 'Then why did you send me all over London looking for the traitor?'

'I'm sorry, Pippa,' Staunton said. 'I knew there was another spy, but not who. I wanted to find him and implicate him, hoping that would be enough to clear me and keep suspicion away from Jane. We still don't know who he is, since Grimod will never talk.'

For the first time since Dev shot the man, they looked at the Frenchman. He lay motionless.

'We'll take his body to London,' Dev finally said. 'It should be proof positive for Wellington that you aren't the spy we're looking for. I'll tell him Grimod said there was a spy in London. Hopefully, the information will be enough to clear your name, but I'd still go to the Continent right now. This may take time.'

'You're letting us go without a fight?' Staunton asked.

Dev stiffened and his arm that held Pippa tightened. 'You're innocent and, no matter how guilty she is, I can't condemn a woman to a traitor's death.'

But instead of watching them get into the boat, he turned away. Pippa thought she understood. His loyalty to his country told him not to let the Marchioness go, but the gentleman in him couldn't punish her as his honour demanded. By letting them go, he did the thing he considered the lesser of two evils.

'Thank you,' she said after the boat pushed away from shore and disappeared into the black night. 'You'll never know what this means to me.'

He grinned his crooked grin that never failed to make
her stomach do somersaults. 'Oh, I think I know. Remember, I'm the man who travelled with you all over France
and chased you around London as you did everything in
your power to find and then save your brother.'

'I'm so sorry I misjudged you,' she said.

'You didn't misjudge me. I intentionally broke your trust
and used you to find your brother. I put my sense of duty
and honour before my love for you. My only excuse was
that many of my friends died fighting Napoleon. I believed,
and still do, that anyone who betrayed England for France
deserves to die.' He looked briefly out to sea in the direction the boat had taken. 'I just couldn't bring myself to turn
in a woman.'

'You tried to clear Philip's name. I know you asked your
father to help and you spoke for my brother at the trial.'

He tipped her chin up. 'I would do the same things over
again, Pippa. Given what I knew at the time, I would ap-
prehend your brother again and send him to the Tower
without hesitation.'

She knew he meant what he said, but in the past few
days she had learned that sometimes you must accept a
person for what they are, even if they have done something
you feel betrays you. It was a hard lesson to learn, but too
many people she loved had seemed to betray her because
of their love for her or for someone else. She hoped she
had grown.

'It doesn't matter any more, Dev. I love you and want
to spend the rest of my life caring for you and proving to
you that what has happened in the past is forgotten.'

He caught her to him and buried his face in the wild
curls of her hair. 'I love you, Pippa.'

With a grunt he lifted her into his arms and started back
the way they had come.

'Put me down,' she gasped. 'You will hurt your leg. You don't need to do this. I can walk with help.'

He laughed at her. 'Are you trying to keep me an invalid forever?'

'No,' she said, tangling her fingers in his hair. 'I just want you able to perform other duties for me.'

He hugged her tight. 'Never fear.'

She pulled his face to hers. He stopped walking to devote his entire attention to her demands.

Epilogue

Rundell Abbey, Boxing Day 1815

Dev looked around the dining table. Everyone was present: his brothers and their wives, his parents, Earl LeClaire and Tabitha and Pippa. Pippa, his wife of one week. She looked at ease amongst his family. The emeralds his mother had given them as a bridal gift were draped round her long neck and dripped from her ears. They were considered the finest in the land, but they were no more brilliant than her eyes which returned his study. He smiled at her and rose to propose a toast.

He lifted his wine glass. 'To marriages of love. May they always prosper.'

His brothers rose and seconded his proposal.

'And may my bride always be glad she gave in to me,' he added, his gaze fixed on Pippa's rosy face. They had made love before coming down to dinner and her lips were still swollen from his kisses. He grinned at her.

Earl LeClaire rose and raised his glass. 'May everyone find a second chance in their life.' He took Tabitha's hand and raised her for his kiss. The room exploded in applause.

Looking very pleased with himself, the Earl added, 'Even my scapegrace grandson, who I hear is in Rome with the woman he loves.'

Lastly, the Duke of Rundell stood up. 'I propose a toast to my lady. Without her gracious meddling, we would not all be here tonight. Nor would I have learned that marriages can be more fulfilling and satisfying than anything else in life.'

Everyone stood and raised their drinks high to the Duchess, who sat looking pleased and embarrassed. When everyone was seated once more, Pippa caught Dev's eye. He nodded so she cleared her throat.

'I...that is, Dev and I have an announcement.' Every face turned her way. Many had a knowing look. She blushed. 'Yes, well, it seems most of you know what I am going to say, but I must say it anyway.' A smile of blinding happiness lit her features. 'Dev and I are to be parents.'

Pandemonium broke out.

The Duchess jumped from her seat and rushed to hug Pippa, scant steps ahead of Tabitha. 'My dear child, I am so delighted.'

Tabitha took the Duchess's place. 'Pippa, darling, nothing could make me happier. Come to us when it is time. I very much want to keep you safe and care for you.' She gave Dev a devilish glance. 'And I am sure your new husband will be frantic and grateful for the calming effects of Julian here.'

At so patent a misrepresentation of the Earl, everyone burst into laughter.

Just as things settled down, Samantha came up to Pippa. 'I am glad we are sisters-in-law.' She glanced at Dev who smiled at her. 'I am even more glad that Dev has found someone he can love with all his heart.'

Pippa fought down the urge to cry from happiness. She

put her arms around Sam and squeezed. 'Thank you. Our babies will be within weeks of one another. I hope they will be good friends.'

Sam wiped away her own tears. 'I know they will.'

A commotion at the door announced the arrival of the nursery bunch. Liza's baby was given to her by the wet nurse. Stephen and Amalie came in, both of them excited at attending a very adult gathering. They moved quickly to Sam, who still stood by Pippa.

'Mama,' Amalie said, 'Stephen says we are all to go riding tomorrow. Is that true?'

Sam smiled and pulled both children into her arms. 'That is what your papa says, and he is always right.' She gave her husband a mischievous grin.

Watching the small exchange, so redolent of love and caring, Pippa was achingly glad she had found Dev. As though sensing her thoughts, he came around the table to her and put his arm around her waist.

'Is it time we went to bed?' he asked softly.

She looked around the room. Everyone was caught up in conversation with someone else. No one would even notice they were gone. 'Yes.'

Arm in arm, they left the room. Tabitha and Alicia watched them before turning to each other. Tabitha winked. Alicia lifted her glass. Both women beamed.

Upstairs in the suite of rooms set aside for their use, Dev turned Pippa around until her face was a breath away from his. 'I love you, Philippa St Simon.'

'And I you.' She burrowed into his embrace, inhaling the scent of bergamot.

He scooped her into his arms and carried her toward the large bed. 'Stop,' she protested. 'What about your leg? 'Tis not good for you to lift me.'

He chuckled. 'It is the best thing for me. Without you I

would not have the thing. Without you I would be wallowing in self-pity.' He set her gently on the feather duvet. 'Without you I would be lost.'

She drew him down to her with a murmur of love and desire. He went willingly.

'I love you more than life itself,' he said.

'I finally know that,' she replied, turning into his arms. 'Nothing will ever part us again.'

'Nothing' he said, meeting her lips with his.

* * * * *

JACK CHILTERN'S WIFE
by
Mary Nichols

Born in Singapore, **Mary Nichols** came to England when she was three, and has spent most of her life in different parts of East Anglia. She has been a radiographer, school secretary, information officer and industrial editor, as well as a writer. She has three grown up children, and four grandchildren.

Also by Mary Nichols
in Mills & Boon Historical Romance™:

THE HONOURABLE EARL
THE INCOMPARABLE COUNTESS★
LADY LAVINIA'S MATCH★
A LADY OF CONSEQUENCE★
THE HEMINGFORD SCANDAL

★ novels have linking characters

Look for Mary Nichols's

MARRYING MISS HEMINGFORD

Coming 2005

Chapter One

1793

The atmosphere in the rectory library was charged with tension. It crackled like lightning in a leaden sky, presaging a storm which threatened to engulf the three people who stood grouped around the hearth. The Reverend William Harston, still in the black evening coat and breeches he had worn to Viscount Beresford's Hunt Ball, stood with his back to the dying fire, facing his niece, Catherine, known to family and friends as Kitty. His dark features were sad and disappointed rather than angry, a fact which filled Kitty with remorse. But that remorse was tinged with defiance.

She, too, was still dressed for the ball in a high-waisted white silk gown with a square neck and three-quarter-length sleeves which ended in lace ruffles, as befitted a young lady of nineteen still in the single state.

Beside them, almost between them, stood Kitty's stepmother, Alice. Her plump frame spilled out of a voluminous gown of pink satin. She wore an old-fashioned white wig and patches on her heavily pow-

dered face. The powder was wearing off and did little
to hide the red spots of anger on her cheeks.

'Sorry! Sorry! Is that all you can say?' Alice's green
eyes gleamed with malice. 'You behaved like a harlot…'

'Madam, you go too far,' William interposed. 'Pray,
moderate your language.'

Alice ignored him and continued her tirade against
Kitty. 'You think "sorry" will see an end of it? We
will never live it down. Never. It makes me quite ill to
think of what we have just witnessed. The most flagrant
impropriety imaginable…'

Kitty had made up her mind not to rise to her stepmother's taunts, to be calm and dutiful and accept whatever punishment her uncle meted out to her. He was her
father's brother and her guardian and she respected him.
But that was too much of an injustice. She looked up,
violet eyes sparkling, and turned to the overbearing
woman who had married her late father.

'That's not fair!' she said. 'It was only a kiss and
meant nothing. Don't tell me you never allowed a gentleman to kiss you before you were wed, because I will
not believe it.'

'That's enough, Catherine!' her uncle snapped.
'Apologise for that at once. You should go down on
your knees in thankfulness to have a mother who cares
for your reputation and the good of your soul.'

It was more than Kitty could bring herself to do and
she hung her head and said nothing. After all, she had
done nothing so very terrible, except allow Edward
Lampeter to dance her straight out of the ballroom on
to the terrace, where he had proceeded to kiss her
soundly.

The trouble was that he had not taken her far enough

and some of the guests at the ball had seen them, had seen, too, that she was enjoying the experience. Her stepmother had been one of them and lost no time in drawing her uncle's attention to the spectacle, and in such a noisy way that even those who had hitherto been oblivious had seen them and either smirked behind fans or chuckled aloud.

Uncle William had forced them apart, pushed Kitty behind him and stood facing Edward in icy control of his temper, before muttering a warning that he would call on him the next day and hustling Kitty from the room and out to his carriage. Alice had been furious at their abrupt departure from so prestigious an event but, in Kitty's eyes, she had made matters far worse by her display of outrage. There was no need to make such a fuss, unless she wanted Kitty to be publicly disgraced.

The carriage ride home from Beresford House, across the park to the rectory, had been made in silence, except for the clop of horses' hooves and the jingle of harness. Only when they were behind closed doors did her uncle speak. 'Do not think you are going to be allowed to go to bed, young lady. Into the library with you.'

Kitty had thrown off her cloak and given it to the waiting Judith, who looked from one to the other and, noticing the black looks of her employer and heightened colour of Mrs Harston, wondered what scrape Miss Kitty had got herself into now.

'Go to bed, Judith,' the Reverend commanded, before ushering his niece and her stepmother into the library.

It was the only room in the house Alice had not been allowed to transform. It was the only room he could go to when he needed solitude, a room for quiet relaxation, a room for doing business and discussing family matters. Here he could put on his stern face and exert his authority as leader of his flock of parishioners and head of the household, something he seemed unable to do anywhere else in the house since he had taken his brother's widow into his home.

Kitty suspected he had not wanted to, but had done so for the sake of the children. Kitty still missed her mother, even after eight years. Her mother had been so gentle, so loving, so understanding of her high-spirited daughter, even though she was often ill and, in the last few months of her life, bedridden.

Her death had changed Kitty's cheerful, easy-going father. He became almost morose, and involved himself more and more with looking after the poor. He had been a country doctor and a good one, just as he had been a good father; too good, she sometimes thought, because it was thinking of his motherless children which had prompted him to marry Alice a little over a year later. And anyone less like her darling mother could not be imagined.

If old Judith was to be believed, Alice had set her cap at Papa before he met and married Anne, the youngest daughter of Lord Beresford, and she had been furious at being spurned.

When the first Mrs Harston died, Alice had, in almost indecent haste, rushed to comfort the widower. And he, needing a mother for his children, James and Catherine, had succumbed. Whether he had regretted making her the second Mrs Harston, Kitty did not know, for he had never given any sign of it.

But he had given way to Alice's demands in every particular, allowing her to redecorate and refurnish the house to her own somewhat flowery taste, connived in the spoiling of their son who arrived a year after their marriage, and pandered to her imaginary ills, so that Kitty became exasperated at his weakness.

But it wasn't Alice's nagging or his weakness that carried him off in the end but typhoid, which he, as a physician, was treating at the infirmary. She had been fourteen at the time and James seventeen, almost a man, while little Johnny was only eighteen months old. On his deathbed Papa had asked Uncle William to look after his children and he, being the good man he was, had undertaken to do so.

Uncle William, unmarried and unworldly, had allowed himself to be persuaded by Alice that he needed a housekeeper as much as she and her fatherless children needed a home. She had taken over the rectory in the same way she had taken over the doctor's home.

But though she tried, she had not been able to subdue Kitty's bright spirit, her love of life, her quest for adventure, for new experiences, almost impossible in the rarefied atmosphere of the rectory of a quiet Berkshire village. Hence, the kiss.

'Just when Lord Beresford was beginning to accept me and her ladyship was showing some friendly feeling towards me, you must perforce disgrace us.' Alice's diatribe went on. 'What must they think? I'll tell you, shall I? They will think I do not know how to go on, that I do not know enough of genteel behaviour to pass it on to my daughter...'

'Stepdaughter,' Kitty murmured.

'Catherine!' warned her uncle in a low voice. 'That is unkind in you. Your stepmama has shown you nothing but kindness and treats you as if you were her own.'

'For which I get no thanks,' Alice put in, addressing Kitty. 'Why, if we had played our cards aright, Lord Beresford might very well have given you a Season;

you are his granddaughter, after all, and he has financed
your brother's Grand Tour. He would have treated you
both even-handedly. We could all have had an enjoyable time going out and about with all the top people.
We might have been presented at court.

'You could have found a suitable husband and set up
your own household,' she went on, hardly pausing for
breath. 'It is too late now—his lordship will not invite
us over his doorstep again and I shall be snubbed by
everyone and not asked anywhere.'

It was obvious to Kitty that her stepmother's concern
was all about her own aspirations to be accepted by the
upper echelons of society. Alice's father had made his
own way up in the world, building up a manufacturing
business and becoming comfortably off. Kitty admired
him for it, but his own daughter had despised him. She
had never written to him and never visited him.

To hear Alice gossiping with her cronies, you would
think she was a duchess at the very least. And she loved
to boast that she had connections with Viscount Beresford, which were tenuous to say the least. Tonight at
the ball, for instance, she had almost hurled herself at
the poor man, gushing and primping and telling him
how she loved dear Kitty like her own, even though she
was often wilful and disobedient.

She had sighed heavily, fluttering her eyelashes at
him over her opened fan. 'Girls need a strong hand, do
you not think so? Not that your dear Anne would not
have been strong if she had been able. She was ill for
so long and dear Henry so engrossed with looking after
her, which was only proper of course. But it is no wonder the children were allowed to run riot.'

It had given Kitty a perverse pleasure when her
grandfather, tall and upright, had pursed his lips and

said, 'Yes, indeed?' in a tone of voice which would have cowed anyone with a thinner skin than her stepmother.

'Oh, yes, my lord. I could see that dear Henry was devastated when she passed away. Being a woman of sensibility, I longed to comfort and succour him and his motherless children after his untimely bereavement; God made it possible.' She had sighed again. 'It was not easy. And after the poor dear man passed away himself, I was left to manage alone and, being a slave to poor health myself...'

There was nothing wrong with Alice's health; it was just an excuse for idleness, to give Kitty more and more to do. She did it willingly for her uncle's sake, and for Johnny, her six-year-old half-brother whom she adored. When the occasion demanded, such as an invitation to Beresford Hall, Alice could be as energetic as anyone there. And certainly her tongue never rested.

'There! You can see how right I have been all along, William,' she went on, when Kitty remained silent. 'She has been thoroughly spoiled. If I were you, I would wash my hands of her, send her to your Aunt Henrietta in Scotland. She will be suitably strict with her and the climate might cool her ardour.'

'No!' Kitty cried, afraid her uncle would do as she suggested. Her great-aunt lived in splendid isolation in the far north west of Scotland. She was almost a recluse, refused to go out and was very rude to any visitors who called. It would be tantamount to a prison sentence. 'Uncle William, am I a criminal to be sent away from you? What have I done that is so very bad, except to be young and want to enjoy my life?'

'Kitty, please don't make matters worse,' he said.

'Apologise to your stepmother and let us discuss what is to be done in a calm and sensible manner.'

For the love and respect she bore him, Kitty turned and gave the apology with as good a grace as she could muster.

'That's better,' he said, giving a sigh of relief, but he did not smile. Indeed, his countenance was even more sombre than usual. 'Now, I will tell you what I have decided.'

Kitty turned towards him, trying to convey a plea in her large, expressive eyes which would soften his heart. Could he not see that Alice wanted to be rid of her and had seized this opportunity to have her sent away? Her stepmother hated her for being too much like her dead mother, whom her father had adored.

Surely Uncle William had noticed the little acts of cruelty Alice had meted out when they first came to the rectory: the stinging rebuke; the quick cuff round the ears; sending her to bed without her supper for the slightest misdemeanour. Even now, when she was grown up, she was subjected to constant reminders of her failure as a daughter.

She was too outspoken, her deportment was a disgrace and her social graces sadly lacking. By social graces Kitty understood she meant the artificial manners in company which went by the name of politeness. Alice was the master of cutting innuendo. Why did her uncle not see it? Or perhaps he saw it and chose to ignore it for the sake of peace and quiet.

Even now he was taking Alice's side and refusing to hear her explanation of what had happened. If they sent her away, Alice could act the injured party. She could almost hear her plaintive voice. 'Why, I did my best with the girl, but she would not have it. We did not want to send her away, but what else could we do?'

Kitty was forced out of her reverie when she realised the Rector had spoken. 'I beg your pardon, Uncle, what did you say?'

'I said you will marry him.'

'Marry? Whom should I marry?'

'Edward Lampeter, of course.'

Kitty's mouth fell open. 'Uncle, I can't do that. He has not offered for me and we do not have that affection which is necessary for a happy marriage.'

'What is that to the point? He is single and of good family, not as well-heeled as I would have liked, but that can't be helped. The money your mother left you will be your dowry and that should suffice…'

'You call that punishment!' Alice broke in, just as surprised as Kitty by her brother-in-law's pronouncement. 'It is more like a reward. What she needs is a little discipline and your Aunt Henrietta is just the person to give it to her.'

'Not while there is a chance to salvage the situation,' he said. 'At least this way we can pass it off as a little premature exuberance on the part of the young couple, that we had intended to announce the betrothal at a gathering of our own later in the year but, in view of the couple's impatience, we have decided to bring it forward…'

'I won't agree to that,' Kitty said. 'And Edward won't agree either. We should not suit. Uncle, please do not put either of us to the humiliation of being refused.'

'Neither of you will refuse,' he said, setting his lips in a thin hard line. 'The young man is honour-bound to make an honest woman of you.'

'I won't. I can't. Oh, Uncle, please don't make me.'

His voice softened as he looked at her. 'Kitty, it won't be so terrible. Edward is not old or ugly, or drunken—at least, no more than any young man of his age—and he will soon settle down.'

'Perhaps he doesn't want to settle down. Have you asked him?'

'No, but before we left Beresford House, I spoke to his father. We are to meet again tomorrow afternoon at his London home to discuss the matter.'

'I won't go.' Now she really was frightened and appalled, but defiant too. 'I won't be party to ruining Edward Lampeter's life or mine, just for one stolen kiss, which meant nothing.'

'You are not expected to go,' he said flatly. 'You will remain here until I return to tell you what arrangements have been made. Now, I suggest you go to your room and reflect on your conduct tonight and what it has brought you to. Then say your prayers and ask forgiveness from Someone who is more able to absolve you than I.'

Kitty knew there was no arguing with him while he was in his present mood, nor while her stepmother stood by to make sure he did not weaken. She curtsied to them both and turned to leave the room. Shutting the door behind her, she gathered her skirts in her hands and ran along the hall and up the oak staircase to her room where she flung herself on her bed.

She would not weep. She would not! Neither, she told herself, would she marry Edward Lampeter. She liked him, was even fond of him, but he was certainly not her idea of a husband. They had known each other ever since they were children; he had been James's playmate and she had often tagged along behind them when they went riding and fishing and getting into the sort of mischief young boys always get into.

He could be fun, but that was half the trouble, he never took anything seriously, and he was only two years older than she was, hardly more than a boy. When she married, it would be someone she could look up to, a man with strength of character, a man who could make her feel like a woman, not a playmate, a man she could love, who loved her.

She smiled suddenly, remembering that kiss. It had been a new experience for her and, she had to admit, a delightful one. She was not the first girl he had kissed, that had been obvious, and it had gone on rather a long time, which suggested he had enjoyed it too. But she was quite sure he had never thought it would lead to marriage.

Was he, even now, being given the same ultimatum as she had been given? She could imagine his reaction and, while it was not very flattering to her, she could hardly expect him meekly to obey. Or would he? Did his light-hearted view of life include an indifference to whom he married? He would not agree, would he? Oh, he must not!

If only James were here, he would know what to do. He would talk to Uncle William and Edward and make everything right again. But James, being a boy and older than Kitty by three years, had escaped to university and after that had taken himself off to Europe to do the Grand Tour, and she missed him dreadfully.

She scrambled off the bed and crossed the room to a small walnut escritoire, where she rifled through the drawers for James's last letter. She found it and took it to the candle to read it. The light was almost unnecessary for she had it almost by heart. Written from Florence, it was full of enthusiasm for his travels. He wrote well, filling his prose with light and colour, peopling the pages with the strange characters he had met.

'I think I shall visit Paris on my way home,' he wrote. 'I am curious to see if it has changed much since the Revolution.' The letter had been written several months before and since then there had been news of riots and beheadings and, worst of all, the imprisonment and coming trial of King Louis.

James, who could be more than a little rash at times, would not be so foolish as to embroil himself in other people's troubles and would surely return by sea. On the other hand, perhaps it was only Paris that was dangerous and the rest of the country was peaceful, in which case, travelling overland would be the safest. Safest of all would be to stay where he was until the troubles came to an end.

He seemed to be enjoying Florence and wrote at length about its antiquities and the hospitality of the people and the social occasions he had attended. That, she knew, was a reference to the young ladies he had met. Had he kissed any of them as Edward had kissed her, for the fun of it?

That was what was so unfair about being a woman; you could not have even the tiniest flirtation, however innocent, without you were branded a wanton. What was it Alice had called her? A harlot. She had only a vague idea of what a harlot was, but she knew it could not be anything but bad, especially as the remark had drawn an exclamation of remonstrance from her uncle.

She wished she were a man; life would be so much more fun. A man could travel the world, without the worry of abigails and chaperons; he could get involved in all sorts of adventures and everyone labelled him a jolly good fellow. Why couldn't a woman do that?

Why not? Why not leave home—it would be better than marrying against her will, wouldn't it? Other women did it, why couldn't she? Alice wanted to be rid of her. She would be rid of her, but not to Scotland.

The prospect began to excite her and she paced the room, trying to think of a way in which it could be accomplished. Her uncle would never agree to let her go and to travel you needed money, a great deal of it.

She had the money her mother had left her, but she could not draw on that until she married and then it would be given to her husband. That was something else that wasn't fair. Her uncle gave her a monthly allowance from the trust her father had set up, but that was only pin money and he could stop it at any time. Could she borrow and, if so, from whom? The idea, when it came to her, was so outrageous, she knew she had to try it.

Judith had long since retired to her own bed and would certainly try to dissuade her from going if she was roused. No one must know where she had gone, no one at all, because she would be fetched back and Alice would have her way about sending her to Scotland. That would be worse than marrying Edward.

She would be sorry to leave the rectory, but lately it had become more a place of confinement than a home, and she would be sorry to leave Judith and little Johnny, whom she loved, but staying would be intolerable whether she agreed to marry Edward or not.

She had to get out of her ballgown and its petticoats, something her uncle had obviously not thought about when he dismissed the maid. It had tiny buttons down the back which she could not reach and after struggling for a few minutes, she took a pair of scissors from her needlework drawer and cut herself out of it. Poor Judith, she had spent hours stitching the lace round the sleeves and neckline and pressing the yards of silk in the skirt; goodness knows what she would say when she saw it had been ruined.

But there was no time to think of that. A coach, on its way from Bath to London, called at the King's Head in Beresford village every morning at five-thirty and she meant to be on it.

It was still dark when she let herself out of the house, wearing a simple blue wool dress and caraco jacket, topped by a blue cloak with a fur-lined hood, for it was bitterly cold. Her feet were encased in half-boots. She carried a small handbag in one gloved hand and a carpet bag containing a change of clothes in the other.

Stealthily she made her way down the steps and along the drive to the London road, hoping no one would go to her room and discover the note she had left on her pillow until she was well on her way.

She had never been about at that time of day before, and never alone, so that the experience was both exhil-arating and frightening, except, of course, that the step she was taking was irrevocable and she had no idea what the future held in store for her.

She arrived at the King's Head just as the coach rat-tled into the yard, its mud-begrimed wheels and sweat-ing horses proclaiming that it had been driven hard through the night in order to reach the metropolis by daybreak. Kitty, having paid her fare, climbed aboard and settled into her seat, while the horses were changed, then they were off, galloping through the countryside as dawn lightened the sky and the domes and spires of London appeared in the distance.

Beresford village was only an hour's ride from the capital, and it was still barely light when she left the coach at the Golden Cross and set out to look for a hackney. It was still very early but already, as she walked up Haymarket, which supplied the nearby stables of the Royal Mews with hay and straw, towards Piccadilly, the streets were becoming busy.

Two milkmaids, their yokes slung across their shoulders, hurried to Green Park where their charges waited patiently to be relieved of their overnight burden. A chimney sweep, with his brushes over his shoulder and his little climbing boy trotting reluctantly at his side, made his way to his first call. Errand boys, clerks, washerwomen passed her, giving her a glance of curiosity, but no more than that.

She crossed the road to avoid a drunk rolling homewards and turned the corner into Piccadilly just as a hire carriage approached. Without thinking, she held up her hand and stepped into the road. The driver, half asleep, pulled on the reins so sharply the horse nearly fell back on its haunches.

'Lunatic!' he yelled. 'D'yer want to be killed?'

'I wish to hire your cab.'

He looked down at what he had taken to be a servant girl on an errand for her mistress and found himself gazing at a raven-haired beauty who, though young and very petite, was obviously not a servant. Her complexion was pale and her oval features perfectly proportioned, framed by the hood of her cloak, which was too expensive a garment for a servant to be wearing. Her agitated manner and the bag in her hand gave away the fact that she was running away. He was not sure he wanted to be any part of that.

'Ain't for hire,' he said, preparing to move on. ''Bin up all night, just going home to me bed.'

'I'll pay you double.'

He hesitated.

'For goodness sake, man,' said a male voice at her elbow. 'Don't dilly-dally, can you not see the lady is in great haste?'

Kitty spun round to see who had spoken and found herself looking into a broad chest which sported the most vivid waistcoat she had ever seen. It was of bright blue velvet, embroidered all over with gold and silver thread and trimmed with scarlet braid. And she was prepared to wager the little buttons cascading down its front like teardrops were diamonds.

Slowly she raised her head to look up over a flamboyantly tied cravat, which spilled over the waistcoat, to the face of its owner. He was handsome…my, he was handsome, dark as a gypsy with a firm chin, almost black eyes which held a hint of amusement, and black hair tied back with a blue velvet ribbon to match the waistcoat. A many-caped overcoat was slung carelessly across his shoulders, as if keeping out the cold was the least of its uses.

Smiling, he reached across her to open the door of the cab. 'Be my guest, ma'am.'

She hesitated, not at all sure how she ought to behave, but then, remembering that the reason she was on the streets of London at this ungodly hour was because she had not behaved as she ought, she decided she might as well continue in the same vein. Her life with her uncle and stepmother had ended the minute she had stepped out of the house; whatever lay before her was of her own making. She smiled, thanked him coolly and stepped up into the vehicle, leaving him to hand in her bag.

The driver, sitting with his hands on the reins, looked on in undisguised amusement as the man stood in the road, still holding the door open, so they could not proceed.

'Where do you wish to go, Miss—?' the stranger queried.

'To Brook Street,' she said, settling herself in her seat and ignoring the hint that she should provide her name.

'What a coincidence, that's just my destination,' he said, jumping in beside her, flinging his coat on the opposite seat and revealing a cutaway jacket. 'We can travel together.' He rapped on the roof with his cane and they were away.

Kitty inched herself as far away from him as she could—which wasn't far, considering the narrowness of the vehicle—her body tense with nerves. What had she done? Supposing he abducted her, or took her for the harlot her stepmother had called her—what could she do? Would it do any good to shout for help?

The few people who were about on the street had seen her climb willingly into the vehicle and were continuing on their way, minding their own business; they would not interfere. It was less than two hours since she left home and already she was in a quandary. She did not look at him, but gazed out of the window as if there was something of great interest to be seen in the road.

'You are nervous,' he said. 'Are you afraid of me?'

'Certainly not!'

'Then perhaps you ought to be.'

She gasped and turned to look at him. 'Why?'

He smiled. She was an innocent. 'No, you are right.

You have nothing to fear from me. I am not in the habit of abduction and I would be a fool to molest a schoolgirl, however pretty and desirable.'

'Sir, you are impertinent. And I am nothing of the sort.'

'Not a schoolgirl, or not pretty and desirable? The first I can only guess at, the other I can certainly vouch for.'

She did not answer, knowing that she should never have entered into conversation with him in the first place. Was he flirting with her?

'Am I to assume you are running away from home?'

She remained silent and was disconcerted when he laughed. 'Your silence is more eloquent than any reply. Why are you running away?'

'I am not running away. I am going to visit Sir George Lampeter in Brook Street,' she said, deciding that mentioning Edward's father might add more respectability to her errand.

'Sir George, eh? He with the handsome son? You are surely not eloping? I must say, it is less than gallant of the gentleman to expect you to call for him. I had always thought it usual for lovesick swains to climb ladders to bedroom windows to rescue those they love from wicked stepmothers.'

She turned to him in surprise. 'What do you know of it?'

So, that was the way of it. He assumed a serious expression; it would not do to laugh at her. 'Nothing, nothing at all, my dear, I was just teasing.'

'Then I beg of you to desist. I am not eloping. It is my uncle's wish that I should marry Edward Lampeter.'

'Your uncle's wish?'

'My guardian.'

'And you and you uncle have crossed swords over it?'

'You could say that. On the other hand, it is none of your business.'

'My, we are sharp, are we not? And so early in the morning too. Have you no liking for Mr Lampeter? I am not acquainted with the gentleman but I know of him, he is personable enough. And eligible.'

'I did not say I did not like him. I like him well enough.'

He sighed melodramatically, enjoying the encounter. 'Ah, then he has done something to annoy you. Stolen a kiss, perhaps?'

She felt the colour flare in her cheeks. How could he possibly know that? 'Sir, you are presumptuous.'

He chuckled. 'When a beautiful young lady is in distress, then I do presume, it would be unchivalrous not to. Tell me, if he has not upset you, why have you no wish to marry him? I assume that is what this is all about.'

'I do not love him.'

'Ah, love!' He leaned back in his seat and surveyed her, from her dark curls, tied back with a velvet ribbon because she had had no one to help her arrange them, to flushed cheeks which gave her a sort of gamine charm, from a sturdy little chin to a slim figure which was far from childish. 'He's a lucky fellow.'

'Edward?'

'No, the man who has your heart.'

'There is no one.' With cheeks flaming, she turned to look out of the window again, wishing she had never allowed herself to be drawn into conversation with him, wishing she had refused to enter the coach.

'Impossible!' He laughed. 'Young ladies are always

falling in and out of love, that is why their elders and betters have to help them make up their minds.'

'You do not understand,' she cried, before she could stop herself. 'It is not like that at all. I do not want to marry anyone.'

'Never?' he teased.

'Not until I meet the right man.'

'Then you are going to Lampeter to give him his *congé*. You know, I could almost feel sorry for him, except that it might be a blessing. In my experience, young ladies are not renowned for their steadfastness. The smallest difficulty and they fly into the boughs and stamp their pretty little feet...'

She gurgled with laughter. 'Quite a difficult accomplishment, stamping one's feet while sitting in a tree. I am sure I could never do it.'

He smiled lopsidedly. So the minx had a sense of humour, even when she was in trouble. Unless he missed his guess, she would need it if she really had run away.

'Is Lampeter expecting you at such an early hour? The house will hardly be astir.'

'No.'

'You propose to go alone and ring the front-door bell?'

'Why not?'

'Why not? My dear Miss...' He paused, still smiling. 'You did not tell me your name, but no matter, I can understand your reluctance. You will set the household on its head if you do anything so outrageous. Do you know what you are about?' He paused and turned in his seat so that he was almost facing her and his knees, clad in slim-fitting breeches and white silk stockings, brushed her skirts, sending a little frisson of alarm through her. 'But perhaps that is your intention. Perhaps you want a scandal?'

'No, of course not.'

'Then, if you would allow me, I might be able to help.'

'How?'

'I could go to the door and fetch Lampeter out of the house on some pretext or other and bring him to you. It would be better than going to him, don't you think?' He was looking at her with his head on one side and broad grin on his face.

'It is not funny!'

He assumed an expression of severity which was even more comical and Kitty, in spite of her annoyance with him, found herself smiling in response.

'That's better,' he said. 'You have a beautiful smile. I cannot think how Lampeter could fail to be moved by it. Now, will you allow me to come to your aid?'

'No.' But it was not a very firm negative.

The carriage turned into Brook Street and slowed to a halt. 'Where to exac'ly?' the driver called, leaning over so that his head was hanging upside down above the window.

'Wait,' his male passenger commanded, then, to Kitty, said, 'Well? Do you want me to fetch the lucky fellow out to you?'

'No… Yes… I don't know.' To Kitty, who had not made up her mind how she was going to make the opportunity of speaking to Edward alone, the stranger seemed the answer to her problem. But did she really wish to be indebted to him? She did not even know his name. He might be the devil himself. Come to think of it, he did look rather devilish with his dark looks, dark hair and equally dark eyes. But the eyes had a glint of gold...and would the devil wear an embroidered blue waistcoat and a mulberry suit?

'What kind of an answer is that?'

'Very well. I shall be much obliged if you would fetch Mr Lampeter here, to me. The house is the one on the far corner.'

Having told the cab driver to wait, he disappeared, leaving Kitty to contemplate her folly, a course which left her feeling more lonely and vulnerable than ever. She sighed heavily. The die had been cast and the only thing she could do was carry through her plan with all the resolve she could muster.

The wait seemed interminable, but just when she thought Edward must have refused to come, or he had perhaps not returned to London after the ball, although he had told her that was his intention, she heard the sound of footsteps and he climbed into the carriage beside her and shut the door.

'Where is...?' She did not know the dark stranger's name and surprised herself by even mentioning him, when there were more important things to be discussed.

'Gone on his way. I must say, Kitty, you do have the most extraordinary calling cards.'

'He seemed a perfectly ordinary gentleman to me.' She was conscious of the irony, even as she spoke. The man was far from ordinary.

'That waistcoat! Did you ever see such a garment? Not one to hide his light under a bushel, is he?'

'You know him?' She was sorry he had not returned; she had not thanked him properly for his trouble. But this was no time to be worrying about a stranger; she had some persuading to do.

'I've seen him at the gaming tables on occasion,' he said. 'Devilish lucky fellow, too, and known for a hard man. The ladies seem to like him, though I can't say why they should. Ain't sure he's even a gentleman. How did you come to meet him?' He looked at her, as a suspicion crossed his mind. 'He's not... Oh, Kitty, I never took you for a...' He paused, unwilling to utter the word.

'Edward! I hope you know me better than that.'

He smiled with relief. 'To be sure I do. But what are you doing here? And so early in the day? Have you been to bed?'

'No.' She turned to look at him and noticed he was still wearing the gold satin evening suit and white stockings he had worn at the ball; his fair hair was tousled and there was a distinct stubble on his chin. 'Then, no more have you.'

'And you chastise me for that! Kitty, I wonder you have the effrontery, considering where you are. Last night was bad enough—do you wish to ruin your reputation entirely?'

'Last night was your fault,' she snapped. 'And it is because of what happened last night that I had to see you today.'

'Can't it wait? I went on to White's for a few hands after the ball and have only just returned home. I'm deucedly tired.'

'You can go to bed when you've heard me out. You know my uncle is most displeased? In fact, he is furious.'

'That much I deduced at the time, but an apology to him and to your good self when he calls on me today will surely set everything to rights. He must know I meant no harm.'

'Whether you meant it or not, it has certainly been the result. He is determined to see us married.'

'Married!' He sat up with a jerk. 'That's going too far!' He leaned forward to search her face. A very pretty face, to be sure, and one he was very fond of, but... 'It's a hoax, that's what it is.'

'It is no hoax, I promise you.'

'But why? You ain't a bad-looking girl. I'd go so far as to say you were one of the handsomest, and your grandpapa is a Viscount and wealthy too, so why pick on me? You can have any of the young bloods in town this year.'

'I don't want any of them.'

'Just me?'

'Not you, either.'

'You don't?'

She laughed at the comical mixture of relief and indignation on his face. 'No, I don't. It is Uncle William's idea and he will brook no argument, possibly because if he does my stepmama will insist on him sending me to my great-aunt in Scotland.'

'No, don't believe that. You're bamming me.'

'No, I'm not. Did you know he is meeting your father this afternoon to discuss arrangements for a wedding?'

'No, by Jupiter, I did not. My father will skin me alive.'

'But he will agree with what my uncle proposes?'

'Very likely,' he said morosely. 'He has been rattling on at me to marry and settle down this past year, but I'm only twenty-one, for heaven's sake, and I want to see something of the world before I do.'

'Why didn't you do as James did? You could have gone with him.'

'James is older than me by more than a year, as you know, and he was sponsored by Viscount Beresford. I have no means to finance a protracted tour. I planned to enter the navy as the next best thing. But to be leg-shackled…' He paused, contemplating the prospect. 'I would make a terrible husband, what with drinking and gambling and staying out all night.'

'I am well aware of that, Edward. If I loved you, I might overlook it, but as I do not love you and never will, not in the way of a wife for a husband, I do not propose to saddle myself with you.'

'You are going to refuse me? Oh, you darling girl, I could kiss you all over again. In fact, I think I will.' And he reached out towards her.

She pushed him away. 'No, Edward, I do not think you should.'

'What would you have me do?'

'You need do nothing, except to act the jilted lover, if you want to. I shall not mind.'

'I say, that's coming it a bit brown, ain't it?'

'You are a nice man, Edward, and we have been friends since we were children and I used to trail after you and James. I would like to think you are still my friend.'

'Always, dear girl, always.'

'Then give me money, as much as you can manage. I want you to buy me off…' She sounded perfectly calm though, inside her blue wool gown, her heart was beating furiously.

'Buy you off?' He was visibly shaken that such a suggestion should come from a young lady who had been carefully nurtured. 'Has your uncle put you up to this?' Noticing the look of consternation on her face, he checked himself. 'No, he would not do such a thing, being a man of the cloth and an honourable one. Your stepmama, perhaps? Now, *she* might.'

She ignored this slur on Alice. 'No one put me up to

it. It was my own idea. They do not know I have left the house, though when Judith goes to my room to wake me she will see the letter I left and take it straight to my uncle. I have no doubt he will look for me, but I do not want him to find me.'

'You surely do not expect me to hide you? God in heaven, the Reverend will scalp me.'

'There is no need for you to hide me or even for my uncle to know I've been to see you. I shall be gone long enough for any scandal to die down, but I must have funds. You do understand, don't you, Edward?'

'And if I can't lay my hands on any?'

She shrugged. 'We will be condemned to a loveless marriage.'

He sighed heavily. 'Very well, I will do my best. Go home and wait for me.'

'No, I am never going home again. And I dare not go to any of my known friends because Uncle William is bound to go looking for me. I want you to take me to an hotel and book a room for me.'

'Out of the question,' he said firmly. 'Do you take me for a mountebank? You are a gentlewoman, you cannot stay in a hotel alone. Nor yet with me. We should never live it down—'

'My stepmama has already said we should never live down what happened last night either. It seems I am to live the rest of my days with my folly. I am past such considerations. Surely you know a discreet little rooming house tucked away somewhere?'

He laughed suddenly. 'You know, Kitty, you really are the most extraordinary girl. I could almost fall in love with you.'

'Well, don't,' she said crisply. 'Just do as I ask.'

'It's unthinkable you should go anywhere unaccompanied,' he said. 'Take a companion or a maid. Ask Judith. Ten to one, your stepmama will turn her off without a character.'

Kitty sighed. He was right and she had been thoughtless to leave without making provision for the servant, who had been nurse and companion to her and her mother before her. Alice would be glad of an excuse to be rid of her. 'I couldn't ask her. It would mean taking her far from home and goodness knows how many adventures we shall have.'

'Far from home,' he repeated in alarm. 'Kitty, where are you going?'

'Better you do not know.'

'Then let me fetch Judith to you.' If anyone could dissuade Kitty from her folly, it would be Judith and, to be honest, he was out of his depth and needed to hand her over to someone more competent to deal with her.

Kitty's bravado was all on the surface and the idea of having a companion on her travels grew on her. Would Judith come? 'Can you ask her without letting anyone else in the house know?'

'I will do my best.'

It was not until she was alone in a bedroom of a small, unfashionable hotel that the enormity of what she had done came to her, and she began to shake uncontrollably. And the thought of what she had yet to do almost made her turn from her resolve and rush straight back home.

But the memory of the scene with her uncle and stepmother in the small hours of the morning, and the countless pinpricks of unkindness meted out to her by Alice over the years, stiffened her spine.

She would not stay where she was not wanted and she would not marry a man she did not love, however many young ladies had done so before her and would do so in the future; if it meant loneliness and hardship, then so be it. She would endure it stoically. Quite how much hardship she was not yet to know.

Chapter Two

If he stopped to think, Edward might guess what was in her mind, Kitty thought, as she climbed into bed that night, having first taken the precaution of hooking a chair back under the door knob, but it might not come to him until it was too late. And he might remain silent, not wanting to implicate himself.

He returned the following morning just as she was finishing a frugal breakfast in her room after a sleepless night. He was accompanied by her maid. Judith Sadler was a woman of middle years, almost as round as she was tall, with reddened cheeks and small blue eyes which easily sprang tears, as they were doing now, as they embraced.

'Oh, Kitty, my love, what have you done?' she cried. 'Your uncle is silent and white-faced and your step-mama is screaming at him what an ungrateful wretch you are. They would have it that I knew aforehand what you were going to do and the mistress bade the Rev-erend beat it out of me. They could not believe I did not know where you were, nor couldn't I believe it my-self. How could you break my poor heart so?'

'I am truly sorry, Judith, but you might have stopped me—'

'For sure, I would.'

'But you came when I sent for you?'

'And why would I not? If ever you needed a body's help it is now, and who else but me could you trust?'

'No one, dear Judith,' Kitty said, looking over the grey head at Edward. 'Was it very difficult?'

He smiled, turning his hat in his hand, anxious to be gone. 'I paid a young girl to call on the rectory and say Judith was needed urgently by her sister who was ill and needed someone to look after her children until she recovered.'

'But Uncle William knows Judith has no sister.'

'Mistress didn't know it and the Rector was out,' the maid said. 'She was glad enough to let me go.'

'Thank you, Edward,' Kitty said.

'My pleasure,' he said, though he looked far from pleased.

'What about that other matter?' she asked, hoping that, in fetching Judith to her, he had not forgotten about the money.

He put a small purse of gold coins and some paper money on the table beside her empty coffee cup. 'I managed to call in a few debts and borrow some more, but I wish I knew what you were going to do. The Reverend is sure to think of me before long and then what shall I say?'

'Nothing. I have written to him again, trying to explain why I have done what I have done. I pray he will understand and forgive me. Will you see that it is delivered to him tomorrow, after mid-day?'

'Why not today?'

'Because I don't want him to stop me.'

'He will say that I should have stopped you. And he would be right. I don't like it, Kitty, not above half I don't.'

'You can have the letter delivered anonymously; he need not know you were involved at all. I told you, you can act the jilted suitor.'

'I shall look a fool.'

'No, everyone will say what a lucky escape you had.' She took his hands in both her own. 'I am truly grateful, Edward. I could not have managed without you.'

He laughed. 'Blackmail is a very strong weapon, my dear. I had no choice.'

'You had, but I am glad you did not take it.'

'Goodbye, my dear, and good luck.' He kissed her lightly on the cheek and left.

Kitty turned to Judith, who stood in the middle of the room with a small travelling bag and a basket at her feet. The poor woman looked pale and worried to death, but she was, above all else, loyal to Kitty and would follow her and look after her through thick and thin, fire and water.

'Fact is, Miss Kitty, I ain't exac'ly sorry to be leaving the rectory. Not that I would have left while you needed me—your poor dead mother asked me to look after you and look after you I will. I suppose that's why your stepmama never did take to me. She would have turned me off the minute you were married.'

'You goose, Judith, I would have taken you with me. Which is what I am doing now. You will come, won't you?'

'I couldn't have borne it if you had asked someone else to look after you.'

'You aren't going to try and tempt me to go back then?'

'Would it serve?'

'No, it would not.'

'Then I shan't waste my breath.'

'Thank you, Judith. You know I was very desolate and frightened, but now you are here, I feel so much better.'

'I took the liberty of bringing some more of your things,' Judith said. 'I thought you might be going somewhere a mite warmer.'

She heaved the basket onto the bed and opened it to reveal two lightweight gowns, one in green silk, the other blue muslin, a thin lawn petticoat, shoes and a pelisse, as well as a carriage dress in brown taffeta for travelling and a flannel petticoat to wear in the January weather then prevailing and which they would not leave behind for some days.

'What made you think that?'

'You left Master James's letter lying on your bed.'

'Did anyone else see it?'

'No, Miss Kitty, I put it in the basket and brought it with me.'

'Oh, now you are here I feel quite cheerful again, so you may take that sorrowful look off your face and smile. We are going to have some high old adventures, you and I, and we are going to enjoy them. Can you imagine James's face when he sees us?'

Judith could not. That meeting was so far in the future that even thinking about what might happen in the mean time filled her with foreboding. But she smiled and began repacking the basket and Kitty's valise.

It was four o'clock the following morning when the two women arrived in Dover after travelling in a public coach since seven the previous evening. They were cold, tired and hungry, not to mention filthy.

'We must bespeak a private room here,' Judith said, as they climbed stiffly from the carriage. 'For I declare I can't go a step further until I have washed, eaten and slept.'

Kitty, who had quite regained her spirits, laughed. 'It is less than twenty-four hours since you left home and already you are complaining.'

'I am not complaining,' Judith denied the accusation sharply. It would never do for her mistress to think she was not up to the rigours of the journey or she might be left behind. Already she had had her own way about crossing the channel by the shortest route, having a great terror of the sea.

She would rather face revolution in France than be drowned trying to sail round it, she had told Kitty. Adding that, if she were sick, how could she look after her darling? And that, she declared, was the one purpose of her life, to look after her charge and protect her from all the dangers that faced them, from lascivious sailors and Frenchmen who would chop off her head, to bad food and bed bugs.

'Very well, we will stop here for a few hours, but then we must go to the harbour and find out when the next packet is due to leave, for I mean to be on it.'

'And what story do we put about for a lady and her maid to be travelling alone without so much as a link-boy for an escort?' Judith demanded, as she picked up Kitty's luggage and followed her into the inn. 'Everyone will know at once that you are running away.'

'I am not running away. I have just lost my parents and am going to Italy to join my brother, he being the only relative I have left in the world. It is as near the truth as makes no difference.'

'Your poor uncle would not think it so.'

'No, but when we reach Calais, I shall entrust the captain of the packetboat with another letter to him, so that his mind is set at rest.'

It was Judith's opinion that a letter from the other side of the Channel was more likely to inflame the Rector's mind than set it at rest, but she did not voice it.

Picking up their luggage, Judith followed her mistress into the inn and demanded a room in a way which brooked no argument. They were soon ensconced in an upper chamber, enjoying a meal of chicken, ham, meat pie, fish and vegetables. What they could not eat they wrapped up and put in their baggage against a future need, not knowing how well provisioned the ship would be, or how difficult it might be to buy food in France. And then they lay down to sleep.

Kitty was woken three hours later by the clatter in the yard outside their window which told her another day had begun.

She padded across the floor to look out of the casement and saw, in the growing light of dawn, that a coach had just arrived from London and its passengers were alighting. There were two portly men in frieze greatcoats and buff breeches and a tall man with dark hair tied back with a black ribbon who was, at that moment, doffing his hat in goodbye to a clerical-looking gentleman and his plump lady.

At first Kitty thought it was her uncle and stepmama come to fetch her back. However, on looking closer realised this was not so, but it served to remind her of the need for haste and she quickly roused Judith; fifteen

minutes later they were out on the street and making
their way down to the harbour.

They had the hoods of their cloaks up over their
heads against the bitter, sleet-laden wind which blew
from the north-east, numbing their fingers and toes. But
it was a good wind for sailing and they hurried to the
quay where they saw a schooner preparing for sea. People were coming and going from it and the sailors were
busy on the deck. Kitty left Judith minding their baggage while she went to the ticket office and paid for
their passage, then urged the reluctant Judith up the
gangplank of the *Faery Queen*.

They were directed below decks to a small dingy
cabin which, so they were told by the crewman who
conducted them there, was usually occupied by several
ladies. 'But you have it all to yourselves,' he said, depositing their baggage on the floor. 'This not bein' the
season for travelling, so cold and wet as it is, and what
with the Frenchies as like to chop your head off as not.
If I was you I should turn right round and go ashore
ag'in.'

They could not have taken his advice even if they
had wanted to because, at that moment, there was a
great crack above their heads as the wind filled the sails
and the deck beneath their feet began to tremble.

'Oh, God be merciful, we're sinking!' Judith exclaimed, clutching at Kitty.

The sailor smiled. 'Bless you, we ain't sinking, we're
under way, as smooth as you please.' And with that he
left them to go about his duties.

'Shall we go on deck and say goodbye to England?'
Kitty suggested. 'I am sure you will feel better if you
can see what is happening.'

They returned to the deck, holding on to superstructure, posts and rigging, anything to help them keep their balance, until they were standing side by side at the rail, watching as the ship slowly made its way out of the shelter of the harbour.

'Well, well, if it isn't my little runaway.'

Kitty whirled round to face the man who had spoken, the man with whom she had shared a cab little more than forty-eight hours previously, the man she had seen getting out of a coach at the inn. She had been so intent on the clerical gentleman, she had not recognised him then.

'*You!*'

He doffed his tall hat with its narrow curly brim and executed a mannerly leg as steadily as if they had been in a London drawing room and not on a heaving deck. He was smiling. 'As you see! Jack Chiltern at your service, ma'am.'

'What are you doing here?' she demanded, unaccountably pleased to see him. He was solidly real in a shifting world; someone from England. How did he know she would be on the packet? Had she let her intentions slip when talking to him in the coach? 'Have you been following me?'

He smiled lazily. 'Why should I do that?'

'To take me back.'

'If that were so, I would surely have made a move before we set sail. I can hardly swim ashore with you. My presence on this ship is pure coincidence, I promise you.'

'Oh.' She turned from him to look at the receding coastline as the ship met the open sea and began to pitch and roll. The unexpected movement flung her towards him. He caught her and steadied her, holding her just a fraction longer than was proper before releasing her.

'But I am curious,' he went on, deliberately setting aside the pleasure her small body next to his had given him. 'Tell me, Kitty, what is so objectionable about Edward Lampeter that you cannot abide being in the same kingdom with him and must flee the country?'

She gasped. 'How do you know my name?'

'Lampeter murmured it when he required me to give a description of the person who commanded his presence so early in the morning. He said he would not stir for any little bit of muslin who might opportune him; his words, not mine, I add. It was not until he had been convinced of your identity that he agreed to go to you.' He sighed melodramatically. 'I am only sorry that it was to so little purpose.'

'What do you mean?'

'Why, that you did not come to an understanding. I should have thought a life with him would be infinitely preferable to the course you have chosen. Or perhaps he did not offer?'

'Sir, you know nothing of it but what I was so foolish as to confide in you. Pray forget it.'

'With pleasure, ma'am. I have more important things to occupy me than a madcap girl who does not seem to realise she is jumping from the frying pan into the fire.'

'Nonsense!' she said with some asperity. She did not know why she continued to converse with him, he was so arrogant and not at all civil, but he had the kind of presence you could not ignore and, if she were honest, she felt a little safer with him beside her. 'I know there is some unrest in Paris, but we mean to bypass the city—'

'You call the bloodiest deed ever to disgrace the name of France *some unrest*!' he interrupted. 'Less than a week ago, they sent their King to the guillotine. Pray, tell me where have you been hiding yourself that something which has cast a cloud over the whole of Europe should be of so little import to you? Do they not have newspapers in your part of the country?'

She was shocked by the news but quickly recovered herself. 'Naturally they do, but I rarely see them. Uncle William thinks they are not fit reading for genteel young ladies. When he spoke of it, he said it would come to nothing; a people could not depose a king and right would prevail.'

'And so you remain in blissful ignorance, which is no bad thing, except that you have taken it into your silly head to hurl yourself into the fray.'

'You overstate the case, sir. We are not hurling ourselves into anything, we intend to stay only at respectable inns and avoid trouble.'

'Easier said than done, Kitty, believe me. But tell me, where are you bound? Purely as a matter of satisfying my curiosity, you understand. Or is this simply a whim to travel without a destination?'

His condescending attitude infuriated her. 'Sir, I did not give you permission to use my given name. But, since you ask, I am going to join my brother in Italy.'

He whistled. 'Right through France? Child, you are mad. Did you not know France is also at war with Austria and half of Europe and will undoubtedly soon be in conflict with England? Do you have papers stating your business? And passports? You will need them to pass through the barriers and cross the borders.'

Before she could tell him that she lacked these requirements, Judith, who had been standing beside her growing paler and paler, was violently sick, and she turned from him to look after her maid. Taking her down to the cabin, she helped her to bed and sat beside her, bathing her brow, until she was calmer and fell asleep.

Later, longing to escape from the malodorous cabin, she returned on deck. The short day had turned to night and she stood by the rail again, breathing deeply, thankful that she appeared to be a good sailor. The sea was calmer now and, above the billowing sails, the stars made a dark pincushion of the sky. They made her think of home, of her uncle and little Johnny.

He would be missing her as she missed him: missed his giggle when she tickled him, his rapt attention when she told him a story. She prayed his mother would have patience with him and perhaps find him a loving nurse-maid. She wondered fleetingly what her grandfather, the Viscount, had made of her disappearance; undoubtedly Alice would have put it in the worst possible light.

'Beautiful, aren't they?' said a voice at her elbow.

She did not need to turn round to know who stood beside her; she recognised the voice, knew the large capable hand that grasped the rail only inches from her own, felt his tall presence overshadowing her. 'Yes, they are.'

'It is strange to think that those same stars are twinkling over the whole northern hemisphere, over France and England, rich and poor, good and evil, faithful and faithless. You would think they would be more discriminating, wouldn't you?'

'We are all God's creation,' she said, wondering at the tinge of irony she detected in his voice.

'Indeed, yes.' He stood looking down at her, seeing the glitter of tears on her lashes in the moonlight and feeling a sudden surge of compassion which he quickly stifled. 'But I believe you are already regretting your precipitous flight.'

'Not at all,' she said, as coolly as she could, though his nearness was making it almost impossible. 'I have always wanted to travel, I'm looking forward to the experience.'

'It is an experience you may learn to regret,' he said. She had courage, he would give her that, and it was courage she would need in the weeks ahead of her. If he was not so pressed for time, he might be tempted to offer to escort her, but then smiled at his own stupidity. Hadn't he learned his lesson yet? 'In those clothes, you will stand out like a beacon. The *sans-culottes* will strip you naked and worse before taking all your money and denouncing you for an aristo.'

Kitty, who considered herself very plainly dressed, looked down at the fur-lined cloak and sturdy half-boots she wore and then back up at him. In the darkness it was difficult to see his expression, but his eyes were watchful. 'What does *sans-culottes* mean?'

He grinned. 'Is your French not up to translating it? It means ''without breeches''. In other words, those who wear *pantalons* and not knee-breeches.'

She found herself blushing. Alice would never use either word and always referred to gentleman's nether garments as Inexpressibles. 'I still don't understand.'

'It is a term applied to the working classes, labourers, shopkeepers, craftsmen. Since they wield a great deal of power these days, it is advisable not to upset them. And being better dressed than they are upsets them.'

'Your puerile attempts to frighten me are wasted,' she said, determined not to let him see how nervous he had made her. 'I am an Englishwoman, not a French aristocrat, so what have I to fear? I have done no wrong and shall do none.'

He laughed suddenly. 'Oh, my eye, a genuine innocent! And you think your haughty manner will be enough to keep you safe? Rest assured, nothing could be further from the truth. Will you, for instance, know how to deal with this?' And before her startled senses could warn her what was coming, he had taken her into his arms and was kissing her.

It was nothing like the gentle kiss Edward had given her which had roused nothing in her but innocent delight at her daring. This man's mouth was hard and demanding, forcing her lips to part, engulfing her, shutting out everything else around her, the wind in the sails, the creak of the rigging, the low voices of the crew, everything except the surge of something growing and expanding deep inside her, something wild and ungovernable which took her breath away.

With one arm still about her waist, he put his other hand up to her neck, caressing it with his thumb from ear to throat, making her shudder. When his fingers found the ribbon that tied her cloak, she suddenly realised what was happening and pulled herself away.

She stood, eyes glittering, breast heaving, unable to speak, unable to think of anything except the effect that kiss had had upon her. She raised both clenched fists to him, but he simply grabbed them and held them fast.

'That was only a small taste of what you might find yourself having to endure,' he said as calmly as he could, though his own heart was pounding. He knew he ought to ask pardon, but apologising would put him in the wrong and render the lesson ineffective. 'Others would not be so careful of you.'

'Careful!' she hissed, unwilling to scream and alert

the crew to her plight. She doubted if they would come to her aid, if she did. 'I cannot think of anything more lacking in care. Do you take me for a…a…?' She could not say the word.

He released her hands. 'No, I meant only to demonstrate to you the dangers which might beset you. Talking seemed to have little effect.'

'All you have demonstrated, sir, is that you are a cur.'

She turned, intending to go down to the cabin, but suddenly realised that the coast of France, which had been a distant line on the dark horizon when she came on deck, now loomed large and she could dimly see buildings and lights and people. Even as she hesitated, the sails were furled and a rope was thrown out and they were being hauled alongside the jetty by a tugboat.

'If you had any sense,' he said, addressing her stiffened back. 'You would not disembark, but stay aboard and return to England. Better the devil you know…'

Kitty might have been tempted to take his advice, if Judith had not been so anxious to have *terra firma* under her feet again that she declared she would rather face a thousand bloodthirsty Frenchmen than spend another minute at sea. Kitty told her nothing of her latest conversation with the tall stranger—she realised she still had no idea who Jack Chiltern was—and, picking up their baggage, helped her maid up on to the deck and down the gangplank on to French soil.

The other passengers had disembarked before them and were each going their separate ways. The two women stood undecided on the quay with their bags at their feet, looking about them for a cab to convey them to a hotel for the remainder of the night. They could see no such vehicle. What they did see was the stranger, who had been striding purposefully ahead of them, stop and turn. He stood for a few seconds, watching them, then strode back.

'Damn you, woman!' he said. 'I cannot abandon you.' Kitty was so thankful to hear his voice, she forgot to reprimand him for his language, although Judith bristled with indignation and would have said something if Kitty had not laid a hand on her arm to restrain her.

'Come with me,' he went on, picking up the valise and basket. 'I'll see you safely settled in a hotel, if you can call it by that name, but more than that I will not undertake to do. I have other more pressing errands.'

'Thank you.' It went against all her inclinations to be civil to him, let alone grateful, but she had to admit she needed help and, as he was the only one to offer any, she should not be too proud to accept.

He conducted them along the street and round a corner, where he stopped in front of a building which looked more like a tavern than a hotel. Above the door the sign of a cockerel creaked in the wind. He ushered them over the threshold into a dimly lit parlour, where several people were drinking. All of them were meanly dressed, the men in pantaloons, rough collarless shirts and a garment that was somewhere between a sleeveless jacket and a waistcoat. Some also wore long overcoats.

The women were in skirts and blouses with red, white and blue shawls tied about their shoulders or waists. All wore the crimson caps of the Revolution, with their tricolour cockades pinned on the side.

'Citizen Chiltern!' The innkeeper came forward and, clasping both their escort's arms, embraced him. 'It is good to see you again, *mon vieux*. Come into the back room and you can tell me all your news.'

'I'll tell you later, Pierre, my friend,' their escort said

in fluent French, stepping aside to allow Kitty and Judith to precede him into the next room where a bright fire burned. He put down their bags. 'First, I must dispose of certain encumbrances. Can you find a room for these two?'

The man looked doubtfully at Kitty and Judith who stood uncertainly just inside the door, looking longingly at the fire. 'Jack, I'll do anything for you, you know that, but…'

'One night, then put them on a south-bound diligence in the morning and forget you ever saw them.' He pulled a purse from the capacious pocket of his greatcoat and extracted some coins which he laid on the table.

'They have passes?'

'No, they travel light.'

'Too light, *citoyen*, too light.' He looked Kitty up and down, noting the warm clothing. 'And in other ways too heavy.'

'I know, but what can I do? They have thrown themselves on my mercy…'

'And you cannot resist a pretty face, I know it. Where do you go in the morning?'

'To Paris.'

'Without them?' He nodded at the two women.

'Without them. But I would not have them molested. They need passports and papers to travel through France. An escort part of the way, if you can provide one.'

'*Mon Dieu!* You do not ask much, do you?'

Jack laughed. 'Put Gerard on to it.' And again gold coins were extracted from the purse and laid beside the others on the table.

'I shall need their names and their destination and a valid reason for travelling.'

Kitty, who had learned a little French in the school-room, had managed to follow the gist of what had been said. 'I am going to Italy to live with my brother, my parents both being dead,' she said, moving to stretch her cold hands towards the blaze. 'Is that reason enough?'

'And this one?' The man pointed a blackened finger at Judith.

'She is my maid, Judith Sadler.'

'Maid, eh?' He smiled at Judith and chucked her under the chin which made her recoil. 'No, not a maid. Citizeness, you are a free woman, free to come and go as you please.'

'Of course she is,' Kitty said, grasping the situation. 'I meant she is my friend. Yes, very definitely my friend.'

'And you, *citoyenne*, who are you?'

'Kitty Harston, plain Kitty Harston. My brother is James Harston, should you need to know that.'

'What!' The exclamation came from Jack.

She turned to look at him. The astonishment on his face was comical. 'Harston,' she repeated. 'Did Mr Lampeter not tell you that when he told you my given name?'

'No, he did not.' He sat down heavily in the nearest chair. '*Mon Dieu*! This alters everything.'

'How so?'

He ignored her and turned to the innkeeper. 'Pierre, we shall have to think again.'

'What do you mean?' Kitty demanded. 'Do you know something of my brother?'

'Shut up, woman, and let me think,' he said in English.

'Did you ever hear such ungentlemanly language?' Judith protested. 'Kitty, I cannot think what we are doing here, allowing ourselves to be bullied in this fashion. I begin to think it was a bad day when you met up with the scoundrel. I am quite sure he is doing all this on purpose to frighten us.'

'Do you know something of my brother?' Kitty asked again, thoroughly alarmed by the thunderous look on Jack Chiltern's face. 'If you do, I beg of you to tell me. He is not…not dead, is he?'

'Not that I know of, but he is certainly not in Italy.' He stood up suddenly and spoke to the innkeeper in French. 'Pierre, give the citizenesses your best room and something to eat. I will go and see when the *Faery Queen* is due to return to England. These two must be on it.'

Kitty, who had followed most of what he had said, was thoroughly alarmed. 'Mr Chiltern, I beg of you to tell me, where is my brother?'

'In Paris, ma'am. At least, he was there two weeks ago.'

'Then we go to Paris tomorrow.'

'Oh, no, we don't. If you think I am going to saddle myself with a couple of *ingénue* tourists, you are mistaken.'

'Then don't. We did not ask for your help and will continue without it.'

Pierre demanded a translation, which Jack furnished him with and which resulted in ribald laughter.

'It is not amusing, my friend,' Jack told him. 'You know how important my business is and how much in haste I am to see it done. I must either return them to

England or take them with me. Either way...' He shrugged.

'Leave it to the morning,' Pierre suggested. 'No one goes anywhere after curfew and the tocsin has long since sounded. And besides, Gerard will need time to forge the papers. Yours, too, because Jack Chiltern is no longer safe in France.'

All of which served to heighten Kitty's anxiety. She realised she knew nothing whatever about Jack Chiltern; he could be anyone, a French nobleman, an English spy, a French spy, a pirate—with his dark complexion he certainly looked piratical enough—a murderer, an adventurer who preyed on helpless women, or simply a gentleman of leisure, making the Grand Tour, just as her brother was doing.

Was that how they had met? Why had he brought her to this inn and how was it that he knew so much about forging papers? And the innkeeper and his patrons were undoubtedly revolutionaries.

Pierre went to the door and shouted for his wife and that good lady, dressed as everyone else was in rough peasant clothes, laid down her knitting and brought in a watery potato soup and some thick black bread and, after Kitty and Judith had tried to swallow some of it, conducted them upstairs to one of the rooms. There was only one bed and no fire, but Kitty was past worrying about such inconveniences. She was beginning to think Jack Chiltern had been right; she had jumped out of the frying pan into the fire.

'Perhaps we ought to go back,' she said, hurriedly taking off her gown and boots and getting beneath the blankets in her underclothes. 'But I am loathe to give him best. And if we went back, where would we go? Not home, for my stepmama would crow like a cock over our downfall and I should be sent to Scotland on the next coach going north. Or Bedlam. She is bound to say I have taken leave of my senses...'

'And who's to say she wouldn't be right?' Judith said, following Kitty's example and joining her in the bed. 'The whole escapade has been madness.'

'You did not have to come with me.'

'I know that, but where else would I go? Mrs Harston would not give me houseroom and, besides, someone must look after you, though I seem to have had little success, so far.'

'Oh, Judith, you have been a tower of strength to me. Now, tell me what you think. Honestly, mind.'

'I am sure, Miss Kitty, that I have always been honest, as you well know.' Her voice, muffled by the bed-clothes, was huffily indignant.

'Go on, then.'

'Your brother would undoubtedly give you welcome and, if the gentleman is right, and he is in Paris, why, that's not so very far to travel and we'd be on good solid ground all the way, would we not?'

Kitty laughed and hugged her. 'Very well. We will not allow ourselves to be bundled back on to that packet like so much cargo. We go to Paris.'

Jack sat before the backroom fire, his long legs thrust out before him, a mug of ale in his hand, listening to Pierre telling him the latest news of Paris. The execution of the King had resulted in popular rejoicing, as if that one act would see an end to all their problems. 'Louis Capet was more fool than traitor, I think,' Pierre said, referring to the King by his popular name. 'Who but a fool would leave incriminating documents in his apartment for all to see? And trying to flee the country, that was the height of folly.'

'He may have been a fool, my friend, but he was also a king,' Jack said. 'The people may come to regret their treatment of him. France will jump from the frying pan into the fire, just as the innocent Miss Kitty Harston has done.'

'How did you come upon her? It is not like you to dally with females when you are working.'

'It was none of my doing,' he said. 'Women are an abomination, always making demands, always interfering...'

Pierre laughed. 'A sweeping statement, *mon vieux*, and one I cannot agree with. I have no fault to find with *madame*, my wife. She has suited me well these twenty years.'

'You have been lucky.'

'So you may yet be. What of the citizeness upstairs?'

'James Harston's sister, God save me, and where is James? Right in the thick of it. They are two of a kind, that pair, impulsive, entirely without sense, but courageous. But there are times when courage is foolhardy.'

'You will send them back?'

'I certainly ought to and I ought to go with them, if only to protect them and try to mitigate the trouble they will surely find themselves in on arriving home.'

'You can't go back now, there is too much at stake.'

'That I know. I must leave as soon as the curfew is lifted.' He paused to drain his glass. 'Is Gerard here yet?'

'Yes, he is in the kitchen, eating—he is always hungry, that one—but he will join us directly. But you must decide on a new identity before he gets to work.'

'What do you suggest?'

Pierre looked thoughtful. 'The time is not far off, I think, when England and France will be at war and *les Anglais* will be even more distrusted than they are now. It is time you took your mother's nationality.' He grinned suddenly. 'But not her noble birth.'

'That poses no difficulty.'

'A farmer, perhaps. You still have that safe house just outside the city?' Jack nodded and he went on. 'If you are seen coming and going daily from the market with your cart, the men on the barriers will become used to you.'

'And my name?'

'Jacques will do, easy to remember. Follow it with… let me see…' He grinned. 'Faucon, how's that?'

'The Hawk. Yes, it will do very well.'

As he spoke a very tall man, thin as a pole, whose rags hung on him like fluttering pennants, came into the room carrying a satchel which he placed upon the table. They turned to watch as he drew out parchment, pens and inks. 'So?' he queried.

'Citizen Jacques Faucon, smallholder,' Jack said, watching him write slowly and laboriously. 'Thirty-one years old.'

'Married?'

'No.'

'Pity. A farmer needs a wife, too much to do alone and no one willing to work any more…'

Pierre looked at Jack and then nodded his head to the room over their heads. 'He has a point. A ready-made wife…'

'No,' Jack said, bluntly. 'They go home.'

'The young one seems determined to go on. You cannot make her go back.'

'I cannot make her come with me either. Nor do I want to be saddled with her.'

'It will help your disguise. Jack Chiltern always works alone. Jacques Faucon is a family man.'

'She would never agree. And what would her brother say?'

'If she is as determined to go as she says she is, it would be safer for her, too. He would understand that.'

'She is not French and, though she can make herself understood, I doubt she speaks the language well enough to pass as a native.'

'Then you once went to England and took an English wife, a foolish lapse and one you have lived to regret many times over, for she is a veritable shrew.'

Jack laughed aloud. 'I think she might enjoy playing that part, for she has no great liking for me. But what of the other one?'

'Her mother, even more of a scold.'

'It is all very well for you to jest, citizens,' Jack said, amid their laughter. 'But I am in the devil of a quandary.'

Pierre stopped laughing. 'Your work is important too, *mon ami*, and personal feelings can have no place in your life. If Providence provides you with a way to make it easier, then you should take it.'

'I wish to God I had never met her.' Even as he spoke he was aware that it was not true. Miss Kitty Harston had attracted him from the first. He admired her beauty, the way she spoke, the artless things she said, her lack of fear, even when he had kissed her. He had done it to frighten her, but instead found himself being roused to a passion he had stifled for too long. And she had not been frightened; in truth, her response had been a delight and he had felt a surge of joy, followed quickly by remorse.

She was an innocent, fragile as porcelain, almost as transparent as glass; he had spoiled something which was beautiful and should have been cherished, had crushed it with his brutality. It was for her future husband to awaken her, not the embittered man he had become.

'Too late, my friend, too late.' Pierre turned to the forger. 'Papers for the women, too.' Then, filling Jack's glass again, he added. 'I'll wager five *livres* that when it comes to it, the women will have the last word.'

'They usually do,' Jack murmured morosely.

Kitty was up at dawn, dressing in the brown taffeta travelling dress and scraping her hair into a bun before repacking their belongings and discarding fripperies. One night in France had shown her that Jack Chiltern was right, they must not stand out in the crowd. She did not fancy being mauled by any of the rough-looking patrons of the Cockerel, and it was her guess they were typical of the population as a whole. When she had finished, she woke Judith and they ate the food they had brought with them.

'Well, do we throw ourselves on Mr Chiltern's mercy this morning, or shall we manage without him?' Kitty asked.

Judith considered the question for some time, looking at Kitty speculatively. 'On the one hand, we know nothing of him. We do not even know if he is trustworthy but, on the other, he helped you without reward when you left the rectory and he seems to know where your brother is. Which weighs the heavier? It is for you to decide but, if we go with him, you must hold yourself aloof and not indulge in battles of words, for you will surely lose.'

Kitty ignored the implication that she was argumentative; she knew that only too well. 'Supposing he has already left without us?'

Judith stood up and helped Kitty on with her cloak. 'Then, child, you will be saved the decision.' She picked up the baggage and made for the door. 'Come, my love, by tomorrow or the next day, you will be with James and he will look after you.'

Kitty followed her out and they went down to the parlour, where *madame* was busy sweeping. She looked up as they approached and nodded her head towards the back room without speaking. Kitty turned and made her way there.

An unshaven Jack was sitting at the table, devouring a hunk of bread. A bottle of red wine and a full glass stood on the table in front of him. The innkeeper was sitting opposite him, watching him eat. Jack rose as soon as the women entered, but it was a Jack much changed. Now he was dressed in grubby black trousers tied about the middle with a length of rope. His shirt was of coarse linen and was topped by a ragged black coat which was so old it was turning green. He wore no hose, but half-boots worn down at the heel.

'Good morning, Miss Harston,' he greeted her. 'Did you sleep well?'

'Tolerably,' she said, unable to take her eyes off him. 'But we were so fatigued we took no note of our miserable accommodation.'

'Breakfast?' he queried, indicating the unappetising loaf and the bottle of wine.

'No, thank you, we have had our breakfast. We took the precaution of bringing food with us.'

He smiled. She was capable of thinking ahead, after all. 'A sensible precaution,' he said. 'And does your good sense extend to returning to England where you will certainly be able to eat more heartily than in this afflicted country?'

'Food is the least of my considerations, sir. I am concerned for my brother. I will not go home without him.' She paused, remembering Judith's admonishment not to have a verbal battle with him. 'I am sorry that we should be such a burden to you, Mr Chiltern, but I entreat you to allow us to accompany you to Paris. We should not be the least trouble, I promise you. And I have a little money…'

'Then hide it well,' he said, wondering if he did not like her better when she was being quarrelsome. 'And address me as Citizen Faucon, if you please.'

Kitty's eyes lit up. 'Then you will take us?'

'Damn you, woman, if you will not turn back, you give me no choice.'

'Sir, you will not swear at my darling,' Judith put in.

'I shall swear when I damn well please,' he snapped. 'And you and your mistress had better become used to it. It is not a picnic we are embarking upon.'

Kitty turned to Judith, who was about to answer back. 'Shush, Judith, remember what you said to me.'

Judith lapsed into silence, though the effort made her feel like bursting.

'You will do exactly as you are told, however uncomfortable and inconvenient, do you hear?' he went on. 'Your lives may depend upon it.'

'Of course.' Kitty thought he would make a great actor; his sense of high drama bordered on the ridiculous, but she managed to stop herself airing her opinion. Perhaps he *was* an actor; she had not thought of that, an actor who seemed not to be able to tell the difference between reality and the stage. And she and Judith were expected to play a part too. She was even more convinced of it when he turned and, picking up what looked like a bundle of rags, handed them to her. 'Put these on.'

'These rags?' Judith demanded, taking them from Kitty and shaking them out. 'Why, they are not fit for beggars.'

'And beggars cannot be choosers,' he said. 'Put them on.'

Kitty took the indignant Judith by the arm and led her upstairs again. 'It is naught but a masquerade, Judith, and we must indulge him,' she said, taking off her dress and donning the peasant costume of skirt, blouse and shawl. 'And, though they look dreadful, they are not verminous.'

'He means to humiliate us.'

'No,' she said. 'He is gruff and ill-tempered to be sure, but I do not think he would do that. I am sure it is necessary not to appear too refined.' She laughed suddenly. 'I promised you high old adventures, did I not?'

'So you did, but I doubt you ever dreamed we should go about looking like riff-raff.' She had been putting on her own costume as she spoke. 'Oh, if your poor mama could see us now.'

'If Mama had been alive, we should not be in this pinch, should we? Now, put on this cap. There is one for each of us.' She handed Judith the red Phrygian cap of the Revolution which seemed to be universal wear for both men and women in France at that time. Thus attired, they bundled up their own clothes and carried them to the lower room where Jack Chiltern was waiting for them.

Chapter Three

Jack walked round them, inspecting them carefully. 'Too clean,' he said and, reaching down to the cold hearth and rubbing his finger along the soot-laden bars, he spread a little on their faces and on the backs of their hands, ignoring Kitty's expression of distaste and Judith's protests. 'Now, let us be off. You may wear your cloaks in the carriage, but take them off and hide them under the seat if we are stopped.'

He shook hands with Pierre and, picking up a small leather valise from the floor and one of the ladies' bags into which they had crammed the clothes they had just removed, he strode from the room. Kitty followed him, head held high, while Judith picked up the basket and went after her mistress to the accompaniment of laughter from Pierre. 'Sooner you than me, my friend!' he shouted.

With the women behind him, Jack made for a battered old carriage which had certainly seen better days. It had once had a coat of arms on the door, but this had been obliterated with red paint. The paintwork on the rest of the vehicle, which had once been a glossy black, was faded and peeling. The upholstery had disappeared and all they had to sit on were slats of rough wood.

The roof had a hole in it and the windows had been replaced by only half-cured hide curtains. Kitty wasn't sure which would be worse, the smell of the skins or the cold she would have to endure if she insisted on having them removed. As for the single horse, it looked ready to drop from starvation. 'Is that the best you can manage?' she asked.

He laughed. 'Why, it is a magnificent carriage, my lady, none better in the whole country. It once belonged to a *comte*, but alas, he no longer has a need for it.' His laughter died. 'Now, get in, I have no time to waste.'

He handed them in, folded the step and shut the door, then climbed up on the seat. A moment later the poor old horse was urged into motion and the wheels began to roll.

'Merciful heaven, I shall eat this filthy cap if we arrive in Paris safely,' Judith said, as they jolted along at little more than walking pace.

'At least we have been spared Mr…Citizen Faucon's company, and we shall see something of the countryside.' She lifted the malodorous curtains so they could look out.

What they saw was devastation. The fields grew lank with weeds, the cattle looked half-starved, the buildings were crumbling and, what was worse for them, the roads were full of potholes so that they were continually being flung about. Judith rummaged in their baggage, which had been put on the opposite seat, and made cushions of some of their clothes.

'I shall be able to press them when we arrive at our lodgings in Paris,' she said, convinced that, once reunited with Master James, their nightmare would end and all would be well.

They travelled all day, stopping at wayside inns where they were thankful to stretch their legs and have something to eat and drink, though it was only thin soup, coarse bread and, at the place where they stopped for the night, one scrawny chicken between them. Only the chink of coins prevented them from having to share a bed with several other women.

Where Jack slept they had no idea, he did not say, but Kitty guessed he would probably prefer to sleep with the horse than share a room with half a dozen other men.

Jack considered the risk of showing they had money against their discomfort and decided that, until they were close to Paris, he could take it, but he made it known he despised the women for their fastidiousness. 'The bitches forget times have changed,' he grumbled to the assembled company. 'But they will know it when we get to Paris. I am escorting them to the Palais de Justice.'

'Aristos?' someone queried.

'No, not so lofty, *citoyen*. But they have been hoarding flour. Can't have that, can we?'

'Where's the flour now?'

'Distributed to the needy in their village,' Jack said, hoping no one would ask for more details.

His listeners lost interest. The women were not nobility and there was no food to be had from them. They turned their backs and continued with the conversation they had been having before the newcomers arrived.

Kitty and Judith, huddling together in a narrow bed, trying to warm each other, had long since realised that high old adventure was not what they had thought it would be. High old adventure was cold and hunger and fear, and not understanding the language, or the people, or their escort who treated them with contempt and called them bitches and refused to allow them to speak. He was a tyrant, every bit as bad as the mob who had chopped off the head of King Louis. Perhaps he was one of them.

But though Kitty told herself with increasing vehemence that she disliked him and wished heartily that they could be rid of him, she knew that they would be lost without him. Within the constrictions imposed by the situation he did try to ensure their comfort and, somehow or other, he found food for them. And, whenever the people they met became too curious, he protected them, shouldering the questioners away and ensuring they were not molested.

At dusk on the fourth evening when they could see the outlines on the city of Paris on the road ahead of them, Kitty's hopes began to rise. They immediately fell again when Jack turned off the road on to a rough track, rank with weeds and overshadowed by uncut hedges. It was so dark they had no idea where they were being taken. Terrified, they clung to each other as the carriage jolted over the ruts.

'Where is he taking us?' Judith asked. 'Does he mean to do away with us here and rob us of all our belongings? Oh, I wish we had never come. I had thought we should be in Paris tonight and instead he takes us heaven knows where.' She began to wail. 'Oh, what is to become of us? It is not the guillotine we should fear, but him. He has frightened us into believing he would help us, when all the time...'

'Oh, Judith, do be quiet,' Kitty said, wondering if her maid might be right after all. But what had the man to gain? They had nothing worth stealing and, whatever he was, she did not think he was a thief. There was more to it than that. Perhaps he was planning some devilment. Did he see her as a threat to those plans? But that was foolish; she had no reason to threaten him. And what could she do anyway?

She had put herself in his power, had begged him to help her, had willingly entered this ramshackle vehicle which was bad enough on what passed for good roads, but which now threatened to fall apart with every bump. She had truly been the architect of her own downfall but, what was worse, she had involved poor Judith.

She thought of trying to jump out and run, but Judith could not do that and Kitty would not leave her. Besides, however fast they ran, he would soon catch up with them. She sat back in her seat, trying to devise a scheme to outwit him, but none came to mind.

Fifteen minutes later, they stopped before the door of a small farmhouse, which appeared deserted. No light shone in the windows and no dogs barked. They heard their escort jump to the ground and then his footsteps as he came to the coach door and opened it. 'This is as far as we go tonight.'

'But this is not an inn,' Kitty protested, making no move to alight. 'Why did you bring us here?'

'We cannot travel after curfew, you must know that by now, and this is a safe house. No one comes here but those I know I can trust. You do understand me, I hope?'

Both women nodded.

'Good. Then get down, if you please, and follow me.' There was nothing to do but obey.

He opened the farmhouse door and ushered them inside. A minute later he had struck a flint and lit an oil lamp which cast its soft glow over what must once have been a comfortable home. There were chairs and tables, even a bookcase and a glass-fronted cupboard containing crockery. A worn carpet covered the middle of the wooden floor and there were curtains at the window. Kindling and logs had been placed in the hearth ready to make a fire and he bent down and put a light to them.

'You will soon be warm.' He moved over to the window and closed the shutters, then returned and lit another lamp from the first. 'I'll show you to your rooms.' He paused on his way to the door to look at Kitty, who stood with her eyes wide and her mouth slightly open in surprise.

She presented a strange but delightful picture. The rags she wore did nothing to diminish her beauty, or the fine lines of her figure, nor did they make her into the coarse peasant she purported to be. She was simply a gentlewoman playing at dressing up and his heart missed a beat. How could he keep her safe? How could he protect her, except by degrading her, bringing her down to the level of those with whom he was obliged to associate?

He must harden his heart, keep his mission in the forefront of his mind, and he could only do that by constantly reminding himself of Gabrielle and the vow he had made to her father to find her and bring her back. Gabrielle…

He shook himself and led the way up the carpeted stairs to the next floor where he flung open one of the doors and ushered them into a bedroom. Putting the lamp on a table by the window, he pulled the curtains closed. 'You may dress in your own clothes tonight,' he said. 'We will dine in a civilised fashion.'

Just this once, he told himself, just this once, he would relax a little, enjoy her company, encourage her to talk, even argue a little; he guessed she had an alert and intelligent mind. Tomorrow…tomorrow was another day.

When Kitty returned downstairs, clad in a rather crumpled green silk gown decorated with rosebuds and with a fine lace shawl to keep her shoulders warm, she was taken aback to see a young woman coming from the room where Jack had lit the fire.

She was dressed in a plain wool gown of a light brown colour with a starched white collar. Her hair, pushed up under a lace cap, was fair and, though she was thin, she was by no means starved. What was so pleasing was that she was spotlessly clean; cleanliness seemed to have been generally abandoned since the Revolution.

She stopped when she saw Kitty and indicated the room she had just left. 'He waits for you,' she said, speaking slowly in French in order that Kitty might understand.

'*Merci.*'

Kitty entered the room and found Jack opening a bottle of wine. He was dressed in black breeches and white silk stockings with black clocks. His shirt ruffles were pristine and he was once again wearing the blue velvet waistcoat. A dark blue coat hung over the back of a chair.

The table in the middle of the room was covered with a white cloth on which were set cutlery and glasses and a covered tureen, which she did not doubt contained the ubiquitous potato soup which might, if they were lucky, contain a few pieces of stringy meat. She guessed it had been cooked by the young woman she had seen, which indicated he had been expected.

Who was she? A servant? But as far as Kitty could tell there were no servants in France any more which, if true, must mean that a great many otherwise deserving people must be out of work. How could the Revolutionary notion of *liberté, egalité, fraternité* justify that? She would ask him over dinner; it might make for a lively debate. But was the woman his sister or his wife?

The thought that he might be married unaccountably depressed her and she pushed it from her mind and turned her attention to her host, as he lifted the lid of the tureen and a delicious aroma of chicken and leeks assailed her nostrils. 'That smells good, Mr... *monsieur*...' She floundered.

He smiled. '*Monsieur* is as bad as Mister, my dear. If you cannot put your tongue round *citoyen*—and who can blame you?—then call me Jacques.'

'I cannot call you that, we are not so well acquainted.'

'Oh, come, Kitty, we are very well acquainted and will become even more so before long...'

She drew in her breath sharply. 'If you think what I think you do, then, sir, you will be sorely disappointed. Just because you had the audacity to take me by surprise and steal a kiss, does not mean I will allow you to...to...' She stopped, unable to put her fear into words.

'You will not allow!' He threw back his head and laughed because she had misunderstood him, but decided against telling her so. It was more entertaining to leave her thinking the worst. 'How, pray, would you prevent me? Scream for help? I assure you, no one will come.'

'There is Judith.'

'Ah, the inestimable Judith. I have no doubt she would be a formidable opponent.'

'Where is she? She was not in her room. I had thought to find her here.'

'What! And have her spoil our little tête-à-tête!' He paused to look at her. Her face was a picture of bewilderment and dismay, her expressive violet eyes open wide, her lovely lips slightly parted, unknowingly inviting more ungentlemanly behaviour, like that kiss. He could not forget it.

What he had intended as a lesson to her, to demonstrate the dreadful fate which could befall her if she continued with her escapade, had been a salutary lesson to him instead. He had meant to be harsh with her, to take some of his own frustration and anger out on her, but instead he had found himself enjoying the taste of her lips, the feel of her softly curved body against his, the warmth of her. She had managed to rouse feelings in him of tenderness and compassion and a desire which had nothing to do with lustful gratification, however hard he tried to convince himself of the contrary.

'Your maid is dining in the kitchen with Lucie,' he went on, because she seemed to be struck dumb. 'They will be company for each other even if they cannot converse.' He smiled, wishing she would relax. She stood there, facing him, every muscle tense, as if waiting for a blow to fall. 'Two silent women, a rare phenomenon, to be sure.'

'It is nothing to jest about. You arranged that so that you might be alone with me.'

'Naturally, I did. Her presence would certainly put a damper on proceedings.'

'What proceedings?'

Was she really as innocent as she seemed, or was it all a ploy to disarm him? 'That depends on you.'

'Sir, I asked you to escort me to Paris because you know my brother and could take me to him, and for no other reason. If you had any notion of anything else, I must disappoint you. If you cannot behave like a gentleman, I will retire to my room.'

'Without your dinner? Are you not hungry?'

'Not so hungry that I will stay and allow you to take liberties.'

He laughed. 'Do you have the least idea what that means?'

'I know I should dislike it intensely.'

'You would not, I guarantee it.' He did not know why he was taunting her so. Was he testing her, seeing how far he could go before she was reduced to tears? He hated seeing a woman in tears; it always made him angry. He could deal with her better if he was angry. Anger was better than compassion. Compassion made you weak. Surprisingly she did not falter, neither did she attempt to leave the room.

'You are insufferably arrogant and conceited,' she said.

'Audacious, arrogant, conceited,' he said softly, changing his tactics. 'Can you find no merit in me at all?'

Unable to lie, she said nothing; she would not let him turn the tables on her and put her in the wrong. She looked from him to the door, and from the door to the table and its steaming tureen. She was very hungry.

'So be it,' he said, cheerfully abandoning his teasing.

'Let us call a truce. It will not serve for us to be forever at odds, we still have some way to go. Now, sit down and eat, it might be the last nourishing meal you have for some time.'

Reluctantly Kitty sat down, knowing she could not fight him physically. Her only recourse was to appeal to his sense of chivalry. He must surely have one, or he would not have brought them thus far without harming them, or allowing them to be harmed by others. But he made a very strange knight.

'Now,' he said, filling a plate from the tureen and putting it in front of her, 'we will stop this cat-and-mouse game and talk sensibly.'

She began picking at her food, but hunger overcame good manners and she tucked into the delicious food with every appearance of enjoyment. But she was still wary. And curious.

'Who is she?' she asked, realising he was not eating himself but was watching her with a delighted smile on his face and eyes twinkling.

'Who?'

'Lucie. I thought at first she might be your wife, but then I thought no, because she would not leave us to dine alone. A servant, perhaps. Are you allowed servants in France these days? Your friend, Pierre, did not seem to think so. Perhaps she is a relative...' She prattled on, not giving him time to answer. 'She is very pretty.'

Not nearly as beautiful as you, my dear, he thought, watching the animated face of his guest and wishing there was some way he could stop time, freeze it so that she need never change, but stay always bright and cheerful, never to know cold and hunger and brutality.

'Yes, Lucie is pretty. And good, which is more important.'

'She is your lover, then?'

He laughed and poured wine in her glass. 'She was what English people might call a serf in the old days, tied to her *seigneur*, but since the Revolution she is free to work for whom she likes, which is good in theory but does not always work in practice.'

'Are you her *seigneur*?'

'No. She chooses to work for me. I pay her wages to keep this house clean and cook for me when I am here. Does that satisfy you?'

'She doesn't wear that hateful red cap.'

'If she went into Paris, she would. As you must.'

'Do you have a wife?'

'Yes.'

'Oh.' She digested this piece of information and wondered what difference it made. None, she told herself sternly, none at all. He was going to take her into Paris and reunite her with James and then she need see him no more. She gave him a brittle smile. 'Where is she? In England?'

Her face was so expressive, the violet eyes seemed to mirror her soul and he understood her thoughts almost as if she had spoken them aloud. It gave him a *frisson* of pleasure which vanished when he thought of Gabrielle, leaving him bitter and morose. 'She is in France.'

'In Paris?'

He shrugged. 'Who knows?'

'Oh, I am so sorry,' she said. 'I have been very selfish, haven't I, burdening you with my troubles and accusing you, when all you must be thinking of is going to your wife? I have delayed you and crossed you at every turn, it is no wonder you are so down in spirits.'

'I am not down in spirits, far from it,' he said, deciding not to correct her misconception. He had never found it easy to talk of Gabrielle and the last thing he wanted was Kitty's sympathy. 'I have no reason to believe she is not safe.' He raised his glass to her. 'We will talk of other things.'

'Very well. This food is delicious, which just goes to show that France is not in such bad straits as you would have us believe.'

'It does nothing of the sort, it shows only that money can still buy a few luxuries if you know where to find them.'

'How much money?' she asked, thinking of her dwindling resources.

'A great deal, I am afraid.'

'Oh. Then how does James go on?'

'He earns his bread and wine, just as we all do.'

'You, too?'

'Yes.'

'How?'

'Better you do not ask.'

'Could I?'

'Could you what?'

'Earn my bread and wine. Edward gave me as much as he could, but it will not last very long with the prices so high here, I must find a way of earning my keep.'

'What can you do?'

'I could teach English. Or sew.'

'Hardly skills in great demand in France at the moment,' he said, smiling at her. 'Have you ever done any play-acting?'

'Of course not. Uncle William would never have allowed it.'

'Not even charades?'

'We did sometimes play charades at Christmas when Mama and Papa were alive. My stepmama does not care for the pastime. Why do you ask?'

'Because, tomorrow, I want you to act my wife for all you are worth.

'Your wife! But how can I? You are already married.'

'Jack Chiltern is married, I give you. But I am not Jack Chiltern, I am Jacques Faucon and my papers state that I am married.'

'Oh, I see,' she said slowly. 'But surely, when you are stopped, you could simply say you had left your wife at home.'

'I could, but how would that help you, my dear? You want to get into Paris, don't you?'

'Yes, of course, but to be your wife…'

'In name only, of course. The last thing I want is an emotional entanglement, I promise you.'

'No more do I,' she retorted. 'Neither do I wish to become embroiled in anything illegal or disreputable. I know nothing about you. Who are you? What are you doing in France? Are you French? You certainly speak it very fluently.'

He smiled. 'You should have asked those questions long ago, before we ever left Calais. It is too late now, don't you think?'

'I thought I could trust you.'

'Trust is a two-way thing, my dear. It must work both ways or it does not work at all. So, think carefully. Do you still trust me?'

She looked at him with her head on one side and considered the question. He *had* been arrogant and conceited, he *had* taken advantage of her naivety to kiss her, he *had* taunted her, *had* been tyrannical and would no doubt be so again but, in spite of all that, she was grateful for his help. Without it, they would never have left Calais. 'I suppose I must.'

He laughed. 'Hardly wholehearted assurance, but no matter. We go on together, eh, *ma petite*?'

'I do not seem to have much choice.'

'Then listen carefully to what I tell you.'

She put her knife and fork down and listened as he outlined his plan, a plan which filled her with trepidation but also gave her a surge of excitement, as if new doors were being opened to her, doors to new experiences, new delights, perhaps new horrors, and it was up to her which she opened.

He emphasised that he would be on hand to support and protect her, but she must follow his lead and do exactly as he said. 'There must be no faltering,' he said. 'Nor must you behave haughtily, however provoked. You must remember you are not of genteel birth—nothing will inflame the Guard more than an aristo pretending to be a peasant. And Judith is your mother, not your servant, is that clear?'

'Yes, yes, but my French is not very good.'

'That could be a problem…we shall have to admit you are English. I married you on a visit to England several years ago. You never think of it now, but cleave to France and the new administration.'

'Do you? Cleave to the new regime, I mean.'

'Jacques Faucon certainly does. He is fanatical about it.'

'But Jack Chiltern?'

'Jack Chiltern does not exist. From now on, we will never mention that name.' He stood up and held his hand out to her. 'I suggest you retire for the night. We have to be away from here by first light. I am afraid you will have to leave your baggage behind, Lucie will take care of it for you until we all come back here, God willing.' He raised her hand to his lips. 'Goodnight and *au revoir*, Miss Harston. Tomorrow I shall greet citoy-enne Faucon, *n'est-ce pas?*'

Kitty went up to her room in a daze, the feel of his lips still tingling on the back of her hand, his soft voice saying goodnight still echoing in her ears. How could he do this to her, make her feel as though she were melting away? She did not want to sleep, she wanted to savour it. But warmth, good food and wine, and the fatigue induced by five days of uncomfortable travelling overcame her and she slept soundly.

'What I want to know is what have we got ourselves into?' Judith demanded, the following morning. 'I never thought I should have to dress in rags and pretend to be your mother while you passed yourself off as that…that charlatan's wife. How could you agree? How could you think I would agree?'

'If you don't want to come, you could stay here with Lucie…'

'No, I could not!' Judith rounded on her. 'If you think I would be so unmindful of my duty, you are mistaken. I came on this jaunt to look after you, and look after you I will.'

She had been dressing in her ragged costume while she spoke, but she was doing it slowly, lacking enthu-siasm for the adventure, unlike Kitty. She set the red cap on her grey curls and, looking in the mirror over Kitty's shoulder, grimaced with distaste. 'We know nothing of him. We have no idea what manner of man he is…'

Kitty looked up and faced the worried reflection in the glass. 'Then how do you know he is a charlatan?'

'He dined with you alone. If Lucie had not insisted you were perfectly safe and looked as though she might hit me over the head with a skillet if I insisted, I should have burst in to rescue you. I wish I had now. Your good reputation will be in shreds.'

Kitty laughed. 'Oh, Judith, I no longer have a good reputation, surely you must know that?'

'But to act his wife? What will you do when…' she gulped '…when the time comes to retire? You cannot possibly share a room with him.'

'Long before then we shall be with James. He will take care of us. It is only so that we may pass safely through the barriers.'

Kitty, who had finished dressing, was surveying the results in the mirror. It was not realistic enough. She lacked the haggard look of most of the women she had come across; her eyes were still bright with untroubled youth, and her hair shone with Judith's brushing. She picked up a pair of scissors from the dressing table and hacked at her long tresses.

Judith was horrified. 'Kitty! What are you doing?'

'Cutting my hair. Have you not noticed that nearly all the women here have short hair? I suppose it is easier to keep free from vermin.'

'Ugh! But I suppose you are right. Here, give me the scissors.'

Kitty handed them over and sat patiently while her long hair was cut short and watched in surprise as it sprang into tight little curls. 'Why, I do believe I like it,' she said, setting the red cap on top. 'Now for the eyes.'

A finger run along the chimney produced enough blacking to smudge her eyes with fatigue, and with the addition of a line or two across her brow, served to make her look older and more careworn. She stood up and slouched slowly across the room, her shoulders drooping. 'How's that?'

'It will serve, though I cannot say I approve.'

'You must do the same.'

Judith was too plump to look haggard, so Kitty contented herself with pulling her hair out of its neat coil and making it stand out round the cap, then blacking one or two of her teeth, which produced loud protests from her maid. 'You are making me look an old hag.'

'Exactly. We cannot afford pride, Judith, which is why I agreed to Mr Chil—' She stopped and corrected herself. 'Jacques' plan. Come on, he will be waiting.'

Outside the front door, they found the old horse harnessed to a farmcart loaded with cabbages, most of which were rotten and gave off a very unpleasant smell. Jacques, once more in ragged trousers and a well-worn greatcoat, thick with grease, was busy burrowing in the produce, hiding his leather bag.

When it was done, he stood and looked at them, surveying them from head to toe, then laughed. 'Very good, my dears, though I fancy you are too well shod. But no matter, a farmer can buy his wife a new pair of boots now and again. Rub them in the mud to make them look more worn and get on the seat. The sun will be up soon and we must join the line at the barrier.'

Lucie came from the house, carrying two small blankets which she handed to Judith. 'To keep out the cold,' she said. *'Au revoir, madame, ma'amselle.'* She turned to Jack. '*Bon chance, monsieur.*' Her grey eyes spoke more than her words; there was in them a look of un-alloyed adoration.

He pulled her to him and kissed her on each cheek. 'Go home to your *maman* until I send you word I need you, *ma chérie.*'

He jumped up beside Kitty and the cart rumbled off along the lane they had traversed the night before. Rain mixed with sleet whipped against their faces and, in spite of Lucie's blankets and the fact that both wore two or three petticoats beneath their rags, their fingers and toes were soon frozen, but they knew it would be useless to protest, nothing could be done about it.

Jack himself seemed impervious to the weather; he was becoming more and more morose, hunching his chin into his coat collar. He appeared to shrink, to grow older and craggier before their eyes, until he hardly seemed the same upright, muscular man who had brought them from Calais. He did not speak. His un-gloved hands, raw with cold, maintained their steady grip on the reins as the old horse plodded on with its burden.

A few minutes later they pulled out on the main road and jolted towards the distant huddle of buildings and spires which Kitty assumed was Paris. Gradually the roads became busier as other carts joined in a procession. There were walkers, too, women and children, carrying produce in baskets. They were poorly clad and looked down at the ground as they walked, as if they had nothing to look forward to. Was this what the great Revolution had done to the people of France? They were the ones who had jumped from the frying pan into the fire.

The line of carts came to a halt as the woods and

fields gave way to a few sparse buildings. 'The *barrière* of Saint-Denis,' Jack murmured, as they stopped. 'Now is the testing time.'

It took half an hour to reach the front of the queue; by then, Kitty was taut with nerves, as she watched some people being let through and others, whose papers, or perhaps only their looks, had been unsatisfactory and they were dragged off to be interrogated.

'Papers, citizen,' one of the guards demanded, holding a grubby hand up to Jack, who silently groped in his pocket and handed over the forged documents. While the guard perused them, his companion walked all round the cart, then stopped to stare up at Kitty.

Kitty looked dully back at him, trying not to let him see she was trembling. She pulled the blanket closer round her and stole a sideways glance at Jack. He seemed totally relaxed although the guard was taking an inordinate time to examine their papers.

'What have you got in the cart?' said the one who was staring at Kitty.

'Potatoes and cabbages,' Jack answered for her.

'Anything else?'

'No.'

The guard moved to the rear of the cart and began throwing the produce out. Kitty was afraid he would soon discover the case. Something must be done or they were lost. She pushed Jack's shoulder and began shouting at him in lamentable French, calling him a pig and a dog and beating her fists against his body, grunting with the effort.

For a second he did nothing, then he turned and cuffed her back, shouting even louder to drown her voice. It brought the guard back to their side.

'The citizeness is a handful, old fellow. Can't you shut her up?'

'Would that I could,' he said, trying to grapple with Kitty's flailing arms. 'Why, this is nothing to what she gives me at home. Grumble, grumble, all day long; I have not done this, I have neglected to do that. I don't know why I didn't leave her behind.'

The first guard had stopped looking at their papers and was standing watching them with a broad grin on his face as Kitty rained blows on Jack. He retaliated by slapping her face, an action which was as sudden as it was unexpected and silenced her.

'What is she complaining of?' the guard asked, while Kitty put her hand up to her cheek and pushed Judith away when she attempted to comfort her.

'Say nothing,' she hissed.

'She complains of the cold, as if I could do anything about the weather.'

The man looked at Judith. 'That one is quiet.'

Jack laughed. 'Being well-padded she does not feel the cold. And she knows better than to hold up the National Guard when they are only doing their duty.'

'Are you going to stand there talking all day?' someone shouted from the cart behind them. 'We've got work to do, even if you haven't.'

'On you go,' the guard said, returning their papers. 'And if you take my advice, citizen, you'll leave the shrew behind tomorrow.'

'I might do that,' Jack called, as the barrier was lifted and they rumbled slowly into the city down the rue Saint-Denis, once a wide street of fine houses, but now looking decidedly dilapidated.

It was several minutes before anyone spoke and then

it was Jack. 'What was all that about?' he demanded of Kitty.

'Charades, you said, act the part.'

'I didn't tell you to bring the whole National Guard down on our heads.'

She grinned. 'No, but I stopped them finding your case, didn't I?'

'What makes you think that it was important enough to take such a terrible risk?'

'You hid it, didn't you? And though it is a matter of indifference to me whether you are arrested or not, I did not want it discovered before we found James.'

He threw back his head and bellowed with laughter. 'Oh, my, you'll be the death of me,' he said, wiping his eyes.

'You ungrateful boor,' she protested. 'You pummel me black and blue and slap my face and then have the gall to laugh. That is the last time I shall try and help you.'

'Good,' he said. 'Your help could have us all guillotined. From now on, remain silent and do nothing.'

She was still smarting, both literally and figuratively, and she would not give him the satisfaction of cowing her. 'And if I don't agree?'

'Then you will be left to your own devices and sooner or later someone will start asking questions; if your answers are not entirely satisfactory, you will be arrested.'

'What would I be accused of?'

'Anything, it does not matter. It would soon be turned to an indictment as a traitor to the Republic.'

'How can I be a traitor to France when I am English?'

'A spy, then.'

'What about you?'

'Me?' He turned to look at her. Beneath the surface dirt her cheeks were pink and he regretted that slap with all his heart, but she had started the scuffle and he had been forced to make it realistic. And he had to make sure she did not repeat the experiment. 'I should deny all knowledge of you.'

'I don't believe you. The devil himself would not stoop to such an act of cowardice. You are bluffing.'

'You think so? I advise you not to call my bluff, my dear, or you might have a rude awakening.'

'Oh, Kitty,' Judith wailed. 'I never thought our position could be worse, but it is getting more dire with every minute. What are we to do?'

'Shut up, woman,' Jack said brusquely.

'Yes, Judith, do be quiet, please. We are in Mr Chiltern's hands and must trust him whether we like to or not.'

'I am not Mr Chiltern, I am Jacques Faucon, your husband. citizen of France. Please remember that.'

'All the same, you might at least acknowledge that I tried.'

'You tried,' he said laconically, staring straight ahead so that he did not have to look at her. She could melt the hardest heart and, though he pretended, he was not hard enough. She had been magnificent, beating him and screaming like any fishwife; if there really had been something of importance in that case, she would have saved the day. 'Do you think I am fool enough to conceal anything incriminating in a pile of cabbages? The case contains nothing but a bottle of brandy.'

'Is that all?'

'That is all.'

'But why hide it?'

'Something hidden is something someone wishes not

to be found. The men would have triumphed in uncovering it. A smuggled bottle of cognac confiscated is a small price to pay for being allowed to pass.'

'It was meant to be found?'

'Yes. Now we will speak of it no more.'

She obeyed, falling silent. In truth, she was already regretting her impulse to show off her acting abilities; it could easily have resulted in tragedy, if he had not been quick thinking enough to answer her blow for blow. She had deserved to have her face slapped.

The streets were busy in spite of the cold and wet. But nearly everyone was dressed poorly and wore the red cap of the Revolution. Many of the men wore black-and-grey striped trousers and coats, while the women were clad in kirtles and wool-shag blouses, with the tricolour scarf knotted round their waists. Some had blankets thrown about their shoulders. All were bare-legged and wore heavy wooden *sabots* on their feet.

'Why are there no gentlefolk?' she asked.

'Oh, there are. What you see is the fashion. Even the wealthy wear it to show they are one with the people.'

'But do they have to appear so dirty?'

'Soap is dear,' he said.

The wide road became narrower and dirtier as they made their way into the heart of the city, towards the river, but before they reached it, they turned off into an alley. It was dark and dismal, its overcrowded tenements leaning against each other, its cobbles wet and greasy, running with rotten vegetation and excrement. Judith flung her apron over her mouth and nose and Kitty did her best to quell the feeling of nausea which rose in her throat.

'Where in God's name are you taking us?'

'Be quiet.' This was a dangerous part of town and he was tense and on edge.

A few minutes later, having passed through with no more than an odd stare of curiosity, they came to the rue Saint-Antoine. 'This is where it all began,' he whispered. 'Up there is the Bastille, taken by the mob in its search for weapons and powder.'

'Surely you are not taking us there?'

'No, but this is the district of the artisan. It is here that some of the grand furniture English homes set so much store by used to be made. The demand has fallen off of late.'

'In these hovels?'

'Yes.' He pulled up outside one of them and jumped down, turning to help them alight. 'You will be safe here.'

He threw a small coin to a ragged urchin to keep an eye on the horse and cart and conducted them into a dingy hallway. An open door to their right revealed a workshop, full of lengths of wood and half-finished chair legs. The floor and benches were covered in sawdust. Two people were at work, but they hardly spared the newcomers a glance as they passed and made their way up to the next floor. Jack knocked on the first of a series of doors.

It was opened by a man of about Jack's age, wearing the universal trousers and rough wool shirt, over which was tied a large leather apron dusted with sawdust. He was a big man with tousled hair and shaggy eyebrows, also covered with sawdust. 'Jacques!' He held out his hand and Jack shook it. 'You are a day late.'

'Yes, Jean, my friend, I know, but it could not be helped. I am not alone.' He turned and beckoned the two women to come forward. 'This is Kitty and this is Judith. We need your help. May we come in?'

'Yes, of course.' The man seemed a little reluctant to Kitty, but she could hardly blame him; she was coming to understand the fear that everyone seemed to have, the need to be vigilant, to view every newcomer with suspicion until they had proved themselves. Without Jack they would not even have passed the barrier, let alone found anyone to help them.

'Kitty, this is citizen Jean Clavier and this...' He turned to a woman who had risen from a chair before the fire. She was warmly clad in a wool gown with a shawl collar and long sleeves. She wore no cap and her short curls were a rich, bright auburn. 'This is Thérèse, his wife. They are good friends of mine.'

Kitty and Judith both bent their knees and inclined their heads in greeting.

'Lord, don't do that!' Jack said. 'No one does that in France now, you will give yourselves away.' He turned to Jean. 'You see the problem I have?'

'Why are they here?' Jean growled, not liking what he saw. 'You're not smuggling aristos, are you?'

Jack laughed. 'Not out of Paris, my friend, they wanted to come in.'

'Then more fools they. And fool you are to help them. They will hinder you.'

'I know, but they have been able to be of some service to me. You see before you citizen Jacques Faucon, his wife Kitty, a shrew if ever there was one, and her mother Judith, who remains silent and eats us out of house and home, which is why she has more meat on her than either of us.'

It was as well this speech was made in French and Judith could not understand a word, except her own name. She smiled at Jean and Thérèse, while Kitty endeavoured to smother a giggle.

'You had better tell me all, *mon ami*,' Jean said, drawing Jack into an adjoining room. 'There have been developments while you have been away.'

What the two men said to each other, Kitty never knew, but it resulted in a grudgingly given agreement that she and Judith could stay there while Jack went out to try and locate James and conduct some business of his own. 'I have to go to the market and sell my produce,' he said. 'It is important to keep up appearances, and the market is a good place to hear the latest news.'

Kitty bade him *au revoir* with a grateful heart; rough-hewn he might be, bad-tempered at times and not apt to spare her maidenly blushes, nor her pride, but he was strong and fearless and, for some reason she could not fathom, his deeds belied his words when it came to caring what became of her. She really did trust him, which was why she was dismayed when he had not returned by nightfall.

Jack's non-appearance seemed to bother Jean Clavier too, for, after a frugal meal of salted herring which they all shared, he paced restlessly about the room, while his wife sat knitting by the fire, her needles clicking in the silence. A log dropped in the hearth, sending forth a shower of sparks, making Kitty jump. Jean pushed the log back with his clogged foot and stamped on the hearthrug which bore testimony to a great many sparks from previous fires; it was pitted with little black holes.

'Well, he'll not come tonight,' he said, as the tocsin sounded over the city. 'He'll not risk being out after curfew.'

His wife put down her knitting on the table at her

side and stood up. 'Come with me, *citoyennes*.' She lit
a candle with a spill from the fire, set it in a holder and
led the way out of the room and up a narrow staircase
to a room in the attic. 'You may sleep here tonight.'
She set the candle down on a chest. 'Snuff this out as
soon as you can, candles cost a fortune and we cannot
afford to waste them. Goodnight, *citoyennes*.' With that
she left, shutting the door behind her.

'She's not exactly welcoming, is she?' Judith said,
surveying the narrow bed, tucked under the sloping roof
and wondering about bugs.

'I expect she is afraid. She sees us as dangerous and
she expected Jack to come back for us long ago.'

'Where is he, do you think?' Judith asked, as the
hours ticked by and neither could sleep.

Kitty sighed. 'I wish I knew, Judith, I wish I knew.'

Chapter Four

Jack was sitting in the back room of a café in the Palais Royal, gambling with as evil-looking a bunch of cutthroats as anyone would wish to meet. They had all been drinking heavily on thin red wine, laced with cognac from the bottle Jack had brought with him. Kitty had saved it from the guard at the *barrière* and he was putting it to good use.

The Palais Royal belonged to the duc d'Orléans, who had converted the ground floor into a colonnade of shops, clubs and cafés. Even though it was near the noisy market of Les Halles, the once-quiet precincts had become popular with idle Parisians for gambling.

The upper classes dared no longer show their faces, but gambling still went on there, and that led to other things: plots, counter-plots, rumours of plots. Here agitators and journalists congregated, talking sedition, writing posters, printing pamphlets and exchanging gossip. It was said that the Revolution had started here in 1789.

Over three years had passed since then and though the Legislative Assembly had tried to govern the country on behalf of the people, nothing much had changed;

prices of bread, soap and candles were still exorbitant
and taxes as crippling as they had been before. Now the
government called itself the National Convention, but
stability was as far away as ever and everyone was angry and afraid.

What could a government prepared to execute a king
be capable of doing? Mere nobles had no chance at all
unless, like the duc d'Orléans, they embraced the new
regime. They were arraigned, found guilty and executed, all in the space of a day or two, but still more
were crammed into the prisons. Jack, who could find
no sign of young Harston, was beginning to wonder if
he were one of their number.

He was acutely aware that Kitty and Judith were
waiting for him, but what he would do if he did not
find James he had no idea. Take them back to Lucie
and hope they would be safe? He certainly could not
go back to England with his mission unaccomplished.
Drat the women!

He had spent some time in the market, selling cabbages and asking questions, but had learned nothing except that France had, while they had been on the road
from Calais, declared war on Britain and Englishmen
were certainly not safe in Paris. James, who loved to
play dangerous games, would not have let that stop him.
He had told Jack he meant to infiltrate the meetings of
the *Enragés*, an extreme revolutionary party, and find
out what they were up to.

'Our Government will pay handsomely for such information,' he had said. 'I will prove I can be of use to
them and that will persuade them to give me other as-
signments. If you go to Horse Guards when you arrive
in London, tell them that.'

Jack, who had been given instructions by the War

Department to stop James from acting the fool and pack him off home, had been sitting at the gaming table most of the night, steadily losing money, hoping to hear news of the young man. The men he played with were *Enragés*, but obtaining information from them was hard work and time consuming, especially as he could not ask them outright.

'Sugar and soap doubled in price,' one of them said, in an interval in the play. 'Coffee up to forty *sous* a pound, candles twenty. The people will not stand for it. It is all a plot to bring us to our knees and restore the aristos.'

'What are you going to do about it, then?' Jack growled, shuffling the cards before dealing.

'Put the food stores in the hands of the people, control the prices, punish hoarders and speculators.'

'Very commendable,' Jack commented drily, dealing expertly. 'But how will you keep law and order? More trials, more people imprisoned? Aren't the prisons overflowing already?'

'Who needs prisons when we have Madame Guillotine?' another said, running a thin finger across his throat.

'And you think that will satisfy the people?'

'No, how can it?' the first man said. 'The lust for blood is insatiable. There are traitors behind every door and even those who are hailed as patriots today will be traitors tomorrow, you mark my words.'

His words were chilling, but Jack recognised the truth of what he was saying. 'But what of the war? How can we hope to defeat *les Anglais* if we are continually watching our backs?'

'*Les Anglais* will defeat themselves. The Revolution

will spread to England and King George will soon know what it is like to bow to the will of the people.'

Jack had to tread carefully now. 'How do you know this?'

'From an Englishman.' He paused to lay a card, while Jack held his breath. 'Young puppy full of fire, hates all aristos, even English ones. He told us all it needs is the spark to ignite it.'

'Where is he now?'

The man shrugged 'Who knows? Gone to light the spark, perhaps. I haven't seen him this last week. We have enough to do looking after our own. Until we are rid of all the aristos, we shall not rest. The Austrian whore must follow her husband to eternity, along with the bastards she has spawned.'

'When will that be, do you suppose?'

'Soon.' He looked closely at Jack. 'What interest do you have in the widow Capet?'

'None at all.' He paused, knowing it was risky to go on, but remembering his promise to his father-in-law, he decided to risk it. 'My interest is in the *ci-devant* comte de Malincourt,' he went on, fingering the handle of a wicked-looking knife he had stuck in his belt. 'I have a score to settle with him.'

'Him!' Another of the four broke in, contempt in his voice. 'He fled with his family to England, in 'eighty-nine, cowards and traitors all of them. I spit on them.' And he spat on the floor at his side before taking another mouthful of wine from the glass at his elbow.

'His daughter married an Englishman, so I heard,' the fourth man put in, then laughed. 'Cuckolded him with a citizen from the French Embassy in London, who brought her back to Paris.'

'That so?' Jack asked lazily. 'Where are they now?'

'Why do you want to know?'

'If the father has escaped, then the daughter will do.'

'I hate to disappoint you, *mon vieux*, but Madame Guillotine got there before you.'

'She's dead?' For a split second he let his shock and horror show, but quickly took control of himself. '*Mon Dieu*, and I had been looking forward to doing the job myself. How did it happen?'

'The diplomat had ambition, he wanted to join the élite of the Jacobin Club. The price was the lady's head. He paid it gladly.' He looked down at the card Jack had just discarded. 'Fool! Why throw away your best trump? Anyone would think you felt sorry for the bitch.'

Jack pulled himself together to answer him. 'No, it's one less Malincourt in the world.' But he felt sick. Gabrielle, the beautiful, the enticing, the siren, his faithless wife, was dead. She had been taken from prison in a tumbril to the Place de la Révolution where, surrounded by a howling mob, her lovely head had been severed from her body. No woman deserved that fate, whatever she had done.

The game ended and the winner scooped up the pot, just as the tocsin sounded the lifting of the curfew. Jack pushed back his chair and stood up. 'I must go to my work.'

'What work is that, citizen?'

'Clerk to citizen Blanchard, the brewer.'

They laughed. 'A good job, citizen. You should hang on to it. Bring a few extra bottles with you tonight.'

He said he would, though he doubted he would see them again. He had to find James Harston and the sooner the better. Life for an Englishman—or an Englishwoman—in France was set to become very uncomfortable; the sooner James took his sister home to England, the better. He told himself that he would be well rid of the pair of them.

By the morning of the third day Kitty was beginning to despair and Madame Clavier was growing more and more tetchy. On one occasion Kitty heard her telling her husband they should turn the Englishwomen out before they themselves were denounced for harbouring them. To give him his due, Jean had turned on her angrily, saying Jack was his friend, a brave and honourable man who had important work to do, and he would not turn his back on him. But even he had sounded worried.

'I think we are a burden to them,' Kitty said, when Judith remarked once again that *madame* was lacking in hospitality. 'It is clear they are very poor.'

They were dressing in their garret room, which was so cold the inside of the windows was patterned with frost and there was a layer of ice on the jug of water which stood on the table beneath it. 'Offer them money, then, for I am heartily sick of fish and vegetable soup.'

'If Mr Chiltern is not back by mid-day today, I shall assume he is not coming and we will leave.'

'You think he has abandoned us?'

'*Madame* thinks so and he did threaten it.'

Judith stared at her. 'But do *you* think it?'

Kitty sighed. She had done nothing but find fault with the man ever since she had met him, but until he had left them, she had not appreciated how much he had done for them, much of it to his own inconvenience. Now, she wished she had showed herself more grateful. Without him to make decisions, to tell her what to do, she felt lost.

And deep down inside her, so deep she refused to acknowledge it, was the memory of that kiss. Had she really reacted so warmly? What must he have thought of her? No wonder he treated her with so much contempt; she deserved it. But she wanted him back. She wanted him back for all sorts of reasons she dare not analyse.

'I don't know what to think, but I cannot just sit here and do nothing,' she said. 'Perhaps he has been taken into custody for having forged papers, perhaps he has been waylaid by cut-throats and thrown in the river, perhaps something terrible has happened to James and…'

'And perhaps you have a lively imagination, miss.'

'What would you have us do?'

'Me? Why ask me?' the maid said huffily. 'You did not ask my opinion before you left home, or I might have given it. You chose to trust a complete stranger, who is most decidedly not a gentleman, so what can I say? You must do as you please.'

'Oh, Judith, please don't let us quarrel, we have troubles enough without that.'

Judith softened. 'I am sorry, my love. It is all this waiting about and idleness. I never could abide being idle. But if we leave, where could we go?'

'To the British Embassy. They must know the whereabouts of all English people in Paris.'

They sat in their room in the cold rather than get under Madame Clavier's feet, but they went down in the middle of the day and were given a bowl of soup made of fish bones and onions, which was so thin it had little nourishment.

Afterwards they offered Jean money and told him

they were leaving. He protested they should wait a little longer for Jack, but his wife contradicted him.

'He must have been discovered,' she said. 'He's in prison or dead. And we shall be next if we give shelter to France's enemies. Let them go.'

It looked as if there might be a serious falling out between husband and wife which Kitty solved by putting a gold sovereign on the table and leaving, followed by Judith. Once outside, Kitty hesitated, wondering which way to go, then decided to walk towards the centre of the city, where they would be able to ask directions.

The noisome alleys were busy and they walked close together to avoid being separated. Bands of women were flocking along the streets, shrieking obscenities and carrying bags of flour and sugar. Some were armed with pikes and knives; a few had muskets. Nervously Kitty and Judith pressed themselves against the wall to allow them to pass.

'I never saw such a bloodthirsty lot,' Judith said after the women had passed on. 'Where are they going with all that stuff? Do you suppose they've looted it?'

'Perhaps, but it need not concern us,' Kitty said, anxious to be away from what was obviously a very unsavoury area and to find somewhere more wholesome. 'Let's hurry.'

But there was no escaping the rioting women. They were everywhere, dashing into shops and coming out loaded with food, shouting, *'Vive la République!'* as if that justified what they were doing. Kitty and Judith, trying to make a way through the crowds, found themselves carried along with the tide.

'Please let me pass,' Kitty said, pushing against the shoulders of one woman who barred her way.

The woman's answer was to knock her to the ground, so that she was almost trampled underfoot.

'Have a care!' Judith shouted, wading in to push aside the women who surrounded her mistress. 'Let my lady up. You will trample her to death.'

'What do you say?' another shrieked, stopping in her tracks. 'What language is that?'

Judith did not understand, so she ignored the harridan and bent over Kitty to help her to her feet, revealing the hem of a warm flannel petticoat beneath her peasant kirtle.

'*Mon Dieu*, what have we here?' the woman cried, lifting Judith's skirt and flinging it over her head. 'Look at this! Petticoats and drawers!' And with that she kicked Judith's backside, toppling her face down into the mud, amid raucous laughter.

'And this!' another said, pulling Kitty to her feet and subjecting her to the same treatment. 'Two petticoats, one flannel and one fine cotton trimmed with lace. And look here, a corset! *Citoyennes*, I do believe we have found ourselves a couple of aristos.'

All this was spoken idiomatically and very quickly, so that Kitty's French was unequal to the task of translation, but she did recognise the word 'aristos'.

'No,' she said in halting French. 'We are not aristocrats, but ordinary British citizens.'

'*Anglais!*' One of the women spat at them. 'Enemies of the Republic. Enemies of France. *À la lanterne!*'

The women seemed to have forgotten their original purpose and abandoned the flour and sugar. They grabbed Kitty and Judith and forced them to march with them, shouting, '*À la lanterne!*'

Kitty struggled in vain and Judith's invective against the heathen scum, as she called them, along with other names Kitty was shocked to hear, only served to inflame the mob even more and Kitty was obliged to tell her to be quiet.

At regular intervals all along the banks of the Seine, facing the Palais de Justice, there were posts erected to hold street lamps, but it was clear they were used as instruments of execution, for many of them held dangling corpses. Kitty was sickened by them and terrified when she realised that the women meant to add her and Judith to their number.

'No! No!' she screamed, trying vainly to break free. 'We have done no wrong.'

Somehow Judith threw off her captors and hurled herself at those who held Kitty. 'You let her go! Let my darling go, you imbeciles!' The last word was easily translated which increased the women's fury; several of them flung themselves at Judith, holding her while others found a rope. In front of Kitty's horrified eyes, they fashioned a noose and put it over Judith's head, then flung the rope over the projecting arm of the lamp post and hauled the struggling woman to the top, screaming with triumphant laughter. *'Voyons l'aristos! Crache donc sur l'aristo.'* And, suiting action to words, they spat on the hem of Judith's skirt as it passed them at face level.

'Oh, God have mercy!' Kitty cried, as others grabbed her and marched her, stumbling, to the next lamp, leaving Judith's still-twitching body swinging in the breeze.

'No! No! No!' Kitty screamed as they slipped a second rope over her head.

'Wait, *citoyennes*,' one of them said. 'Let us not spoil those beautiful petticoats.'

In seconds Kitty's clothes had been stripped from her, leaving her in nothing but a shift. She felt the rope

tighten about her neck as they began to haul on it. The
breath was forced from her body and blessed darkness
closed in on her.

The women who crowded the streets impeded Jack's
progress. He encountered them everywhere he went: the
Palais Royal, the Palais de Justice, the Tuileries, scene
of so much destruction and bloodshed when the King
was arrested, along the rue Saint-Antoine to the Arsenal
and in every connecting road. It was clear that this was
what his fellow card-players had predicted, probably in-
cited.

It would be foolhardy to continue his search for
James; it was more important to return to Kitty and
Judith and ensure their safety. He was thankful that at
the moment the rioting women were only interested in
food shops, but it would not be long before they began
systematically raiding other premises and the wood-
workers might easily be next. If the ladies were found
on Pierre's property, then his life would also be forfeit.

But when he arrived, he was shocked to learn the
English women had left. Pierre told him he had tried to
detain them, but they insisted.

'Where have they gone?'

Pierre shrugged. 'I heard the young one say something about the British Embassy.'

'Didn't you tell them we are at war? That makes them
enemy aliens. You should have made them stay.'

'And lost our own heads for our pains?' Madame
Clavier put in. 'No, citizen, and though we do not condone the killing of a king, it is done now, and we are
loyal citizens of France.'

'Yes, I beg your pardon,' he said, realising his anger
was unjustified. They had helped him only so long as

they thought his first consideration was for France and the French people, but now France and Britain were at war, he could no longer rely on their support. He did not blame them, but it did mean the sooner Kitty and Judith left Paris, the better.

'Jean, I will go now, but make sure you have no evidence for anyone to find. You understand me?'

'Yes, rest easy, there is nothing to find except this.' He held out the sovereign. 'The young one left it as payment for their board. Gold it may be, but I dare not spend it. Take it, I do not want it.'

Jack delved in his overcoat pocket and extracted a small leather bag. From this he selected two *louis d'or* which he dropped into Jean's palm. 'Two for one, is that fair?'

'Thank you.' He took Jack's hand and held it in a firm grip. '*Bon chance, mon ami.*'

Jack clattered down the stairs and out into the street. Resisting the temptation to run, he strode purposefully down the street, passing knots of women on the way. '*Vive la République!*' they shouted at him.

Laughing, he answered them and passed on his way unmolested, but his thoughts were not on the women, but on Kitty. What had become of her? If she found the British Embassy closed because of the declaration of war, what would she do? Look for her brother? But James was not to be found and Jack feared he might have been arrested. The same fate might well fall to Kitty and her maid.

There were a dozen overcrowded and ill-documented prisons in Paris and anyone could easily be locked up and never heard of again. Or guillotined. The shock and revulsion he had felt on learning of Gabrielle's fate rolled over him once again and he realised he was not as hard-hearted as he liked people to believe, and if, through his negligence and uncaring attitude, Kitty also died, then he would be twice damned.

He had taught himself to smother his emotions, believing them to be a sign of weakness, especially since Gabrielle had taken all the love he had lavished on her and thrown it in his face. He had sworn never to allow another human being to rule his heart, but now he was forced to admit he did have a heart and one that could feel pain and tenderness. And, if that were so, what else could it feel?

He began to run, pounding the slippery street, unmindful of the strident yelling of a band of women, who congregated along the Quai de la Mégisserie opposite the Palais de Justice. He had almost passed them when a glimpse of white lace carried on the top of a pike caught his eye. White lace was not the usual material used for their banners and he paused to look. It was then he heard a voice screaming in English. 'No! No! No!'

He turned and dashed into their midst, just in time to see Kitty, almost naked, hoisted to the top of the lamp post. For one terrible second he stood still, staring up at her, feeling sick and hating himself for bringing her to this. Then the need for action forced him to his senses and pushed his way forward, grabbing the rope from the women who had not yet tied it off. 'What are you doing, citoyennes?' he demanded. 'What has this woman done?'

'She is an enemy of the Republic. *Une Anglaise* and an aristo.'

He knew he could not fight them off and must persuade them to let him have her body. And quickly. Already Kitty's face was blue and though he tried to let her down, the women were pulling against him. 'No, she is a poor misguided simpleton, whom I have the misfortune to have married.'

'Are you rich enough to clothe her in lace?'

'No, as you see, I am a humble farm labourer.'

'Then where did she get this?' One of the women waved a petticoat under his nose.

In the last two or three years he had learned to think fast and if there was any hesitation in his answer it did not show. 'She stole that from the home of our former *seigneur* after he and his wife were arrested. Don't all women like pretty things? They took her eye and what must she do but put them on.

'I told her it would lead to her downfall. I warned her but...' He paused and shrugged, not wanting to appear in a rush, though every second was critical. 'Please, *citoyennes*, you have done what you had to do, let me have her body for burial. Fool that she was, she was my wife and I cannot bear to see her left there to be pecked by hungry birds.'

They looked from one to the other. 'Oh, you might as well have her,' their leader said, suddenly letting go of the rope so that Jack found himself almost bowled over as Kitty dropped into his arms. 'We are more interested in food. Come, *citoyennes*, to the warehouses next.'

Jack put Kitty on the ground and knelt beside her to take the rope from her neck. The knot was tight and it was some seconds, which felt like hours, before she was free of it. He breathed a sigh of relief when he saw a light pulse fluttering in her throat. He grabbed her scattered clothes and scooped her up in his arms before looking about for Judith. 'Where is her mother?'

One of the women who remained pointed along the

street and for the first time he saw the dangling body. He would have to come and fetch it later for burial, but now he had to get Kitty to a safe place where she could be revived. He started to walk away, not hurrying, not daring to, but as soon as he had turned the corner, he began to run.

'Don't die on me,' he murmured, as he ran. 'Please don't die. Oh, why did I ever bring you to this God-forsaken place? It is all my fault.'

Telling himself that he wasn't to know how much worse things had become since the King's execution, that he had expected to find James easily, that she was headstrong enough to have come without him, did nothing to ease his conscience. He had made a mess of it. He should have put her back on the packet to England, he should not have allowed the forger to sway his judgement and he should have told Jean to keep her indoors by force if necessary.

He looked down at her. She was still unconscious and there was a dreadful bruise round her neck, but she was beginning to breathe again in a ragged kind of way, gulping air. 'Oh, my love,' he said, hardly aware of the endearment. 'You are going to have a dreadful sore throat, but thank God you will live.'

A few minutes later he turned the corner into the market and ran under an archway to what had once been some stables and there, to his unbounded relief, he found his horse and cart and gently laid his burden in the back. He had thrown Lucie's blankets over the horse to keep it warm, and now he pulled them off, folded one under Kitty's head and put the other over her, adding his dirty old overcoat for extra warmth.

He had a flask under the driving seat, but he dare not try to give her anything to drink while she remained unconscious. She was breathing a little more easily and he bent to kiss her before slipping off the back of the cart and going to the driver's seat. It was not safe to stay in Paris, he could not burden any more of his contacts with his personal problems. Nor would his superiors condone it. There was too much at stake. But Kitty must be saved and there was no time to lose.

It was not just that she was another human being needing help—it was far more than that. She had taken that hard-shelled heart of his in her small hands and cracked it wide open to reveal the core of him, the need in him, the capacity for love he had stifled for so long.

How had she done it, when he had put up a solid wall against such a happening? By being herself, he realised. There was nothing half-hearted about anything she did; that business with the guards at the barriers had proved that. Tiny as she was, she had immense courage. Her laughter was full-bodied, her anger red-hot. She was infuriating sometimes, but loyal and capable of infinite tenderness. Her hatred, he guessed, could be terrible, but her love steadfast to death. He knew it and he knew also that he loved her.

'Oh, Kitty, what have you done to me?' he murmured as he picked up the reins and the cart jolted out into the market place and made its way northwards to the Porte Saint-Denis.

Kitty felt as though her throat was on fire and her body ached with every jolt of the cart. What had happened? Where was she being taken? Where was Judith? She tried to cry out, but could not. She was beset by images of women's faces, of noise and a pounding in her ears, of her feet leaving the ground. Slowly, the horror of it all came back to her. She had been hanged and now, believing her dead, they were taking her for burial. She tried once again to move, to cry out.

'You are safe,' said a disembodied voice, somewhere above her. 'Lie still. Don't try to talk.'

She knew the voice. Oh, blessed, blessed relief!

The jolting of the cart increased until she could hardly bear it. 'I'm sorry,' he said, hearing her groan and wishing he could take her pain on himself. 'We'll soon have you comfortable again.'

They stopped at last. Jack came round to the back of the cart and picked her up in his arms as if she weighed nothing at all. She tried to speak, to thank him, but could not. He carried her into the farmhouse they had left only three days before, though it seemed like a lifetime. Up the stairs they went to the room she had occupied before, where he put her gently on the bed and covered her before turning to light a candle.

'You must stay here until you have fully recovered,' he said, his voice thick with emotion. 'Then we will talk.'

He took the candle to the window and stood passing it from side to side, before setting it down and returning to sit on the side of the bed. 'Lucie will see the light from her mother's house and know that I need her. She will be here soon. Shall I fetch you a drink?'

She managed to croak 'Please', but it hurt dreadfully and she put up her hand to her throat. She could feel the ridges left by the rope and shuddered.

He took her hand away and held it in his own. 'Don't talk. I will get you a drink of water with a few drops of laudanum in it and that will help you sleep.' He raised her hand to his lips, then got up and left the room.

As soon as he had gone and she was alone, the terror returned. Every shadow caused by the flickering candle held a menace, the sound of the wind in the trees out-side the window was threatening voices. The creak of the stair was her executioner coming for her. She sat up, opening her mouth to scream, but no sound emerged. She was dumb.

And she had lost the one person she held dear, the one person who cared enough to give her life for her. Judith. Judith had tried to protect her. She had died, hadn't she? It wasn't a terrible nightmare. What had happened to her body? Had someone taken her down and buried her? Poor, poor Judith. She had not wanted to come to France but, staunchly loyal, she had been prepared to follow her mistress wherever she went, whatever mad scheme she dreamed up.

It was all her fault. All of it. Kitty flung herself face down and sobbed, thumping her pillow with a clenched fist.

'Now, that will do you no good at all,' Jack said, returning with a glass of cloudy liquid and sitting on the side of the bed to help her to drink it. 'You must stay calm.'

'Calm!' she mouthed, turning to face him. 'How can you talk of being calm? I don't feel calm. I feel angry. Angry! Angry! Angry!' With every silent word, she thumped the pillow.

'Good,' he said, grinning. 'That's more like the old Kitty. Now drink this and go to sleep. Tomorrow will be time enough to talk.'

He held the glass to her lips and she sipped it very slowly, forcing herself to swallow, but the fire in her throat made every tiny mouthful agony. He was very patient, taking the glass away from time to time so that she could recover a little, then beginning again, until it had all gone. Then he put her back on the pillows and covered her up.

'Sleep is what you need,' he said softly. 'Sleep and time to forget.' He rose to leave, but she clung to his hand and would not let it go. He smiled. 'Very well, I will stay.'

He sat and held her hand until her even breathing told him she had fallen asleep but, instead of tiptoeing softly from the room, he sat on, watching her.

There was no colour in her cheeks, or even in her lips, which made the red, mauve and yellow on her neck seem more pronounced. Her expressive eyes he could not see, but he noticed the long lashes and the finely drawn brows, the smooth forehead and the mop of dark hair framing her piquant face. One hand was flung out, the other lay in his palm, like a tiny bird in its nest. She was lovely and so innocent. It was that innocence which made her so vulnerable and so trusting, that and her courageous spirit which did not take caution or discretion into account.

He must teach her not to trust; he must teach her to doubt all men, not to rely on anyone. For her own safety, he must teach her wisdom and cunning and how to be deceitful, because a time might come when he could not protect her. And in doing so he would spoil her. It had happened to Gabrielle.

Oh, he had not corrupted his wife, others had. She had early learned to make demands and to turn to whomever would satisfy them. He didn't understand it, her parents were not like that. The *comte*, whom he had—God forgive him—vilified to his card-playing companions, was a good man and he loved the *comtesse* like a second mother. If it hadn't been for them, he would never have undertaken to find their wayward daughter, his wife, and embarked on his career as an agent.

As he sat watching the sleeping Kitty, his mind went back over the years and he was once again a young man. He wasn't old now, a mere thirty-one, but there had been so much pain and suffering, so many delusions shattered in that time that he felt ancient. Already there was grey in the hair at his temples.

But ten years ago he had been carefree and in love and staying with his mother's sister, Anne-Marie, and her husband, the Marquis de Saint-Gilbert, at their château above the village of Haute Saint-Gilbert just north of Lyons. Comte de Malincourt was their near neighbour and, during the course of that visit, he had been introduced to the *comte*'s daughter, Gabrielle. She had captivated him on sight and, before long, with the enthusiastic support of her parents, he had proposed and been accepted.

He had taken her home to England, to his father's estate in Wiltshire, but she hated it. It was too dull for her and she was not used to the strict etiquette prevailing in England. She, who was like an exotic butterfly, wanted to preen herself, to be the centre of attention, to go to balls and meet the top One Hundred, to flirt.

At first he had humoured her, spending more time in London than he ought, alienating his father, who told him he should be stricter with her, and upsetting his mother, whom Gabrielle made no secret of disliking. There had been constant friction. And then she had taken a lover. His hurt when he learned of it had penetrated deep into his soul, making him withdrawn and bad-tempered.

'I cannot see why you are in such a state about it,' she had said, when he confronted her. 'It is the natural thing to do. In France every man of any consequence has a mistress and every woman a lover.'

'This is not France.'

'More's the pity. If we were in Paris, we could have a gay time and see whom we pleased and no one would think anything of it. We should be accepted at court and visit Versailles and…' She had scolded on and on until, in order to try and save his marriage, he had moved to France, spending half the year at Malincourt with her parents and half the year in Paris. It made little difference. Until the Revolution.

Always one to keep abreast of current affairs, he had seen it coming, though not until the riots, which included the storming of the Bastille, was he able to persuade Gabrielle to return to England and then only because her parents had decided to flee the new regime and become part of that vast army of *emigrés*.

His father had several properties in London and one of these he leased to the *comte* and that, together with the proceeds from the gold and jewellery they had managed to bring out of France, allowed them to live in some degree of comfort. He had taken Gabrielle back to the family estate in Wiltshire, but his hopes that she would settle down to life in England were dashed when, less than two years later, she disappeared with a new lover. Jack had followed her to France and been arrested leaving his uncle's town villa.

It was while he was in prison that he learned that his wife had told the authorities he was a spy. At that time it had never entered his head to do anything of the kind. After all, he was half-French himself. It was only later, after his escape, when the Minister for War approached him, that he agreed to do what he could.

The danger excited him, made him forget his wife's

perfidy, and he believed he was doing some good, not only for England, but for France and all the oppressed people in that troubled country. He had tried to forget Gabrielle, to put her from his mind. Until yesterday in the Palais Royal, over a game of cards.

It was as if a door had closed on his past, but it had not freed him, because another had opened and he had been fool enough to enter it. He looked down at the slight form sleeping so peacefully, her hand in his, and wondered how he could harden his heart again, temper it like a blacksmith forging a shoe, when every fibre of him wanted to protect her, to see her safe, to hold her close to him, unchanged and unchanging, to love and cherish her.

But it was already too late. She had had her first taste of bestiality and man's inhumanity to man, and he did not suppose it would be her last. He bent to put his lips to her forehead as he heard a step on the stair which was followed by a light tap at the door. He got up to open it.

'Lucie, thank you for coming. *Ma'amselle* needs your help. She has had an unfortunate accident.' He stood aside and the girl hurried to the bed, gasping when she realised what had happened to Kitty.

'She will live?'

'Praise God, she will live, but she must stay here until she mends. Will you look after her?'

'Of course, *monsieur*.' She stopped to correct herself. '*Citoyen.* But where is her *maman*?'

'Dead.'

'Not…?' She looked down at Kitty's neck. 'Not that…?'

'Yes, I am afraid so. I do not know if she realises it

yet, but when she wakes, we must break it to her gently.'

'Oh, *la pauvre*! We must fetch a doctor.'

'No.' The word was almost snapped and he regretted it instantly. 'I'm sorry, Lucie, but it is obvious what has happened to her and the doctor would not treat her without informing the authorities. We cannot afford to be investigated. In truth, no one must know we are here…'

'But if she should die?'

'She will not die. She had already started to recover when I gave her a sleeping draught.' He smiled to reassure her. 'We will see how she goes tomorrow, eh?'

'Very well. I will watch over her. You must go to your own bed, you look exhausted.'

'I am. *Merci, ma petite*.' He dropped a kiss on the top of her head and went to his own room. Three days and nights with hardly any sleep had taken their toll, and he had hardly pulled off his clothes and flung himself on his bed before he was out to the world.

A weak winter sun was shining in at the window when Kitty woke. She turned her head and saw Lucie sitting in an armchair beside the bed. The light played on her blonde hair, turning it to iridescent gold; she made Kitty think of angels. 'Where am I?' she croaked.

'*Dieu soit béni!* You are awake. Do not try to talk. I will fetch *monsieur*.'

She hurried away and presently Jack came into the room. Lucie had evidently caught him in the middle of dressing for he was wearing black trousers and a rough shirt, but no neckcloth or waistcoat.

'How are you?' he said, sitting on the side of the bed.

'Sore.' It was no more than a whisper. 'I can't talk.'

He grinned. 'A silent woman, now there's a thing!'

He paused and looked closely at her, putting his hand on her brow. Thank heaven, there was no fever, her eyes were bright and there was a little more colour in her cheeks. 'You do know how lucky you are, don't you?'

'Yes, and I must thank you. If you hadn't come when you did I...' She shuddered. 'Judith...?'

His heart was wrenched with pity, but he could see no way to soften the blow. 'I am sorry I was too late to save her.'

'What...will...happen to her? Will someone take her down?'

'Yes. I will see that she is buried.'

'Those dreadful women. Like animals, screeching for blood...'

'They were hungry and their children starving.'

She was astonished. 'You condone what they did?'

'No, of course not, but they have been taught to hate the aristocracy as the cause of all their ills and hate dies hard.'

'They had no reason to hate us. I was pushed over. Judith tried to stop them trampling on me.'

'That was all?'

'They did not like our petticoats.'

'Petticoats!'

'Said they were too fine and we must be aristos.'

'You had them on under your rags?' If he had known that before they left Calais, he would have insisted on them being removed.

'Yes. We were cold without them.'

'You didn't give your name, or that of Faucon?' If his cover was blown, he must find a new identity and quickly.

'No.' She began to cough and he picked up a glass of water and held it to her lips. When she had swallowed a little she pushed his hand away. 'We said nothing.'

He scrutinised her carefully, deciding that being soft would not do, he had to make her realise her predicament or they would all be lost. 'Did you not realise that when I told you to stay with Jean, I had a very good reason for doing so and expected to be obeyed?'

'You did not come back.'

'I was detained. You should have waited.'

'Your friends did not want us, they were afraid.'

'Everyone is afraid. Now, in future, you will obey me to the letter, do you hear?'

She nodded. What else could she do? She was virtually his prisoner. All her money had been taken; she was penniless and entirely in his hands. She was not even sure that he had her welfare at heart. Had he even looked for her brother or simply gone about his own business, whatever that was?

'James…?'

'Your brother has disappeared.'

'You looked for him?'

'Of course I looked for him. Do you think I wanted to be saddled with a couple of silly women? There is nothing I wish for more than for him to take charge of you. I could find no sign of him.'

She could not believe that, after all she had been through, she was not to be reunited with James. 'Do you think he has been arrested? Or…' she gulped, feeling the rawness of her throat '…hanged?'

'I have certainly found no evidence of it. He may have sensed danger and decided to go home. I have yet to find out.'

'What must I do?'

'Nothing. You will stay here and get well. Lucie will

look after you, but you will not attempt to go out and, if anyone comes to the house, you will hide. Lucie will show you where. Is that understood?'

She nodded. She must have imagined his tenderness of the night before, dreamed that he had kissed her; there was nothing tender about him now. What was he up to, that there had to be so much secrecy? Was he a criminal? She knew he would not answer if she asked him, but he could not be all bad because he had saved her life. Why had he bothered, if she was such a burden to him?

'Good. Here is Lucie with some chicken broth for you. You must try and swallow it. I must go.'

'Go? Go where?'

He smiled. 'That's another rule. No questions. The less you know, the better. You won't always be dumb.'

He stood up and made way for Lucie to sit in his place. 'Be good until I return.' And, to Lucie, 'She is not to get up. If she attempts it, you are to tie her to the bed.'

Lucie smiled at Kitty. 'He does not mean it.'

'Oh, yes, he does,' he said. And with that he was gone.

Lucie sat by the bed and slowly spooned broth into Kitty's mouth until she had drunk nearly a whole bowlful, then she helped Kitty to lie down and tucked the bedclothes about her.

'Goodnight, *ma'amselle*,' she whispered. 'I will be in the next room, if you need me.'

Kitty watched her as she glided silently from the room and gently shut the door. She smiled as she heard the key turn in the lock; Lucie was going to make quite sure she obeyed Jack's command.

Chapter Five

During the next two weeks, Kitty mended slowly. The bruises on her neck, though fading, were still visible and she still spoke with a rasping voice, but her hurt went deeper than bruises and that would take longer to heal. And the longer she stayed inactive, the more time she had to dwell on her culpability.

Oh, if only Judith had been saved too! She missed the old servant, she missed her warm affection, even her scolding, and wished she had taken more notice of her. Judith's death was on her conscience and she would have nightmares about it for the rest of her life. She turned her head into the pillow and wept silent tears of remorse and misery. 'Forgive me, Judith, forgive me.'

Her confinement frustrated her and she longed to be able to dress and go downstairs, to go out and breathe fresh air, but Lucie would have none of it. '*Monsieur* said you must stay indoors,' she said firmly.

'He is a tyrant,' Kitty whispered, when her latest request was denied her.

'No, *ma'amselle*,' Lucie said, putting a tray containing a bowl of soup in front of her and handing her a spoon to feed herself. 'He is gentle and kind, but it is sometimes necessary for him to be firm. It is for our own good.'

'Do you always obey him?'

'Always.'

'When did you meet him? Is he your kin?'

Lucie laughed. 'Kin? No, I am far, far beneath him.'

'But you do love him.'

'*Naturellement*, I do. I owe him my life. Just as you do.'

'Tell me about it.'

'There is little to tell. I worked in the household of a *duc*, as a maid to the *duchesse*. They were ardent Royalists and were accused of taking part in the plot to help King Louis and his family flee the country. When they were arrested, the Duchess entrusted me with a letter to take to the Comte de Malincourt, a friend she thought might be able to help them. Unfortunately, I was searched on my way out of the château and arrested too.

'Citizen Faucon heard of it and he came to my trial and told the court I could not read or write and did not know the importance of what I had been given. He said I was on my way to deliver the letter to the captain of the guard, believing it to be my duty. They believed him and I was released.' She paused to make sure Kitty was swallowing the soup. 'It was very brave of him to stand up in public like that. He risked his own safety for me and I can never sufficiently repay him.'

'And now he has saved my life too,' Kitty croaked.

'Yes.'

'Why was it such a risk for him to defend you?'

'It is always a risk to cross the Public Prosecutor. It will be held against him if he is ever caught.'

'Caught doing what?'

'That I cannot tell you, *ma'amselle*.'

'Cannot or will not?'

Lucie blushed crimson. 'I have not asked him and I entreat you not to do so.' She took the tray with the empty bowl from Kitty and stood up. 'We have talked long enough and you must rest.'

The more Kitty learned about the enigmatic Jack Chiltern, the more puzzling she found him. The man Lucie had described was hardly the man she knew. The Jack Chiltern she knew hadn't a sympathetic bone in his body. He had saved her life but, even after that, when she thanked him, he had cross-questioned her, more concerned with what she might have told those dreadful women about him than about how she felt. And he had made no secret of the fact that he wanted to be rid of her. And yet, in spite of that, he had rescued her.

Lucie stayed in the house and occasionally her mother arrived with provisions and gossip, but no one else came to the farmhouse and, so far, Kitty had not had to resort to hiding behind the wood panelling under the stairs. It had no window and was cramped and airless; on the one occasion she had rehearsed going into it, she had been beset by a horror of the dark, something that had never bothered her before coming to France, and only just managed to refrain from screaming.

Jack's return, at the end of three weeks, was a great relief.

Lucie had allowed her to dress and go downstairs on her promise not to try and leave the house, a promise she gave willingly because all thoughts of trying to proceed alone had been driven from her by her terrible ordeal at the hands of the mob. It could so easily happen again. She was thankful Jack had made her leave her luggage at the farmhouse, so that she still had some clothes to wear.

As soon as he entered the room where she was struggling with the French in a book she had found on the shelf, she stood up, wanting to run into his arms, to tell him how pleased she was to see him and how much she had missed him, but she dare not. There was a moment of awkward silence while they stood and looked at each other, before she gave him a little curtsy. 'I am glad to see you back, sir.'

He smiled. It had not taken her long to forget their intimacy and become once more a cool young lady of manners. But also a very beautiful young lady in her green silk dress, which fitted her slim waist and flowed over her hips to almost cover her dainty shoes. She had allowed her hair to fall loose on her shoulders, held back from her face with combs, and had filled the neckline of her dress with a lace fichu, in order to hide her throat, but he could still see a little of the purple bruising.

He gave her a sweeping bow. 'Ma'am, your obedient. I hope I find you recovered.'

'Indeed, yes. You see, I can speak again.'

The slight huskiness in her voice enhanced it and he was tempted to tell her so, to admit that he found her enchanting, but it was a temptation he stifled. 'You will be pleased to know that I have news of your brother.'

'You have?' Her eyes lit with hope and she forgot their stiffness with each other. 'Where is he? Is he well? What did he say?'

'I have not seen or spoken to him, but I believe I know where he is.'

'Then let us go to him at once.'

He smiled at her eagerness; she was simply asking to be teased. 'Is my hospitality so lacking, my dear?'

'No, no, I did not mean...' She stopped, confused. 'You have been very kind and I am not ungrateful, but I do so want to see my brother again. It is why I came to France in the first place.'

'Is that so?' he said laconically, seating himself on the sofa beside her. 'Now, I thought it was something to do with a distaste for marriage...'

She coloured. 'I have no distaste for marriage, I did not want to marry Edward Lampeter simply because he kissed me.'

'Kisses mean nothing to you, then? Anyone may kiss you with impunity so long as they do not ask for your hand in marriage? I am relieved to hear that I shall not be expected to offer for you, after all.'

She stared at him, uncomprehending, making him laugh. 'Had you forgot so soon? Perhaps I should remind you.' He put a hand either side of her face, drawing it towards him. The temptation was almost overwhelming; her soft lips, slightly parted in surprise, were only inches from his. He smiled, tipped her head down and kissed her forehead before releasing her.

'Sir,' she said, refusing to admit, even to herself, that she had wanted him to kiss her, to experience again that extraordinary feeling of dizziness, of floating on air, of being moulded to his body as if they were one being, of hot sweet melting deep inside her. She wanted to know it if were real or she had dreamed it. But her behaviour on that occasion had not been ladylike and she did not want him to think she was always so wanton. 'I do not need reminding that you are not a gentleman and care little for a lady's sensibilities, and I should certainly refuse you should you have the impertinence to propose.'

He threw back his head and laughed aloud. 'Oh, well said, *ma petite*, but don't you think it is too late? You are already my wife, or had you forgot?' He paused and became serious. 'Citizeness Faucon.'

'Jacques Faucon does not exist, so how can he have a wife?'

'I have papers to prove he exists.'

'Forged.'

'You know that for sure, do you?'

'Of course I do. Jacques Faucon is not your name and, besides, you told me you were married.'

'How do you know what my name is? How do you know that, in these heathen times, a wife cannot be discarded as easily as a grubby cravat, that a marriage ceremony is necessary? If the Jacobins have their way, the Church will become defunct. They have already confiscated the assets of many churches and sold off their lands to the highest bidders.'

'I don't believe that. You are just trying to frighten me, to make me do as you wish.'

He sat back and surveyed her, looking from her dainty feet, up over yards of green silk and her poor bruised neck to her face and expressive violet eyes, which betrayed her bewilderment. Did she really believe he could be so callous? She might be grateful to him for saving her life, but gratitude was not love or trust. He had nothing to complain of; he had done nothing to deserve either.

'Enough of this banter,' he said brusquely. 'I am not coercing you into anything, but if you want to see your brother again, we have a long journey ahead of us and it were better you believed in Jacques Faucon.'

'Long journey?' she queried. 'He is not in Paris?'

'No, he has gone south to Lyons. We leave tomorrow. Be ready.' He paused to pick up a handful of her silk skirt and rub it between finger and thumb. 'As Citizeness Faucon.'

They set out at dawn, travelling in the old coach. Kitty, dressed in the common dress of a *sans-culottes*, sat on a cushion provided by Lucie. A rough blanket was tucked about her legs and there was a warm brick on the floor at her feet, though the balmy air was showing the first signs of spring. Her remaining clothes had been packed into her basket and were stowed away under the seat on which she sat.

'If we are stopped, do not speak,' Jack said, as he shut the door. 'I do not want a repeat of your performance at the Paris *barrière*.'

'Supposing I am asked a question?'

'Then groan. I shall say you have a contagious fever. It might be enough to make inquisitive people keep their distance.'

'How far do we have to go?'

'Three hundred miles.'

'Three hundred!' She was aghast. 'How long will that take?'

He grinned. 'At six miles an hour, you work it out.' He turned from her to make a final check of the harness. 'And don't forget the poor horse has to be rested regularly and we have to sleep.'

She stuck her head out of the window as he climbed on the driver's seat. 'Couldn't we go post chaise?'

The question seemed to afford him a great deal of amusement; he chuckled but did not answer as he flicked the reins. 'Walk on, Samson, my beauty.'

Kitty sat back on her cushion as they jolted down the lane to the road. They had hardly gone a mile when he turned off it again to avoid going through Paris.

Kitty did not want to go to Paris; she never wanted to see the place again, but three hundred miles in this bone-shaker was going to be an appalling journey and she would be black and blue after one day, let alone…how many? She shut her eyes, doing the arithmetic. How many miles a day? How many stops and for how long?

Even in March, the days were still short; they could not start out until it grew light enough for horse and driver to see or they would stumble into the huge pot-holes and ridges which were a feature of the roads. And darkness fell soon after four, earlier on an overcast day, that meant eight or nine hours, not counting rest periods and if the poor horse did not need them, she surely would. Why, they would be lucky if they made thirty miles in a day. Ten days, probably more.

No, she would not believe it; he was teasing her again. That was the trouble with him, he changed so quickly. One minute he was being brutally frank, the tyrant, the next he was the courtier, laughing and teasing her, both equally annoying. There was a third side to him, which she had glimpsed once or twice, and that was the thinker, the quiet man, the man who had sadness and pain in his eyes; the man he kept hidden beneath the veneer of the other two.

They turned off the road into a wood at mid-day and he lit a fire to warm them and heat a little soup that Lucie had packed for them. There was also half a loaf and some cold chicken wrapped in a clean cloth. The fire was welcome and Kitty huddled on the ground beside it, warming her frozen hands and toes, while the horse munched its way through a handful of hay and some mouldy carrots. An hour later Jack hitched up the horse and they set off again.

Just as Kitty was wondering if they were going to sleep under the stars, they pulled up in the courtyard of an inn. Jack jumped down and came to the door to help her alight. 'Now, guard your tongue,' he murmured in an undertone. 'I do not think we are in any danger, but it is as well to be prepared.'

He did not take her arm, nor show any particular concern for her, as he strode ahead of her into what she could only describe as a hovel. But it was cleaner than she expected and as soon as Jack produced good hard coinage, the innkeeper and his wife were all smiles.

'Our best room, of course, citizen. Come with me,' the landlord said, picking up a lamp and leading the way through a brick-floored parlour and up some rickety stairs to a landing, where he opened the first door he came to.

'Fresh linen on the bed this very morning,' he lied, putting the lamp on a table and going over to the hearth to set light to a few sticks. Straightening up, he grinned at Kitty and then at Jack. 'Don't suppose you need a bedwarmer.'

Jack laughed, not so much at the man's crude joke but at Kitty's look of dismay. 'I'd say no, but we have been on the road some time in bitter weather and the citizeness has terrible cold feet, which she delights in putting on my back, so a hot brick would be appreciated.'

'Very well, citizen. And do you want food?'

'Naturally we want food. Bring a tray up here, the best you've got. And a bottle of wine.'

The man left, closing the door behind him.

'If you think I am going to share a room with you—' Kitty began as soon as he had gone.

'Only the nobility can afford the luxury of separate quarters,' he said. 'Would you have these good people think we are aristos?'

His use of the word aristos served to remind her of what had happened in Paris and she shuddered. Surely the whole countryside was not infected by this madness? 'You did not have to say we were married.'

'Our passports say we are, you know that. How else can I protect you? A woman alone, and not just any woman, but a very young and beautiful one, would fall prey to the first lecher who knocked on her door. And standing on your dignity would avail you nothing.' He came over and took the blanket and shawl from her to throw them on a chair, standing for a moment with his hands on her shoulders and looking down into her up-turned face.

Her eyes were bright and her cheeks rosy with cold; her lips were slightly parted and the pink tip of her tongue protruded between her teeth. Did she have any idea of what she was doing to him? Did she know that her mixture of hauteur and innocence was having a profound effect upon him, turning him into a quivering mass of indecisiveness and desire? He was rapidly losing the initiative.

He dropped his hands to his sides and took a deep breath to regain control of the situation. 'Now come and sit by the fire and warm yourself. It is not necessary for us to fight.'

He pulled a chair close to the meagre blaze and motioned her to sit. 'I told you before and I shall tell you again, I have more important things to do than seduce an unwilling chit. We share the room and that's an end of it.'

She had seen that look in his eyes again, the look of pain and doubt, as if he were undecided whether to take her into his confidence or not, but before she could say anything the innkeeper returned with a tray of food and a hot brick wrapped in flannel. Jack took both from him and thanking him, ushered him out again.

'Now, eat,' he commanded, pulling a small table close to her chair and setting the tray on it. He put the brick in the bed and returned to add another log to the fire before bringing up another chair for himself. The meal was only a thin stew, with a few grisly pieces of meat, some onions and carrots, accompanied by cabbage and a couple of tiny potatoes, but it was nourishing in its way and she knew they would not even have had that if Jack had not given the couple more money than they could earn in a month.

He poured the wine which was surprisingly good and they ate and drank in silence. She wanted to ask him what his business was and, if it was so important, why was he taking time to escort her on this journey? Why wasn't he concerned about his wife? Shouldn't he be searching for her? Unless she was in Lyons too, or somewhere on the way. Was James even in Lyons? She had only Jack's word for it.

So many questions buzzing round in her head, but she knew it was no good asking them. He told her only what he wanted her to know. Besides, she was feeling replete and sleepy, but unwilling to admit she wanted to go to bed. 'I worked it out,' she said.

'Worked what out?'

'At six miles an hour with stops we shall cover no

more than thirty miles a day. We shall be on the road for ten days at least.'

'Two weeks would be nearer the mark.'

'And we go all the way like this?'

'Like what?'

'Plodding along all day with you on the driving seat and me rattling round inside and the nights spent…' She spread her hands to encompass the room.

'If we are lucky.'

'If we are lucky!' she repeated. 'You call this miserable existence lucky? I should hate to encounter illluck.'

'So should I,' he said laconically. 'A broken axle, perhaps, a lame horse, bad weather, brigands…'

'Stop! Stop! I really do not want to know.'

He smiled. 'If you had known what was ahead, I'll wager you would never have left home, would you?'

She looked at him with her head on one side, pondering the question and he found himself holding his breath for her answer. 'No, for I would not then have been the cause of Judith's death and I can never forgive myself for that.'

He supposed it was the kind of answer he should have expected from her. She said nothing of her own ordeal, or the discomfort she was being forced to suffer, the poor food, the filth, his overbearing manner. 'You should not blame yourself,' he said. 'She chose to come with you.'

'She was loyal and my stepmother would have turned her out of the house in any case, so what choice did she have? And it was my decision to leave Monsieur Clavier's, not hers.'

'You could as easily blame me for taking you to Paris. I should have forced you to return to England.'

She smiled mischievously. 'Do you really think I would have gone? It seems to me I gave you no choice either because, in spite of your efforts to prove the contrary, I do believe you have some gentlemanly feelings...'

He inclined his head, amusement in his brown eyes. 'Thank you, ma'am.'

She stood up, trying not to let him see how nervous she was. 'Now, I think I must put that to the test. I am going to bed.' She went over to the four-poster and removed a blanket and a pillow which she dropped into his lap. 'It will be warm by the hearth. I bid you goodnight, sir.'

He scrambled to his feet and watched her clamber on to the bed and draw the curtains round her, dislodging a thick film of dust which made her cough. They had obviously not been drawn for a very long time and she was lucky they did not fall down about her head. He thought about going to help her but such a move would undoubtedly be misunderstood.

He heard the bed creaking as she endeavoured to undress on it and then there was silence.

'Goodnight, my dear Kitty,' he murmured, putting out the lamp before taking off his coat and boots and stretching himself on the hearthrug in shirt and trousers and pulling the thin blanket over him.

Kitty had removed her skirt and blouse and lay down in her shift and petticoat, but in spite of her fatigue she could not sleep. She was acutely aware of his presence in the room. The fire went out and the wind began to rattle the window panes and creep into the cracks around the door; she could hear the inn sign creaking as it swung to and fro. The moon rose and cast long shadows on the curtains that surrounded her. She felt closed in, unable to breathe and at the same time shivering with cold.

She pulled the curtains to one side so that she could see the window. Clouds were gathering, obscuring the moon. Tomorrow, there would be rain. The brick at her feet lost its warmth and she pulled it out and put it on the floor, glancing between the bed hangings at the huddled form on the hearthrug. He must be even colder than she was. She lay back on the pillows and shut her eyes, trying to empty her mind of all that had happened, so that she could sleep. She was so tired…

Her own screams woke her. Woke Jack, too. He rushed to her side, pulling aside the curtains and sitting on the bed to hold her in his arms. 'Hush, hush, *ma petite*, you are safe. I have you safe. Look, there is no one here but me. Hush, hush…'

She clung to him as her screams subsided into sobs and the sobs into long heaving breaths, as she tried to throw off the nightmare. It had been so real, so terrifying. She was being buried alive in a dark cellar with hundreds of dead bodies. They were all about her, mangled, grotesque. She saw Judith's face, her mouth and eyes wide open. There was a door and James stood by it, looking for her, but she could not move, could not cry out to let him know she was there, alive, not dead like everyone else.

'That's better,' he said, stroking her hair. 'Try and go back to sleep.' He laid her back on the pillow and pulled the blanket over her, but she continued to shake. 'You are cold.' He fetched the blanket she had given him and tucked it round her.

'No, no,' she murmured. 'You will freeze.'

He smiled and climbed in beside her, taking her shivering body into his arms and holding her close against him. 'We will share. Go to sleep. No more nightmares.'

His voice was so soothing, the warmth of his body so comforting, she forgot to be afraid. A tiny voice in her head reminded her that what they were doing was scandalous in the extreme, but the voice had no strength and was lost among the screeching of the demons of her nightmare. She was tired and afraid and he comforted her. She put her head on his shoulder and risked shutting her eyes. The nightmare did not return and she slept.

When she woke again, dawn was breaking and rain was beating against the window pane. Had she dreamed that Jack Chiltern had lain beside her, that he had held her in his arms and soothed her? Or was that a dream too? She turned her head. The imprint of his head dented the pillow beside her, but of Jack Chiltern there was no sign.

She sat up in a sudden panic. His boots and coat had gone. He had abandoned her, gone on without her. She scrambled out of bed and reached for her skirt and blouse just as the door opened. He came in bearing a tray.

'Good morning, sleepy head,' he said, smiling. 'I thought you would never wake. Now, come and have breakfast, we must be on our way as soon as you are ready.'

It was all so very normal.

That day and night were the first of many, all very similar. Sometimes it rained; sometimes the sun shone; sometimes they made only half a dozen miles a day because the poor old horse could do no more. When that happened, they had walked beside it, talking in desultory fashion.

Without once mentioning his wife, he spoke of his parents and his boyhood which had been spent in England, of the countryside, the hunting and fishing with which he had filled his leisure, of his liking for books and learning and his assessment of the political situation. He talked of France under the *ancien régime* which he seemed to know just as well as England, and the changes brought about by the Revolution.

'Theory and practice do not always go hand in hand,' he said on one occasion. 'Equality when applied unequally does not work. The new regime was supposed to have addressed the problem, made things more even, but the rich still escape while the poor still pay. They pay taxes to the state, taxes to the church, taxes to their *seigneur*. The cost of the intervention in the American War was bad enough, but now France is at war with half of Europe and the cost in money and lives is crippling. The country is all but bankrupt.'

She smiled. 'You care, don't you?'

'Of course I care. Ardent patriotism soon turns to fanaticism, and fanaticism to despotism in the hands of powerful men, especially when the supreme authority is weak.'

'You mean the King?'

'Yes, the King. He was made the symbol of repression and it was easy to incite the poorer sections of the community into believing he was the author of all their ills.'

'Now he is dead, has anything changed?'

'No, of course not, so they turn their attention to the Queen and anyone seen to sympathise with her.'

'They will never execute her, surely?'

'Who knows?'

'Poor woman.'

'As you say, poor woman. If England were to win this war...' He stopped, realising he was getting dangerously close to confiding in her and that would be bad for her safety. 'It's beginning to rain again and Samson has had his rest, so into the coach with you.'

She had returned to the vehicle and he had climbed on to the driving seat again, and they had continued their bone-shaking journey. But she was slowly beginning to understand him, and in that understanding there was a flicker of something more. Of love.

During the day she could set aside the terrible memory of Judith being hoisted up to the top of the lantern; during daylight hours, she could pretend there was nothing wrong, but when night came, when she went to sleep, the nightmares returned and then she was glad that he slept in a chair in the same room or across the foot of the bed.

Hearing her cries, he would wake her and murmur softly and lay beside her and both would sleep. She no longer argued against sharing a room with him. If they derived comfort and warmth from each other, that was good. She was as chaste as the day she left the vicarage, though she doubted if anyone would believe it. But England seemed far away and the proprieties she had been brought up to observe hardly seemed relevant.

They travelled almost due south, passing through the forest of Fontainebleu, favourite hunting ground of kings, on through Sens, with its tall cathedral and half-timbered houses, to Auxerre and Avallon, set on a promontory jutting out over the river valley along which they meandered, as if they had all the time in the world, then through forests, stopping to rest beside lakes, where Jack caught fish for their mid-day meal.

Sometimes he snared a hare to supplement their diet of onions, peas, beans and cabbages and whatever they could glean from the hedgerows. Bread was in very short supply and very dear.

The days became a little warmer and the bare fields changed to sloping vineyards, each overlooked by its château, some quite small, others as big as castles. Beaune gave way to Chalon-sur-Saône, then Tournus and Macon, and still they journeyed on, following the banks of the river, sometimes hemmed in by towering cliffs, at other times gentle rolling hills, dotted with little villages.

The people they met on the roads and on the river barges pretended little interest, but Kitty was sure that they were watched and their presence commented upon. Occasionally they met soldiers on the march and Jack pulled off the road to let them pass. But even then the violence of Paris seemed a long way off; the gentle pace they had maintained for the benefit of an old horse also served to calm their own separate conflicts and produce a kind of euphoria.

But as they neared the city of Lyons, Jack fell silent and Kitty began to think more and more about her brother and what lay ahead. What would James say to her? What was he doing in France that prevented him from going home? He had always been headstrong, even more so than she was, so had he become involved in revolution or counter-revolution? Why Lyons?

It was nearer three weeks than two when they stopped at Villefranche-sur-Saône, capital of the Beaujolais region, and next morning turned off what was euphemistically called the high road on to one that was even worse. Here the land was marshy and dotted with lakes, home of thousands of wild birds: waders, herons, birds of prey. Their pace became even slower.

'Why are we going this way?' she asked when he stopped the carriage at mid-day. 'Is it a short cut?'

'No, not a short cut, but beautiful, don't you think?'

'We have made a detour in order to admire the scenery?'

He smiled, fetching out the bread and cold chicken which had cost him a small fortune at the hostelry they stayed at the night before. 'No, this is the only way.'

'To Lyons?'

'No, to our destination. You will soon see…'

'But you said we were going to Lyons.'

'Later, perhaps. After I have made certain inquiries. Now eat up, we will soon be there.'

After they had finished their meal they set out again and began to climb into the hills. To save the horse, they both got down to walk. The road became steeper and more broken and Jack began to fear for the carriage, as it jolted out of one pothole into another. There was a single roadmender half-heartedly throwing rocks into the worst of the holes and even as they passed him, he stopped and sat down on the side of the road to drink from a flask, watching them out of sight.

Halfway up the hill they came to a village, surrounded by a broken wall. At the gate Kitty turned to look about her. The view over the valley below was breathtaking: rocky outcrops, stands of trees, shimmering lakes and terraced vineyards.

'Our destination,' Jack said, pointing at a large château which overlooked the town from the tree-clad hills above it.

The old carriage rumbled over the cobbled streets of the little town with Kitty and Jack walking at the horse's head. It seemed a typical hillside community, with lop-sided wooden houses, a church with a very tall spire, a mill, a town hall, a fountain in the middle of the central square and an inn with a stableyard. She could not imagine many wayfarers passing through; the only road out of it, apart from the one climbing up from the valley, seemed to lead to the château.

'What is this place?' she asked. 'And who lives at the château? Is James supposed to be here?'

He smiled; never content with one question, she must always ask several at a time. 'The village is called Haute Saint-Gilbert and the château is the home of my mother's sister and her husband, the Marquis and Marchioness de Saint-Gilbert, or I should say the *ci-devant* Marquis and Marchioness, since titles have been abolished and he is simply a citizen like everyone else. And, yes, we may very well find your brother here.'

'What is he doing here?'

'You must ask him that.'

As they climbed the last steep hill of their long journey, she began to wonder what Jack would do next. Would he hand her over to her brother and leave her? Six weeks before she had not wished for anything else, but now she realised she would miss him dreadfully. He had become necessary to her existence and without him she would crumble to dust and be borne away on the wind.

He had kept her sane when nightmares troubled her; he had provided her with food and warmth, had entertained her with discourse and laughter, instructed her on the countryside, pointing out places of interest. He had been her guide on her very own Grand Tour. And now it was coming to an end.

He had protected her from prying eyes, lied gallantly to ensure her safety as well as his own and, if he had sometimes been tyrannical, it was a tyranny of love not hate. She loved him. She knew hardly anything about him and yet she loved him. He was married and yet she loved him. Her footsteps slowed as she realised the enormity of her discovery and the hopelessness of it.

'Come, I would have thought you would be all ea-gerness to be there,' he said, stopping to wait for her to catch up.

'Of course I am,' she retorted. 'But this slope is so steep I hardly know how to climb it.'

'Nonsense! You have walked up far steeper ones in the last three weeks.' He reached out to take her arm. 'Here, let me help you.'

She wrenched herself from his grasp, unable to bear his touch for fear of giving herself away. 'I'm all right.'

He looked sideways at her, wondering what had come over her. She was ill at ease, walking with her head down, as if she did not want to look at him or speak to him. He sighed. 'What have I done wrong now?'

'Nothing.'

'Then I wish you would look more cheerful. Your brother may see us coming and will surely think I have been ill-treating you.'

'Don't be silly. Why should he think that?'

'You have a face like thunder and I do believe I could strike a tinder from the sparks in your eyes.' He stopped and took her chin between his fingers and thumb and forced her to look at him. 'Or are they tears?'

'Of course not. Please release me.'

He dropped his hand and pulled on the horse's harness. 'Come, Samson, just a few more yards and your work is done, then you may rest as long as you want.'

Kitty looked up as he spoke and realised they were within a stone's throw of the château, every bit as imposing at close quarters as it had been from the village below. It looked like a fairytale castle with steeply sloping roofs and several turrets and a huge oaken door which stood open to reveal a paved courtyard and a fountain. Jack led the horse and cart through it.

A door opened to one side and a young lady flew out of it and ran towards them. 'Jack! Jack!' He stood with his feet apart, holding out his arms and she flung herself into them. Laughing joyously, he picked her up and swung her round and round, revealing a frou-frou of lace petticoats and silk stockings, while Kitty watched, her heart growing as heavy as lead.

This must be his wife. She was so young, hardly more than eighteen, and Kitty's notion that he had not talked about her because he did not care flew away. He had not spoken because he cared too much to share his thoughts with a mere stranger. This lovely girl was petite and pretty and beautifully dressed in pale aquamarine silk, with ribbons in her very pale hair.

Kitty became acutely conscious of her rough peasant skirt and blouse and the darned shawl which she had draped about her shoulders. And, unlike the girl's satin pumps, her shoes were so thin that even the smallest stone imprinted itself on the soles of her feet. She could not bear to look and turned away to pat Samson's nose.

'Oh, Jack, you do not know how I have longed to see you again.' Kitty could turn away, but she could not shut out the sound of the young lady's voice. 'But how did you manage it? Are you going to stay this time?'

'Questions, questions, questions,' he said, setting her back on her feet. 'Why are women so full of them?' Reminded of Kitty he turned to her, only to realise she had disappeared. 'Where is the pesky woman?'

'You mean the *citoyenne*. Why, she went round to the back of the carriage. I must say, Jack, it is the most dilapidated vehicle I ever did see. And as for that animal…' Her laughter pealed out, making him smile.

'He brought us safely from Paris,' he said. 'Three hundred miles, as Kitty will vouch if I could only persuade her to come out of hiding.' He went round the carriage and found her trying to pull her basket out from under the seat where it was wedged fast. 'Leave that,' he said, taking her hand. 'A servant will see to it. Come and meet Nanette.'

'Nanette,' he said, drawing her forward. 'This is Miss Kitty Harston.'

'Kitty Harston,' she repeated in astonishment. 'You mean Jamie's sister?'

'I do, indeed.'

She stared at Kitty, taking in her rough clothes and tangled hair, obviously doubtful as to the truth of the young woman's identity. 'But I thought you were a peasant. Whatever are you doing here?'

'Now, that is hardly a welcome, *ma petite*,' Jack remonstrated. 'We have come a long way and we are dirty and tired…'

'Oh, please forgive me, Miss Harston. I was so taken aback I forgot my manners. And Jack has forgotten his, too, for he has not introduced me. I am Nanette de Saint-Gilbert.' She smiled at Jack. 'And for my sins I am Jack's French cousin.'

'His cousin.' The day was overcast but it seemed as

though the sun had come out and flooded the courtyard with its warmth. This lovely girl was not Jack's wife.

'Yes. You do speak French, do you not?'

'A little.' Kitty curtseyed. 'How do you do, *ma'amselle*.'

'Come in. Come in. A bath and a meal first, I think. Papa and Mama are out visiting, but they will be back directly, and we will save the story of your journey until they arrive and we can all hear it together.' She took Kitty's arm as she spoke and led her into the house.

'*Mon frère…?*'

'You have just missed him. Jamie went to Lyons this morning. There is to be a meeting tomorrow.'

'When do you expect him back?' Jack asked, as he followed them into a vast marble-floored vestibule with an enormous fire which burned a log as big as a tree trunk.

'I don't know. The day after, perhaps. He was a little vague.'

Jack groaned. The man was as elusive as a butterfly. What was he up to? What meeting? If he was stirring the mutterings of discontent into more rebellion, he must be stopped. It was too late to do anything tonight and he was dog-tired. Tomorrow he must find him and make him understand that people who went off at half-cock without proper orders were a danger to themselves and everyone else. James must take Kitty home.

Nanette clapped her hands and servants appeared from everywhere. One was despatched to see to the fires in bedrooms, another to make up the beds, two others to fetch hot water and another to summon the cook for new instructions. The Revolution did not seem to have touched this out-of-the-way place; everything spoke of opulence. The furniture, the hangings, the carpets, the huge fires, the myriad of crystals in the chandeliers, the paintings on the walls, the carved oak staircase, the long windows, all spoke of great wealth.

Kitty was led upstairs to a huge bedroom which had a magnificent view of the town nestling on the hillside. From here she could also see that there was another road down the mountain, small and winding and hidden for most of its length by trees.

Servants bustled in to fill a bath before the fire, which was already warming the room. Kitty suspected that it was kept alight and only needed stirring up and more fuel added.

'Take your time,' Nanette told her, as a male servant arrived with her basket. 'Let me have the gown you mean to wear, I will have it pressed for you.'

'Thank you.' Kitty, who had very little choice in her basket, picked out a short-sleeved dress of blue muslin, with a deep frill at the hem and a fichu of white lace to fill its low neck. She handed it to Nanette, together with a fine lawn petticoat trimmed with lace, the same undergarment she had been wearing in Paris. She shuddered as she touched it, remembering again the humiliation of having it flung over her head, but pulled herself together and smiled at her young hostess.

'You don't know how much I have been looking forward to being clean and civilised again.'

'I suppose that reprobate cousin of mine insisted on you dressing like that? It really is too bad of him.'

'I believe it was necessary.'

'Then you shall tell me all about it later.' She turned for the door with the clothes. 'I admire your courage, *ma'amselle*. I am quite sure I should never have endured it. Marie will help you dress and conduct you downstairs when you are ready.'

The water was hot and scented with jasmine. Kitty soaked herself for nearly half an hour, until every vestige of grime from her journey had been washed away. The maid washed her hair and she sat before the fire to dry it, musing on the events which had brought her here. Less than two months before, she had been sitting in a bath and having her hair done before dressing for the Viscount's ball.

Young and naive, she had set out in a mood of excitement, looking forward to the dancing and the supper, of meeting one or two local eligibles, perhaps even the man of her dreams. He would be handsome and gallant and fall in love with her on sight. Instead she had been kissed by Edward Lampeter, whom she had known since childhood and who was definitely not the man her fantasies were made of.

It was strange how something as innocent as a kiss could lead to this. A château in the middle of France in the company of a married man. She had no money, only two dresses and a filthy skirt to her name and that name tarnished forever. Would she, given her time over again, have stayed at home?

No, a thousand times no. If she had stayed she would be betrothed to Edward by now, her future mapped out for her and she would not have met Jack. Chiltern or de Saint-Gilbert or Faucon, it did not matter; she loved him whatever his name. But she did have two regrets: Judith had died needlessly and Jack was married. Both gave her nightmares.

Marie, the maid Nanette had assigned to her, returned with her petticoat and dress and laid them on the bed. 'Shall I brush your hair, *ma'amselle*?' Her voice impinged on Kitty's reverie and she shook her sad thoughts from her. She must think of happy things, of

James and their coming reunion. He was obviously staying at the castle and expected back so it would not be long now.

She sat in her shift and petticoat while the maid did her best with her hair, which was inclined to be wayward and would not stay where it was put. Since Judith had cut it, it curled all over her head like a mop. 'Do you wish for powder?' the servant asked. 'It might help it to stay down.'

'No, thank you. A ribbon band will suffice.'

Her reflection in the glass revealed a much thinner Kitty Harston than the one who had set out on what she had so naively called high old adventure, but it suited her, made her look older. She supposed she had matured. In a few short weeks she had changed from a schoolgirl into a woman. She stood up and allowed herself to be helped into her gown, then slipped on some pumps which Judith had packed for her and picked up her fan. 'I am ready.'

Chapter Six

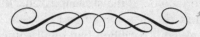

Kitty was conducted downstairs and along a wide corridor to a large room which overlooked terraced gardens, just beginning to show the green shoots of spring. It was luxuriously furnished, making her wonder again how it had escaped the ministrations of the *sans-culottes*.

At first she thought she was alone, but a slight sound made her turn and she saw Jack standing by a bookcase with an open book in his hand. He had shaved and changed into black superfine breeches with white silk stockings and buckled shoes. His black velvet coat had diamond buttons; his jabot of fine lace cascaded over his embroidered blue waistcoat and ruffles of lace fell over his wrists. His hair, washed and brushed to a black sheen, was unpowdered and held back by a velvet ribbon. She was surprised that he had such finery in his small valise. Did it mean he meant to come here all along?

He bowed formally. *'Ma'amselle.'*

She curtsied. *'Monsieur.* I may call you *monsieur* now and not citizen?'

'You may call me Jack, as you have been doing for

the past few weeks.' He put the book back on the shelf and walked towards her, surveying her from her dainty feet to her mop of dark curls and smiled. 'The cygnet has become an elegant swan and I am overwhelmed.'

It was true. He had always thought her beautiful in a gamine sort of way, an innocent, but now she took his breath away. Here was no schoolgirl, but a woman of startling attractions. The oval shape of her face, the expressive eyes, the firm mouth and clear-cut brows, the heavenly curved body filled him with desire.

He had not been unaware of it when he held her in his arms each night, trying to keep her warm, to comfort her when nightmares invaded her sleep, but it was easier to think of her as a child. He could only thank God for the rough clothes, the lack of hot water to wash, the cold, and her fear of the bad dreams that had brought out the gentler side of his nature. Why had she come into his life when she had? The timing of it was all wrong. What future could they have?

'Kitty…' He took a step towards her, just as the door opened and Nanette came into the room, and whatever he had been going to say remained unsaid.

Nanette, innocently unaware that she had interrupted anything, crossed the carpet and took both Kitty's hands in her own and held them out to look at her. 'Why, you are quite lovely,' she said. 'Jack, how could you bear to disguise her in that horrible garb she arrived in?'

'It had to be done,' he said. 'Paris is a hotbed of revolutionaries. No one is safe.'

'So Jamie told me, which was why he decided to come back with Papa after his visit to Paris last year.'

'And found the delights of Haute Saint-Gilbert so beguiling he forgot he was supposed to meet me in Paris,' Jack said. 'It was damnably inconsiderate of him.'

'He said there was plenty of time,' she said, blushing and looking down at the toe of her slipper, peeping out from the hem of her gathered satin skirt. 'He did not expect you so soon and he was not to know his sister would come looking for him, was he?'

Jack smiled, noticing the flush in her cheeks. 'Oh, I see. That is the way the wind blows, is it? And what does my illustrious Uncle Louis think of that?'

'He is perfectly at ease with it. James is the grandson of an English viscount, after all, and he is a very presentable young man.'

'With no prospects.'

Kitty could not let that go. '*Monsieur*, I protest. Prospects are not everything, if two people are in love. He will come into something from our grandfather, even if it is not a great deal.'

'I was not referring to material wealth, so much as his penchant for hurling himself into every adventure that comes his way with no thought for the outcome,' Jack said; then, to Nanette, 'Where is he now? What is this meeting all about?'

Nanette shrugged. 'I do not know.'

'You think he is in danger?' Kitty asked. 'Oh, I don't think I could bear it if anything happened to him.'

'What is going to happen?' said a booming voice from the door.

All three looked round to see a portly man in a square-cut blue frockcoat, short brocade waistcoat and cream cashmere breeches. His hair was long and heavily powdered.

'Papa, look who is here,' Nanette said. 'Jack has brought Jamie's sister to stay with us.'

'His sister, eh?' The Marquis advanced into the room

and stood facing Kitty before inclining his head towards her. '*Enchanté, ma'amselle.*'

Kitty curtsied. 'My lord.'

'Hush, child, there are no titles now. I am citizen along with everyone else.' He turned to Jack and held out his hand. 'Good to see you, boy. How goes it in Paris?'

'Bad, I'm afraid. Anarchy. Hangings and beheadings and likely to be worse before it is better.'

'That is precisely why I keep my head down. I give the peasants most of what they want and they leave us alone, it is as simple as that.' He paused. 'You were speaking of that pup Harston, I believe?'

'Yes. Miss Harston has travelled all the way from London to find him and now it seems he has gone off on some errand of his own. She is concerned for his safety.'

'Oh, he is safe enough under my patronage. He has only gone to his club.'

'And what club would that be? It wouldn't be counter-revolutionary, would it?'

The Marquis laughed. 'Now, you know me for a patriot, Jack. Would I countenance a counter-revolutionary under my roof?' He turned to take Kitty's hand and pat it. 'Now don't worry, my dear, he will be back tomorrow and you will be reunited with him. But I am curious to know why you found it necessary to venture so far in search of him.'

'Here is *maman*,' Nanette said, as her mother came into the room, saving Kitty from having to reply immediately. 'Mama, this is Miss Kitty Harston.' She giggled and pointed at Jack. 'And this is citizen Jacques Faucon, a perfect stranger to me.'

The Marchioness, unlike her husband, was very tall

and thin, and made taller by the two feathers which she wore on a band in her hair. The hair itself was thick and dressed in fat round curls. Her brown taffeta was striped horizontally with red satin ribbon. A white silk shawl covered her shoulders and upper arms. She wore a quizzing glass on a ribbon about her neck and now picked it up to examine Kitty.

'How do you do, my dear. You are very welcome. As for you...' She turned to Jack. 'Still playing at charades, nephew? What was it last year? A colonel in the... What regiment was it? I forget.'

He grinned and went to kiss her on both cheeks. 'It was the National Guard, Aunt Anne-Marie.'

'And now you are dressed like a turkey cock. Such finery in this day and age. Dear me, you are taking a risk, are you not?'

'I have changed since I arrived, Aunt. You would not have had me at your table dressed as a *sans-culottes*, unshaven and dirty.'

'No. I do not believe in this universal lowering of standards. France was always a civilised country and I deplore what is happening to her. But I believe supper is ready, so we will adjourn to the dining room and you can tell us all about it.' She offered her arm to her nephew and he escorted her in to supper, while the Marquis followed between the two young ladies.

The food was better than anything Kitty had tasted since leaving England, but it was certainly not a banquet. 'I am sorry for such poor fare,' the Marchioness said. 'But even here, we have been beset by shortages and it does not do for our servants to report to those who govern us that we live a life of luxury. We have had to tighten our belts.'

'It is quite delicious,' Kitty murmured, tucking into

roast chicken in a light creamy sauce and several kinds of vegetable. If this was belt-tightening, what was it like in the old days?

'Now, Jack,' the Marquis said. 'Tell us everything. How did Miss Harston meet you and persuade you to bring her here?'

While they ate, Jack told the tale very simply, saying nothing about their habit of sharing a room, making their journey sound almost commonplace. Kitty was quizzed about her reasons for leaving home and, though she tried to explain, she sensed their condemnation of her conduct for which she could hardly blame them.

They did not understand about her stepmother and she didn't think they believed that nothing had happened between her and Jack, especially as she blushed crimson whenever she mentioned that journey. He had done nothing but hold her, but if he had kissed her again, caressed her as a lover, she might very well have allowed her own burgeoning passion to get the better of her. Young ladies of quality were not supposed to feel passion, were they?

But he hadn't made any advance at all. Oh, she knew he loved his wife and guessed that he was not the sort of man to take his marriage vows lightly but, apart from that kiss on board the cross-Channel packet, he had given no indication that he found her desirable, that he had even been tempted. His compliments were always teasing and not meant to be taken seriously. He looked on her as an overgrown child and had kissed her to teach her a lesson. The knowledge did nothing for her self-confidence.

'And you lost your maid,' Nanette said. 'It must have been dreadful. However did you manage to dress?'

'Dressing was not the problem—after all, I could

only wear peasant clothes. The worst of it was the manner of her death. I am afraid it still gives me nightmares.'

'Ma pauvre,' Nanette murmured. 'No wonder you wanted to find James. He will be here tomorrow or the day after and will be very surprised to see you, I think.'

Jack smiled. James would be astonished and, if he guessed aright, not particularly pleased. Having to take his sister home would curtail whatever he was up to, political or personal.

'And you, Jack,' his aunt put in, 'what are your plans? Will you spend some time with us?'

'I think I will go into Lyons tomorrow and bring James back,' Jack said, smiling at her. 'The sooner he takes his sister home the better.'

Kitty's heart sank. He wanted to be rid of her after all; though she loved her brother dearly, he would be no substitute for the man she really loved. A married man. She must never allow herself to forget that.

He had gone by the time she rose next morning and he did not come back that night. Although her host and hostess were polite and pretended to make her welcome, she felt undercurrents of disapproval, of tension. She was sure they would be glad when she left. If only Jack had taken her with him, they could have shared whatever danger was out there…if danger there was. In the isolated château above the peaceful village, it was difficult to imagine there was conflict all around them.

The following day Nanette suggested a walk and Kitty was happy to agree. She felt stifled in the house and decided a little fresh air might make her feel better.

They put on hats, coats and half-boots and set off up the slope behind the château into the forest.

The days were becoming longer and warmer. The scent of hyacinths filled the borders near the house; early clematis was already covering the walls of the château and the bougainvillea and jasmine were in bud. On the slopes, the vines were green and down in the valley the fields were beginning to reveal shoots of corn, peas and beans.

'You know,' Kitty said when they had been walking in silence for several minutes. 'I never did know how Jack and James came to know each other. I thought James was in Italy. Is that where they met?'

'No, it was in Paris last year. Jamie told me about it.' She took Kitty's arm as she spoke. 'He is very resourceful and brave, you know.'

'Jack?'

She laughed. 'Jack, too, but I meant Jamie. He saved Jack's life. Didn't Jack tell you?'

'No. I didn't even know he was in France last year. I met him in London and assumed he had been there some time. He did speak of his home in Wiltshire and I thought…' She stopped. She had already made too many false assumptions about Jack Chiltern and here was another proved wrong.

'Oh, he comes and goes all the time. I am not quite sure what he does, it is better not to ask, but I think he has been helping *emigrés* to escape. He was caught last year, did you know?'

'No.'

'He was denounced and the Guard went to arrest him at our town villa in the rue Saint-Honoré, where he had been staying with Papa. Papa had gone to Paris to see the King and speak to citizen Danton. He thought he might act as an intermediary but the King was arrested…'

'What has that to do with my brother?'

'Jamie was in the street when Jack was brought out of the house. He told me he was on his way to visit him. He had an introduction from a mutual friend and he thought Jack might show him the sights. He also intended to write a first-hand account of what was happening under the Revolutionary Government for the English newspapers.'

It was typical of her brother to discount the fact that the city was full of unrest and violence and seize on what he saw as an opportunity to make a name for himself. 'Then what? Did James rescue him?'

'Not right away, there were half a dozen guards and they were all armed. He followed them to the Conciergerie prison and later bribed a guard to lend him his uniform. When Jack was brought out to be taken to his trial, Jamie said he had been ordered to take charge of the escort.

'He pretended to treat him roughly and knocked him to the ground. Then, when he hauled him up again, he whispered who he was and cut his bonds with a knife he had in his belt. Before they reached the Palais de Justice, they overpowered the other two guards and dived into the river. I believe shots were fired, but neither was hit and they crawled out half a mile downstream.'

'Goodness, what a tale! I wonder why Jack did not speak of it?'

'I expect he found it difficult. You see, the woman who denounced him was his wife, Gabrielle.'

Kitty stopped walking and turned to face Nanette, her

face betraying her shock. 'Oh, no! How dreadful! Surely she would not do such a thing?'

'I think Jack is convinced she was forced into it. You see, Gabrielle's father, the *comte* de Malincourt, was one of the *ci-devant* King's most useful courtiers and was privy to a great many of his secrets. After the Revolution began in eighty-nine, he was in danger of arrest and Jack persuaded him to take his family to England. They lived in one of the Earl of Beauworth's properties in London.'

'Earl of Beauworth?'

'Jack's father.'

'His father is an Earl?' Kitty gasped.

'Yes, did you not know?'

'No, he told me his name was Jack Chiltern.'

'So it is. Chiltern is the family name. He is Viscount Chiltern. His name is John, but as that is also his father's name, he is called Jack by the family.'

'I had no idea,' Kitty said. So the mysterious Jack Chiltern was of noble birth. Why was she surprised? Shouldn't she have guessed? She had called him arrogant, but that was how he had been brought up, to command, to lead, to stand no nonsense from those below him and that included her. 'And is he really your cousin?'

'Yes, that is true. Mama and his mother are sisters. Aunt Justine went to live in England when the Earl married her. He wasn't the Earl then, of course, his father was still alive. He inherited the title when Jack was a boy and then Jack, who is an only child, became the Viscount. Is that not the way of English nobility; the son takes his father's lesser title?'

'In some cases, yes. But I never heard anyone call

Jack…' she paused to correct herself '…his lordship by his title.'

Nanette smiled. 'It is not a good idea to admit to being an aristocrat in France at this moment, especially an English one. I think you had better forget I told you. It is dangerous knowledge.'

'I shall certainly say nothing. I would not for the world put him in danger. But if his wife was in England, how did she betray him?'

'Gabrielle was abducted by someone from our Embassy in London on one occasion when she was visiting her parents. She sometimes used to leave Jack at home on their country estate in Beauworth and stay with them in London. I think she found country life a little dull.'

'Abducted? But why?'

'Well, nothing was said officially and I do not think the Revolutionary Government would ever have admitted they had a hand in her disappearance, but I suppose they thought they could hold her hostage to force the *comte* to return to France and stand trial. Naturally, Jack went after her. Papa said they must have freed her on condition she led them to him.'

'And James saved him. I am very proud of my brother for that. But what happened then?'

Nanette shrugged. 'I don't know. Papa deemed it prudent to leave Paris and return home and James came with him. He feared he might be arrested for his part in Jack's escape and he also wanted to write about the counter-revolutionaries in this part of France. We heard nothing of Jack and assumed he had taken Gabrielle back to England.'

'No, he told me he thought she was in France. I assumed he was still looking for her.'

'Oh, then that accounts for him not coming back last

night. He would have gone to Malincourt to see if she had gone to her old home. It is only ten kilometres from here. But I should be surprised if he found her there. No one lives there now and the land has been sold off in small lots.'

'He loved her very much, then?' The words were wrung out of her, though she could not keep the huskiness from her voice. She tried pretending it was the result of the attempted hanging, but she could not deceive herself.

'Oh, yes. You should have seen them when they were first married—so close, they had eyes only for each other. He showered her with gifts and even lived in France rather than England because she didn't like the English climate, but the Revolution changed all that and they had to return to England. How Gabrielle came to fall into the clutches of the man at the Embassy, I do not know.'

Kitty felt wretched. Nanette's revelations had helped her to understand the man beneath the rough exterior, but left her feeling desolate. His love was for his wife. His careful protection of her on their long journey was no more than a heightened sense of chivalry. When she rescued her from those bloodthirsty women and looked after her, when he warmed her with his own body, when he paid the exorbitant prices demanded for food and lodging for her, he had been doing no more than repay the debt he owed her brother for his life. A life saved for a life saved.

'He is a wanted man, then?' she said. 'No wonder he took such great care to play the *sans-culottes*.'

Nanette laughed. 'And made you play it too. Oh, Kitty, what adventures you have had. I think you are very brave. I know I should not have been able to do it.'

'Now we are here, what do you suppose he means to do?'

'Has he not told you?'

'No. He has undertaken to reunite me with James, no more. My brother and I have still to leave the country.'

'True, and it will be even more difficult now. In the last few weeks, there have been even more repressive measures passed by the ruling committees in Lyons. They are so afraid of counter-revolution they have ordered the National Guard to arrest anyone they consider suspect and that includes anyone without a passport.'

'Oh, but I have one of those.' Kitty laughed in spite of her low spirits. 'In the name of citizeness Kitty Faucon. Jack keeps it with his.'

Nanette stared at her with her mouth open in surprise, then she laughed delightedly. 'Oh, how clever of him! But it is doubtless forged?'

'Yes, but it served me well whenever we were asked for it.'

'You had Jack with you then.'

'Yes, but James will be with me on the return journey.' Although she spoke with confidence, she knew James was not Jack and his French was only a little better than hers. Without Jack the journey would be doubly difficult. Without Jack she would be miserable, even if there were no danger at all.

'Yes, Jamie must go with you.' Nanette's voice was wistful.

'Oh, you must think me very selfish,' Kitty said, taking Nanette's arm, as they picked their way over fallen pine needles. 'Of course, you do not want him to leave.'

'Oh, I do. And he must,' Nanette cried. 'I think he

has become very involved with politics here and that could be very dangerous. There are counter-revolutionaries plotting to overthrow the regime and restore the monarchy and he goes to their meetings.'

'Is that where he was going when he left here?'

'Yes, I think so. He says it is only so that he can write it all down to make a book, but no one is going to believe that. If they catch him, they will say he is spying. I am very afraid for him. You must make sure he leaves with you.'

'You could come with us.'

'I would not leave my parents. We are in no danger as long as we do as we are told. Papa has been forced to give nearly all his money to the poor and waived his seigneural dues. He is accepted as a good patriot.'

'Poor Nanette,' Kitty said softly. 'You are torn between them, aren't you?'

'Yes, but I know where my duty lies. And I have always been a dutiful daughter.'

Kitty laughed suddenly. 'And I have not. And look what has happened to me.'

'I did not mean that as a criticism of you, Kitty. You have no parents living and we are very different in character, are we not? I have not half your courage and independence.'

'Nonsense. You have not yet been tested, that is all.'

'Then I hope I never am.' She paused. 'Now, I think we have gone far enough, don't you? Let us turn for home. Perhaps they will both be back.'

Jack returned in the middle of the afternoon without James. He looked tired and was not in the best of tempers. 'The silly young fool has gone off to rally the other sections and communes to join the federalists,' he told Kitty and Nanette. They had seen him coming from an upper window and had gone down to the hall to meet him. 'He is asking for trouble. They will never unite, they differ too much about what they want to achieve.'

'Someone ought to let the world know what is going on,' Kitty said. 'If he wants to write about it, then he needs to be in among them. It doesn't make him a conspirator.'

'Write about it!' he scoffed. He had been riding hard and his scuffed boots and long coat were covered in caked mud. He had been looking forward to a bath and was not in the mood to be cross-examined. 'Stirring up the populace with rumour and plots and inciting them to rise against their elected rulers will achieve nothing and will only bring the wrath of the National Assembly down on them.'

'Is that what he is doing?' she asked, becoming alarmed for her brother's safety.

'So I am led to believe. They are too disorganised to succeed and it will only result in the chaos we have seen in Paris.'

'I am surprised at you,' Kitty said, a little waspishly. 'If they need organising, why are you not doing it? People listen to you. You are—'

'I am an Englishman and it is not my business,' he interrupted her. Better she should think him indifferent than know the truth. The less she knew, the safer she was. 'Nor should it be your brother's. He is interfering in what does not concern him.'

'I do not understand you,' she said. 'When we were in Paris, I was sure you were a Royalist, now I begin to wonder…'

'The King is dead, that is a fact. And the country must be brought to peace. James has been in the country less than a year, how can he understand? This is not England. It is nothing like England and it is useless to try and impose English thinking on French people who have been sorely tried over a great many years. And they are afraid.'

'At least James is trying.' She didn't know why she was arguing with him when in many ways she agreed with him. It was not what she wanted to do. She wanted...she wanted him. She loved a man who loved his wife and loved his duty even more; there was no place in his life for her. England and home suddenly seemed very desirable and very far away.

'Very trying,' he said laconically.

'You are in a very disagreeable mood,' Nanette said. 'Have you been to Malincourt?'

He looked at her sharply. 'What made you say that?'

'I thought you might have gone there to look for Gabrielle and that has made you miserable.'

'Gabrielle.' There was a ragged tone to his voice which betrayed his emotion; he was not as cold and hard as he would have them believe. 'She is not at Malincourt. Now, if you will excuse me, I must change.' He bowed to both girls and left them looking at each other in bewilderment.

'I told you, didn't I?' Nanette said, as soon as he had gone. 'Jamie is involved with the counter-revolutionaries. Oh, I wish he would come back, then Jack would persuade him to leave.'

'And what about Gabrielle? Would Jack go without her?'

'I don't know. If he has no idea where she is...'

'In that case he must be worried to death,' Kitty said.

Jack's worries had nothing to do with his wife, they were for Kitty. He sat in the hip bath which had been brought up to his room and took stock of a situation which was rapidly getting out of hand.

He was half-French, half-English, and he hated this war, but not so much as he loathed the despots who had taken over his beloved France and made it into a place of fear and reprisal. When he told Nanette and Kitty that he wanted peace, he had been telling the truth, but not peace at any price, not if it meant destroying everything that was great and good.

He had been instructed to see that James returned to England before he clumsily upset everything, but obeying that was secondary to his orders to scout out the strength of the Royalist faction, to find out what they needed and which of the leading men could be relied upon to welcome British intervention, if it were offered.

Admiral Hood was in the Mediterranean with the British fleet and he was successfully blockading the port of Toulon and preventing essential food stuffs, including the desperately needed grain, from reaching the people. How far were they prepared to go to obtain those supplies? Would they welcome an invasion for bread to put in their children's mouths?

And he had no orders at all about Miss Kitty Harston. Kitty. She was rapidly undermining his ability to think dispassionately, to function as an agent. What should have been his last concern had become his first. He loved her.

In spite of his promise to himself never to let another woman rule his heart, to stick rigidly to what he conceived to be his duty, he had succumbed to those deep violet eyes and inviting mouth. But, more than that, he loved the person she was, bright, independent and thoroughly infuriating.

When he first met her, he had thought of her only as a spoiled child, used to having her own way, protected from the evils of the world to such an extent she could not recognise danger even when it was thrust under her nose. To a degree that was right, but she was far from unintelligent and she had learned quickly. Now he knew he could trust her in a tight situation and she would not panic; there had been enough sticky moments on their journey to convince him of that.

And every day he had grown closer to her, admired her more, chided her less, and every day he had been tempted to tell her that he loved her. But he could not. Once the words were out of his mouth, she would change, just as Gabrielle had changed. She would become the tyrant and he would be like clay in her hands. He could not afford to lose control. If she were arrested and let it be known, however inadvertently, that he loved her, they might use it, use it as bait as they had used Gabrielle. Except his wife had co-operated willingly.

On the other hand, could he rely on James to take Kitty safely home? James would turn aside whenever the opportunity for fresh adventure showed itself. His presence among the counter-revolutionaries proved that. Did James think he led a charmed life and nothing could touch him? He was in for a rude awakening if he did. He might very well forfeit his life. And Kitty's.

The bath water was becoming cold and he heaved himself out of it and towelled himself dry. He must finish his business, find James and take them both south to Toulon. There were allied sympathisers there who would help them to join the British fleet.

Dressed once more in respectable breeches and stockings, a clean white shirt and neckcloth and striped waistcoat, he shrugged himself into a frockcoat and went down to join the ladies. Kitty was alone in the withdrawing room.

'Nanette not here?' he queried.

'No, my lord…'

'Oh, it's my lord now, is it? What happened to Jack?'

'I don't know. He has gone. He disappeared when Nanette told me who you really are. I had no idea you were Viscount Chiltern and the son of an Earl. Why didn't you tell me?'

'Would it have made any difference if I had?'

'No, I suppose not,' she said slowly. She would still have fallen in love with him.

'Then, I beg of you, forget it. Titles are never mentioned in France unless they have *ci-devant* in front of them.'

'One time,' she translated. 'No, there is nothing of the past about you.'

He laughed and took her hand to kiss it, sending shivers of desire coursing through her. To hide her confusion, she turned away from him just as the door opened and the Marquis joined them.

'My boy, there you are. Tell me the latest news…'

Kitty became increasingly concerned for her brother over the next few weeks. According to Jack, he had been seen in one place, heard of in another, was reported to be riding south, then north, then west to the Vendée where there were other counter-revolutionaries. 'Mind, it might not be James,' he told Kitty one day when they were walking in the garden with no other company but each other.

Neither was prepared to speak of what was in their hearts. To do so would have set off an avalanche of emotions which would engulf them and leave them gasping, unable to continue the roles they had set themselves. Keeping their relationship on an impersonal level was the only way they could survive.

It was almost midsummer and the flowers in the untended garden were a riot of colour: red geraniums, mauve bougainvillea, bright yellow mimosa, heavily scented jasmine. The uncut grass was parched and brown, and the roses a tangle of thorns and spilled petals. Kitty could imagine it in its heyday before the gardeners had disappeared.

'He is not using his own name,' Jack went on. 'And I have only a description which is vague to say the least.'

He did not add that there was a price on the Englishman's head and the people were so poor that they would denounce anyone for a precious loaf of bread.

'Does he know I am here?' Kitty asked him. 'Have you been able to send a message to him?'

'I dare not. It is impossible to know whom to trust.'

'But he is safe?'

'I have heard nothing to the contrary.' Which was an evasive answer, but the only one he was prepared to give.

'He will come back to Nanette, I am sure. He loves her. Love is the greatest force of all, don't you think?'

He smiled wryly, looking down into her upturned face and forcing himself not to succumb to the urge to kiss her again, to enjoy the taste of her lips, the feel of her clinging to him as she had done that first time. 'And naturally, you know all about it.'

'I…' She stopped, unable to go on.

'Love is a tyranny,' he said. 'It commands obedience, it stifles free will, it makes a man act irrationally.'

'How cynical you are,' she said, wondering why he was so vehement about it if he loved his wife so dearly. 'But I do not think you mean it.'

'Oh, I do, believe me, and I have more important things on my mind than love. If I cannot find James in the next two days, we must leave without him.'

'Why? What has happened? Are we not safe here?'

'For the moment, but the situation is changing all the time and we shall soon have outstayed our welcome. I cannot put my uncle at risk. He is not a man who enjoys risk, which is why he has obeyed all the edicts of the Revolutionary government in return for being allowed to keep his home but...'

'That might change? Is it because of what James is doing?'

She was extraordinarily perspicacious, he decided. James was stirring up a hornet's nest and the outcome, if the bees buzzed too noisily, would be civil war. He dreaded that.

'No, not altogether. I have heard that General Dumouriez has been driven back from the Netherlands and instead of rallying his army for a counter-attack, he tried to persuade them to march on to Paris and restore the monarchy. Louis's young son is still held in the Temple prison, you know; he is the rightful king. But the troops refused to follow him and Dumouriez has fled to the allies. His desertion has started a wave of anti-Royalist agitation.'

'Is that not good?'

'No. A Committee of Public Safety and a Revolutionary Tribunal have been set up in Paris to prevent any more dissension. I hear the guillotine is becoming increasingly busy.'

'But that is Paris, not here.'

'Like a plague, it will spread. Representatives have been despatched throughout the country to make sure its decrees are obeyed and enforce the conscription of all able-bodied men into the army. Soon they will be combing this district and our presence here will not remain a secret much longer. Any strong young man not in uniform will be suspect.

'Already there is a brand new guillotine in Lyons ready to execute the so-called enemies of equality, hoarders, capitalists, members of the nobility and priests who refuse to conform.' He smiled wryly. 'Not to mention Englishmen and women.'

'You are worried on my behalf?'

'Naturally I am. Until I find your brother, you are my responsibility.'

'How can that be? I forced myself on you. It was not your choice.'

'What would you have me do?' he asked, his mouth lifting in the ghost of a smile. She was the most provocative woman he had ever met. 'Should I have left you to hang? Should I abandon you now?'

'You could.'

'Don't think I haven't thought of that,' he said grimly. 'But I must also consider my uncle and aunt.'

'I am sorry,' she said. 'Nanette told me the Marquis has already forfeited his title and his dues as a *seigneur* in order to appease the local government. She said they were safe as long as they did as they were told.'

'Perhaps they are, but we are not helping by being here.'

'You are suspect?'

He smiled grimly. 'Jack Chiltern may be. Jacques Faucon is a true patriot.'

She giggled. 'Are you still using that ridiculous name?'

'Of course. It is what keeps us safe. For the moment.'

'Does anyone know Jacques Faucon is staying here at the château?'

'No, I do not think so. I live in a labourer's cottage on the far side of the estate and make a living rearing pigs and growing cabbages.'

'But then who am I? How did I arrive here?'

'You are simply a visitor, a relative staying with the family. My uncle brought you back with him from Paris last year.'

'I see. He brought a young lady back, not a man.' She laughed suddenly. 'I could say I came disguised as a boy—my brother and I are alike.'

He was forced to smile, though the situation was serious. 'I sincerely hope you are not thinking of repeating your playacting performance at the Paris barriers, my dear.'

'No, I have learned my lesson. But do you think we might be questioned?'

'It is always possible.' He reached for her hand, making her shiver with pleasure. His touch always affected her like that, but he seemed totally unaware of it. 'While you are here, you are not citizeness Faucon, but Catherine Gilbert, a distant cousin of the Marquis, do you understand? It is why I keep your passport. If it was found in your possession…' He stopped.

'I understand. I know nothing of Jacques Faucon. I have never heard of him.'

'Good. I am leaving now for a last look for James. I should be back in two days. Be ready to leave.'

There were visitors to the château the day after he had gone: six men in grubby pantaloons and red caps with tricolour cockades pinned to them. They had muskets in their hands and pistols in their belts. Kitty kept herself hidden while they spoke to the Marquis, the Marchioness and Nanette and, although they left soon afterwards, apparently satisfied with the answers they had received, they served to reinforce what Jack had said. There was danger everywhere.

She stood on the gallery above the vestibule as the Marquis and his wife watched them leave. 'She can't stay here,' he said, turning to come back into the house. 'She'll have to go. We should never have let Jack persuade us to take her in. We have to think of our own skins…'

Kitty did not wait to hear any more. She ran to her room, changed into her old peasant skirt and packed everything else in her basket; Nanette would come looking for her soon and she must make haste. She scribbled a letter to her host and hostess, then went down the back way to the stables and hitched Samson to the old carriage, thankful that Jack had taught her how to do it while they had been on the road and had even allowed her to drive along some of the better roads.

Carefully she drew out of the yard and started off down the steep, winding hill. This was the most dangerous time because in some places the road could be seen from the château and from the town and she was not sure how far the guards had gone. But she passed no one except the lazy roadmender who sat beside his heap of stones, smoking a clay pipe and surveying the scenery as if filling holes was the last thing on his mind.

Remembering the alternative road she had seen from above the château, she decided to take that. It was more wooded and less open to prying eyes and with luck she would join the main road in the valley without being seen. From then on, she would have to say she had come direct from Paris. Her destination was... Where could she possibly be going? Italy. If she could cross the border, she would be safe.

But what about James? And Jack Chiltern? Jack was resourceful enough to survive, especially when he did not have her to hinder him. He would be glad she was no longer his responsibility and he could go and search for his wife with a clear conscience.

She did not consider how and when she would eat, where she would sleep, what she would do for money. She had not used any of her own since Jack had taken charge of her; he had even returned the sovereign she had left with the Claviers, saying it was useless. But it was gold, wasn't it? Someone must accept it. And she had a pearl necklace her grandfather had given her—that might fetch something.

The road she had taken was even worse than the other one, steep and twisting, and she sat on the driving seat, hanging on for all she was worth, allowing the old horse to pick his own way down. She shouldn't be here, she should never have come, never allowed Jack Chiltern to bring her here. It was a wild goose chase. He had no idea where her brother was and even less idea of how she felt.

She loved him. Hopelessly. She hated him, too, for making her love him. She hated France. She hated this dreadful flannel skirt which made her itch, hated the horrible red cap. She pulled it off and flung it into the trees. She hated the women who had killed Judith, a kind gentle soul who had never done anyone any harm. She hated her brother for disappearing, Edward Lampeter for kissing her.

It was that kiss that started it and another which had

enslaved her. Jack had said love was a tyrant; well, he was right there. She felt so helpless and lonely and so angry, she was weeping. Tears cascaded down her face, as the old carriage rumbled on. She did nothing to wipe them away, was hardly aware of them.

Immersed in misery for which she could blame no one but herself, she plodded on until she suddenly became aware that the track had widened; lying by the side of the road was a pair of iron gates, pulled off their hinges and flung into the undergrowth. She scrubbed at her tear-streaked face with the edge of her skirt and urged Samson on, but then she caught sight of the name interwoven in the scrolling of the gate: Malincourt. Looking to her left, she saw a weed-encrusted drive at the end of which stood a château.

Curiosity quenched her anger. She turned and went in past the gates. Nanette had been right; the house was much bigger than the Saint-Gilbert château. Its turrets soared above the surrounding trees; it must have once been very grand. But now weeds and overgrown shrubs had encroached almost up to the building itself.

Every window was broken, the great front door missing and the walls smoke-blackened. She stopped and climbed down, hitching the horse to an overgrown lilac bush. Picking her way over broken glass, roof tiles and smashed furniture, she stepped into the hall. It was black with soot and littered with debris and she could see the darkening sky through its roof. There wasn't a whole piece of furniture, a picture or an ornament left. She supposed they had been looted.

No wonder Jack had been in such a miserable mood. It was enough to break anyone's heart. She turned to go, to leave the place to its ghosts, but it was growing dark and she could not continue without the risk of toppling the horse and carriage into a pothole or turning it over the side of the road down the steep mountainside. She would find a corner to sleep in and go on in the morning.

The stable at the back still had its roof and it was big enough to hide the horse and the carriage. There was a little straw there, too, and a trough of water, but no hay. Sensibly she had thought of that; the inside of the coach, besides her basket, contained a few armfuls of hay and some carrots which she had taken from the Saint-Gilbert stables. The horse was fed, but she remained hungry. Stealing food for herself had not occurred to her.

She looked after the animal and was about to make herself comfortable in the straw when a sound disturbed her. She whirled round to find herself face to face with a man in the garb of a *sans-culottes* who blocked the doorway. He carried a musket which he was pointing at her. She froze.

Chapter Seven

'She's in here, citizen Santerre,' he called to someone behind him. He stepped forward and walked round her as three more men entered.

'Who…who are you?' Kitty managed to ask, not daring to move, although her knees were shaking so much she was afraid they would let her down.

'We ask the questions,' a second man said. The cockade on his cap had a gold edging and she supposed that was a sign of authority. 'You are under arrest.'

'*Pourquoi?*'

'That we will discover when you have been questioned. It is enough that you are suspect. Come with us.' He grabbed her arm and dragged her out into the open where two more men waited on guard. It appeared they had arrived on foot; she supposed they were the men she had seen at the château. They must have looked back and seen her leave and followed her.

They harnessed the horse to the carriage again and bundled her inside. Two climbed in with her, two sat on the driver's seat and two more walked either side of the horse's head to guide it in the dark. And thus they arrived in Lyons just as dawn was breaking.

If Kitty had not been so immersed in her own seemingly insurmountable problems, she might have been able to admire the view from the steep cliffs above the city of Lyons. They were breathtaking. Lyons lay below them at the confluence of two rivers, the Saône and the Rhône, a sprawl of old and new, low red roofs, a church spire here and there, open tree-lined squares.

It was France's second city and, according to Jack, had always prided itself on its independence from the central government, but now all that was changing. Paris was dictating policy.

Jack. Had these men been looking for Jack when they found her? Jack Chiltern or Jacques Faucon? Did they think she would betray him? If so, they would be disappointed. She was alone now and, whatever she did, she must not implicate him or say anything to endanger the Saint-Gilberts. She must remember what Jack had told her. She was an innocent visitor. She had simply been out for a drive and was drawn to the deserted château out of curiosity.

She knew there were huge holes in her story that any good lawyer would probe, but she would have to trust to luck. She could protest her innocence, pretend to be younger than she was, perhaps a little simple. Would that do?

She did not need to force the tears that ran down her cheeks as the old carriage bumped down the mountain track, on to a lower road and into the old town, through its warren of narrow streets and alleys, to a small square lined with elegant old houses built for the town's rich bankers and silk weavers.

Years ago Kitty remembered her mother speaking of Lyons silk and showing her a lovely puce-coloured gown. What had happened to the silk weavers since the

Revolution? she wondered. Had they, like Jack's uncle, embraced the new regime or had they aligned themselves with the counter-revolutionaries?

Her captors, who smelled of sweat and drink, offered no conversation at all and seemed relieved to hand her over to the warder of the town prison when they arrived at its doors a few minutes later.

Here she was taken to a cell and locked in to await interrogation. She did not struggle; it was better to seem bemused. Her trial was the place to act the innocent. She would have a trial, wouldn't she?

Although the room was small, it was crowded. Men and women jostled for places to sit against the walls or stood to breathe what little air came from the tiny barred window. It was unbelievably hot and Kitty could feel the perspiration running between her shoulder blades, making her clothes stick to her.

One woman, dressed almost identically to everyone else in the cell in black skirt and red peasant blouse topped with a shawl in the ubiquitous colours of the Revolution, edged up to make room for her on a narrow bench. 'Another one for Madame Guillotine,' she said cheerfully. 'What are you accused of?'

'I don't know.' Kitty smiled wanly, trying not to retch from the stench which assailed her nostrils. 'They said I was being arrested on suspicion of being a suspect, which doesn't make sense, does it?'

The woman cackled. 'To them it does. You don't come from round here, I can tell by the way you speak. Up north, was it?'

'Yes.' No sense in saying she was English. In fact, the less she spoke the better. 'What are you accused of?'

'Hoarding flour. Two kilos I had in my cupboard.

Two kilos and me with ten mouths to feed. And my husband conscripted into the army.'

'Oh, that is terrible. Surely they will not condemn you for that?'

'I sent my eldest to fetch the *curé*. He'll speak up for me. I've done my share for the Revolution, they know that. I am hopeful.'

Kitty, who had no one to defend her, was not so sanguine of her own chances. She had had one taste of revolutionary justice already, she certainly did not want another. But this time she was not being tried by rioting women but a court of law. Surely her accusers would realise their mistake and set her free?

A very small plate of food was brought to everyone later in the day, but Kitty had no idea what the time was, except that the light was fading. The food was cooked in oil which was rank and she could not swallow it. There was nothing to lie on, nowhere to be comfortable, and she spent the night sitting on the bench with her back against the wall. Sleep was impossible.

She tried to pass the time thinking of summer in England, of her childhood and her mother, but that made her sad. She tried to think of what she would do when she returned home and that led to wondering if she would ever go home and made her sadder still. She listened to the woman beside her chattering until the *curé* came and the prisoner was released. Others in the cell were crying, others singing loudly and raucously to cover their fear.

Dawn came and the prisoners began to stir and scratch, making Kitty itch too. Some thin gruel was served to them, but it was greasy and tasted foul. As with the meal the night before Kitty gave hers away.

One by one, the prisoners were led out to be tried. One by one they came back, crying, screaming or numbly silent. It was late afternoon and Kitty was just beginning to think that she would have to spend another night in uncertainty, when her turn came.

She was marched to a large hall where three men, dressed in unrelieved black, sat at a table on a dais. At a table below them was another man whom she supposed was the clerk to the court: he had pen, ink and papers on the table in front of him. There was a dock and a public gallery, but she soon discovered that was as far as the system went in following normally accepted legal procedure.

Her jailer pushed her into the dock. 'Citizen Judge,' he said, addressing the man who sat in the centre of the three on the dais. 'This citizeness refuses to give her name and carries no passport. She was found looting at the Château Malincourt. Also she had stolen a horse and carriage, the carriage being that of the *ci-devant comte* de Malincourt, with the arms painted over. She was also carrying English gold coins.'

The judge peered down at her. She was weeping copious false tears and looking at her feet. 'What do you say to that?'

Kitty did not know what to say. The horse and carriage were not hers and to say where she had come by them would implicate Jack. As for the money, that was perhaps the most damning evidence of all. This was not suspicion of being a suspect, this was real evidence and she had no answer that would satisfy them.

The crowd began to shout. '*Traître! Traître! À la guillotine!*'

The clerk to the court shouted for silence and, when order had been restored enough for him to be heard, the judge spoke to Kitty. 'You are condemned by your own silence. Guilty! The sentence is death.'

That was too much. The tears were miraculously dried by anger. 'Am I not to be allowed to say anything in my own defence?'

'You were caught red-handed,' the judge went on. 'You have no defence. Take her away.'

The whole bizarre business had taken less than five minutes and she was dragged out and returned to her cell to await execution. It had happened so quickly, she thought it must be one of her nightmares, but after a few minutes back in the cell, the reality of her situation swept over her like a huge black cloud.

So this was the end. Was the guillotine quicker and more merciful than hanging? She was going to lose her life miles away from home, and no one would know what had become of her. Not her uncle, or James. Not even Jack. She had refused to give her name. She was going to die unknown and unmourned. Jack would never know how much she had loved him, or why she had decided to leave the château when he had told her not to. But at least she had not implicated him. He was safe.

'Damn it all,' James said for the hundredth time. He was riding up the winding road towards the Château de Saint-Gilbert beside Jack. The two men were wearing nondescript black clothing and were riding scrawny mounts which plodded along, as much affected by the heat as the men who had been riding all night and most of the morning.

James continually removed his tricorne hat to wipe

the sweat from his brow with his sleeve. He was a good-looking young man with short dark curls, brown eyes and a ready smile, features which young ladies found attractive and which he often used to charm his way out of trouble. And he seemed to invite trouble. How he had survived as long as he had was a mystery to Jack.

'Are you sure it is Kitty?'

'Of course I'm sure.'

'But I cannot imagine her running away. She's always been a dutiful little thing, wouldn't say boo to a goose…'

'When did you see her last?'

'Oh, it must have been three years ago, maybe more. I didn't go home very often when I was at Cambridge. Didn't like the old stepmama, don't you know. Then I went off on the Grand Tour and stopped off in Paris on the way home. You know all that.'

'I was only pointing out that she was a child when you last saw her, but she's a woman now. And a woman with a mind of her own.'

'Dangerous, that,' James mused. 'Women with minds of their own.'

'Quite. Which is why she must be got home as soon as possible.'

'You brought her. You take her home. In fact, I think you should. There'll be an almighty scandal.'

Jack turned in the saddle to look at the young man. Was he really as callous as he sounded? 'Don't you care?'

'Of course I care. She's m'sister, after all. But to bring her all this way unchaperoned…'

'I would not have done if you had stayed in Paris as we arranged.'

'The place got too hot for me.' He laughed. 'Now, I've got rather fond of your little cousin and…'

He stopped speaking as they approached the front of the château and the door was flung open. He dismounted as Nanette came running down the steps and threw herself into his arms. Jack, still sitting his horse, watched with a wry smile, wondering why Kitty had not also come out of the house to greet them.

'Oh, I am so pleased to see you safe, Jamie,' she cried. 'But now Kitty has disappeared.'

Jack was off his horse in an instant. 'Disappeared? When? What happened?'

'It was after the gendarmes came…'

'What did they want?'

'Something to do with capitation tax. They had heard we had a visitor. Papa told them what you said, that Mama's cousin's daughter, Catherine Gilbert, was staying with us for a week or two, but would soon be leaving.'

'And—' He could hardly contain his impatience. 'Did they see Kitty?'

'No. She stayed out of sight, but when they had gone I went to find her and she had disappeared. She left a note for Papa…'

Jack did not wait to hear more. He left the two young people to make their own way into the house and hurried to find his uncle.

'What's this about Kitty going off alone?'

The Marquis shrugged. 'Gone. Taken the old horse and carriage. Left a letter thanking me for my hospitality. Signed it Catherine.'

'That's all?'

'Yes.'

Jack squashed his mounting exasperation in favour of

action. Kitty must be found before she got herself and everyone else into more trouble. He turned went straight out of the house and remounted. There was only one road down the mountainside, discounting the track that went past Malincourt; she would not attempt that with the old top-heavy carriage.

Halfway down the hill he encountered the roadmender, shovelling stones into the potholes. 'If you're looking for the English *ma'amselle*,' he said without bothering with a greeting, 'she went down the old road.'

'The old road?' Jack drew up beside the man. 'Are you sure?'

'Yes.'

'God in heaven, she'd never make it. We'll find her at the bottom of the ravine.'

'No, she made it,' the man said laconically. 'With a little help.'

'Help—what do you mean?' His heart was thumping in his throat and he had to force himself not to go rushing off at half-cock.

'The local National Guard found her and escorted her down. Took her to Lyons gaol.'

'They arrested her?'

'Yes. Your cover's blown, old man. It's time to beat a hasty retreat.'

'Not without Kitty.'

'But they'll know everything by now. Who you are, what you are, what you know.'

'She knows nothing except my name.'

'And that's enough. Jack Chiltern was the man who engineered the escape of the Malincourts and that coach was last seen thundering along the road to Calais with the National Guard in hot pursuit. Now it's back at Malincourt and even these dimwits can add two and two.

Jack Chiltern is back in France...' He left the end of the sentence unfinished.

'I'll lay odds she won't talk.'

'Then you've more faith in her than I have.'

'I'm going into Lyons. I've got to get her out.'

'You'll be putting your own head in the jaws of Madame Guillotine.'

'Then I die with Kitty. You can take the despatches back to England.' He fetched a bundle of papers from the capacious pocket of his frock coat and handed them down to the roadmender.

'What are you going to do?'

'I don't know until I get there. If I succeed, I'll meet you at your cottage and take those back.' He nodded at the papers.

'You're mad, you know that, don't you?'

Jack laughed, wheeling his horse round. 'Tell James to meet us at the cottage.' And with that he was gone.

Kitty heard the key grating in the lock and the door opened. 'Where is the English bitch?' the turnkey demanded.

The woman next to her poked her in the side. 'I think he means you.'

Kitty tried to stand. Her legs felt boneless and there was a knot of pain in her stomach that almost doubled her up; she did not know how she was going to walk. She forced herself upright and stepped forward.

'Come with me,' the jailer said, grabbing her arm and pushing her in front of him. 'This way.'

She shrugged him off to walk unaided. At least she could die with dignity. Her shoulders went back and her head went up. I am not afraid, she said to herself. Then, aloud, 'I am not afraid.'

He laughed.

Outside in the street a horse and cart stood ready to convey her to the guillotine. Beside it stood Jack, looking very fierce in his red cap and dirty old greatcoat. Shocked to the core to see him, she stumbled and would have fallen if the jailer had not taken her arm again.

'She's all yours, citizen,' he said, pushing her towards Jack who gave her a look which told her to say nothing. Not that she could have uttered a word; she was too bewildered. Was Jack planning on a rescue from the very jaws of the guillotine? Oh, what a terrible risk. Especially when she had been at such pains not to involve him. But, oh, how glad she was to see him!

None too gently he grabbed her from the jailer. 'My thanks, citizen, though why I should bother my head with her, I do not know.'

'You're welcome. And if I were you I'd beat her for wasting everyone's time.'

'That I will do,' Jack said, grinning at him. 'Good day to you, citizen.' He picked Kitty up and heaved her into the cart with no more care than he would a sack of potatoes. 'Get in there with you, woman. And be quiet.'

He climbed up on the cross bench and Kitty felt the cart jolt into motion. 'Keep down,' he muttered in a low voice. 'The people will not like being deprived of their spectacle.'

They moved agonisingly slowly. Unable to see where they were going, she lay in the bottom of the cart, and gave thanks for her deliverance. Once again, Jack Chiltern had saved her life. But the risk to himself was enormous. Why had he bothered?

They left the town behind; she could no longer see buildings between the cracks in the side of the cart and the smooth road had become a rutted track, she could tell by the added jolting. Still she dare not lift her head. There were trees blotting out the sky now and she wondered if they were going back to the château of Saint-Gilbert. She ought to tell him what she had overheard; there would be no welcome there, she was sure.

'Jack, you must not—'

'Save the talking for later, madam,' he said so brusquely she felt it was wise to obey.

Half an hour later, he turned to look over his shoulder at her. She was crouched in the cart, looking crushed. He wanted desperately to soothe her, to comfort her, to tell her that he would go to the ends of the earth for her, but that would only make her think she could twist him round her little finger and behave with even less circumspection. It was too risky. 'You can sit up now, if you like.'

She scrambled up beside him and impulsively took his arm. For a moment he looked down at her and then put his arm about her shoulders and pressed her to him. His bulk and warmth enveloped her like a comforting mantle and she laid her head against his chest and allowed herself the luxury of feeling protected. He was her bulwark, strong and steadfast, and she needed someone like that. But sometimes she needed a little tenderness, too, and he did not seem able to provide that.

'Thank you,' she said, looking up at him. He was looking straight ahead, almost as if he were embarrassed by that simple show of affection.

'For what?'

'For saving my life again. Once more I am in your debt and I don't know how to thank you.'

He removed his arm and took up the reins in both hands again. 'You could try doing as you're told.'

She drew back from him and looked into his face, expecting thunderous looks to match his words, but there was no sign of anger, only a quiet desperation. 'I know. I am truly sorry. But I didn't know what to do. I couldn't stay at the château. I had to leave.'

'Why?'

'To protect you.'

'Protect me!' He laughed. 'How could you possibly protect me?'

'By relieving you of a responsibility you find onerous and because you were right, we had outstayed our welcome. Men came to question your uncle after you left; after they had gone I heard the Marquis say you should never have brought me to them and he had to think of the safety of everyone else. I dared not wait for you to return.'

'I half expected it. But my uncle satisfied them, I dare say.'

'I think so, but then I thought of the risk my presence was causing them and you and so I decided to leave.'

'And where did you think you were going?'

'To Italy. I thought if I could cross the frontier...'

'Without me? Without your brother?'

'You could not find him. And the longer you searched, the greater the risk.'

He grinned. 'You may set your mind at rest. Your brother is safe.'

'Why didn't you say so before?' she cried, eyes bright with eagerness. 'Where is he? Where did you find him? He's not in trouble, is he?'

'No more than he was before, but he will not leave

Nanette and has gone back to the château to try and persuade her to come with us.'

'Oh, no! He'll be caught, just as I was.' She paused, suddenly realising that no one at the château could have known she had been arrested. She had refused to give her name. And if that were so, how had Jack known where to look for her? 'How did you know where to find me?'

'You were seen leaving.'

'Oh, I was followed. I guessed as much. Those men were the same ones who had been at the château. They found me in the stables at Malincourt.'

He twisted in his seat to face her. 'What, in the name of all that's holy, were you doing there?'

'I was looking for somewhere to sleep for the night and I saw the gates and decided to go in.'

'The place is in ruins.'

'Yes, it must be very sad for you,' she said gently.

'Sadder for the *ci-devant comte* de Malincourt.'

'Yes, to be sure. Did you know that coach had once belonged to the *comte*?'

'Yes. We used it when we escaped the first time. We hid it in the barn of a deserted farm near Calais when we embarked for England. I remembered it when I needed a conveyance to get us to Paris.'

'You didn't want to take me to Paris, did you?'

'Of course not. But as soon as you knew your brother was there, you were determined to go, with or without me. I could not allow you to run into danger, which you surely would have done had you gone alone.'

'And then I did, in spite of your care. Oh, how angry you must have been that I had disobeyed you.'

'Not angry,' he said softly, remembering how he had felt when he had seen her hanging from the lantern.

'There was no time for anger and afterwards…' He shrugged and flicked the reins across the horse's back, though, if he were honest with himself, he did not want it to go any faster. He was content for the moment just to have her safely by his side again.

When he had learned that she had been arrested, it had taken all his self-control not to dash after her and make a scene in the courtroom. He had pictured her in a crowded cell and then put up before the court and all the onlookers baying for blood like so many thirsty hounds. His first task had been to discover how much was known about her and what she had been accused of and then to devise a plan.

'And then I went and did it again,' she said. 'How did you manage to save me this time? That jailer handed me over to you without a qualm. He was laughing.'

He smiled crookedly. 'I used the same story that worked before. I told them you were my foolish wife, a complete scatterbrain. You were in the forest gathering firewood when you came upon the old coach. It had obviously been abandoned and so you came home and fetched the horse and harnessed it up and brought it to our cottage.'

'How clever of you. They obviously believed you.'

'Yes, I said I had told you to put it back where you found it, that we could be in grave trouble if we kept it.'

'But what about my English sovereigns?'

'You found them hidden in the coach. We quarrelled when you wanted to keep them. You went off in a temper while I was working in the fields and I did not know you had gone until a neighbour came and told me you had been arrested.'

'I am so sorry, but the more I realise all the risks you have taken to rescue me, the more I wonder why.'

He threw back his head and laughed. 'I should have thought that was self-evident, you keep putting yourself in need of rescuing.'

'I am grateful, of course I am, but that doesn't answer my question. You did not need to do it. I have no claim on you.'

He smiled slowly. The claim she had was unbreakable; it tied him to her with bonds stronger than chains. He would die for her. 'Let us say I must and leave it at that, shall we?'

'Because of James?'

'James?' He was puzzled. 'What has he to do with it?'

'He saved your life when you were arrested last year. Maybe you thought you owed it to him.'

'Who told you about that?'

'Nanette.'

'My goodness, you did have a pretty little coze about me, didn't you? What else did she say?'

'That you had been betrayed. Is it true?'

'You could say that. Did she say why and by whom?'

'By your wife. Nanette said she was forced into it.' She looked up at him, waiting for his comment but the only reaction was a slight twitch in his jaw and a tightening of his hands on the reins. He obviously still found it difficult to talk about. 'It is a terrible situation to be in, being so frightened you say things you don't mean.'

'True. But you did not, did you? You were not so frightened that you confessed all you knew. That was very brave of you.'

She must have been terrified and he would not have blamed her if she had spoken out, but as soon as he got to the court and started telling his cock-and-bull story, he knew she had remained silent. And he had been so proud of her when he saw her emerging into the sunlit street with her head high. Gabrielle had not even been under duress and, in any case, what she had told the prosecutor had been a tissue of lies.

'I know very little.'

'Enough. I shall have to devise a way of making you safer.'

'How?'

'I shall think of something.'

He fell silent, as if cogitating on the problem, and Kitty used the opportunity to look about her. They were climbing steadily along a dusty track. The sun beat down and the heat shimmered on the distant hills. Either side of them were terraced vineyards with people hoeing between the bushes. It was too soon to be gathering grapes, but they hung in clusters on the stems of the bushes, small and green. She wondered if the harvest was going to be good and hoped so for the people's sake.

As they approached a crossroads, she noticed a man sitting on the ground beside a heap of stones which had been collected from the fields. He was eating a hunk of black bread, but stuffed it into his bag and rose as they approached. She gasped when she saw it was the road-mender.

'Jack, that man…' She nodded in his direction.

He laughed and pulled the horse to a halt. 'It is my good friend, Thomas Trent.'

'Your friend?'

'Yes.' He reached out and shook the man's hand. '*Bonjour*, Thomas.'

'*Bonjour, mon vieux.* Did you have any trouble?'

'None at all. This, as you have no doubt guessed, is *citoyenne* Kitty Faucon, the bane of my life. Kitty, may I introduce Captain Thomas Trent.'

The captain smiled and climbed up beside her. '*Bonjour, citoyenne.* I am glad to make your acquaintance and only sorry you had to wait so long for rescue.' His English was perfect and she realised, with a little sense of shock, that he was an Englishman.

'You knew? Was it you who told Jack I had been arrested?'

'Yes.'

'I am glad you were there.' She smiled. 'You seem to be everywhere.'

He laughed, but made no comment. Jack set the horse off again, turning right and making for a stand of trees on the hills above the vineyards. She wondered where they were going, but did not dare ask.

Now there were three of them the intimacy she had shared with Jack was gone and she regretted its passing. For a little while he had seemed relaxed, willing to talk. He had almost dropped his guard. Almost. Now it was back again, as impenetrable as before.

'Anything to report?' he asked the roadmender.

'No. I gave James your message.'

'Any sign of the gendarmes?'

'No, but they cannot be far away.'

'Do you think they will be looking for us?' Kitty asked.

'Perhaps.'

'But if they believed Jacques's story…'

'They would still follow it up.'

'Then James is in danger. Jack, we must warn him. Where are we? How far is it to your uncle's?'

He laughed. 'You see, Thomas, what I have to contend with? She can't help herself, you know. As soon as she scents an adventure, she must rush headlong into it…'

'It's no more than you do,' she retorted.

'I never rush headlong anywhere,' he said, laconically. 'I stop and think first.'

'What are you thinking now?'

He smiled. 'I am thinking that somehow, God knows how, I must cure you of your impetuosity.'

'That's not what I meant. I was speaking of warning James.'

'Oh, that,' he said calmly. 'You must leave that to me, my dear. After all, there is nothing to connect Jacques Faucon and his erring wife with the *ci-devant* Marquis de Saint-Gilbert. Is there?' He turned to look at her, requiring confirmation that she had said nothing to her captors.

'No, I suppose not. If it was Monsieur Trent and not the gendarmes who saw me leave.'

'Quite.'

'But you told me to forget Jacques Faucon, to deny all knowledge of him.'

'That was while we were at my uncle's, where I expected you to stay. Your flight changed everything. We have left there now and nothing we say or do must lead anyone back there, you understand?'

'Yes. I would not for the world betray his hospitality.' She was a little hurt that he had even thought that she might, but, remembering what Gabrielle had done, she could understand why.

'Turn left here,' Thomas said, as they reached the edge of the woods. 'The track is rough, but the cart will make it if you are careful.'

It was an understatement. It took all Kitty's efforts to

retain her seat and several times she grabbed Jack's coat sleeve to save herself as they bumped their way between the trees. The only consolation was that they were now out of the sun and it was cooler. After several more concisely given directions they reached a clearing and there before them was a tiny cottage, dappled in sunlight.

They stopped in front of it and the Captain jumped down. 'Here we are, safe as houses.'

Jack climbed down and turned to Kitty, holding out his hands to help her. 'Come, my dear. This is as far as we go for the moment.'

She grasped his hand and jumped straight into his arms. After the relief of being rescued and sitting so long on the hard bench, she felt weak at the knees and unable to stand.

He held her for a moment longer than he needed to, savouring the feel of her small body against his, wishing he could claim it, to make love to her, to tell her she need never be afraid again. But that was foolish; they had a long way still to go and heaven knew what dangers still faced them. If only he could keep her safe. He had to, whatever it cost. She was dearer than life to him. He bent to put a kiss on her untidy curls and then released her.

'Come inside,' Thomas called to them from the door.

The little cottage was very primitive, having only one room downstairs, with a lean-to addition at the back, but it was clean and warm and the food Thomas prepared, though simple, was good and hot. Jack would not allow her to speak until she had eaten her fill, by which time she was feeling decidedly sleepy, although it was barely dusk.

'Did you sleep last night?' Jack asked, smiling at her.

'No. There was no room to lie down and too much
to think about.'

'Then it's time you went to bed.' He reached out his
hand towards her.

'But what about James...?'

'Leave your brother to us. Come along.'

It had been a long day. She had lived through terror
and isolation even in the crowded cell, had felt herself
slowly giving up hope. And then there had been the
immeasurable relief at seeing Jack waiting for her, followed by that bone-shaking ride which had numbed her
bottom. And meeting Captain Trent and eating and
drinking while the two men talked generalities and
never once mentioned their plans. It was all too much.

She took Jack's proffered hand and allowed him to
lead her across the room to a narrow staircase which
led up to the loft. 'Up you go.'

He followed as she climbed the stairs. There was only
one room which contained a narrow bed and very little
else. She stared at it, then turned to face him, noticing
how tired he looked. His face seemed grey and the lines
about his mouth and on his forehead were more pronounced, though his eyes still seemed able to see deep
into hers and winkle out whatever thoughts she might
be trying to keep hidden.

And the thoughts she were trying to hide were shame-
ful. She wanted him to sleep with her, to hold her and
make love to her, and she knew if they shared a bed
again, it would happen. Since they had been at the château, they had behaved correctly towards each other,
putting on a semblance of gentility with their good
clothes, bowing and referring to each other by their titles and avoiding being alone together. Which was as it

should be, she told herself, but it put a distance between them.

'You may have the bed,' she said. 'You need it more than I do. I shall go downstairs. There is a settle...'

She turned to go down but he grabbed her arm, forcing her to face him. His own emotions were so ragged, he could only control them with levity, by teasing her; he could not handle tenderness, not now, not yet. 'No. You will have my friend Thomas wondering what sort of a wife you are if you cannot be pleased to see me after the ordeal you have endured.'

'You are despicable!' Why, after all the time they had been together, she should choose this particular moment to think about propriety, she did not know.

'You would rather I had left you to the mercy of Madame Guillotine?'

'No, of course not. I am grateful for your timely rescue, but that doesn't mean I am prepared to...to...' She stopped because he was doubled up with mirth. 'What are you laughing at?'

'My poor dear Kitty, we travelled three hundred miles and spent—how many nights was it?—on the road, often in the same bed, what is so different now?'

She wanted to say, Because now I know I love you, because now I know that what I want most is to be your wife in reality and not just pretend, that if I lie beside you, I should surely give myself away. Because you are married and love your wife and I could never respect a man who betrayed his wife with me, however much I loved him. And because you are a nobleman and I am nothing, a nobody. Instead she said, 'That was an expediency for the duration of our journey—'

'Which is not yet ended. In fact, this is less than

halfway. The second half will, I hope, take us back to England.'

'Us? You mean you are coming too?' She could not keep the pleasure from her voice.

'Yes.'

'And we go on as before?'

'How can we? Things are different…'

'Yes,' she said. Did he mean different in the same way that she meant it? 'Tomorrow, James will come and…'

'And what will James do? Will he be able to make everything right again? James says he loves Nanette and wants to take her to England.'

'She told me she would not leave her parents,' she said.

'Then James might want to stay here.'

'It is too dangerous.'

'Love conquers all, you said that yourself, or something very similar.'

She looked up at him then and he thought his heart would burst. She was extremely pale; there was no colour in her cheeks and there were dark smudges beneath her eyes and tears glistening on her lashes. He reached out and wiped them away with the back of his forefinger.

'What are you trying to tell me?' she asked. 'That I have been on a wild goose chase? Do you think I don't know that? I know I never should have come. I know I should have turned back at Calais. Judith would still be alive if I had. And even after you rescued me the first time, I could have said I did not want to go on to Lyons. It was not too late to turn back.'

'Yes, it was. There was no one to accompany you,

not even Judith, and I could not return with my mission unaccomplished…'

'Intelligence gathering?'

'Yes,' he admitted. 'Finding James seemed to be the only solution.'

'And now you are telling me it was not?'

'I am telling you that, for me, there was no alternative. From the moment you stepped ashore at Calais, our lives were inextricably linked.' He smiled wearily. 'Call it fate, if you like.'

He possessed himself of her hands and drew her to sit on the bed beside him. 'Now, let us have no more teasing because I want to talk to you very seriously and I want you to understand.'

'I am listening.'

'Play-acting is all very well here in France where we are not known and where everyone is more concerned with their own lives than with propriety, but what happens when we return to England? Had you thought of that? You have spent days and nights in my company unchaperoned—what do you think that will do for your reputation and how will your grandfather, the Viscount, react, do you suppose? Will he cut James off? Will he turn your uncle from his living?'

'He would surely not punish them for something I have done?'

'Mud sticks, my dear.'

'Oh, that is so hypercritical. And it isn't fair. James has done nothing wrong. And neither have we.'

He smiled. Was she being deliberately naive? 'Will anyone believe that?'

'Perhaps not, but as I have no intention of going home, not to Beresford…'

'Then where will you go?'

'I shall find somewhere. You need not concern your-self about me.'

'No? What do you think I have been doing these past six months?'

'Six months? Is it as long as that?'

'January to July. I am sure it must seem a lifetime to you…'

'No, it seems shorter.' She spoke softly, not daring to look up at him. 'You have looked after me so well, I hardly noticed the days passing.'

'Some would say otherwise. Some would say I had ill used you.' He knew he should have found some other way, he should not have insisted on her playing his wife, or on sharing a room. The first night he had done it to drive home his message that she was not safe alone, which was true. The second night, he had sat in a chair by the hearth, listening to her tossing and turning and crying out in her sleep. Once, he fancied she had called his name. And he had answered her, gone to take her in his arms, to comfort her, sleeping beside her. He had known what he was doing; she had not.

'Jack, please don't make it sound sordid when it was nothing of the sort. What you did was good and chiv-alrous…'

He laughed harshly. 'Chivalrous! Chivalrous to share a room, sometimes a bed…'

'You did it for my protection. I had nightmares…' She shuddered. 'You have no idea how bad they were. Thanks to you they are far less frequent now and not half as frightening.'

'For heaven's sake, don't make me into some kind of saint. I am nothing of the sort.'

'Jack, I am very tired. Please tell me what all this talk is leading to.'

'A way out of our dilemma,' he said, stroking the back of her hand idly with his thumb. 'You could marry me. I mean a real marriage, not this charade we have been playing.'

'Marriage!' She was so startled she pulled her hands from his and gaped at him. He had the grace to look sheepish. 'Are you mad? Or is bigamy accepted in this Godforsaken country now?'

'Bigamy?'

She laughed shrilly. 'Had you forgotten you are married? I believe her name is Gabrielle. Nanette told me all about her. She said you were devoted to each other.'

'Gabrielle is dead,' he said flatly. 'She died last year.'

'Oh.' She was so shocked she could not go on, but pulled herself together quickly. 'I didn't know. Oh, Jack, I am so sorry. Please forgive me.'

'There is nothing to forgive.'

'When did you find out? How did it happen?'

'She went to the guillotine. I learned of it while we were in Paris. Now we will talk of her no more.'

'Of course. I can see it is a painful subject. But how can you talk of marriage to me? You do not love me and…'

'What has love to do with it?' he broke in before she could force a confession out of him. How could he tell her that ever since he had saved her from that hanging, perhaps even before that, the one thing he had wanted was to make love to her? That his desire that been overwhelming and could only be controlled by teasing her or being harsh with her?

He wanted to marry her, to have her legitimately in his bed. And James, hearing how they had come this far without a chaperon of any kind, had insisted on it. 'My sister is an innocent,' he had said when Jack finally caught up with him two days before. 'She doesn't understand that she can never go back to England unmarried. You must make an honest wife of her.'

Jack did not need to be told; it had been occupying his mind for some time and the solution he had offered was the only one. It was also the one he most wanted. She was looking at him now, hurt and puzzlement in her lovely eyes, and a dash of anger too. He could hardly bear it.

'Is this another tease?'

'No, far from it. I am in deadly earnest.' He retrieved her hand and lifted it to his lips. 'I'm sorry, my dear, that was not the most romantic of proposals, but you must know me by now. I am not a romantic man, and the circumstances are hardly conducive to tender declarations. Perhaps if we were in England...'

'If we were in England,' she snapped, 'I would not even entertain such a proposal.'

It was such a set-down, he gave up the struggle to redeem himself, but neither could he withdraw the proposal. 'Then let us come to an amicable agreement,' he said brusquely. 'We will marry tomorrow. Thomas will fetch the *curé* and he and James can be witnesses. And though I do not hold with breaking marriage vows, I shall raise no objection if you decide to ask for an annulment after we arrive safely in England.'

She was staring at him as if he had run mad and he supposed he had, mad enough to think they might be able to find happiness together in spite of the circumstances. 'Think about it,' he said, getting to his feet. 'Think about the alternatives and give me your answer tomorrow.' Then he bent to kiss the top of her head and left her.

He joined his friend downstairs. The roadmender was

sitting by the hearth, smoking a clay pipe, but knocked it out on the fender when he saw Jack. 'All is well?'

'I think so. What do you think happened to James?' Jack asked, taking a seat at the table. 'He should have been here hours ago. Do you think there's trouble up at the château?'

'Could be. After all, the guards know you are related to the Marquis and if they think you are in the area...'

'By me, you mean Jack Chiltern, not Jacques Faucon?'

'Either. The two will be connected before long. You can't afford to hang about waiting for someone who may never come.'

'Kitty won't go without him. Not willingly.'

'Then you'll have to make her. Marry her or something.' Thomas stood up and pocketed his pipe. 'I'll take the horse and see if I can find out what is happening. If I ride over the top of the hill, it should only take a couple of hours. But whether I come back or not, you must leave at dawn.'

He went from the room, leaving Jack with his elbows on the table and his head in his hands. It had been a nerve-racking day and he was exhausted. So was Kitty and he should have waited until they had both had a good night's sleep before proposing to her. He had handled it very badly, stressing the practical arguments instead of opening his heart to her. 'I am not a romantic man.' He grimaced as he remembered his words.

It would serve him right if she turned him down.

Chapter Eight

Kitty was exhausted, mentally and physically. She lay on the hard bed, her head buzzing with everything that had happened to her since her precipitous and unthinking flight from the rectory: the poverty and dirt and, worst of all, Judith's death, which had robbed her of a good friend as well as a chaperon, and now a proposal of marriage which, as Jack had pointed out, was far from romantic.

Just how much did it mean to him? It seemed extraordinary that he should be prepared to sacrifice his future happiness, perhaps even his inheritance, for her sake. He did not even like her; he found her a nuisance, a responsibility he would rather be without.

She could not forget what Nanette had told her about how Jack behaved towards Gabrielle, how close they had been, how he had done all he could to please her. It was almost as if she were talking about another man, not the Jack she knew. Could the loss of his wife have changed him so much, that he was harsh and uncaring about every other woman he met?

And yet he had offered to marry her, to try and mitigate the scandal. He was so deeply immersed in his grief for his wife that he did not consider it much of a sacrifice. But she did. She must say no. She must take the consequences of her own actions and face the shame when they returned to England.

But, oh, how she loved him! She knew that beneath that harsh exterior there was a man who could feel deeply, who could put someone else before himself, who was honourable. After all, there had been countless occasions when he could have forced himself on her and had not. She smiled wryly to herself in the darkness—not much force would have been needed because she loved and wanted him.

His touch, however fleeting, sent shivers down her spine, and she longed to dispel that look of pain she sometimes saw in his eyes. Could she make him forget Gabrielle with her own love? Could she make him love again?

If she said yes, then it would be a genuine commitment on her part to make the marriage work and hope that in time he would come to love her. If she failed, if he continued to be cold and hard, then she would be trapped in a loveless union because she would not go into marriage with the intention of ending it if it went wrong. Dare she chance it?

She fell asleep, dreaming of pale English skies, of gentle rain in summer, of the peaceful countryside and the placid pattern of life there, of friends and family. If she could find that again, she would never again long for adventure.

She woke suddenly before dawn to the sound of horses and voices. Scrambling from her bed, she hurried to the tiny dormer window, but it was in the slope of the roof and she could see nothing. She turned back, pulled on her clothes and crept down the stairs. Jack was fast asleep in a chair at the table, his head on his folded arms. She shook him. 'Jack, someone's coming.'

He was awake in an instant and on his feet. 'Stay there.'

He went outside. She could hear voices and then laughter and the next moment the tiny room was full of people: Jack and Captain Trent and a man she had not seen before, besides Nanette, who was hanging onto the hand of another young man.

'James,' Kitty cried, flinging herself at her brother. 'You're safe.'

'Of course I'm safe, silly.' He grinned at her and held her at arm's length. 'My, how you've grown! If you didn't look so horribly like a peasant, I'd say quite the lady.'

'The disguise was necessary,' Jack said, defending her. 'But you may take my word for it, she is quite the lady.'

James turned to him. 'And are you going to make an honest one of her?'

'James!' Kitty remonstrated. 'Don't be so tactless.'

'Sorry,' he said quickly. 'But it is better to be blunt, don't you think?'

'It is none of your business.'

'Oh, but it is. I am your brother and in the absence of our guardian…'

'Shut up, James,' Jack said sharply. 'Kitty left home because she did not want to be forced into a marriage and here you are, only five minutes reunited, trying to do the same. Let her make up her own mind.'

'Well, she had better make haste. The Marquis has betrayed us all…'

'My uncle? I can't believe that.'

'He has,' Nanette put in. 'The guards came back and I heard him talking to them. They seemed to know you were in France. It had something to do with the *comte*'s carriage and knowing we were related...' She paused. 'Papa told them all about Jacques Faucon and what James was doing, everything. He did not need to, he could have pleaded ignorance.'

'Have they arrested him?'

'No, because he convinced them he intended to hand you over. He told them they could find you at Malincourt.'

'But we are not at Malincourt,' Kitty said.

'We are not far from it,' Jack said. 'We had better make a move.'

'We have time for a wedding,' James said, nodding towards the fourth man. 'The *curé* is prepared to conduct the ceremony.'

'You take too much upon yourself,' Kitty said. 'I have not agreed.'

'You may do as you please,' James said. 'But I do not intend to stir unless Nanette and I are married. Not for the world would I expose her to the kind of scandal you will be subjected to if you return to England unwed.'

'Oh, I am sorry, I did not think of that.'

'No, that is just your trouble,' her brother said. 'You never stop to think—'

'And you always consider the consequences of your actions, do you?'

'Children! Children!' Jack laughed. 'Do not quarrel over it, for I declare you are as bad as one another.' He turned to Nanette. 'Is it your wish to marry James?'

'Yes, it is.'

'It means leaving your parents and your home. You may not see them again for a very long time...'

'I know, but Papa betrayed James and you and Kitty, who is so brave to follow her heart. Even if he is afraid to lose his house and lands as the *comte* de Malincourt did, it is no excuse. You are my cousin and James is my own true love. I have aligned myself with you.'

'So be it.' Jack turned to the priest. 'Will you marry the young couple?'

'With pleasure, *monsieur*.' He smiled and corrected himself. 'I mean, *citoyen*.' He opened a canvas bag he carried with him and began to take out his vestments.

'Can it be done here?' Kitty asked. 'Will it be legal?'

'The place is unimportant, *citoyenne*,' the *curé* said. 'It is as binding as a marriage solemnized in church. And as I now have no church, I must serve my God and my people wherever I can.'

Jack took Kitty's hand. 'Well, my dear, do we follow their example?'

She looked up into his face and it seemed as though there was a new softness there. His eyes were searching hers, asking for understanding, and her heart swelled with love. She wanted it, wanted it in spite of all the arguments against it. Arguments did not count. Risks did not count. What mattered was what she felt deep inside her. There was no doubt there. He had said love conquers all and, though he had been teasing as usual, she had a feeling he did believe it. She must put her faith in that.

'You really mean it?' she asked.

'I do not say things I do not mean.'

'Then tell the priest to make it a double wedding.'

It was far from the wedding of her dreams. She was not in her uncle's church with its high-vaulted roof and multi-coloured altar window. She was not wearing a lavish gown and costly jewels loaned to her, or perhaps even gifted to her, by her grandfather. There were no flowers, although the priest had brought out some incense and the tiny room was filled with its heady scent, almost overwhelming her. And the ring Jack slipped on her finger was his signet ring and much too big. But none of that mattered because she was giving herself to the man she loved.

He kissed her when it was all over, kissed her for the first time as her husband, and it was a joyful and sensuous sensation, but a little constrained by the knowledge that they were being watched. She did not care. They had the rest of their lives together. He might talk of annulment, but she would never ask for it. As far as she was concerned, this marriage was going to last into eternity.

There was time for nothing else. The *curé* packed up his bag and departed, riding an ancient mule. The horse was reharnessed to the cart which had brought Kitty from the prison and brought to the door. Kitty and Nanette said goodbye to the Captain who was staying behind, then climbed into the back with their meagre luggage and a parcel of food.

Jack and James, who had remained behind in the cottage, reappeared in the uniform of French cavalry officers, resplendent in dark blue double-breasted jackets with rows and rows of silver frogging and heavy silver-fringed epaulettes. Their breeches, tucked into shining leather boots, were tightly fitting and set off muscular thighs. They each wore a sword belt and a pistol and a shako with the regimental insignia on the front. The girls gaped at them and then began to laugh.

'Oh, you are the very top of the trees,' Kitty said. 'The handsomest of heroes.'

'*Vraiment épatant*,' Nanette said, giggling. 'Truly stunning. *Magnifique*. I am overcome with admiration.'

James grinned and punched Jack on the arm. 'There, my friend! We have made a conquest each.'

Jack smiled and made no comment as he shook the roadmender by the hand and took his place on the driving seat. Laughing, James climbed up beside him and they were off.

Thus they journeyed the whole of the day, taking byroads and cart tracks. Sometimes Nanette sat beside James while he drove and Jack joined Kitty in the cart, sometimes she sat with Jack on the driving seat. Sometimes they walked.

In some ways it was like their journey from Paris except that she had been reunited with her brother and, what was more important, she need no longer worry about the impropriety of sharing this strange nomadic life with Jack. He was truly her husband now. She began to look forward to the night with a mixture of trepidation and eager anticipation.

They passed through the ancient Roman town of Vienne without stopping and by dusk had reached Roussillon where they drew up outside an inn. It seemed untouched by either the Revolution or the war, but they all knew appearances could be deceptive and were on their guard.

Going ahead of the others to reconnoitre, Jack approached the inn with caution. If anyone asked their business, they had agreed to say they were going to Toulon. The men were going to rejoin their regiment defending the city against the British navy and their wives had every intention of following them. Once there, they could discard the uniforms and make contact with the men who could take them out to the British fleet.

The innkeeper welcomed them if only because they paid him with a gold *louis d'or*, the equivalent of two English sovereigns, and far more acceptable than the paper *assignat*. He prepared his two best rooms and produced a meal of chicken and fish, with leeks and potatoes, a basket of fruit and a bottle of wine. There were no other guests and they sat over the repast for two hours, but Kitty could see that James was wriggling with impatience to have Nanette to himself; in the end, he could contain himself no longer.

'We have an early start tomorrow,' he said, smiling at his wife. 'I think it is time to retire.'

She rose willingly and took his hand. Jack, too, was on his feet. He watched them pick up a candle from a side table, light it and leave the room before he turned to Kitty. 'Well, my dear, shall we follow suit?'

Without waiting for her answer, he went to light a second candle and stood by the door. Suddenly she was nervous and afraid. She looked across at him, her eyes mutely appealing. He smiled and held out his hand. 'Come, my dear.' His voice was gentle.

She went to him and slipped her hand into his. Together they climbed the stairs to their room.

Once in their bedchamber with the door closed, he seemed to hesitate, uncertain what he should do. He had offered her an annulment and he supposed that was what she wanted. To share her bed would be construed as consummation, even if he managed to refrain from touching her. It was ironic that what had been acceptable when they were unmarried could not be countenanced now.

What he wanted most was to be a proper husband to her, to love, honour and cherish her to the end of their days. Why had he never told her so? Because he was afraid of rejection, of being spurned, because he hoped she would change her mind about the annulment when they reached England. In England he could woo her as a man should woo the woman he loved, unhampered by rough living and danger, which made people say and do things they did not mean.

'You go to bed,' he said, putting the candle down on a chest. 'I must see to the horse.'

She was bewildered. He had never been irresolute before, he had always known exactly what to do. Surely the presence of his ring on her finger hadn't changed that? It ought to have made it easier for him to share her bed, not more difficult. 'But the hotel ostler has done that,' she said. 'Why go out again?'

He smiled, but it was a smile that did not reach his eyes. They were blank, almost as if he had deliberately shut her out. 'You did not think I should be so unfeeling as to assert my rights, did you?'

'Unfeeling?' Her own heightened sensitivity, her mental preparation for the night to come, her disappointment, made her so angry she was almost shouting. 'Yes, you are unfeeling. You play with people, do you know that? You treat them as if they have no more feelings than a piece of furniture. Do this, do that, don't do this, don't do that. Get up. Be quiet. Go to bed. Did it ever occur to you to wonder how I felt about it all?'

He stared at her, completely taken aback by her outburst, as she was herself. She had not meant to let fly at him, especially not tonight, their first night of marriage. She did not understand herself, let alone him.

'I did not need to wonder,' he snapped. 'You made

it abundantly plain. I was conveniently to hand when you needed an escort. I was there to shield you from the grimmer realities of life, rescue you, even to marry you to prevent scandal…'

Instead of telling him that he meant far more than an escort to her, which would have defused the situation, she seized on his last unflattering statement. 'That was your idea, not mine. I would have continued as we were.'

'And I could not. The world would never believe we had not become lovers in the months we have been together. For your sake…'

'For my sake! Are you sure you are not thinking of your own reputation?'

'You are surely not suggesting I coerced you into marriage in order to—' He stopped. He hadn't done that, had he? 'Oh, no, my dear, nothing was further from my thoughts. You cannot annul a marriage that has been consummated, you know.'

'And you think it makes me feel better to know that I am so unattractive I cannot compete with a dead wife.' It was not her speaking, she told herself, it was the little green god of jealousy and she hated herself for it.

'Leave my wife out of it.' He did not want to talk about Gabrielle; she had no part to play in the present situation.

'Why should I? You evidently cannot.'

'God, woman, what do you want from me? You are the most trying, the most provoking, the most…' He grabbed hold of her shoulders. 'I am not a saint. I cannot stand much more of this. Look at me, damn you.'

She tilted her head to look at him. His dark eyes were pinpoints of steel flashing in the light from the candle flame. His jaw was rigid, his mouth grim. For the first time ever, she began to feel a little afraid of him. 'Let me go, you're hurting me.'

Her mouth was slightly open, almost inviting him to do his worst. 'Heaven help me,' he said, lowering his mouth to hers in a bruising kiss.

It went on a long time. She beat her hands on his chest but he simply wrapped his arms about her, imprisoning her and taking the breath from her body. His mouth explored hers, setting up sensations in her belly she could not control. Every fibre of her was shouting its own needs, making her respond, making her lean in to him, to feel his heartbeat, his strength subjugating hers; she wanted him. She stopped struggling.

He picked her up and carried her to the bed, flinging himself down on top of her. Holding her down with the weight of his own body, he lifted her skirt and parted her legs. 'You want proof I am not made of stone, do you? You shall have it.' He undid the buttons on the flap of his pantaloons and began to thrust into her. He did not look into her face, did not see the pain and horror there; he was too intent on releasing months of frustration and anger.

Afterwards came the remorse, the burning shame, the knowledge that he had spoiled everything that had been good about their relationship, the trust they had always had in each other. He would never forgive himself, so how could he expect her to forgive him? He turned towards her, not knowing how to make amends.

She was lying on her back looking at the ceiling, silent tears streaming down her face. How tiny she was; small pointed breasts, slim thighs, little feet. He had great strength and he had used it to subdue her. He had taken something which was precious as life to him and crushed it savagely.

'Oh, God, what have I done? I didn't mean it, I didn't mean to hurt you. I was out of my mind.' He reached out to wipe the tears away, but she knocked his hand from her.

'Kitty, I am truly sorry.'

'For what? For acting like the tyrant you are?' She gave a cracked laugh. 'Am I supposed to complain when my husband takes only what is his by right?'

'But I had no right to hurt you. I beg you to forgive me. It will never happen again, I promise you.' He tried again to reach out to her.

She turned her back on him. 'Go away.'

After a moment, he left the bed and she heard him fumbling with his clothes, then he was gone, taking the guttering candle with him.

She pulled off the ring and flung it into the darkness in the corner of the room and sobbed in total despair. There was no love in him, there never would be for her and she had made the greatest mistake of a life already over-full of mistakes. She had thought she could make him love her. How conceited, how foolish she had been!

She had wanted him to make love to her, would have given herself happily and willingly if he had asked it of her. He did not need to be cruel. It was the mention of his wife that had triggered it and that was her fault. And now she must live with his contempt.

She rose next morning, her eyes, heart and feet as heavy as lead, and sat looking in the cracked mirror above the dressing table, then smiled crookedly at her reflection. She had not slept and she looked terrible.

Would James guess what had happened? Would Nanette notice? She could not bear the thought of their pity.

Turning her basket upside down, she began flinging clothes this way and that. Judith would have packed some rouge and powder, she was sure of it; she could not have known they would not need these essential requisites to a lady's toilette. Grabbing the little pot, she returned to the mirror and coloured her cheeks and lips. It made her look a little less wan, but could not disguise the misery in her eyes.

Five minutes later, dressed in her blue muslin, she made her way downstairs. James and Nanette were sitting at the breakfast table, gazing into each other's eyes and smiling dreamily. Their night had obviously been all they had hoped for.

'Kitty, good morning,' James said, rising. 'Come and have some breakfast. I just saw Jack, he said you wouldn't be long. He's gone to give orders about the horse.'

'Yes, he told me,' she lied.

She sat down but she could not eat. Her mouth was too dry to swallow. She gulped coffee. She must behave normally. She must not let them see that her wedding night had been a disaster. She smiled. 'Well, you two seemed pleased with the world this morning.'

'Why shouldn't we be?' James said, smiling at Nanette. 'We are as happy as two lovebirds can be. We can face anything so long as we are together, rain, wind, rough seas, even Madame Guillotine, it doesn't matter. Don't tell me you don't feel the same.'

'Of course I do,' she said, just as Jack came into the room to join them.

He walked over to Kitty and bent to kiss her cheek. 'Good morning, sweetheart. You looked so peaceful, I let you sleep, but we must not be long before we move off.' His voice was perfectly normal—he was much better at playacting than she was, she decided.

'I am ready when you are,' she said, surprised that he had not suggested she should change into the peasant costume. After all, that's how he liked to have her. Well beneath him, under his control. 'My basket is packed and only needs fetching from the bedchamber.'

'I'll get it, my love,' Jack said. 'You go and get in the cart. It's ready at the door.'

James had already brought Nanette's bag and his own valise downstairs. He picked them up and led the way into the street. Unwilling to be parted even by a couple of feet, he settled himself in the cart beside Nanette, leaving Kitty to climb up on to the crossbench to wait for Jack. He joined them five minutes later, put Kitty's basket and his own small bag into the cart and jumped nimbly up beside his wife.

'Right,' he said with false cheerfulness as he picked up the reins. 'Let's be off.'

She noticed he was wearing his signet ring. It was why he had been gone so long; he had noticed she was not wearing it and had been searching the room for it. He would take that as a sign that the marriage was over before it had ever begun. He was too proud to ask her forgiveness again and the future looked bleak indeed.

The horse was younger and stronger than old Samson, and they were able to cover many more miles a day than they had from Paris to Haute Saint-Gilbert. And, as they were so far from the capital and in pro-Royalist country, there was less danger too. But Kitty could not appreciate that; she was so overcome with misery, she could think of nothing else.

Jack treated her with the utmost courtesy, worrying

about her comfort, running little errands for her, speaking gently, doing everything a considerate husband should do for a wife. Except love her. At night, he slept in a chair or huddled on the floor of whatever hotel, inn or deserted cottage they chose for their night's lodging, while she occupied the bed alone. He had said it would not happen again and he meant to keep his word.

Each morning he rose, apparently refreshed, and went to see to the horse, to pay the innkeeper, to shop for food for the day, leaving her to her toilette. James and Nanette, immersed in each other, knew nothing of the anguish they both suffered. Life for them was good and, now that they were out of the district of Lyons, they did not even worry about the danger or the Reign of Terror beginning far to the north.

They followed the river bank to Tournon, with its granite hills and steep vineyards, and from there climbed a tortuous road with breathtaking views. At its highest point they could see Mont Blanc in the east and Mont Ventoux to the south.

On they went, through Valence and then Montelimar, where they were caught in a violent rainstorm which turned the tiny stream which ran through it into a torrent of swirling water. They stopped here, earlier than they might, in order to take shelter and dry their clothes.

Sitting in the porch of an empty villa, looking out at the brilliant flashes of lightning, listening to the thunder reverberating through the hills, they chatted of other storms in other places. And that led on to tales of home, summers in England. Kitty, listening to Jack speaking of his home, was filled with longing. Would it ever be her home too? Would his father and mother welcome her? Did she even want to go there under the circumstances?

She did not know, was not sure of anything any more. Her high-flown plans to make her marriage work, to make Jack forget his dead wife and learn to love the one who was alive and wanted and needed him, would come to nothing. Vanity, that's what it had been. Conceit. Pride. And now she must pay the price.

She must live with the tyrant love. She did not know whether she wanted this journey to end, so that she might know what fate he had in store for her, or whether she wanted it to go on and on, that she might never have to face it.

Their progress southwards continued in brilliant sunshine the next day and James sang snatches of *The Beggar's Opera* as they went. Nanette joined in, trying to learn the English words, making him laugh. They were so happy, it hurt Kitty to watch them. She dare not look at Jack for fear he could read the envy in her eyes, and he would not look at her, for the guilt was still with him.

Why had she provoked him on their wedding night, taunted him about his wife? That had been the crack which had burst the dam. All his hurt and frustration, all his iron self-control, had come spilling out. It was not Kitty, he had wanted to hurt, but Gabrielle. Gabrielle who had spurned him, who had wanted him dead so that she could impress her lover, had injured his pride. His pride had retaliated, had punished Kitty whom he loved beyond reason.

How could he explain that to her, when she would not even speak to him, except in the day-to-day polite discourse of passing acquaintances? And at night, when they should have been opening their hearts to each other, they did not talk at all. Nights were silent tor-

ment. But he could not blame her. He had brought it
on himself and must pay the penalty: her contempt.

When they moved into Provence they felt a distinct
rise in temperature. As the old cart with its single plodding horse took them through the little town of Orange
with its ancient Roman theatre and steep terraces, the
north was left behind. The days were hot and even the
nights too warm for comfortable sleep.

The sky was a deep blue, the light very clear, putting
the white houses with their red roofs into sharp focus.
Oleander and bougainvillea climbed over walls. Cicadas
screeched, a hawk swooped and rose with a tiny mouse
in its claws; and they could smell the wild thyme, the
rosemary and lavender growing on the roadside verges.

After a night spent in yet another country inn, they
continued through a rocky countryside dotted with vineyards and olive groves and on to Avignon, which had
been Papal property until two years before when the
Revolutionary government had appropriated it.

James, who was sitting in the back of the cart with
Nanette, began to sing again.

—Sur le pont d'Avignon,
—L'on y danse, l'on y danse;
—Sur le pont d'Avignon
—L'on y danse tous en rond.

Laughing, Nanette joined in and then Jack, who was
driving, accompanied then in a surprisingly good tenor
voice. Kitty stole a glance at him. Was he as relaxed as
he seemed? Had that dreadful night left no mark upon
him at all?

They turned away from the river and, at the end of a

long day, came to Aix-en-Provence with its narrow medieval streets. Soon they would reach the sea and then would come the difficult part of their escape, moving from land to water and persuading Admiral Hood to take them on board. After that, their return to England was in his hands. Not even Jack could influence it.

Wanting them to have a good view of the bay and its shipping before going down into the town of Toulon, he took them through a spectacular gorge overshadowed by huge rock formations and up a steep hill at the top of which he stopped. They climbed out and stood looking down at the bay of Toulon sparkling beneath them. It was crowded with shipping, none of it able to move because of the British ships that blocked the entrance to the bay. They could just make them out on the horizon.

'What a sight!' James said.

'Let's hope they don't decide to lift the blockade before we get out to them,' Jack said.

'How are we going to do it?' Kitty asked. 'All those ships. There must be hundreds of French sailors in the town with nothing more to do than catch spies and traitors.'

'Then we shall have to avoid them,' Jack said, as if it were the easiest thing in the world. 'Come on, back in the cart. In a few hours we shall have no more need of it.'

They rumbled into the town and Jack, who seemed to know where he was going, drove the cart along the twisting old streets and stopped at a blacksmith's forge. 'This tired old nag needs new shoes,' he said to the farrier, a big burly man in a leather apron, who came out to meet them.

'Now why should he bother with new shoes?' Nanette whispered to Kitty. The two girls were sitting in the cart with their legs dangling over the back. 'We don't need the horse any more.'

Kitty shrugged, knowing how Jack operated. He seemed to have contacts the length and breadth of the country, knew who could help him, whom to avoid. She recognised a password when she heard it.

She was right. Half an hour later they were all seated in the back parlour, eating a hastily cooked meal of fish, listening to the blacksmith telling them the latest situation in impeccable English.

'The town is being systematically starved into submission,' he said. 'Nothing is coming in by sea and nothing comes down from the north because Paris commandeers what there is. There is talk of surrender. Admiral Hood's launch comes almost daily to offer terms and the local government is on the point of accepting.'

'Can you get me aboard the launch when it comes next?' Jack asked.

'Get *you* aboard!' James exclaimed. 'What about us?'

'It will have to be arranged,' Jack said. 'Four extra passengers in a small launch would not go unnoticed by the port authorities.'

'That is true, Mr Harston,' their host put in. 'If his lordship goes first, something can be arranged. Though how you expect to get to England once aboard, I don't know. There are no plans that I know of to lift the siege.'

'Despatches have to be sent home regularly,' Jack said. 'We go with the despatches.'

'You too?' the blacksmith demanded. 'Do you not stay behind and continue your work?'

'I have done what has been asked of me. Now I must take my wife home.' He looked at Kitty as he spoke, smiling a little crookedly. His wife! What a mockery! 'We have not long been married.'

'Is that so? Then may I offer my felicitations to you both.' He looked from Jack to Kitty as he spoke, forcing her to smile and bow her head in acknowledgement.

'It is the same for us,' James said, reaching across the table to take Nanette's hand. 'I cannot wait to get out of this barbarous country and return to my homeland. Begging your pardon, *monsieur*.'

'Oh, you do not have to spare my feelings, Mr Harston. Now, I will go and find out when the Admiral's launch is expected and let us hope he has not given up trying to negotiate. You must wait here and you'll oblige me by staying indoors.'

They wiled away the time by playing whist, at the end of which James had lost several guineas. 'I don't mind in the least,' he said when Jack commiserated with him. 'Unlucky at cards, lucky in love. I know which I would rather be.'

Kitty stole a glance at Jack, who was gathering up his winnings, but he did not look at her. She had lost too, so the old saying could not be true. Her luck was abysmal on both counts.

Towards evening the blacksmith returned to tell Jack to be ready to leave the following morning. 'I told the bo'swain in charge of the launch that you had important information which you would only impart to the Admiral himself.'

'That is true.'

They listened as he explained how Jack was to be smuggled aboard while the launch was tied to the quay, waiting for the Admiral's party to return to the flagship.

Once on board it was up to the Admiral whether he helped them or not.

'You mean he might not?' Kitty asked, her hopes plummeting again. 'Surely he would not leave us here to fend for ourselves? Supposing he won't let Jack come back for us?'

Jack smiled crookedly. 'Why, I do believe my loving wife cannot bear to be parted from me.' He rose from the table and took her hand to kiss it, making her shiver with desire. She hated herself for her weakness. 'You don't know how gratifying that is.'

James gave him a curious glance and then laughed in an embarrassed way. 'Are you surprised? You have hardly been married a se'ennight. I know Nan would feel the same if I went off on my own.'

'Of course. Leaving Kitty, even for a minute, breaks my heart. But you know how I like to tease.' Jack's little show of temperament was over almost as soon as it had begun, but it left Kitty feeling more uneasy than ever, if such a thing were possible. It seemed there was to be no expunging of that dreadful wedding night from their memories.

She freely admitted she had been as much at fault as he had, but she had not been able to tell him so because he made sure he was alone with her as little as possible and, when it could not be avoided, he discouraged conversation by pretending to be busy with other things, or asleep, or so deep in contemplation that she could not interrupt him. Gone was their earlier affinity—now they could not communicate at all.

Not wishing to intrude on James and Nanette, she spent the waiting time alone, pacing up and down their room or sitting in the corner of the forge, away from the heat of the fire, pretending to read. Most of the time she was mentally rehearsing conversations with Jack, conversations in which she was open and eloquent in explaining her feelings and he listened attentively and told her how much he loved her. All fantasy.

He returned late the following afternoon with the news that a boat would be sent secretly at dead of night to pick them up at a little cove further along the bay and take them directly to the sloop which was due to sail for England, just as soon as the wind was favourable. The blacksmith would guide them along the top of the cliff and show them a way down. After that it was up to them to make the rendezvous on time.

With Kitty and Nanette wearing dark clothes and hoods, provided by the blacksmith, and the men in naval coats with no embellishments, they set off at dusk, following the bulky shape of the blacksmith. By the time they reached the tortuous path which led from the cliffs to the beach, the moon was up, lighting their way.

The blacksmith pointed. 'Down there. *Bon chance, mes amis.*' Before anyone could thank him, he had melted away, making no sound.

'Look!' James said, pointing out to sea. 'There's a small craft, rowing out from that ship. We must make haste.'

They scrambled down. Jack went first, stopping every now and again to help the ladies over a difficult piece of ground, leaving James to bring up the rear. Several times they dislodged loose scree which went tumbling down, making a noise that sounded loud in the silence of the night. They waited to see if any sentries had been alerted, then continued down.

Once on the beach, they made for the water's edge,

standing with their feet in water, ready to jump into the rowing boat which was only a few feet from the shore. 'Chiltern?' queried a voice from the boat as the oars were shipped and one of the rowers jumped out to pull the small craft inshore.

'Yes. All present and correct.'

'In with you then, quick as you can. If this night's work becomes known to the local citizenry, it might well foil the negotiations.'

They needed no second bidding, but waded knee-deep to scramble into the boat. The rowers had dipped their oars almost before they were safely aboard and Jack had to be hauled in by James as they began to pull away again.

Twenty minutes later they were among the British ships and making for a sloop on the outer edge of the fleet. A rope ladder was flung over the side and caught by Jack as they came alongside. He turned to Kitty, holding out his hand and smiling reassuringly. 'Up you go, my dear. James will be right behind you.'

Now was not the time to have qualms, to have doubts about her fitness or wonder whether she might fall. Now was the time to grit her teeth and climb. She took a deep breath and began, one rung at a time, while Jack steadied the swaying ladder from below. She could hear James's heavy breathing as he followed her. As her head reached the top, many hands reached out and un-ceremoniously hauled her on board.

James came next, then Nanette, sobbing because she had almost slipped and had looked down to see the sea, inky black below her, and lost her nerve. Only Jack, climbing almost over her to steady her, had kept her going. But now all four were aboard.

'I'll take you down to the Captain's cabin,' one of

the sailors said, as Kitty and Nanette shook out their skirts and patted ineffectually at their hair.

They followed him down the companionway and were soon being ushered into the Captain's presence, a young man with untidy blond hair and very blue eyes.

'Edward!' Kitty and James exclaimed in unison.

He laughed. 'The last person you expected to see, eh? I have the honour of commanding this vessel, His Britannic Majesty's sloop, *Lady Lucia*.' He bowed with as much of a flourish as he could manage given the size of the cabin and the number of people in it.

To Jack he offered his hand. 'Good to see you again, my lord.'

'And I you. May I present my cousin, Nanette.'

'My wife,' James announced proudly.

Edward bowed to her. 'My felicitations, ma'am. I hope I may make you comfortable.' He turned to Kitty. 'And you, Miss Harston...'

'Lady Chiltern,' Jack corrected him.

'Is that so?' Edward looked from one to the other with amusement. 'Then may I wish you happy?'

'Thank you.' Kitty said, her voice slightly too brittle to be natural.

'Who would have thought when I last saw you that it would all turn out so well?' Edward said, beaming at her. 'I must say, I am vastly relieved. I often wondered if I was right to help you escape. I would certainly have thought twice about it if I had known where you intended to go.'

'Did my uncle know it was you?' she asked.

'I do not think so. He never said, though I have seen little of him since because of my naval duties. War keeps a man from home, you know.'

'Quite,' Jack said cryptically. 'Kitty's debt to you will be repaid just as soon as we reach home.'

'Pray, think no more of it,' he said. 'It was a gift, and if it has made Kitty happy, then I am content.'

Kitty did not reply and neither did Jack. There was nothing they could say. The silence stretched uncomfortably.

'I shall look forward to hearing all about your adventures tomorrow.' Edward said, smiling round at them all, making Kitty wonder if he had detected the strained atmosphere or whether it was her imagination. 'Now, I am afraid duty calls. We are sailing at once. The intelligence I have for the War Department cannot wait. The second lieutenant will show you to your quarters. This is a ship of war and not built for passengers, so the accommodation is somewhat spartan. On the plus side, we are fast and will have you in Portsmouth in no time.'

Portsmouth. England. Kitty viewed the prospect with mixed feelings. Not for the first time she began to wonder about her uncle and stepmother. What had happened in her absence? How was little Johnny? What would be said about her marriage? Would she be forgiven? Had her uncle received her last letter sent from Calais? Seeing Edward Lampeter again had brought it all home to her, long before she had expected to face it.

James seemed unconcerned when she found him alone, looking over the ship's rail at the oil-dark sea. She had delayed going down to her cabin, knowing Jack would be there. On board ship there were no horses to see to, no provisions to buy, no more despatches to write. They could not escape each other and the tension between them was tearing her to shreds.

'There will be no scandal,' James said. 'Why, you

have made a catch, don't you know that? Married to the Earl of Beauworth's heir. You won't be living at home any more, will you? You will be with your husband in Wiltshire. Alice won't be able to say a word against you. You have come up trumps. Edward did you a good turn.'

Her brother would not have said that, she told herself, if he had known the truth. She had gambled and lost and all because of one wrong move. 'I am not so sure…'

'What are you saying? You love Jack, don't you? You are not sorry you married him?'

'No, no, of course not. I was thinking of the manner it came about.'

'Oh, you will soon live that down, don't worry. Jack will be there to protect you from gossip. And so will I. If anything is said, I shall tell everyone I was with you the whole time. Now, go to bed.' He kissed her cool cheek. 'Goodnight and God bless.'

Only partly soothed, she went down to her cabin. Jack was in the upper bunk, apparently fast asleep. She undressed in the dark and crept into the lower one.

He heard her settle down, wondered whether to ask her where she had been, but decided against it. It might provoke another argument, she might say it was none of his business and he could not bear that.

They rose next morning to a calm sea and warm sunshine. After breakfast they went on deck where they met James and Nanette. Chairs were found for them and they sat down to a day of idleness. James was looking forward to taking his bride home and, confident that his reports of life in Revolutionary France would be accepted by a publisher, was full of plans to become a writer.

He had given Kitty his manuscripts to read and that furnished her with an excuse not to join in the general chatter. How could she talk of the future when she could see no further than the end of each day?

Towards noon, Edward joined them. 'All's well,' he said. 'We're on course in a good following wind, so now I have a little time to hear all about your adventures. How difficult is life in France these days? One hears such dreadful tales of the guillotine and rivers of blood. Surely they have been exaggerated?'

'Not knowing what accounts have reached England, it is difficult to say,' Jack said. 'Our own experiences were hair-raising enough. Kitty still bears the scars of an attempted hanging.'

'Good God! I beg your pardon, ladies, but that has really shocked me. How did it happen? How did you two come to be together in France? Surely that was not coincidence.'

'It was,' Kitty said, and told him how she had met Jack on board the packet, how Judith had died and her own ordeal. 'Jack looked after me, until we joined James,' she said.

'The last time I was home, my father told me that your uncle had had news of you,' he said. 'He knew you had gone to stay with the Marquis de Saint-Gilbert; your stepmama even boasted of it.'

'How could he possibly have known that? The last time I wrote was from Calais.'

'I wrote to him from Paris,' Jack said. 'I had intelligence to send, and enclosed news of you and told him where we were going, so that he would not worry about you.'

'Why didn't you tell me?' she demanded. 'I could have written myself.'

He smiled enigmatically. 'I could not tell you I was in touch with London, could I? It would have contravened all the rules of espionage and put you in very grave danger if the despatches had been intercepted. It was all done in code. By the time we reached Haute Saint-Gilbert, it became too difficult to send word overland, so I am afraid your uncle does not know we are married. That is something we shall have to tell him when we arrive, my dear.'

It was the longest speech he had made to her since their wedding night and the most exasperating. Long after Edward had left them to return to his duties, she went over and over it. Why had he taken all that trouble? The risk must have been enormous. Nanette said she thought he had been helping aristocrats to escape, but it was much more than that.

Wherever he went, he was known. There was the couple at Calais, the Claviers, Thomas Trent, the blacksmith and others along the route. And there had been times when he left her at their lodging in the evening, telling her to go to bed and not wait up for him. She imagined him relieving the boredom of escorting her by drinking and gambling. Sometimes he had called for pen and ink and wrote far into the night. Despatches. Letters to her uncle.

And there was Gabrielle. He had learned of her death in Paris and yet he had kept it to himself, bottled it up. Why could he not have confided in her? Why, oh, why had he married her?

Chapter Nine

Edward was right; the *Lady Lucia* was fast. Five days later they docked in Portsmouth with nothing to complain of but a little rough weather in the Bay of Biscay. The formalities were soon concluded, they said goodbye to Edward and stepped ashore, back in peaceful England at last.

Jack hired a coach to convey them all to his home where James and Nanette were to stay overnight before proceeding on to London. It was taken for granted that Kitty would remain at Chiltern Hall when James and Nanette left. Why wouldn't she? She was Jack's wife and, however brutal the circumstances of it, the marriage had been consummated.

She was filled with apprehension and misery, wondering what the Earl of Beauworth and his wife would think of their son's new wife. She looked like a peasant, had lived like one for so long she was even beginning to think and behave like one: ill clad, rough and unmannerly.

Both the gowns she had taken with her were torn and dirty, her stockings were full of holes, though she had tried mending them. She had no hat and her hair, a little longer than when Judith had cut it for her, stuck out like a bush. How could she face her new in-laws like that?'

Jack smiled when she ventured to express her concern. 'My dear, clothes mean nothing. You are who you are whatever you wear and my parents will understand. Nanette is also dishevelled and as for James and me...' He spread his hands, laughing at his disreputable appearance in black trousers, second-hand naval jacket and a plain tricorne hat. 'Hardly the stuff of gentlemen, are we? We are not returning from just a grand social occasion, but an adventure of epic proportions.'

An adventure, she thought, an adventure of my own making. Did I once envy James his independence? Did I really long to test my mettle in new experiences? Did I once wish I were a man? How foolish of me! Now I shall be labelled a hoyden and, if it had not been for Jack Chiltern, it would be much worse. She sighed. There was nothing to be done but brave it out.

'What you need, what we all need, is a bath and a good meal and a day or two to recuperate,' he went on. 'After that, you can go shopping for your immediate necessities in Winchester and, later, you can go to London and buy whatever fripperies take your fancy.'

Not one word about how he was going to explain their marriage so soon after he learned about the loss of his first wife, not one word about an annulment, or how they were going to go on, when they were so obviously not going to suit.

Chiltern Hall was a huge mansion set in acres and acres of parkland and reached by a private road lined with ancient elms. It had hundreds of windows and almost as many chimneys.

'Home,' Jack said, as the coach came to a stop outside the porticoed main entrance. He opened the carriage door and jumped down almost before the wheels had come to a stop and ran up the steps just as the door opened and a footman appeared.

'My lord! Oh, her ladyship will be so pleased to see you safe. She is in the blue parlour.'

'Oh, no, she is not,' said a female voice in a slight French accent. Kitty, who was being helped from the coach by James, looked up to see a woman, of perhaps a little over fifty, run and throw her arms about Jack. She was slim and elegant in a round gown of dark blue silk trimmed with bands of coloured ribbon. Her dark hair, with hardly a trace of grey, was piled high, on top of which was perched a tiny lace cap from which floated more ribbons. 'When did you get back? Oh, I am so glad to see you safe.'

She caught sight of the trio on the gravel beside coach. 'Who are these people?'

He smiled. 'Mother, here is Nanette. You remember her, don't you?'

'Nanette! *Quelle surprise!* Of course I remember you. Come 'ere, child, let me kiss you. Why, it must be seven or eight years since I saw you at Haute Saint-Gilbert. You are quite grown up. I am so pleased to see you safe. Is my sister with you? And the Marquis?'

Nanette curtsied and kissed her aunt. 'No, Aunt, Papa would not come, he feels his place is at home. *Maman* would not leave him.'

'No, she would not. But you are 'ere and for that I give thanks.'

Nanette turned towards James. 'Aunt Justine, this is my husband, James Harston.'

James swept an elegant bow. 'Your obedient, my lady.'

''Arston? Are you not the young man who saved my son in France?'

'It was fortuitous that I was in the right place at the right time, my lady.'

'Then you are doubly welcome.'

Jack reached out to take Kitty's hand and draw her forward. The gentle pressure of his hand, the warmth of his smile, made her insides melt, as they always did whenever he touched her. It was pleasure and torment together, heightening her sense of isolation and loss, feeding her desire. If he took her violently again, she would welcome it, welcome any sign that he wanted her for his true wife. If that was what the marriage bed was all about, so be it. But she could never tell him that.

'Mother, this is James's sister, Kitty. She is my wife.'

'Wife?' She looked from one to the other in confusion. ''Ow can she be? Gabrielle…'

'Gabrielle is dead, Mother. She died over a year ago.'

'Oh. Then I am sorry for it, but to marry again so soon…' She sighed. 'But I suppose you know what you are about.'

Did he? Kitty wondered as she curtsied. 'My lady, my presence must be a shock to you and I am sorry for that…'

'Oh, Jack is always giving me shocks. I am used to them,' Lady Beauworth said. Her smile was so like Jack's and her eyes were so like reflections of her son's that Kitty found herself warming to her. 'You are welcome. Come in and tell me all about it. But first some refreshment.' She led the way as she spoke.

'No, Mother,' Jack said. 'First a bath and clean clothes and then we can think of refreshment.'

'Of course,' she said. She turned to the footman. 'Fletcher, fetch Mrs Gordon.'

When the housekeeper arrived, crying with pleasure to see Jack safely home, her ladyship issued instructions one after another; fires were to be lit, water heated, beds made, food prepared. Servants ran hither and thither, obeying her commands, and, in no time at all, Kitty was in a vast bedroom being helped out of her filthy clothes and into a scented bath by her ladyship's own maid, Susan, whom she had brought with her from France when she married and who had never managed to get her tongue round the English language.

An hour later, with her blue gown cleaned, mended and pressed and her hair looking surprisingly neat after being washed, brushed and dressed, she ventured downstairs. Now she could converse with her hostess in a civilised fashion, to try and reverse what must have been a very poor first impression.

Her mother-in-law had taken the news of Gabrielle's death very calmly. It was almost as if she had half-expected it. And not a word of censure, only a warm welcome for her new daughter-in-law. If she and Jack had married in normal circumstances, if they had loved one another, she could be very happy here.

She was even more sure of it when she met the Earl of Beauworth, who was an older version of Jack, still very handsome though his hair was white. At dinner he questioned Jack carefully about the situation in France and what he had learned, especially about the situation around Lyons, his wife's former home.

'I hear Toulon has surrendered to Admiral Hood,' he

said. 'And the revolutionary government has ordered every able-bodied man into the army. Do you suppose that is the beginning of the end of this dreadful business?'

'No,' Jack said. 'I am convinced it will be worse before it is better. The revolt in the Vendée and Lyons has the government worried. They have tried to stir up more anti-Royalist hatred and ordered all the tombs and mausoleums of the kings to be destroyed. The bodies of Louis's ancestors have been dragged out and tipped into a lime-filled common grave. And the Queen has been taken to the Conciergerie and reduced to the status of a common criminal.'

'Oh, the poor, dear lady!' the Countess cried. 'And what of the Dauphin? Oh, but 'e is not the heir anymore, is 'e? 'E is the King. 'As 'e gone with her?'

'No one thinks of him as King; he is simply another Capet. By all accounts he was separated from his mother some time ago. He is still in the Temple, being brought up as a good *sans-culottes*.'

'Poor child. 'Ow can the world allow it? 'Ow can Britain stand by and do nothing?'

'We are doing what we can,' the Earl said. 'Now, tell us how you came to meet Kitty.'

This was a far happier subject and they listened with rapt attention as Jack gave them the facts in his dry, impassive voice. 'I know it was perhaps not ideal that we had to travel so far unchaperoned,' he said. 'But, until I learned of Gabrielle's death…'

'Yes, how did she meet her death?' his father asked.

'She went to the guillotine,' Jack said, his voice devoid of emotion. 'Denouncing me did not save her.'

'And have her parents been informed?' the Earl asked, while Kitty digested this piece of information.

Why had Jack never told her the manner of his wife's demise? It must have made it doubly difficult to bear. No wonder he had been so crusty.

'No, it is not something I could convey in a letter,' Jack said. 'I have decided to go with James and Nanette tomorrow and see them.'

'Tomorrow?' Kitty queried. 'But I thought…'

'It is not something that can be postponed, my love,' he said, speaking gently. 'They deserve to know the truth face to face. I will not be gone long and Mother will look after you until I return.'

'Of course,' her ladyship said. 'We will send for my dressmaker and have 'er make up some gowns, and then go into Winchester and shop for everything else. Then I shall show you all over the estate. We'll go riding and visiting in the phaeton. Will you like that?'

'Yes, very much. Thank you.'

'No need to thank me. You are my daughter now and it will give me great pleasure. You must 'ave a maid. Rose is a good girl and she 'elped me when Susan was indisposed last year. She will suit you very well, I think. I will send 'er up to you when you retire.'

Jack took his leave the very next day, kissing her goodbye at the front door with every appearance of tenderness. 'I will be back,' he said, looking into her violet eyes and wondering when the sparkle would return to them, when he would once again see the humour and spirit of her shining from them. It was his fault they had disappeared; perhaps absenting himself from her for a time might bring the roses back into her cheeks.

'Mother, you will look after her, won't you? She has been through so much and is very tired.'

'Of course, she shall have everything she needs and

wants. Now, off you go. And God bring you swiftly back.'

He climbed into the family coach with James and Nanette who had already said their goodbyes. They were taking a letter from Kitty to her uncle and step-mother, telling them of her marriage and asking their forgiveness.

She waved them out of sight and then turned back to her mother-in-law, who put an arm about her shoulders and smiled. 'Now, Kitty, you are not to grieve. 'E is only going to fulfil an unpleasant task and will be back before you know it.'

'What will your friends and neighbours think of me?' Kitty asked the Countess, two days later, when they were enjoying a ride in the phaeton. The estate was very extensive and covered parkland, pasture, woods, several farms, the river bank where the fishing was exceptional and the whole village of Beauworth. The weather was dry and warm and the workers were in the fields cutting the corn.

'They will love you, why should they not?'

'But they knew Gabrielle and that Jack loved her...'

'Jack was a fool.' It was said with such vehemence Kitty turned to look at her in surprise.

'I'm sorry, I don't understand.'

''As Jack not told you?'

Kitty smiled. 'He is hardly going to admit being a fool, is he?'

The Countess smiled. 'No, I suppose not. But 'e should 'ave said something instead of leaving you to think it was a happy marriage.'

'Nanette seemed to think it was. She said Jack was devoted to Gabrielle.'

'What does Nanette know of it? She only saw them together very briefly at the start of the marriage when she was only a child. And Jack would never complain. 'E is very good at 'iding his feelings, but that does not mean 'e does not feel deeply. Only we who are close to 'im know how much she made 'im suffer.'

Suffering. She had detected that in his eyes on several occasions. 'What did she do?'

'She was a virago, a taker. She gave nothing. Poor Jack tried to satisfy her, but the more 'e gave, the more she demanded. She would not live 'ere, said it was too dull, quarrelled with me, made Jack quarrel with me too...'

'But it is Jack's home,' Kitty exclaimed. 'And it is so beautiful and so peaceful, I cannot think how anyone could dislike it.'

'She did not want peace, Kitty, she wanted excitement. She could not live without it and turned to anyone who could give it to her. She loved risk...'

'She gambled?'

'Yes, and not just with money, Jack could have borne that in moderation. She gambled with 'is love, made 'im live in France and, when the war came and the family was forced to flee, she spent more time with 'er parents in London than 'ere.'

'It was from there she was abducted, wasn't it? Nanette told me she was kidnapped by someone from the French Embassy.'

'Abducted!' Her ladyship gave a short bark of a laugh. 'Jack told his cousin that, I expect. 'Is pride. No, Kitty, you should know the truth. The man was her lover. She ran off with 'im back to France. Her parents were distraught, as you can imagine, and they persuaded Jack to go after 'er, to try and bring 'er back. She betrayed 'is whereabouts to the Revolutionary government and 'e was arrested for 'elping the *comte* de Malincourt to escape the year previously.'

'That was when my brother saved him.'

'Yes. Jack came back without Gabrielle, but 'e was a changed man. His former sunny disposition turned to bitterness and anger. 'E could not settle to anything. 'E offered his services to the government as an agent and made several trips to France. Whether 'e was still looking for 'er, I do not know.' She sighed heavily. 'I was desolate every time 'e went, afraid 'e would never return.'

'Why did he never tell me all this?' Kitty asked. 'It would have explained so much.'

''E is a proud man, *chérie*. And you must not tell him of this conversation. 'E would see it as betrayal. No doubt 'e will tell you 'imself in time.'

'It does not matter. Now you have told me I understand.' She could understand why he found it so difficult to love, to give his heart to someone else. When he came home, she would make a special effort to be loving, to make him see that he could trust her and she would not fail him.

'I am so pleased 'e 'as found you,' her ladyship said, squeezing her hand. ''E deserves a little 'appiness.'

Kitty stared down at their two hands, one heavily ringed and the other with none at all, wondering if she ought to tell this dear, kind lady that the marriage was no more than one of convenience, that her husband disliked her and that, if it had not been for that one terrible night, it could have been annulled. She looked at her and smiled wanly, but remained silent.

'I can see you are still tired after your ordeal,' her ladyship said. 'We will forgo our visits today and go 'ome so that you can rest. And, Kitty, I know Jack could not buy you a proper wedding ring, but I think you ought to wear one. I will find one for you, until Jack comes 'ome and can buy you one.'

Kitty could hardly thank her for the tears which choked her.

A week passed in which she grew closer to her mother-in-law, learned the names of all the servants and was accepted by them and bought a wardrobe of new clothes, more than she needed or felt she ought to have, but the Countess would not listen to her protests. 'You must dress befitting your rank, my dear,' she said. 'There is no question that Jack can afford it. And it will please me.'

She gave in and allowed the Countess to help her choose gowns, pelisses, cloaks, undergarments, shoes, boots, shawls, even things like fans and feathers and jewellery. 'Of course, you will one day come into the family jewels,' she told Kitty. 'But, for now, I think a few pearls and simple gems will suffice, don't you agree?'

'Most assuredly I do. I am not used to so much.'

'But you deserve it for making my son 'appy.'

Kitty felt a fraud. She had not made Jack happy. He had shown no sign of being happy. Oh, he did not show his aversion to her in front of his parents or anyone else, but she knew it was there and it broke her heart.

Three days later, a letter arrived from her uncle. It was a long and loving letter. Jack had been to visit them and explained everything. They approved of the marriage and of course she was forgiven and the sooner she paid them a visit the happier they would be.

James and Nanette had arrived and were looking for a home in London. They had been most graciously received by Viscount Beresford, who had helped to find a publisher for James's account of his travels in France, and now James was planning other works.

'Jack has been to see Uncle William,' Kitty told Lady Beauworth.

'Well, naturally 'e would,' her ladyship said. ''E would want to obtain your guardian's blessing, even if it is a little late, and 'e would want to smooth the way for you to go 'ome for a visit. I would have expected nothing else from 'im.'

The letter and Lady Beauworth's comments cheered Kitty immensely and she began to look forward to making a visit to her old home. But not before Jack returned. Surely he would not have gone to see her uncle if he did not mean to remain her husband?

She began to watch for him every day. He would come home and they would make a fresh start. If she wanted her marriage to work, she must fight for it. She would risk a rejection and tell him she loved him, offer herself to him, tell him she asked nothing of him, but his good will. Love had blossomed from much less.

Her hopes were dashed when a letter arrived from Jack. She was in the breakfast parlour with her ladyship, when a servant brought the mail on a silver salver. The Earl had already left the house for the stables. One of his mares was foaling and he was particularly anxious over it.

Kitty turned the letter over in her hand, puzzled that Jack should write to her when he was expected home any day. But he wasn't coming home, she discovered when she broke the seal and began to read.

'Jack's gone back to France,' she gasped. 'Oh, why did he do that? I can't believe the War Department would make him go again.'

'Oh, *ma chérie*, I am so sorry,' her ladyship said. ''E was always doing that to me, rushing off without a by-your-leave, but I never thought 'e would do it to you. It is most inconsiderate of 'im.'

'And it's dangerous,' Kitty said. 'If he's caught…'

'Oh, you must not think of that. 'E will not take risks, not now 'e 'as you to come 'ome to. We must be patient.'

But patience was not one of Kitty's strong suits. She endured two days of idleness and then announced she was going to London. 'I must find out why he went,' she told Lord and Lady Beauworth. 'I need to know what is so important that none but Jack may be trusted with it. It isn't fair. He has already done enough.'

His lordship looked from Kitty to his wife, a question in his lifted brow. She nodded.

'I think I should also like answers to those questions,' he said. 'I will accompany you. They will be more forthcoming with me at Horse Guards than with you. We will set off tomorrow.'

'Take Rose to look after you,' Lady Beauworth said. 'I will go and tell 'er to pack.'

On Jack's instructions, the coachman had returned with the empty coach two days previously and it was soon made ready for the journey, with grooms sent ahead to arrange for changes of horses along the way.

The next day Kitty left her mother-in-law and Chiltern Hall, wondering if she would ever see them again. Jack had obviously decided to absent himself so long as she was there and she could not be so selfish as to deprive him of his home. Her grand plans to welcome him back with love and forbearance, to be a proper wife to him, had fallen about her ears. There would be no reconciliation.

She sat in the corner of the comfortable coach, staring out of the window, hardly noticing the countryside they passed. Her mind was filled with Jack, going over and over things he had done and said on their travels through France, remembering the way he had protected her and made it possible for her to return to her home with her reputation intact. Her eyes filled with tears.

'Oh, my dear, do not grieve,' his lordship said. 'He will come safely home.'

She fumbled for a handkerchief in the pocket of her gown and scrubbed at her eyes, unable to tell him the true reason for her tears. 'Yes. I am sorry.'

'Nothing to be sorry for,' he said, patting her hand. 'We will soon be there and then perhaps I can persuade the War Minister to recall him, eh?'

They stopped only to change the horses and have something to eat, and arrived at Beauworth House in Hertford Street late the same night. The Earl kept a number of servants there even when he was not in residence and their rooms were soon prepared and a meal put before them.

'Tomorrow I shall go to Horse Guards,' his lordship told her, as they ate. 'You will want to visit your uncle and stepmama. Take the coach. I can hire a chair.'

'Thank you, my lord,' she said, wishing Jack could have been there to accompany her. She needed his support. But visiting her old home would take her mind off what might be happening at Horse Guards.

* * *

It certainly did that. She dressed in the finest of her new gowns, a pale lemon silk with a deep fringe at the hem and a wide yellow-and-amber striped sash at the waist. The narrow sleeves ended in a deep frill and her shoulders were draped with a gathered scarf pinned above the cleft of her breasts with a large ornamental brooch. It was one Lady Beauworth had persuaded her to buy in Winchester and was only moderately expensive. Her hat had a tall crown and was trimmed with curling feathers. An amber-coloured pelisse, satin pumps and fine yellow kid gloves completed the outfit.

She smiled to herself as the Earl's carriage drew up at the rectory door. That would set her stepmother in a flurry and she would be dashing about giving orders about how her illustrious caller was to be received, not realising who it was.

Kitty was unable to suppress a smile when she saw the thunderstruck look on the maidservant's face when she opened the door. 'Miss Kitty!'

'Lady Chiltern,' Kitty corrected her with a smile. 'Would you please tell my uncle I am here.'

'Yes, miss—I mean, my lady.' The door was flung wide. 'I'll fetch him. Don't go away.' And she went running off to the rector's study, quite forgetting to show Kitty into the presence of Mrs Harston.

Alice, unable to contain herself in patience, came out into the hall to see an elegant young lady dressed in the height of fashion, standing alone peeling off her gloves. 'Oh, forgive me, ma'am. Where has that stupid girl gone? She should have brought you straight to me. Servants these days are so useless, one is in despair of finding one who knows what is expected of her. Do come in. Oh...' Her voice faded in shock as Kitty turned to face her. 'It's you.'

'Yes, Stepmama, it is Kitty. And Annie has gone to fetch Uncle William.'

'Oh, then you had better come into the drawing room. He will be down directly, though you are lucky to find him in. He is more often than not at Beresford Hall. Your grandfather has asked him to catalogue the library, you know.'

She led the way into the drawing room. 'As you see, nothing has changed. Sit down. When your uncle comes we will have tea. I must say, you have done very well for yourself. How did you manage to persuade Viscount Chiltern to take you on, I wonder? You had nothing to commend you. I never would have believed it if I had not met his lordship himself.

'Such a gentleman,' she went on, giving Kitty no opportunity to reply, not even when Annie came in with the tea tray and set it on the table at her side. She waved the maid away and continued without pause. 'He and the Reverend spent a long time closeted together in the study, though what they had to talk about, I cannot imagine. There could be no question of a dowry. You had left home, cut yourself off...' She looked up as the Reverend came into the room. 'Ah, here is your uncle.'

Kitty rose and ran to her uncle, dropping him a full curtsy. 'Uncle William.' She was too choked to go on.

'Get up, Kitty, do. And give your uncle a kiss.'

He was holding out his arms. She flung herself into them. 'Oh, Uncle, it is so good to see you again. I am truly sorry if I hurt you. Please say you forgive me.'

'Of course I forgive you. You are my niece, though why James should write to you of his problems and not to me, I do not know. And to swear you to secrecy! I have given him a very great scold.'

Kitty had no idea what he was talking about, but dare not say so. 'Oh, but you should not blame James.'

'No, for some of it must be put at the door of young Chiltern. Spies, agents, I never heard the like. If James needed money for his clandestine work, why did he not ask me for it? He should have known you would have to borrow it.'

She was beginning to see daylight. 'I think he did not want to trouble you, especially as you do not approve of war and fighting. And I don't suppose he thought I would be so foolish as to take it to him myself.'

'So he said.' He sighed. 'Ah, well, we will say no more of it. Edward Lampeter has been repaid and you have come back married. Are you happy, child?'

'Yes,' she lied.

'Who wouldn't be, married to the heir to an earldom?' Alice put in, pouring tea. 'That can't be bad. I am so thankful I advised your uncle against that match with Edward Lampeter. After all, he is nothing but a sea captain and his father a mere baronet.'

'He is also a very nice man, Stepmama,' Kitty said. Her stepmother did not change; she was still manipulating the truth to suit herself, forgetting that she was the one who had wanted to send Kitty away. Now it pleased her to think she had been instrumental in marrying Kitty off so advantageously.

'Yes, of course. Now, drink your tea and we will go up to the nursery to see Johnny. I wonder if he will remember you. Children forget so easily, do they not?'

Johnny had not forgotten her. He showered her with kisses and exclaimed rapturously over the toy soldiers she had brought him as a present, asking her if she was going to stay.

'No, my love, but I shall visit you again and you may come and visit me soon.'

She took her leave and returned to Beauworth House, thankful to escape Alice's sharp tongue. How her uncle bore it, she did not know. Even if she and Jack never lived together, if the marriage came to an end, she would not live at home again. Too much had happened and she knew Alice would never let her forget her infamous conduct, whatever her uncle said; there would be hints and innuendo and cruel taunts, just as there always had been. Whatever happened, she would keep her hard-won independence.

Her father-in-law had only in the last hour returned from Horse Guards. 'All day I've been there,' he complained to Kitty, as soon as she had taken off her pelisse and hat and joined him in the withdrawing room. 'Everyone seemed intent on passing me on to someone else. They were too polite to tell me to go away, but too cautious to tell me what I wanted to know. I had to go right to the top, the Minister himself.'

'What did he say? Is he going to recall Jack?'

'He said he could not. He said communication was so bad, he could do nothing until Jack himself sent word.'

'But what is he doing in France? He cannot save the whole French nobility single-handed.'

His lordship smiled a little grimly. 'No, but he might try to save one in particular, someone extra special…' He paused.

'The Queen?' she queried. 'The young King?'

'I am sworn to secrecy,' he said enigmatically, but she knew she was right by the look in his eyes.

'It is, though, isn't it? Oh, how could they ask it of him? Surely her Majesty is closely guarded?'

'Undoubtedly she is. We must pray for a successful outcome.' He paused and reached across to take her hand. 'I have been told that the *Lady Lucia* with Captain Lampeter on board is standing by off the coast of Brittany to take them all to safety.'

'If they succeed.'

'Even if they do not, the sloop will wait two days for Jack.'

'When is the attempt to be made?'

'I was not told the exact date. The Minister told me he had already given me more information than he should have done and we must be content with that.'

'Yes, I understand.' But it was so very difficult to accept and her imagination was already running riot with all the things that could go wrong.

He smiled reassuringly. 'We will go home tomorrow and wait and pray for Jack's safe return. And Kitty…' He paused. 'We will say nothing of this to anyone, do you understand?'

'Of course.'

'Not even the Countess. Especially not the Countess. We must shield her from worry, she has had to endure enough already. Her country torn apart by bloodshed and her son so confused and unhappy, he must expunge it by flinging himself into ever more dangerous situations. But now he has you and a chance to settle down. To be honest, I am a little peeved with him for volunteering to go. He had no business to leave you so soon after your wedding.'

'I expect he thought it was his duty.'

'Duty, bah! His duty is to you and his family. He is my only son and heir and I want to see a grandson before I call in my accounts. If I lost him…'

'Oh, pray that you do not,' Kitty said, reaching out to touch his arm.

He took her hand from his sleeve and squeezed it. 'This is no way to go on, is it? We will be patient and cheerful.'

'Yes, my lord.'

'Can you not call me Father? I should like that very much.'

'Yes, Father,' she said, shyly. She was beginning to love this man and the thought of disappointing him as a daughter-in-law weighed heavily on her. She sensed that he needed her, that her presence was a comfort to him in the absence of his beloved son. 'We will go home.'

If only Jack would come back, if only they could somehow learn to get along together.

The forger had been busy again and Jack now had a new identity. His cover as Jacques Faucon was blown. Now he was Pierre Bandol, a gunsmith. Because there had been mass conscription of all young men to fight the war that was sapping the country's life-blood along with that spilled daily in the Place de la Guillotine, he was obliged to pretend to be lame and had practised a strange limping gait, as if one leg were longer than the other. It was tiring, but it did mean he was left alone when recruits were rounded up and marched off to be soldiers.

The Luxembourg and Tuilleries Gardens had been turned into massive forges and the fires were kept going night and day, making weapons. In the buildings nearby women were set to work stitching tents and uniforms, and children were making bandages. Men too old to fight were directed to repair roads and public places and encouraged to preach patriotism, the invincibility of the Republic and the hatred of kings.

The need for more and more weapons made it easy for Jack to find work, to listen to gossip, to find out exactly where in the Conciergerie the Queen was held. It was becoming even more urgent that something was done because there was open talk of putting her on trial for treason. But it seemed no one had any communication with the prisoner. She was kept in solitary confinement and even her guards had guards and were watched.

It was the end of August before any progress could be made. After weeks of careful nurturing the prison administrator, a former lemonade seller called Michonis, was persuaded to let the Queen have a visitor.

The Chevalier de Rougeville, who had led the Queen to safety from the attack on the Tuilleries just before the royal family were taken to the Temple prison, was allowed to have a few words with Antoinette and left her a message hidden in a carnation. 'We have men and money at your service. I will come Friday.'

'Now, we wait,' he said to Jack and the other conspirators when he met them afterwards in the cellars of a wine merchant. 'And pray she found the message. I was watched all the time and could give no indication that she should examine the flower.'

It was one of her guards, a man named Gilbert and a distant cousin of Jack's, who brought her reply, pricked out with a pin on a scrap of paper. 'I am watched. I speak to no one. I trust you. I shall come.'

The scene was set for one of the most daring attempts of rescue Jack had ever been involved in. Shortly before eleven on Friday the second of September, dressed as a guard, he accompanied Michonis and Gilbert to the Queen's cell, deep inside the prison.

The room was only a few feet square, sparsely furnished with three beds, one for the Queen, one for her woman and one for the two guards who never left her. It had no fireplace and no lighting, save for a glimmer of light which came from a lamp in the courtyard. It was bitterly cold and had a sour-sweet smell of medicines and herbal concoctions, having once been the prison pharmacy.

Jack was shocked that the queen of a great country like France should be treated so harshly, but he could say nothing, nor show her any politeness or good manners. He did not speak at all and neither did Gilbert.

'I have orders to conduct the Widow Capet back to the Temple,' Michonis told the guards.

Flanked by Gilbert and Jack, dressed as a gendarme, and preceded by Michonis, the Queen left the cell and began to walk down a long corridor and through several gates, each of which had to be unlocked. So far so good. There was only one more to be unlocked and then they would be at the main exit, where Rougeville waited with a carriage. Nervously Michonis fumbled with the keys, but at last they were through and could see the dim outline of a vehicle in the courtyard.

Suddenly Gilbert stopped. 'What ails you, man?' Jack demanded.

'I saw something,' he whispered, shaking from head to toe with fear. 'A guard with a musket, hiding in the shadows.'

Jack looked. 'There is no one there. Come on, we have no time to lose.'

'I can't. It is not right…'

Jack was all for knocking him down and continuing without him, but Michonis himself seemed to lose his nerve. He placed himself before the Queen, who appeared to be on the verge of fainting. 'Go back.' He glanced towards the main gate as he spoke. The sentries there were watching them intently, their muskets off their shoulders, ready for use. 'Our bluff has been called. Go back, *citoyenne*, back to your room.'

The Queen gave one despairing look at Jack, turned and walked slowly back through the gates they had just left, followed by Michonis and Gilbert. The sentries moved forward, muskets pointing. Jack could not go back into the prison; his only hope of escape lay with Rougeville, who was pacing impatiently beside the carriage, wondering what had delayed them.

He strode towards the sentries, hoping they had not recognised the Queen. 'A slight hitch,' he said, and passed them at a run. They levelled their muskets and called to him to halt. 'Get into the coach!' he yelled at Rougeville, as bullets spattered round him. Rougeville, startled, ran back to the coach and scrambled inside, holding the door open for Jack, while the driver whipped up the horses.

They rattled out of the courtyard followed by musket fire, across the bridge and into the maze of alleys on the north side of the river. Behind them they could hear shouts of command and the sound of horses in pursuit.

'What happened in there?' Rougeville demanded.

'Gilbert got cold feet.' Jack had been hit by a musket ball and his arm was hurting him. 'We were within a hair's-breadth of pulling it off and the spineless fool has to go and be frightened by a shadow. Michonis realised the game was up and quietly took the Queen back where she came from.'

'Damn! We'll never have another chance to save her. They'll be doubly watchful now. Did they recognise you?'

'I don't know, but it is of little consequence. I am not going to go anywhere for a little while.'

Alerted by his tone, his companion turned to look at him. 'You've been wounded?'

'Yes. And please do not suggest taking me to a hospital.'

'You need attention.'

'I've had all the attention I need, I thank you, sir. I'll get out here.' He put his head out to tell the driver to stop. 'You save yourself.'

'Where are you going?'

'Best you don't know.' He opened the door and yelled at the driver. 'I told you to stop, damn you. At least slow down.'

Reluctantly the man pulled the horses up, but long before the wheels had stopped turning Jack had jumped into the road. He stumbled and put his hand against a wall to save himself, jarring his injured arm, forcing a grunt of pain from him. The coach rattled on and he dashed into an alley as their pursuers passed.

Ten minutes later he half-walked, half-fell into Jean Clavier's furniture workshop among the wood shavings and chair legs.

'Jack! What in heaven's name are you doing here?' his friend demanded. 'And wounded too. Well, do not say I did not warn you. Come on, let me get you upstairs. Thérèse will bind you up.' He put Jack's good arm about his shoulder and helped him up the stairs and into his living quarters. 'But do not tell us what happened. We do not want to know.' He gave a cracked laugh, as he guided him through the sitting room into a bedroom beyond it. 'Not that it would help much if a wounded man were seen coming in. There is a new law. Anyone can denounce anyone anonymously. They call it the Law of the Suspect.'

'I know. I do not ask you to hide me. Simply bind me up and let me be on my way.'

Jean let him down onto a bed. 'Where do you go?'

'Home.' The sound of the word conjured up visions of England, of Chiltern Hall, of his parents and Kitty. Most of all, of Kitty. He had been a fool not to tell her he loved her, a bigger fool not to stay at home where it was safe and where they could learn to love each other. She had a great capacity for love, he knew that without being told; all he had to do was make her fix some of it on him.

Edward Lampeter on *Lady Lucia* was standing by off the coast of Brittany, watching for the signal to send a boat ashore to pick up the Queen and her rescuers. They had failed, but he must still make it to the rendezvous and then home. Home and Kitty.

Thérèse was digging around in his wound, trying to find the musket ball, and the pain was making him sick and dizzy. Jean handed him a bottle of cognac and he gulped at it. It dulled the edge of the pain. Kitty hovered in a kind of fog just out of his reach. He lifted an arm feebly beckoning her to come to him. Thérèse put it back under the covers.

'To England?' she demanded. 'How will you get there? You will be lucky if you do not catch a fever from this wound.'

'No, no fever...' He yelped as the ball came out and Jean fetched the poker from the fire to cauterize the wound.

'Be quiet, would you have the whole *armée revolutionaire* down on us? Drink some more brandy.'

'You're a hard woman Thérèse Clavier,' he murmured, half-drunk, half-fainting. 'But an angel.'

'You can stay here tonight, tomorrow you go, understand?'

'Yes.' He rolled his head towards Jean. 'Get me a cart.'

He was far from fit to travel the next day, but it was not because of Thérèse's insistence that he went, but his own determination to reach the coast. They dressed him up as an old woman, an old woman with a fever, so that no one would come near him, then they loaded him on to the back of an empty farm cart and covered him with sacks which had once held potatoes. The stench made him feel sicker than ever.

The owner drove him through the *barrière* at Saint-Denis and took him to the farmhouse on the Calais road, where, having been paid generously in gold coin, he left his passenger to the tender mercy of Lucie and her mother.

The jolting had made his wound bleed again and he was only semi-conscious. It took all their strength to haul him from the downstair room where the farmer had dumped him like a sack of potatoes, up to his own bedroom, by which time he was past caring.

Lucie, who loved him, would not let him die. She would take any risk for him and set off for Paris to buy salve and ointment and laudanum for his pain, hiding her purchases in her petticoats in case she was stopped. She did not go through the barriers, but out over a broken wall and through a cemetery. As soon as she was clear she began to run.

He was worse by the time she arrived. Her mother had been sitting at his side all day, bathing his brow with cool water, giving him sips of water to drink, and praying loudly to every saint she could think of who might help. 'He has been calling Kitty's name in his delirium,' she told her daughter, when she returned. 'And he thrashed about and made his wound bleed. What shall we do if he dies? How shall we get word to his family?'

'He is not going to die, *Maman*. I will not let him. Come let us wash him down and dress that wound again with this new ointment and see if we can get him to swallow a little laudunum.'

It was three days before he came to his senses; by then he knew it was useless to go to the coast. Edward Lampeter had his orders not to wait above two days and he would obey those orders. Now everyone would know the attempt to rescue Antoinette had failed and they would assume he had died. He might do so even now, if news of his whereabouts reached the Revolutionary government.

He must escape, if only for the sake of Lucie and her mother, who would forfeit their lives for giving him succour; it would take only a malicious neighbour to denounce them. All the ports were blocked. Save one. Toulon was in the hands of Admiral Hood. Five hundred miles away. Five hundred miles across enemy terrain, and this time without the woman whose company had delighted him before. Did he have the strength for it?

Chapter Ten

It was September and the leaves were beginning to turn colour in the woods on the estate before the news reached Chiltern Hall that the attempt to rescue Antoinette had failed.

Kitty had gone downstairs to breakfast as she was in the habit of doing, though Lady Beauworth rarely rose before midday. She found his lordship alone, eating toast and reading his mail. Bidding him good morning, she seated herself at the table to be served her own breakfast.

'This is a letter from Captain Lampeter,' he told her. 'He docked at Portsmouth two days ago.'

Her heart began to beat so fast she could hardly breathe. The sloop had been in two days, long enough for Jack to have reached home if he had been on board. Where was he? Had he had taken one risk too many? 'Jack?' she queried. 'Oh, tell me he is all right. Tell me has has only gone to London to report and will be here soon.'

'I only wish that were so.'

'What does Edward say?' She could only pick at her

food; her stomach was too queasy in the mornings to eat heartily.

'Only that the sloop waited a full twenty-four hours longer than the allotted time, but there was no signal from the shore. They had to leave without any of our people.'

'That doesn't mean anything, does it?' she said, clutching at straws. 'There could be any number of reasons why he missed the rendezvous. It is early days yet.'

'Of course,' his lordship agreed, sounding positively cheerful. 'If the Revolutionaries had captured him, they would not have kept silent about it, the French papers would have been full of it. An English peer, trying to free the Queen! My goodness, the whole world would have heard of it by now.'

'What shall we tell her ladyship?'

'Nothing. Not yet. I shall invite Captain Lampeter to visit us. He will perhaps be able to tell us more.'

But when Edward came there was little else he could tell them. He had landed Jack secretly on the coast of Brittany where the remnants of a counter-revolution had not yet been entirely eradicated. 'There were sympathisers there waiting for him,' he said.

'And that was the last you saw of him?' Kitty asked. They were talking in the library where his lordship had received his visitor. It was afternoon and her ladyship had taken the carriage to call on friends. Kitty had declined to go with her, preferring to stroll round the grounds. Seeing Edward arriving, she had hurried back to the house to join the two men, knowing her father-in-law would not exclude her.

'Yes.'

'So you do not know if he even reached Paris?' his lordship asked.

'No, but we know the attempt to free Antoinette was made and one must suppose he had a hand in it. It was his mission, after all.' He paused, knowing something more was expected of him, but unable to give them the reassurance they needed. 'It is a pity it failed. If it had succeeded, it would have been a great coup and every exiled Frenchman would have rallied to her. The other great powers might have renewed their efforts to rid France of the scourge. As it is…' He shrugged.

'Do you think Jack stayed behind to try again?' Kitty asked him.

'It is possible, but very unlikely. The Queen will be more closely guarded than ever and the latest intelligence is that she is to be tried for treason. Our sources say it was talked of at a secret session of the Committee of Public Safety, but as the man most wanting the Queen's execution, besides being a *procureur* of the Paris Commune, is also the editor of *Père Duchesne*, a popular newspaper, it did not remain a secret very long.

'He is reported to have said he promised his readers Antoinette's head and, if there was any further delay in giving it to them, he would go and cut it off himself. The Public Prosecutor has been called in to make a case against her.'

'Have they one?' Kitty asked.

'I don't know. The report is non-committal, but no doubt they will fabricate one.'

'Jack is missing, not dead,' Kitty said stubbornly. 'He has simply gone to ground. He knows where he can be safe.'

With Lucie, perhaps?

The thought of Lucie and Jack together in that shabby

but comfortable farmhouse filled her with jealousy. Lucie loved Jack, she had made no secret of it. How long before Jack, in hiding and cut off from home, came to reciprocate that feeling? He was not made of stone, he had told her so, had demonstrated it in no uncertain way.

Lucie had known Jack longer than she had; Lucie had made no demands on him, she had simply given him her love. And if Jack chose to ignore his clandestine marriage… What had he said? 'How do you know that, in these heathen times, a wife cannot be discarded as easily as a grubby cravat?' Oh, she did not want to think of that. She would not.

They had unfinished business, she and Jack, and he must come home. He must. She had put their quarrel firmly behind her, pretending it was nothing but a tiff, her innocent reaction to the act of love which she had not understood, and she wanted to tell him that. She wanted to tell him that the result of that one night's union, unnerving as it had been, was to be a child. And the waiting was tearing her to shreds.

Her theory that Jack had stayed behind to make a second attempt to free the Queen was blown away a month later when they learned she had been tried and executed.

'A week ago on October the sixteenth,' his lordship said, tapping the newspaper which had been delivered that morning. 'She was accused of conspiring with her brother, King Leopold of Austria, against France and sending him money; organising a counter-revolution; forcing Louis to veto the deportation of priests; having a hand in appointing her husband's ministers favourable to herself and trying to start a civil war.'

'*C'est incroyable,*' Justine said. They were seated at nuncheon and this time the Countess was included in the discussion. ''Ow can anyone believe that nonsense? Why, she is nothing but an empty-headed pleasure seeker. I 'ave met her and anyone less likely to meddle in politics I cannot imagine.'

'They tried at the preliminary examination to trap her into a confession, but she came out of it very well,' her husband went on, referring to the report. 'At the trial itself the prosecution maintained that she had influenced the King into doing whatever she wished, that she made use of his weak character to carry out her evil deeds. They called dozens of witnesses, including her son. His evidence was vile.'

'Poor little Louis loved his mother,' the Countess said. ''E must 'ave been coerced into giving evidence.'

'Was she not allowed to say anything in her own defence?' Kitty asked, remembering her own so-called trial.

'She was allowed to speak at the end, but it did no good. The jury took only an hour to find her guilty and she was sent to the guillotine the very next day. The report says it took nearly an hour for the tumbril to reach the Place de la Guillotine because of the press of the crowd. She had to be helped out of the cart and up the ladder to the scaffold. Four minutes later she was dead and her head held up for all to see. According to this, the crowd cheered themselves hoarse.'

Kitty shuddered. 'Whatever is the world coming to? Where is their Christianity?'

'Denounced, along with everything else.' He sounded weary and dispirited. 'Sunday has been abolished, the churches closed or turned into what they call Temples of Reason.' He laughed suddenly. 'It is bizarre. All the months now have thirty days divided into ten-day periods. *Décades*, they call them. And they have new names. October is called *brumaire* now.'

'I cannot imagine anything more likely to cause chaos,' his wife said. 'Surely the people will rise up against that? They are most of them Catholic, they will want to say Mass and go to confession.'

'They will do it secretly,' Kitty said. 'The priest who conducted the marriage ceremony for us at Haute Saint-Gilbert did it in secret because he was one of those who would not take the new oath, but he said it was no less legal.'

'When Jack gets back we'll make doubly sure,' his lordship said. 'We will have another ceremony.'

'Oh,' she said, shocked. 'Do you think it wasn't legal?'

He smiled and reached out to pat her hand. 'Of course it was, my dear. You and Jack believed it was and that is good enough for me. Think no more of it.'

But now the doubt had been planted in her head, Kitty could not shake it off. Had Jack known the marriage wasn't legal? Was that why he was able to say they could have it annulled and why he was so angry with her on their wedding night? Now, added to the worries over Jack's absence was added the anguish of a marriage that was no marriage at all and of bringing an illegitimate child into the world. How could she be sanguine about that? She had not told anyone of her condition, but it would soon become obvious, and then what? Would they accept the child?

'Now perhaps Jack will come 'ome,' the Countess said, then smiled when she saw the startled look her husband and daughter-in-law gave each other. 'Do not look so surprised. Did you think I did not know 'e 'ad gone back to France?'

Kitty smiled. 'We hoped to save you distress.'

'What about your own distress, Kitty? You must be as worried and afraid as I am.'

'No, Mama, I am not afraid,' she lied. 'Jack will come back soon. I have no doubt he has gone south to Toulon, as we did before.'

'Then perhaps 'e has gone to Haute Saint-Gilbert and will bring us news of Anne-Marie.'

Kitty agreed, not daring to say what was in her mind. With the whole of France undoubtedly searching for the conspirators, Toulon, in British hands, was an obvious place to look for them. And if Jack's identity was known, they would also be watching Haute Saint-Gilbert and Malincourt.

For his lordship's sake and for the Countess's, she had to sound confident, but inside she was crying.

As the autumn days shortened towards winter and still there was no news of Jack, hope began to die inch by inch.

France was slipping into anarchy. According to some reports reaching England, the Law of the Suspect was being used to feed the guillotine, often several at a time, and those who had been at the forefront of the Revolution were themselves being put to death. No aristocrat was safe and even men of letters and science were obliged to watch their tongues and be continually looking over their shoulders. What hope had a foreign agent of staying undiscovered?

The Earl wrote frequently to the War Department, but they had nothing to tell him, except that the situation in France was so confused that there was little information coming through. 'We are forced to the conclusion that Viscount Chiltern has been apprehended and may have met his death,' they wrote. 'Until lines of communication are reopened, we cannot confirm this but must counsel you against false hope.'

Kitty, in her fourth month of pregnancy, was in despair. Had Jack died? Had he given his life for a foreign queen, not knowing she loved him, that he was to be a father? Knowing about the baby helped the Earl and Countess to bear their loss and Kitty herself was a little comforted by the small being growing inside her. She must live for her child, watch him grow healthy and happy and pray that the dreadful deeds being perpetrated against humanity in France would never be repeated.

She corresponded with James and Nanette frequently, and that November they arrived for a short visit. Nanette, too, was expecting a baby, though she was not as far advanced in pregnancy as Kitty, and the two young women were able to talk and even laugh a little over it so that the dreary atmosphere was lightened a little.

James and the Earl talked a great deal about the war with France, expressing the hope that, when it was won, the monarchy could be restored in France and that it would be safe for Nanette to visit her parents, or for them to come on a visit to England. She worried about them constantly.

They were two weeks into their stay when everyone's rest was disturbed at eight one morning by a loud knocking at the front door. Apart from the servants, Kitty was the only one already astir.

She had slept badly and had decided to dress and go down to the kitchen rather than summon a maid to bring her a dish of hot chocolate. She paused on the stairs as Fletcher, slow and ponderous, went to open the door.

The man who stood on the step was tall and gangly, dressed in a plain dark suit of clothes over which he wore a cloak and a black tricorne hat, both of which glistened with damp. It had rained during the night and now a thin mist covered the ground and hung in the air.

'Captain Trent!' Kitty cried, dashing down the rest of the stairs. 'How good it is to see you! Have you news of Jack?'

'My lady.' The one-time roadmender bowed to her, while his cloak dripped on the tiled floor. 'No, I am afraid not, but I have brought someone to see you.'

He turned back to a hired coach which stood on the drive and opened its door to assist a lady to alight. She was of middle years dressed in a rich taffeta gown with a woollen riding cloak, both of which were creased and travel-stained. The long feathers in her high-crowned hat drooped in the damp air. It was a moment or two before Kitty recognised the Marchioness de Saint-Gilbert.

'My lady!'

Anne-Marie smiled feebly. '*Bonjour*, Kitty.'

Although it was only a few months since Kitty had last seen her, she had aged. She seemed smaller, shrunken almost; her eyes were dull and there were deep lines about her mouth.

Kitty ran forward to help her into the house. 'Come in. Come into the morning parlour. I believe there is already a fire in there. Take off your cloak. Fletcher will have it dried for you. You too, Captain Trent.' Then, to Fletcher, 'Please tell the Earl and Countess and Mrs Harston we have visitors.'

She led the Marchioness and the Captain into the parlour and invited them to sit down by the fire. 'I'll have some refreshment brought in. You must be cold and hungry. Lord and Lady Beauworth will be here soon.' She rang a bell and ordered coffee and food to be prepared, then sat down, biting her lip in an effort not to bombard them with questions.

'Nanette is here,' she said in French. 'Did you know?'

'No, I didn't.' Anne-Marie's eyes lit briefly with pleasure. 'I came here first because I did not have her direction. I assumed my sister would have it.'

At that moment the Countess came into the room, clad in a dressing robe over her nightgown, and with a cry of joy ran to her sister and embraced her. 'Oh, my dear, dear Anne-Marie, I am so pleased to see you. But how did you get here? Where is Louis?'

'Louis is dead.' She spoke flatly as if repeating something someone had told her.

'Oh, no! I am so sorry. How did it happen? No, do not tell me now. Here is Annie with some refreshment. Eat and drink first. When John and Nanette come, you must tell us together.'

Kitty, suddenly remembering Thomas, who was sitting silently contemplating the fire, turned to her mother-in-law. 'Mama, may I present Captain Thomas Trent, a friend of Jack's.'

The Countess turned to face him, her face alight. 'Captain Trent,' she said, reverting to English. 'You 'ave news of Jack? You 'ave seen 'im?'

'Yes, I have seen him.'

The Earl came in at that point. He had dressed in breeches and shirt, but no neckcloth, and his feet were encased in soft slippers. Fletcher must have told him their visitor came from France, for he would never normally appear in a state of undress. Like Kitty, his first thought had been of Jack. He was closely followed by Nanette who had hastily flung on a muslin day gown and pulled a brush through her hair.

'*Maman!*' She flung herself on her knees in front of her mother's chair. 'Oh, *Maman*! I could not believe it when the maid told me. It is so good to see you.' She paused and looked round the room. 'But where is Papa?'

Her mother reached out to stroke her daughter's hair. 'My darling, your papa…' She paused to swallow. 'He is dead.'

'Dead?' She looked wildly round the room. 'How? What happened? Was he ill?'

Her mother leaned wearily back in her chair. 'Let Captain Trent tell you. I don't think I can bear to recount it.'

Everyone turned to Thomas, who cleared his throat before beginning the tale. He was aware of Kitty watching him, knowing she was anxious to learn what he had to say about Jack, but holding back for Nanette's sake. In any case, the two stories were really one.

'The Marquis was denounced,' he said. 'I don't know who it was, one of the servants, I suspect. He and his wife were arrested.'

Nanette turned to her mother. 'You too?'

'Yes. They took us to Lyons prison. They said Louis was a friend of the *ci-devant* King and went to Paris last year with the purpose of helping in the escape of the Royal family. When they failed, he had connived in the escape of a wanted criminal and an English spy.'

'I can hardly believe it,' Kitty said. 'Why, he was at great pains always to placate the new regime, you know that. Thomas, you were there when he informed on Jack…'

'He informed on Jack!' his lordship repeated. 'You did not tell me this.'

'No, it would have made no difference and I wanted to spare the Countess.'

'Continue,' his lordship instructed Thomas.

'They had been in prison less than two days awaiting trial when Jack turned up unexpectedly…'

'At the château?' Kitty asked.

'No, he had more sense than to do that. He came to my cottage. He was injured. During the abortive attempt to free Antoinette, he took a musket ball in the shoulder.' He ignored Kitty's gasp and the little cry from the Countess, who was sitting bolt upright in her chair, with the Earl standing behind her, his hand on her shoulder. 'He had friends who took the bullet out and other friends who nursed him, but he missed the rendezvous—'

'I knew it,' Kitty interrupted. 'Oh, please go on.'

'He decided to try for Toulon, which was why he came to me. He was very weak, having walked most of the way, and had not dared to call on his old contacts for help.' He paused to sip his coffee. No one else spoke.

'As soon as he heard about the arrest of his uncle and aunt, he insisted on trying to free them. It was madness. The Marquis…' He bowed his head towards the Marchioness. 'Begging your pardon, my lady. The Marquis had already betrayed Jack to the authorities; they knew who he was and would be only too eager to get their hands on him. I tried to dissuade him, but it was useless.'

Kitty hardly dared breathe. This story was looking

more and more like the tale of a man determined on death. Thomas's next words seemed to confirm that. 'His plan was nothing short of reckless. I told him it would fail, that he would forfeit his life, but he didn't seem to care. He had a wild sort of look about him. I thought he had a fever from his wound.'

'He went ahead despite that?' Kitty murmured.

'Yes. His idea was to waylay the tumbril on the way to the guillotine.'

'By 'imself?' Justine gasped.

'No, I helped him and two others. There was a big crowd round the guillotine and all along the route, all very noisy and shouting for blood. We planned to ambush the cart when it passed the end of a narrow alley that went under the houses to the road on a lower level. Lyons is like that, you know, full of secret little tunnels and alleyways. One of us would pull the horse up and tackle the driver, two others were detailed to pull the prisoners out of the cart and bundle them away. Jack was to fight off anyone who tried to come after us.'

'They managed to free me because I was on the near side,' Anne-Marie said in French. 'But they could not reach Louis. One of the guards clubbed him over the head with his musket so that he fell unconscious into the bottom of the cart.'

'Jack struggled with the guards,' Thomas said. 'He fired his pistols, but I do not know if he hit anyone. He shouted to us to go, he would follow.' He paused. 'I am sorry. I wanted to stay with him, but I had the Marchioness to look after and she was all but fainting in my arms.'

'You think he died?' the Earl asked.

'I don't know how he can have survived. I am sorry, but the last I saw of him one of the guards had floored him and…' He looked doubtfully from Kitty to the Countess.

'Go on,' her ladyship said. 'I want to know it all.'

'He was sticking his bayonet into him. I went back into the town later, after I had taken the Marchioness to safety. The Marquis had been guillotined, that much I could confirm, but no one would admit to knowing anything about Jack. I dared not tarry.'

'No, of course not,' Kitty reassured him, though it was an effort to speak at all. She could imagine the scene, could imagine her brave, proud husband taking on the guards single-handed. If he had not been suffering from a wound, he might even have succeeded. 'You did your best.'

'We came by sea from Toulon,' he went on. 'It is still in British hands, though how much longer it will stay that way I do not know. The Revolutionary Army with all its conscripts is being surprisingly successful.'

'Thank you for telling us,' the Earl said as his wife began to sob quietly. He sat down beside her and put his arm about her. 'Let us hope his end was mercifully quick.'

'You were very brave,' Kitty said.

'No braver than Jack,' he said. 'He was truly a great man. And I can do no better than follow his example. I have to return, there is still work to be done.'

'You must stay and rest first,' his lordship said. 'Nanette, take your mother up to your room until one can be prepared for her.' He bent to his wife. 'Come, my dear, you need to rest too. I shall have a tisane sent to you.'

He gave orders to the servants, a task his wife would normally have done, but she was clearly incapable of it. And Kitty, who might have deputised for her, was numb, though dry-eyed. She could not believe they had really been talking about Jack's death. She could not mourn him; it seemed too unreal. How could he have died and she not know it? She had been living with hope for so long that it would take time to realise it had been dashed.

Thomas left again and a few days later Nanette and James took Anne-Marie to Richmond where they had acquired a little house not far from the park. It was peaceful there and yet within a day's ride of London, a good place for the Marchioness to recover and for James to continue his chosen career as a writer.

Their departure left Chiltern Hall very quiet. Kitty tried to lead a normal life, keeping her mother-in-law company, sewing, visiting friends and neighbours and writing letters during the day, reading or playing the harpsichord and singing a little in the evenings. But her thoughts constantly returned to France, to the château on the hill at Haute Saint-Gilbert. To Jack. Her husband. The man she loved.

She found herself more and more thinking back over what had happened. She had run from home. Anyone could have taken advantage of her. She could have been robbed or raped; she could have been flung into the gutter and left to die. Instead, a kindly fate had sent Jack Chiltern. It was not so much that first meeting of strangers, but the later one on the packet to France which had sealed her fate.

Something had passed between them when he kissed her, a flash of something akin to lightning. No, she decided on reflection, it was nothing so violent. A thread perhaps, passing from fingers to fingers, lips to lips, or heart to heart, a thread so fine it was invisible, so strong

it could never be severed. It had been there all through
their long journey from Paris to Lyons, even when they
quarrelled, even when he had taken her so forcefully on
their wedding night.

It had survived the journey to Toulon, and home. She
was quite sure it was still there, linking them when he
left again. If he was somewhere, alive and well,
wouldn't he be able to feel it too? Had it at last been
broken? Would she have felt it go? But how could it,
when she carried his child in her womb? That link was
unbreakable.

For her child's sake, she must be strong, to accept
what had to be accepted, but, oh, how she wished she
had told Jack of her love before he disappeared. They
would not have parted so coolly. Or would they? He
had shown no sign of wanting to end their estrange-
ment. 'It will not happen again,' he had said. And he
was a man of his word.

When, the week before Christmas, they learned that
a French army officer named Napoleon Bonaparte had
recaptured Toulon, that all foreign invaders had been
forced to retreat from French soil and all counter-
revolution suppressed, even the Countess admitted she
had given up hope of seeing her son again. Kitty, seeing
the dull misery in her mother-in-law's eyes, felt the last
vestige of her own hope shrivel to nothing.

'It will soon be Christmas,' her ladyship said, sitting
with Kitty in her boudoir, staring into the fire, as if
conjuring up images in its flames. 'Jack loved the fes-
tival when he was a child. We would help bring in the
Yule log and deck the hall with holly. And after we had
been to church, we would eat goose and roast beef and
apples and nuts. All the servants would put on their best

clothes and come to eat with us. Jack was such a favourite. I could not have any more children and...'

'Please, don't,' Kitty said, putting her arm round the
older woman's shoulders, weeping herself. 'I can't bear
to see you cry.'

'No, I must not. It upsets 'is lordship and I would not
for the world upset 'im. 'E is such a strength to me, but
underneath 'e is as miserable as we are, more because
Jack was his heir.' She sniffed and rubbed at her cheeks
with a minuscule lace handkerchief, forcing herself to
smile. 'But we shall soon have another heir and we must
look to 'im.'

Kate did not have the heart to wonder whether it
might be a girl and not a boy. Whichever it was, it
would be an only child. 'We can still enjoy Christmas,'
she said. 'I am sure Jack will be with us in spirit. He
will always be with us, don't you think?'

'Of course. You are right. Life must go on and it is
expected of us. We cannot let our people down, can
we?' She got up from her chair. 'I must go and give
the orders. We must cook festive pies and cakes and
kill the goose.'

'And tomorrow, we will bring in the holly and the
Yule log,' Kitty said. 'It will be a pleasant diversion
decorating the house.'

Her ladyship, her hand on the door knob, turned back
to Kitty. 'You are so good for me, Kitty. Every day I
thank God Jack brought you to me. It is almost as if 'e
knew.'

'Knew what?'

'That I should need comfort and solace and that you
were the one to provide it. I think 'e must have loved
you very much.'

And that was more than enough to make Kitty cry.

She managed to hold back her tears until Justine had left the room, and then she sank to her knees on the hearthrug and allowed them to fall unheeded. She did not deserve their good opinion of her. If she had had a little more sense, been a little more mature about it, she and Jack would not have quarrelled and he would not have made that last trip to France. They could have had a good marriage. Now it was too late.

No one knew of her tears, she told no one of her feeling of guilt, she simply scolded herself and joined in the preparations for Christmas as if her sanity depended on it.

The next day, dressed in a voluminous cloak which disguised her condition, she set out for the nearby woods with half a dozen servants to take part in the traditional task of dragging home the Yule log. The day was crisp and frosty and the sun shone, gleaming on the crystals which hung from the branches.

They selected a huge branch which would fill the hearth of the hall and everyone had a hand on it, dragging it through the fallen leaves, laughing as they went, their breath hanging in the frosty air. Kitty gave only token assistance, but she was happy to be involved and walked alongside the workers, carrying an armful of berry-laden holly wrapped in canvas to protect her from its prickles.

When they came out of the wood and could see across the park, they stopped to rest a moment and it was then Kitty looked up and saw a hired carriage bowling along the road towards the gates of Chiltern Hall. She stood a moment, watching it, shielding her eyes with her hand, the better to see it in the strong sunlight.

Strange carriages were a rarity at Beauworth, where everyone instantly recognised a neighbour's equipage.

It turned into the gates and made its way up the drive. It stopped at the front door and a man alighted. 'Jack!' she cried aloud, dropping the holly and gathering up her skirts in order to run.

It was not her husband, she decided, as she came a little nearer; this was an older man. He walked slowly and stiffly, his shoulders hunched. She paused, panting for breath. But supposing he had news? Good news or bad? From a distance he did not look joyful. She watched as the door was opened and Fletcher came out and hurried down the steps to help the caller inside. The carriage was driven away. He was obviously known to the footman. She began to run again and, reaching the front door, raced in in time to see the newcomer disappearing into the library. He turned when he heard her.

She stood and stared for several moments before she found the voice to speak. '*Jack!* It is you!'

He was as thin as a beanpole, his normally tanned face ashen, his eyes sunk deep in their sockets, his clothes hanging on him in loose folds. One arm was tucked uselessly inside his coat. He could hardly stand and was still being supported by Fletcher. She curbed her inclination to throw herself at him; she would bowl him over. A feather would fell him.

She stopped. 'Jack! Oh, how good it is to see you!'

'Good?' he queried with a twisted smile. 'A wreck of a man appears on the step and you call it good.'

'At least you are alive. Fletcher, does the Countess know he is here?'

'I was about to inform her, my lady, as soon as his lordship was seated.'

'I'll go and tell her. Jack, can you climb the stairs?
You should go straight to bed.'

'Later,' he said, pushing the footman away and walking unaided towards the library. 'I need a drink first.'
Kitty ran to support him. He waved her away. 'I can
manage, I am not ill.'

She stood back and watched him, afraid he would
fall. 'Fetch the Countess,' she said to Fletcher. 'Then
see that his lordship's room is made ready.'

Fletcher disappeared at a run as Jack sank into an
armchair before the hearth. Kitty went and knelt beside
him, taking his hand in both her own. 'Oh, Jack, we
have been so worried, especially when Thomas arrived
with the Marchioness…'

He gave a twisted smile. 'They made it, did they?'

'Yes. Nanette and James were here when she arrived.
She went back to live with them.'

'Not an entirely wasted trip, then.'

'No. Thomas said you were very courageous. In fact,
he said you were reckless considering you had been
wounded in the attempt to free Antoinette.'

'That very nearly succeeded,' he said. 'It would have
if certain people had had a little more backbone.'

'Not everyone can be as brave as you are, Jack. But
do not talk about it now. It will tire you and you need
to rest.'

'Rest,' he murmured. 'Yes, I think I may rest now.'

'Jack! Jack!' Lady Beauworth ran into the room, her
skirts bunched in her hand. 'Fletcher tells me…' She
stopped at the sight of her son. 'Oh, my dearest, what
'as happened to you?'

He tried to rise, to make his obeisance, but sank back
into the chair. 'A slight wound, Mother, nothing serious…'

'Not serious! You look at death's door.' She came forward to kneel at his feet and take the hand Kitty had relinquished. 'You must go to bed at once and Dr Seward sent for.'

'Don't fuss, Mother. All I need is rest.' But it was evident there was more than fatigue wrong with him. He was in a state of collapse.

The Countess called Fletcher back to carry Jack to his bedchamber, sent his valet to him, sent a groom on horseback to fetch the doctor, another to find the Earl who was out riding somewhere on the estate, and ordered the cook to prepare nourishing broth.

Kitty waited until the valet came out of Jack's room and then went to sit with him. He was delirious and did not know her; he hardly seemed to know where he was. She sat watching him, wringing out a cloth and mopping his brow every so often, trying to stop him thrashing about.

The doctor arrived half an hour later. Kitty left the room while he made his examination and paced up and down the corridor outside. Justine came to her, her soft skirts rustling. 'How is he?'

'I cannot tell, he is not fully conscious. Dr Seward is with him now.'

''Ow did he manage to come home like that? Fletcher said 'e came alone, there was no one else in the carriage that brought 'im.'

'He is in no condition for explanations. We must wait until he has recovered.'

'Yes, of course. Let us give thanks that 'e is back with us.'

'No! I will not have it!' The sound of Jack's voice

came clearly through the closed door. 'Clean it up, then leave me.'

They looked at each other, wondering whether to go in, but before either could do so, Dr Seward came out of the bedchamber looking grave. 'He has sustained a wound, perhaps more than one, which was not properly attended to. I cannot be sure, but it looks as if a musket ball is lodged in his upper arm and has been there some time. The area round the wound has putrified. I have told him he must lose the arm.'

'And he has refused?' Kitty queried. 'Is there no alternative?'

'I think it will be unwise to wait. I tried to explain to him, but I fear he is not fully aware of his condition.'

'Go to 'im, Kitty,' her ladyship said. 'Talk to 'im.

Kitty crept into the room. Jack was lying on his back, his face a pale mask. 'You still here?' he queried weakly. 'I had thought you would be long gone.'

'Why should I go? I am your wife. This is our home.'

'So it is.' His tone was full of wry irony.

'You wish me gone?'

She waited, with her heart in her mouth for his reply. He smiled lop-sidedly. 'That fool wants to take off my arm.'

'Yes, I know.'

'I won't have it. It will heal, given time.'

'Jack, please, do not take any more risks. You are home now and I would rather have a husband with one arm than no husband at all.'

'I am not your husband, I never have been.'

She rose and ran from the room. He knew. He had known all along. He had arranged that ceremony simply to make her conform, to obey him. She passed the Countess, still pacing up and down the corridor, and fled to her room, where she laid herself on her bed. To have him home when they thought him lost, to see him so obviously in pain and be able to do nothing to help, to have continued to hope when all hope should have faded—surely she deserved a reward for that?

While he had been away, she had been able to convince herself that, as soon as he came home, all would be well and he would love her and their child. She had been deluding herself. Now what could she do? Where could she go? How could she explain to the Earl and the Countess, who had both been so good to her, that her marriage was a sham?

Jack lay back exhausted. What had made him say such a terrible thing to her? Why didn't she understand that he loved her, that he had been to hell and back and all he wanted was the peace and quiet of Chiltern Hall, his parents and a wife who loved him and wanted him? She didn't want him, she had not even tried to touch him when he arrived.

He could not blame her for that; he must be a ghastly sight, but if she cared for him at all, she would have ignored that. It had been his disappointment that made him lash out. It had been the thought of being reunited with Kitty which had driven him on, helped him to ignore the pain, the hunger, the sore feet from walking miles every day, the danger of being spotted. Kitty, always Kitty. Now he was home and too weak to say and do the things he had planned.

His mother came into the room and sat beside the bed, not speaking, just watching him tenderly. He smiled lop-sidedly. 'I do not make a good patient.'

'Are you going to let the doctor amputate your arm?'

'No.'

'He says the ball is still in there and is poisoning your system.'

'He is wrong. It was taken out. The wound never healed properly because I could not rest. And in Lyons a gendarme stuck his bayonet into it. Filthy it was, so I don't wonder the wound has gone bad. But, now I am home, it will mend.' He paused to gather his strength. 'See, already I am growing stronger.'

She sighed. 'Why did you send Kitty away?'

'I didn't. She went. Mother, keep her away. She only stays from duty…'

'I never heard such nonsense! You are delirious. Why, she loves you. She 'as been beside herself worrying about you, worrying about the child…'

'Child?'

'Did you not notice? Oh, Jack, I can only think your fever has affected your eyes.'

'She is expecting a child? But how could she? We…' This was something he had never envisaged. It put a completely different light on the matter. 'Where is she? Fetch her back.'

'Later.' She stood up as the doctor came back into the room. 'Here is Dr Seward come back.'

'With his chopper and his saw, no doubt.' He lifted his head. 'Take them away. You may clean the wound, no more.'

'But, Jack…' his mother protested.

'You risk your life by refusing,' the doctor said.

Jack's smile was more a grimace of pain as the doctor removed the bandage which had been strapping his arm to his body and peeled off the dressing. 'I have risked my life many times in the last three years, sir. I am… used to it…' His voice faded away as he fainted.

'Good,' the doctor said. 'Now we can get on.'

'No.' The Countess's voice was quite firm. 'I will not let you do it against 'is wishes. Clean the wound and bind 'im again. We shall see how 'e does.'

Dr Seward sighed. He had seen brave men brought down when it came to amputation and many had at first refused, but when the pain and putrefaction became too much to bear they had been willing enough. The trouble was that delay usually meant the infection spread and the final cut was all the more severe; because the patient had been weakened by his obstinacy, he frequently did not survive the operation.

'I will take the responsibility,' she added, when he hesitated. 'Tell me what we must do to nurse 'im and we will do it.'

Reluctantly he gave in.

For three days Justine and Kitty nursed him in turns, never leaving him alone for a second. He grew more and more feverish and restless, tossing this way and that, crying out and mumbling in delirium. Sometimes Kitty thought he called her name.

'He cannot go on much longer like this,' Kitty said to her mother-in-law. 'Are you sure we are doing the right thing?'

'No, I am not, but Jack would not forgive me if 'e came to 'is senses and found we 'ad agreed to let the doctor take 'is arm off.'

'It is better than letting him die.'

''E did not die in France when there was no one to nurse 'im. 'Ere, where 'e 'as every attention, 'e will survive.'

'You are as stubborn as he is,' Kitty said. 'I think he would rather die than stay married to me.'

'What? What nonsense is this? You must not say

such dreadful things. 'E came 'ome to you. It is for you 'e wants to get better…'

'Then why is he getting worse?'

'Is 'e?' Justine stood looking down at the form in the bed. For once Jack had stopped thrashing about, as if his soul had already accepted death and welcomed it. He was no longer fighting.

'Yes. Please, send for the doctor again,' Kitty whispered. 'Tell him to do as he thinks fit. I would rather die myself than be the cause of his death…'

'Kitty, go to bed,' the Countess commanded. 'You are so exhausted, you talk as much nonsense as Jack. It is not good for the child.'

'Send for the doctor, please.'

'Very well. But go to bed, child. I'll send Rose to you with a tisane. I will call you if there is any change.'

Slowly Kitty dragged herself to her own room. Jack was dying and, whichever way you looked at it, it was her fault. His innate sense of chivalry had made him offer to escort her in the first place, to try and take her to freedom, to marry her. And having done so, he had brought her to safety, left her in possession of his home and gone off again, risking his life to save a doomed queen.

It was all her fault. He thought so too. She could not forget his words: 'I am not your husband, I never have been.'

Rose came into her room with a glass in her hand and persuaded her to drink the bitter draught it contained. She needed oblivion. She would not be able to think clearly until she had slept. She stripped off her gown and lay down in her petticoat. Her last conscious thought was of her child.

How much were unborn children affected by their

mother's upsets? Did the little one know the anguish she suffered? Was he equally disturbed? She felt him kick, quite violently. 'Oh, you do know,' she murmured. 'You are determined to punish me too.'

Forced into sleep by the drug, she did not wake until the next day. The sun was shining through the fabric of the curtains and she could hear the church bells ringing. For a moment she was confused, wondering what day it was. Then she remembered it was Christmas Day. She rose and went to the window, pulling back the curtains to peer out.

It had snowed a little in the night. The path was glittering with it and it hung on the branches of the bare trees and piled itself against the hedgerows, white and pure. Today was a day of purity; the birthday of the Saviour. 'A child is born,' she murmured, turning back towards the room as Rose came in.

'I thought I heard you about, my lady. I've brought you hot chocolate and water to wash. Shall I help you dress?'

'Yes, please. Lord Chiltern?'

'The Earl sat with him during the night while her ladyship rested, my lady. I believe she went back to him after she had breakfasted.'

'Has the doctor been?'

'Expected any minute.'

'Then let us make haste.'

Fifteen minutes later, Kitty crept into the sick room. It was uncannily silent. The Countess sat beside the bed, watching her son, with tears raining down her cheeks. He lay very still, a hump in the bedclothes, no more. The single candle left burning all night guttered and went out.

Kitty gasped and moved forward to fall on her knees beside the bed, her heart screaming against the outrage, but no sound came from her throat. What she felt was beyond speech.

Justine put a hand on her shoulder and gripped it. 'He sleeps,' she said.

At first Kitty did not comprehend; she thought of eternal sleep, not the sleep from which one awoke refreshed. 'Yes,' she said softly.

'Thank God. Now he will not lose his arm. We can send the doctor away again.' She looked down at Kitty. 'Oh, this is so wonderful. Happy Christmas, daughter.'

A small sound from the bed made Kitty turn startled eyes towards it. Jack was looking straight at her, his dark eyes clear and bright.

'You still here,' he murmured, just as if there had not been four full days since the first time he had uttered the phrase.

It was a second chance. She had a second chance to frame her reply. It was worth fighting for, she told herself. If fate had been kind enough to give you what you most desired, then you would be a fool to throw it away for want of a little honesty. 'It is the only place I want to be, the only place I shall ever want to be.' She smiled and bent to kiss his forehead. 'I am afraid, my darling, you are stuck with me.'

He grinned. 'You mean that? I cannot drive you away, however boorish I become?'

'No. I love you.'

'I do not know what you are talking about,' the Countess said brightly. 'Why should you drive Kitty away? And you are never boorish. Why, you are the most even-tempered of men.' She paused and gave a light laugh. 'Most of the time, anyway. I own you were dreadfully ill-tempered when you arrived, but that was because you were so ill. I am sure Kitty has forgiven you, for I 'ave.'

'Have you?' he queried, looking at his wife.

'Yes.'

He raised his eyebrow at her. 'For everything?'

She knew what he meant. 'For everything.'

He grinned lop-sidedly. 'Love is the strongest force of all, isn't that what you once said to me?'

'Yes, though you said it was a tyrant.'

'I was wrong. And you were right. I love you, Lady Chiltern. I have loved you since the moment you berated me at the Paris *barrière*, a veritable fishwife.'

'But you were not at all pleased with me for that.'

'Oh, indeed I was. I thought you were wonderful.' He reached out and put his good hand up round her neck, drawing her face down towards him so that he could kiss her. 'My little tyrant.'

The Countess crept from the room. They hardly noticed her go.

Epilogue

The sun was shining and the daffodils were nodding on the day Justin James Chiltern was christened. Wearing the christening robe Jack himself had worn, he was taken to the church by his proud parents in the family coach, where the ceremony was witnessed by his doting grandparents, his Uncle James, who had provided one of his names, and his Aunt Nanette, determined to be present though the birth of her own child was imminent.

Great-aunt Anne-Marie was also present, and Great-uncle William and Kitty's stepmother, who, unusually for her, was overawed by the grandeur of the occasion and had little to say, apart from cooing over the baby. Captain Trent and Edward Lampeter also arrived, both resplendent in uniform. And all along the way almost the whole population of Beauforth stood to cheer the new heir.

It was a day on which to be happy and Kitty was happy. She could hardly believe there had been that appalling quarrel on her wedding night. Her first wedding night, for there had been a second that was very different.

* * *

When Jack had been sufficiently well to speak of what was on his mind and had been on his mind ever since it happened, he had once again begged Kitty's pardon. It was the first time he had dressed and come downstairs and, though he was still pale and a little weak, he was making rapid strides towards a full recovery. She had wrapped a rug about his knees and put a cushion behind his injured shoulder, before sitting in a chair beside him.

'I was so sure you wanted an annulment and that was the last thing I wanted,' he went on. 'It made me feel so frustrated and confused, I wanted to lash out against it, against the circumstances that had brought us to such a pass, at myself for being such a fool as to think I could win your love after we were married when I had not succeeded before. It was a feeling that was new to me and I suppose I needed to prove I was my own master. Instead, I lost control.'

'Why did you not say so? It was a strange way to ensure the marriage endured. And so unnecessary. I would have given myself to you willingly.'

'I did not know that. I thought you had agreed to the marriage simply to help us get out of France and keep your reputation intact.'

'Jack, that was how you put it to me when you suggested it. It was not what was in my mind. I wanted a true marriage. And when you…when you…' She could not bring herself to put into words the horror of that night.

'I must have been out of my mind, there is no other explanation. And I knew, as soon as it was over, that I had forfeited your love for ever. Nothing I did afterwards could redress the wrong.'

'So, instead of trying to work things out, you brought

me home and disappeared again. Jack, we were so worried about you and, when the War Department as good as said you must be dead, we almost lost hope.'

He smiled wryly. 'Only almost?'

'I could not bring myself to accept it. I had this strange feeling that we were joined in some way, and that if the thread that bound us had been severed by death, I should know it when it happened. I know that sounds fanciful, but I was right, wasn't I?'

'Yes, thank God. When I found you still here…'

'Where else would I be? I am your wife. This is our home. It will be the home of our child.' She paused. They had to be open and honest with each other, or any doubts they had would never be quite erased. 'But the question is, do you want to be bound to me?'

'Do you need to ask? My bonds are easy to live with. I loved you in France, I love you now, I will love you in a hundred years if we should live so long.'

'Oh, Jack, how I have longed to hear you say that!'

'In spite of what I did to you?'

'I cannot believe the marriage bed is always like that.'

'Oh, believe me, it is not. If only you would forgive me, then I could show you a very different husband, one who cares deeply for you. I would hope, in time, to expunge the memory of that dreadful wedding night.'

She looked at him shyly. 'Jack, it was a proper wedding, wasn't it? Legal, I mean?'

'Yes.' He looked at her sharply. 'You surely do not think I contrived it to—'

'Now, don't fly into the boughs, all I meant was that we could make doubly sure. It was your papa put the idea into my head. He said we could have a second ceremony, here, in Beauworth church, and then there could never be any doubt about it.'

'And you would like that?'

'I should like it very much.'

'Then, this time, I must do the job properly.' He flung the rug from him and slipped from his seat to kneel in front of her, taking both her hands in his. 'My darling Kitty, I adore you, I cannot live without you. Will you make me very happy and consent to become my wife?'

'La, sir,' she said, entering into the spirit of the occasion. 'I shall have to think about it and give you an answer later.'

'How much later?'

'Oh, I think thirty seconds will suffice.'

He waited the prescribed time, his eyes dancing with happiness, while she smiled down at him. 'And your answer?'

'Yes, of course, silly. And do get up, you will soil your beautiful clothes.'

He stood up, drawing her to her feet to kiss her very gently, very tenderly, afraid of being too forceful. 'When, my love? Tell me when.'

'As soon as maybe.' She laughed. 'After all, our child must be born in wedlock.'

The ceremony, witnessed by Lord and Lady Beauworth, took place a week later, a year almost to the day since they had first met. And that night, in spite of her ungainly bulk, he had taken her in his arms in their bed and kissed her tenderly, beginning with her face and working his way down to her throat and breasts, putting his hand to her swollen stomach and laughing delightedly when he felt the baby kick. 'I am half afraid to touch you,' he murmured.

She lifted his head in both her hands and smiled at

him. 'He is tougher than you might think. He will not mind.'

'You are sure it will be a boy?'

'No, but it does not matter in the least, there will be others. We are going to be one big happy family, God willing.'

'Amen to that.'

He kissed her rounded stomach and stroked her breasts and thighs, gently and tenderly, taking infinite pains not to alarm her. But their love was not to be denied; she was as passionate as he was and she had waited too long already. Instinct told her what to do and instinct served her well. It was all about loving and being loved and when they came together in one glorious frenzied peak of fulfilment, they both knew that this wedding night was one not to be forgotten.

* * * * *

When she was good,
she was very, very good.
And when she was bad, she was...

NAUGHTY MARIETTA

NAN RYAN

Published 17th September 2004

Published 17th December 2004

THE CHARM SCHOOL

From wallflower to belle of the ball...

...Michelle Reid

.....Jane Porter

Susan Stephens...

One
Christmas
Night

On sale 3rd December 2004

*Available at most branches of WHSmith, Tesco, ASDA, Martins,
Borders, Eason, Sainsbury's and all good paperback bookshops.*